THE I TATTI
RENAISSANCE LIBRARY

James Hankins, General Editor

HUMANIST COMEDIES

ITRL 19

HUMANIST
COMEDIES

EDITED AND TRANSLATED BY

GARY R. GRUND

THE I TATTI RENAISSANCE LIBRARY
HARVARD UNIVERSITY PRESS
CAMBRIDGE, MASSACHUSETTS
LONDON, ENGLAND

2005

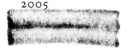

Series design by Dean Bornstein

Library of Congress Cataloging-in-Publication Data

Humanist comedies / edited and translated by Gary R. Grund.
p. cm. — (I Tatti Renaissance library ; 19)
Includes bibliographical references (p.) and index.
Contents: Paulus / Pier Paolo Vergerio —
The play of Philodoxus / Leon Battista Alberti —
Philogenia and Epiphebus / Ugolino Pisani —
Chrysis / Enea Silvio Piccolomini — The epirote / Tommaso Mezzo.
ISBN 0-674-01744-7 (cloth : alk. paper)
1. Latin drama, Medieval and modern—Translations into English.
2. Latin drama (Comedy)—Translations into English.
3. Latin drama, Medieval and modern.
4. Latin drama (Comedy)   5. Humanists.
I. Grund, Gary R. (Gary Robert), 1946–   II. Series.
PA8165.H86 2005
872'.0308—dc22   2005040408

Contents

ক৭৭ক

Introduction   vii

Pier Paolo Vergerio, *Paulus*   2

Leon Battista Alberti, *The Play of Philodoxus*   70

Ugolino Pisani, *Philogenia and Epiphebus*   170

Enea Silvio Piccolomini, *Chrysis*   284

Tommaso Mezzo, *The Epirote*   348

Note on the Text   433

Notes to the Text   437

Notes to the Translation   441

Bibliography   451

Index   457

Introduction

Origins

The history of humanist Latin drama in the Quattrocento is largely a story of the imitation and adaptation of Seneca (first century AD) in tragedy and Plautus (third century BC) and Terence (second century BC) in comedy. Tragedy was always about great ones, men and women caught in the throes of impossible choices; it made perfect sense that an aristocratic genre like tragedy would appeal to the courtly audiences in Renaissance Italy before whom it was performed. As it turned out, though, the Latin New Comedy of Plautus and Terence proved much more attractive to Latin humanists — as well as to later vernacular writers — because, unlike Senecan tragedy, it presented narratives drawn from ordinary life that proved easily adaptable to the daily life of contemporary Italy. Comedy turned on human imperfections; its events were unheroic; and it drew its inspiration from the ageless commonplaces of love, money, sex, and manners.

For comedy, the plays of Plautus and especially of Terence provided Italian humanists with a reservoir of characters, plots, and themes that had continued to enrich the culture of the West long after the performing traditions of Latin New Comedy had died out. It was a literary genre, too, that was grounded in a style of unabashed colloquialism, especially so in Plautus, and was characterized by vitality, wit, and coarse puns. Both Plautus and Terence assembled their characters in three recurring groups: the males — a young man (*adulescens*), an aged parent (*senex*), and a cunning slave (*servus callidus*); the females — a young heroine (*virgo*) or a courtesan (*meretrix*) who is the object of the young man's desire, a wife or a mother (*matrona*), and the maidservant (*ancilla*); and professional

caricatures—the parasite (*parasitus*), the whoremaster or slave-dealer (*leno/lena*), the soldier (*miles*), the money-lender (*trapezita* or *danista*), the doctor (*medicus*) and cook (*cocus*).[1] The plotting of New Comedy was always concerned with the maneuvering of a young man toward a young woman, and marriage was the typical ending, so that its main theme was his successful effort in outwitting an opponent, usually the father as *senex*, to possess the girl of his choice.

The five comedies included in this volume—*Paulus* (ca. 1390) by Pier Paolo Vergerio (1370–1444), *The Play of Philodoxus* (1424/ 1437) by Leon Battista Alberti (1404–72), *Philogenia and Epiphebus* (1437/38) by Ugolino Pisani (1405?–1445?), *Chrysis* (1444) by Enea Silvio Piccolomini (1405–64)—the later Pope Pius II—and *The Epirote* (1483) by Tommaso Mezzo (b. ca. 1447)—constitute a representative sampling of comedy during the Quattrocento as it was interpreted by some of the most important Latin humanists. Petrarch wrote the earliest Neo-Latin comedy, the now-lost *Philologia*, sometime before 1336, and the few fragments which have survived reveal his interest in the standard metrical form of Terentian comedy, the iambic senarius. Written over the course of nearly a century, the earliest comedies in this volume were more than half-medieval in form and intention while at the end of the period Mezzo's Plautine comedy—perhaps the best of them all—looked forward to the more modern, sophisticated comedies written in the vernacular during the Cinquecento. As we shall see, most Latin comedies were recited rather than acted in front of an audience, although in the final decades of the century a number of them were presented as grand courtly spectacles in Florence, Rome, and Ferrara. Latin humanist comedy had an important historical moment in the Quattrocento. Even though it reworked and ultimately perfected the comic spirit and forms of Plautus and Terence upon which it drew, it also made serviceable use of many native forms, *novelle*, goliardic poetry, and scenes from everyday

Italian life which Ariosto, Machiavelli, and Aretino would rely on in the next century. In a broader sense it may very well be that because comedy always pits those in the grip of convention against those who desire to love and flourish (*bene esse*), it will always find a deeper resonance in the hearts of those living in times of political authoritarianism and strict social codes. The ending of comedy is always a release from bondage, a liberation from some kind of constraint, an overthrowing of those who would tyrannize us.

There were many influences that formed the character of Quattrocento Latin comedy, but none so pervasive as that of Latin New Comedy. Even in their decline the plays of Plautus and Terence continued to have a powerful effect on the Christianized West. Despite the animosity of some Christian authorities, Latin New Comedy continued to be read, but read as a literary genre, especially in the classroom. As late as the tenth century, Hrotsvitha, a nun at Gandersheim, rewrote in Latin the plays of Terence "substituting for so many incestuous vices of feminine lusts the chaste actions of holy virgins."[2] Still, with the gradual transformation of the ancient Roman *ludi* of Plautus and Terence from performance-texts into lexical texts, not only was the vitality of the theatre inevitably dissipated but the audience now was composed of readers, not spectators. Drama became a privileged literary exercise.

At the same time, generic distinctions were eroding so that comedy was classified not as drama but as narrative, defined largely by its language, subject and style, a notion that was transferred to vernacular compositions as well, and medieval and Renaissance curricula reflect this adjustment.[3] Terence had a prominent place in Renaissance pedagogy, but not for his dramatic skills: Gasparino Barzizza (1360–1430), a famous humanist schoolmaster based in Padua, Milan and Pavia, praised Terence for the soundness of his moral judgments; and Guarino da Verona (1374–1460), court tutor to the Este family and a friend of Ver-

gerio, extolled Terence for the purity of his style. For such reasons as these, Terence's plays exerted a much wider influence on the first generation of Latin humanist writers than Plautus. In an age that aimed to revive the spoken as well as the written language of the ancients, Roman comedy provided useful models for colloquial Latin speech.[4]

To read Terence in the schools also meant reading the most important of his commentators, Donatus (fourth century AD), whose notes on dramatic structure were soon combined with others' in the extant scholia on Terence. Though known to the humanists in manuscript as early as 1433, Donatus' commentary was first printed in Venice in 1472 and first printed along with Terence's six plays in Venice in 1476 by Giovanni Calfurnio (the *editio princeps* of Terence was published at Strasbourg in 1470). An edition by Rafaele Regio in 1473 was the first to include the act-divisions recommended by Donatus for Terence's texts. In most of the manuscripts (and in many editions) of the plays there are no act- or scene-divisions, and Terence's verse appears as prose. In 1498, Angelo Poliziano was the first to emend Terence by restoring his meters and maintaining the act-divisions.

The manuscripts of Plautus are like those of Terence in that the act-divisions are not indicated although scene-divisions are. The act-divisions were not added until the sixteenth century, and his commentators generally followed Terence's lead in matters of structure. Most of the codices date from the eleventh and twelfth centuries and present considerable difficulties. While eight of the plays of Plautus were familiar to Italian humanists at the beginning of the Quattrocento, twelve were completely unknown for centuries until the exciting discovery (1429), by Poggio Bracciolini (1380–1459) and Nicolaus Cusanus (1401–64), of a codex in Germany containing them, the Codex Ursinianus, now in the Vatican; very soon thereafter, they were being recited along with Terence's

comedies at the courts of princes. The *editio princeps* (1472), edited by Giorgio Merula (1431–94) in Venice, followed a few decades later.

The manuscripts and printed editions of the comedies of Plautus and Terence, their accessibility and adaptability, are crucial elements in understanding Latin humanist comedy in the Quattrocento. Terence had a remarkable currency at the beginning of the century in forming the tastes and dramatic principles of the first writers of Latin comedy in Italy; however, by mid-century dramatists were fashioning their comedies on Plautine models. While familiar with Terence, the first writer in this volume, Pier Paolo Vergerio, has barely a reference to Plautus (perhaps only his character Stichus from the *Stichus*), while in Enea Silvio Piccolomini's *Chrysis* (1444) the language and structure of Plautus have been assimilated into the comic mainstream.

There were other dramatic forces at work in the immediate background of humanist Latin comedy. Paralleling the decline of Roman dramatic art and perhaps rising from its ashes was the ascendancy of devotional representation within the Church that produced the great mystery cycles of the Middle Ages. In their manifestation in Renaissance Italy, religious dramas were called *sacre rappresentazioni*. They belonged to a popular genre created for the instruction of the people and were written, therefore, in the vernacular. Their origins may be traced to the *laudi* of thirteenth-century Umbria, religious poems based on the liturgy and on the songs of praise in the morning Office, and to its later form, the *devozioni*.

In Florence, such plays were given in churches, piazzas, convent refectories, even on barges floating down the Arno. So great was the crowd of spectators assembled in Florence on the Ponte alla Carraia on May 1, 1304, to view the representation of Hell on pontoons, Giovanni Villani tells us, that the bridge collapsed. Antonio

Pucci commemorated the occasion in verse, describing in great detail such effects as the cauldrons and grills tended to by the devil as cook who was ready to roast the souls of the impenitent (in reality, shirts stuffed with straw or inflated ox-bladders). Many wept in terror at the sight.[5] Besides the use of Biblical and allegorical characters many plays recalled the secular caricatures (like the cook) of Latin New Comedy — midwives, courtesans, doctors, merchants, soldiers, vagabonds, innkeepers, monks, and priests. During the Quattrocento the scenic effects that were part of religious representations were increasingly used as elements in various secular festivals, processions (*trionfi*), and on other special occasions, the profane entertainments in time overshadowing the sacred. It was a curious but characteristically Renaissance kind of blending: Christ with Apollo. As had been the case in ancient Rome, when mimic drama and the pantomime overtook other forms of entertainment in popularity, secular presentations that were originally meant as *intermezzi* superseded the religious drama they were designed to enhance. Old and new, sacred and profane, found themselves in potent combination during the Quattrocento.

Performance

Unfortunately, the performance records of Latin humanist drama during the Quattrocento are scanty. None of the comedies included in this volume can be proven with any certainty to have been presented publicly. There can be little doubt, however, that they circulated privately and widely. Ugolino Pisani's *Philogenia and Epiphebus*, written about 1438 and set in Pavia, has survived in more than forty manuscripts and was described as one of his many "finely wrought, delightful, and most pleasant comedies." Surprisingly, it was another work, the much less distinguished academic farce, *A Culinary Confabulation* (*De coquinaria confabulatione*)

that was performed; it was one of many presentations at a Shrove Tuesday carnival in the *studium* at Pavia in 1435 (where Pisani was attending university). The work was also quite conspicuously dedicated to Leonello d'Este, almost assuring its longevity, whose court at Ferrara Pisani had traveled to in 1437 seeking patronage. (One of the manuscripts of the *Philogenia* from the Este collection in Modena has in fact survived.) A year earlier, Leon Battista Alberti had sent Leonello a copy of his comedy, *The Play of Philodoxus* (1424) and an important accompanying commentary on the origins of his play. Aristocratic recognition played an extremely useful role in the advancement of literary careers and in the survival of Latin humanist drama.

The humanist plays that were performed, like Pisani's pre-Lenten comedy, were often presented as part of academic ceremonies, courtly entertainments, or religious spectacles in cities across Italy. Many were presented in the open air as well as in the halls of the nobility and in the palaces of the pope and his cardinals. The possibilities for grand scenic display inherent in the sacred drama of the Church quickly spilled over into the realm of political and social compliment. When the princesses of the house of Este arrived in Venice in 1491, a classical pantomime on the legend of Meleager was performed in the ducal palace as boat-races took place on the Grand Canal. After the publication of the works of Plautus and Terence in the 1470s, their plays were adapted for similar social festivities. At the nuptials of Alfonso I d'Este and Anna Maria Sforza at Ferrara in 1491, for example, Plautus' *Amphitruo* was carefully selected for performance—the comedy has Jupiter, disguised as the titular character, fathering remarkable twin sons, one of whom was Hercules, with Amphitruo's chaste and dignified wife —concluding with a prediction of the future birth of a Hercules in the family (Duke Ercole II). It was understandable that the plays of the Latin humanists which were performed would be adapted and performed in similar aristocratic venues.

Literary academies, too, such as the famous Accademia Romana under the leadership of Giulio Pomponio Leto (1425–98), vigorously encouraged the accurate representation of Latin New Comedy as well as the production of the works of the Latin humanists in less informal and private settings outside the confines of the university or the Church. The founder of the contemporary Accademia Pontaniana in Naples was the friend of Alberti's who may have circulated his *Play of Philodoxus* privately: Antonio Beccadelli, called "il Panormita" from Palermo, his city of birth. Leto's fanatical dedication to all things Roman—he refused to learn Greek for fear it would contaminate his Latin style and had his fellow academicians don Roman names and Roman garb—caused Pope Paul II to disband the academy in 1468 believing, probably with some justification, that Leto had taken the "pagan spirit" too far. The pope had Leto and his followers imprisoned for subversion and tortured them mercilessly. The academy was reestablished a few years later in 1471 by order of Pope Sixtus IV.[6]

Naturally enough, there was a good deal of interaction between signorial courts, the academies, and the papacy in matters of dramatic representation. Cardinal Pietro Riario, the nephew of Pope Sixtus IV, was impressed by Leto's researches into ancient Rome and utilized the Accademia Romana in the lavish entertainment given Eleanora of Aragon en route to her marriage to Duke Ercole d'Este of Ferrara in 1473. When Pietro died in 1474, his nephew, Raffaele Sansoni, was appointed his successor. Under the patronage of Cardinal Raffaele Riario, the academy took up the performance of Latin New Comedy and the authentic recreation of the ancient Roman stage as its chief interests. Leto had been especially drawn to Plautus and every year commemorated the founding of Rome with speeches, sermons, and the performance of Roman comedy. Some of Leto's disciples not only acted in these plays but

also wrote others, and it seems that under the sponsorship of Cardinal Riario these practices continued.

In his quest to revive Latin New Comedy in all its richness Leto was very interested in the manner of presentation. Many of the earliest performances of Latin humanist comedy during the Quattrocento involved the recitation of plays to an audience, not their being acted out in a modern sense. For example, Pisani's *Philogenia and Epiphebus* concludes by naming the reciter of the play, "Alphius," also the name of a character in the play. The task of the *recitator* or *recensor* was to read the text of the play aloud, imitating the voice of each character in turn, while actors pantomimed the action. This practice seems most unclassical to us, but the contemporary reasons for it are worth discussing. Senecan tragedy is made up of long speeches, primarily, punctuated by choral moralizing that takes place only when there is no more than one actor on the stage. With the chorus completely cut off from the action, such drama lent itself to declamatory presentation, most suitable to reading aloud. Although Latin New Comedy was based not on oratory but on conversational dialogue, during the Middle Ages a misconception arose that Terence or a friend of his named Calliopius recited the play from a raised platform (*pulpitum*) while a group of mimes placed below the stage gesticulated their accompaniment. This misunderstanding was probably compounded by a passage in Livy (7.2) in which was told the story of the playwright Livius Andronicus, one of the predecessors of Plautus during the third century BC, who had strained his voice after taking too many encores (he was an actor in his own works as well). He employed a young boy, thereupon, to sing as Livius Andronicus acted out the song by means of gestures alone. Livy said that as a result there evolved a distinction between songs (*cantica*) and dialogue (*diverbium*) and, thus, a tradition of two complementary modes of presentation.

In an early fifteenth-century manuscript preserved in the Bibliothèque de l'Arsenal in Paris, the *Térence des ducs* codex, there is a picture representing a performance of one of Terence's comedies. Within an enclosure (*theatrum*) are positioned members of the audience (*populus Romanus*) who are listening to Calliopius on a *scena* read (recite) the play while below him are four grotesques, who are remarkably like the stock characters of the *fabulae Atellanae*, presumably miming the actions by emphatic movements of their bodies.[7] The method of the pantomime was well known to Quattrocento humanists and was surely related to the conventions of the *sacre rappresentazioni* and of various native spectacles employed on social or political occasions.

At the Accademia Romana, Leto was untiring in his research and aided in the restoration, not only of acted drama, but also in the recreation of visualized, scenic drama. The production of plays before an audience was greatly stimulated, of course, by the printed editions of Plautus and Terence in the 1470s. Terence's *Andria* was performed at least three times in 1476 in Florence: in the school of Giorgio Antonio Vespucci, at the Medici palace, and at the Palazzo della Signoria. But the actual staging and scenic design of Latin New Comedy and Latin humanist comedy were revolutionized by the publication in 1486 of Vitruvius' first-century BC *On Architecture (De architectura)*, a work edited by Sulpizio da Veroli and dedicated to Cardinal Raffaele Riario and the Accademia Romana. A second edition appeared in Florence in 1496 and a third in Venice a year later. Vitruvius had been known in manuscript at the beginning of the century — Bracciolini had discovered a codex at St. Gall in 1414 — and was very influential in the development of Renaissance architecture; but besides dealing with the construction of temples and private houses he also devoted time to the building of theatres. And in this area, his influence was explosive. For instance, while Plautus' *Menaechmi* was performed in 1486 at Ferrara amidst great pomp, when it was

given again in 1491, the name of the scenic designer, Niccolò del Cogo, was preserved and handed down. This was no longer closet drama.

In Book V Vitruvius described the actual performance area, the *scena*, of the ancient Roman theater:

> The scenery itself is so arranged that the doors in the middle are like those of a royal palace, while those on the right and left are for strangers. On either side are the spaces prepared for scenery. These are called revolving wings [*periaktoi*] by the Greeks because they have three-sided machines which turn and display on each side as many subjects . . . Next to these spaces angular walls run out which contain the entrances to the stage, one from the public square and the other from the country . . . There are three styles of scenery: one that is called tragic, another comic, and the third satyric . . . The comic scenery has the appearance of private buildings and balconies and projections with windows made to imitate reality in the fashion of ordinary buildings.[8]

Interpretation of this passage during the Quattrocento varied. For the most part, stage scenery had involved the painting of a flat façade, a screen, with various columns, pediments, and statues. The arcades and colonnades used in different kinds of public street-performance and political processions—and prevalent in much Quattrocento painting—were easily adapted to dramatic scene-painting. In the 1491 performance of the *Menaechmi* at Ferrara, Plautus' comedy was put on before a façade depicting four castles. The people were the audience, as was the case in the *sacre rappresentazioni*, and the entrance of the king was the climax of the show, so to speak. Most often, though, the arcade façade depicted four or five houses on an open street, each covered with a curtain at its entrance, because the early designers assumed after reading Latin New Comedy that each character should have his own

house. The houses were attached, so that the street scene looked like an elongated booth. In the ancient Roman theater the audience was in the open air, and the actors had to come out in front of some outdoor structure, such as the royal palace Vitruvius described, to speak their lines. When the play called for an interior scene, a special machine, the *periaktos*, would move the background. During the Quattrocento interior scenes were presented by simply opening the curtains and playing the scene in front of the background screen. In Tommaso Mezzo's *The Epirote* (1483) the opening scene is clearly an interior one but set on an exterior forestage on which Lesbia applies make-up to her mistress Pamphila as the old woman lies on a couch in front of a mirror with her cosmetics spread out in front of her on a dressing-table. The conventions of the arcade façade made it an extremely flexible stage medium, and it was employed in academic settings and various courtly spectacles.

Vitruvius was very specific, too, in assigning doors to the central façade of the stage building, which itself was set on a street and to which access was gained from two side entrances. Though he was not as clear about which was which, the convention seems to have been that the entrance to the spectators' right led to the forum and the entrance to the spectators' left led in the opposite direction to the countryside or the harbor. Thus, the classical *mise-en-scène* emphasized the center of the stage, and there were characteristically five means of access. When characters entered, they did so from side-houses located in the projecting wings which added further breadth to the central space; their approach onto the stage was usually announced by one of the other characters or foreshadowed by the creaking of a door.

During the Renaissance, Terence's comedies were regarded as requiring two or three houses which were typically set on opposite sides of the stage. The earliest of the extant humanist comedies, *Paulus* (ca. 1390) largely followed the Terentian design with the

house of Paulus, the *adulescens*, opposite the house of Nicolosa, the *lena*; the only exception to classical practice was that the two houses had upper storeys and were elevated above street-level. It also appears that Vergerio was aware of the device of the *angiportum*, the alley-way leading back between the houses that faced the audience. Such a design aided the frequent entrances and exits in the play of the *callidus servus*, Herotes, and offered many possibilities for eavesdropping. The two opposing houses intensified the action center-stage by creating a symbolic thematic field of sober self-restraint and unfettered license.[9]

Contributing spatially to this tension was the emerging interest in perspective, an interest underscored by Vitruvius (7.11). The first theoretical treatise on the subject was Leon Battista Alberti's *On Painting* (*Della pittura*, 1436), originally published in Latin in 1435. Vasari attributed the discovery of the artistic uses of perspective to Filippo Brunelleschi (1377–1461), the designer of the dome of the Florentine cathedral, and, indeed, there was much discussion about the handling of space between Alberti and Brunelleschi. In the perspective scene as it was applied to drama, the scenic designer attempted to put on stage an illusionistic picture of an actual place. This kind of verisimilitude was possible when an audience saw the performance from the same vantage-point, a development that was initially embraced by well-to-do aristocrats who could afford such extravagance. The first formal attempts at producing plays on the perspective stage occurred during the early years of the Cinquecento, but judging from a remark about perspective design by Sulpizio da Veroli, the first editor of Vitruvius, upon seeing a performance of the *Menaechmi* at Rome in 1486 which employed "painted scenes (*picturatae scenae*) . . . the first in our time,"[10] contemporary enthusiasm for perspective scenery was widespread and contagious.

There can be little doubt, then, that humanist drama from the later Quattrocento employed the technique of stage perspective; at

the very least, it is probable that an architect like Alberti had the current theories of perspective in mind in the creation of his *Play of Philodoxus* (1424/37). In fact, his later work *On the Art of Building* (*De re aedificatoria*, 1452) faithfully recreated the stage-designs he found in *On Architecture*, earning him the title of "the Florentine Vitruvius." Even though it was written well after the *Play of Philodoxus*, *On the Art of Building* exemplified the principles Alberti employed in his earlier comedy and anticipated later theatrical designs.[11] For example, the architect proposed for the stage a richly decorated central acting space that was defined by side-structures, each with a door. The central space was imagined as a street onto which fronted houses where the action took place. In the case of the *The Play of Philodoxus*, the house of Doxia is opposite that of Ditonus behind which are porticos revealing a doctor's office (a barber-shop) and a tavern. Alberti's stage was the most classical of all.

At the same time, perspective must have seemed an inevitable scenographical choice for both the architect and the dramatist, and Vitruvius provided the authority: "Scene-painting is a shading of the foreground and sides receding and congruent with the center of all the lines of an arc" (1.2).[10] Perspective and scene-painting were one and the same. It has been recorded that Alberti built a *theatrum* in the Vatican palace in 1452 for Pope Nicholas V although there are no records of any performance there until about 1485, when the students of Pomponio Leto began using the space.[11] In the dedicatory letter that Sulpizio da Veroli wrote along with Leto to Cardinal Riario in the preface to the first printed edition of Vitruvius in 1486, what stood out was his enthusiastic hope for the future: If Vitruvius were alive, he says, "he'd be working for you, building camps, villas, churches, porticoes, castles, and palaces, but in the first place theaters . . . Go ahead, then, and build a theatre! We need a theater . . . Of churches we have a goodly number and you can build them when you are old . . . What then

is left for our time to do . . . but to set up a theater?"[12] In the final years of the century the convergence of Vitruvian studies, the theatrical revival of Plautus and Terence, and the increasing attention paid to the varieties of theatrical design provided a fertile seed-ground for the blossoming of the vernacular drama of Ariosto, Machiavelli, and Aretino during the Cinquecento.

Structure and Style

Because the five comedies included in this volume were written over the course of almost a century, they represent an important gauge of the changing literary tastes of the period and of the variety of approaches in the adaptation of Latin New Comedy. This is especially true in matters of dramatic structure and language. Three of them, for instance, are in prose of varying levels of sophistication; of the two verse plays one, the *Paulus* was modeled in substance and form on Terence while the *Chrysis* relied more on Plautus. Only one, Vergerio's *Paulus*, was found adaptable by a later scribe to the five-act structure common to Latin New Comedy,[13] while others were written episodically in scenes and are much more reminiscent of medieval drama. Alberti's *Play of Philodoxus* was rigorous in its observance of the Aristotelian unities and yet organized itself allegorically around the quest of Philodoxus ("lover of glory") for the girl of his choice Doxia ("glory"), a match which, though much complicated by Fortunius ("fortune"), was finally achieved through the help of Chronos ("time"). In contrast, Pisani's *Philogenia and Epiphebus* (ca. 1438), with its gritty realism, could have been taken from a contemporary *novella*: a reckless, wealthy young man named Epiphebus violently seduces Philogenia, a sensitive and honorable girl, carries her off, then marries her off her to a peasant with a view to continuing his illicit liaison. In the arrangement of his fifteen scenes on Pisani's stage we find at least five multi-leveled houses, a church, and a forum, the action

moving from city to country, outdoors to indoors, upstairs and down, with little concern for the unity of place. At the end of the period Tommaso Mezzo advertised *The Epirote* (1483) as "a play constructed in a new way" (*novo modo conditam fabellam*), that is, by daring to employ jokes in a comedy written in prose; sixty years earlier a version of Alberti's comedy circulated under his pseudonym of Lepidus and was thought to be an authentic classical comedy taken from an ancient manuscript (*ex vetustissimo illam [fabulam] esse codice excerptam*) despite its cumbersome medieval trappings. Of the humanist playwrights whose five plays fill this volume, Vergerio was an educator, Alberti a writer, artist and architect, Pisani a courtier, Piccolomini a diplomat and future pope, and Mezzo an antiquarian—men as varied as the traditions and conventions on which they drew.

For example, the allegorizing of ancient texts which was a staple of Renaissance pedagogy surfaces clearly in *The Play of Philodoxus*. Besides presenting the audience with allegorical characters who tend to declaim more than converse, Alberti went out of his way to make his moral explicit: "This play deals with conduct, for it teaches the diligent and hard-working man no less than the rich and fortunate one how to attain glory." Despite its seeming medievalism, the play, however, depended upon classical models: the intrigue plot, for example, is the mainspring of the action in both. Because of his reliance on *sententiae* and the purity of his diction Terence represented to the Quattrocento a fusion of thought and expression very much in keeping with the ethical vision of the time.

For Latin humanist drama written in verse—Vergerio's *Paulus* and Piccolomini's *Chrysis*—Plautus and Terence were the masters of colloquial dialogue, of language that was in the service of the everyday situations of comedy. The Latin metrical structure which gave this impression was rather complicated and employed very differently by the two ancient writers. Aristotle had said in the

Poetics (1449a24–26): "The iambic is indeed the most colloquial of all the meters: proof of this is that we most often use the iambic when we talk to each other." The iambic format that he referred to here, the iambic trimeter (a dodecasyllabic line of six iambic feet |∪∪ – ∪ – |∪ – ∪ – |∪ – ∪ – |), was the standard dialogue form found in Menander's comedies, and it made its way into Roman comedy as the iambic senarius; it is roughly equivalent to English blank verse although the English line is decasyllabic. The final foot of the line was invariably an iambus, but the metrical scheme admitted a number of variations: trochaic (– ∪) or spondaic (– –) feet were often substituted for the expected iambic sequence; at the same time, both iambic and trochaic rhythms could be altered by lengthening the short elements (∪ – ∪ – to – – – – or – ∪ – ∪ to – – – –) or the resolution of long syllables into its short elements, the iambic format, then, looking like ∪ ∪ ∪ ∪ ∪ ∪ ; occasionally, entire scenes were made up of longer lines in either iambic or trochaic patterns (the septenarius or octonarius) which seemed to have been accompanied by the flute and were used to evoke a special liveliness. Iambic measures were common, but a feature found in Terence but not in Plautus was his desire to interweave metrical patterns over quite short stretches of writing as a way of controlling tone and tempo. Thus, the varieties of rhythm were almost unlimited.[14]

The Latin playwrights of the Quattrocento who wrote in verse made little consistent use of the iambic and trochaic rhythms typical of Latin New Comedy. To begin with, only a few plays were written in verse at all, probably because, as we have seen, most of Terence's manuscripts were arranged as prose—Hrotsvitha's six adaptations were also composed in prose—so that it would only be at the end of the century that any serious complaint would be heard. Poliziano wrote in a prologue he added for the production of Plautus' *Menaechmi* in Florence in 1488 that a comedy written in prose was no comedy at all. Polemics followed, and the question of

the proper medium for comedy was hotly debated in the Cinque-cento. In the vernacular *commedia erudita* of Ariosto, for example, both prose and poetic versions of several of his comedies have sur-vived. When Vergerio wrote his *Paulus* about 1390 in verse, he was familiar with ancient prosody; a few years later in 1395 he and Francesco Zabarella composed a treatise on the subject, the *On the Metrical Art* (*De arte metrica*). However, only about five per cent of the 865 lines in his play are in the classical senarius. Vergerio pre-ferred, instead, to adapt Terence's construction of plot and charac-ter, especially his *Andria* and *Eunuchus*, citing Terentian meter (*Andria*, 66) only once in the *On the Metrical Art*.[15] His verse does attempt to reproduce the line-length of Terence's comic verse, and, at times, he is very careful to alternate short and long lines, espe-cially in scenes involving complicated intrigue where the fast-talk-ing slave Herotes is center-stage (e.g., Scene VIII). In one in-stance of comic irony, when Herotes is pantomiming his enjoyment of Ursula in front of the audience at Nicolosa's house on one side of the stage, on the other side at Paulus' house Herotes' master is simultaneously and unwittingly cheering him on: "Herotes, fight as hard as you can; you have to deliver on this deal." Still, in most instances, Vergerio's poetry sounds more like the rhythmical prose of a medieval academic farce.

Piccolomini's *Chrysis* of 1444 is much more dependent on Plautus in form and matter, but still metrically uneven. Line-length is more consistently based on the senarius, and Piccolomini maintains an iambus in the final foot of his regular lines; never-theless, he had a tendency to use other metrical patterns, not be-cause the scene called for variation but probably for the simple reason that they appeared in Plautus. Thus, *Chrysis* employs ana-pestic ($\cup\ \cup\ -$) rhythms for the set-piece of Charinus' monologue in Scene VIII, the bacchiac ($\cup\ -\ -$) in Scene XV, and the cretic ($-\ \cup\ -$), a pattern often found in the lyrics of comedy and used by Piccolomini in Canthara's exaltation of wine in Scene V and

Dyophanes' lamentation one scene later. Piccolomini's *Chrysis* represents the emergence of the Plautine model in Quattrocento Latin comedy. Piccolomini's characters, situations, and language are faithful renderings of the ancient Plautine comedies he knew.

The plot of the play is centered on the kind of love intrigue common to Latin New Comedy and set, for the most part, in a bordello, whose three adjoining spaces form a kind of comic triptych: the vestibule, the bedroom, and the kitchen-dining area. The intermingling of prurience, overindulgence, and moral pomposity symbolically expressed by these spaces is Plautine and cleverly enhanced by Piccolomini's timing of character entrances and exits. The vitality of Piccolomini's adaptation of Plautus is expressed not only in his realistic orchestration of detail that borders on obscenity but also in its anti-clerical cynicism. Two of the lovers of the courtesans, Chrysis and Cassina, for example, are the ecclesiastics Dyophanes and Theobolus who tout their privilege:

We live for ourselves; others live for others.
Beautiful Venus is more favorable to us than to anyone else.

Even though Piccolomini tried to wrest a hollow moral from the sensuality through the character of Archimenides in the final verses of the play — "Virtue excels all things, and the virtuous man lacks for nothing" — it wasn't the moralism that his critics remembered.[16]

The three prose comedies included in this collection — Alberti's *Play of Philodoxus* of 1424/37 , Pisani's *Philogenia and Epiphebus* from about 1438, and Mezzo's *The Epirote* of 1483 — testify to the increasing importance attached not only to Latin New Comedy but also to the evolving definition of classicism itself. They were all written in scenes, without any act-divisions, and largely because of their episodic structure, look more medieval than classical. Alberti's characters may have ancient names and the setting may duplicate ancient Rome at the time of the Punic Wars, but its allegory

was clearly inspired by more medieval motives. Pisani's characters have ancient names, too, but they are also realistic figures drawn from Italian life, and his comedy deftly mirrors contemporary attitudes towards women, marriage, social class, and clerical hypocrisy. The wedding scene of Philogenia and her oafish fiancé Gobius is a comic *tour de force*, while the seduction scene between Philogenia and Epiphebus employs all the commonplaces of courtly love. Pisani, whom Angelo Decembrio (?1415–after 1467) had dubbed "a mighty imitator of the plays of Plautus and of comic style,"[17] adapted for his *Philogenia and Epiphebus* the plot of Plautus' *Casina*, in which the protagonist hopes to bed his wife's maid by marrying her off to his own slave. The latest of the three prose comedies, Mezzo's *The Epirote*, is the most successful in its reworking of ancient conventions.[18] The play takes place in Syracuse where the *virgo* Antiphila (who never appears in the play) is unable to wed Clitipho, the *adulescens*, because she lacks a dowry. At just the right moment, the uncle of Antiphila — the man from Epirus of the title — who thought his niece was dead, arrives, discovers that the girl is alive, and provides not only the finances but the happy ending as well. The action of the play is completely simple. The characters are recognizable types from the ancient Roman theater — there is a second Clitipho who complicates the intrigue — and they all fit into the plot seamlessly.

All of the Latin comedies included in this volume attempted to recapture the appeal of the ancient theater by means of careful imitation. The retrieval and dissemination of ancient texts played an obvious role, but we have seen, too, that ideas about comic structure and the proper instrument for comic form were still unsettled at the beginning of the Cinquecento. The modes of literary expression in Latin humanist comedy are personal, varied, and dynamic, and offer us a meaningful vantage-point for assessing its achievements. The evolving standards of proper structure and

proper Latinity, *latinitas*, represent not just a stylistic debate but a cultural one that mirrors the intellectual history of Quattrocento humanism and its attempt to define and recover its own idealized past.

One of the most pleasant of any writer's tasks is to thank those who through their knowledge, support, and kindness have made his labors easier. The research for the volume was carried out at a number of libraries: the Widener and Houghton Libraries of Harvard University, the James P. Adams Library of Rhode Island College, the University of Rhode Island Library, the John Hay and John D. Rockefeller, Jr., Libraries of Brown University, the Biblioteca Apostolica Vaticana, the Biblioteca Medicea Laurenziana and Biblioteca Riccardiana in Florence, the Biblioteca Comunale of Piacenza, the Biblioteca Municipale in Reggio nell'Emilia, the Biblioteca Nazionale Marciana in Venice, and the Bibliothèque Nationale de France. I am indebted to the directors and research staffs of these institutions for their unflinching services on my behalf. To Myra Blank of Rhode Island College I am particularly grateful. I have also benefited from the kindness of dott.ssa Alessandra Tizzi Barbanti of the University of Bologna and her staff for their hospitality and graciousness. Professor Emeritus Joseph P. McSweeney of Rhode Island College and Professor Joseph Carroll of Providence College have helped me shape and clarify my ideas over many months (and many dinners) by offering their time and individual talents to my project. Professor Stephen Barber of the University of Rhode Island has always been an avid supporter and helped me reconnoiter my way through some German documents. I am also indebted, in ways great and small, to Professors Harold Bloom of Yale University, Barbara Lewalski of Harvard University, and Olga Juzyn of Rhode Island College as well as to Dr. Margaret Fogel. To my colleague and friend at Rhode

Island College, Professor Robert E. Hogan, I owe the greatest debt for his unwavering enthusiasm, careful proofing, and technical expertise. All of the errors and omissions that my friends tried to forestall are, of course, my own. The Faculty Research Fund and the Faculty Development Fund at Rhode Island College provided me with financial support that gave me time to work; I am very thankful for the assistance and friendship of President John Nazarian. Finally, although the many labors of my wife, Carrie Mitzel, shall be nameless, without them this volume would never have been written:

ὄστρακα ἀντὶ χρυσωμάτων

NOTES

1. The structural details concerning Latin New Comedy and its sources are drawn from Duckworth, *The Nature of Roman Comedy*, esp. pp. 236–71; David Konstan, *Roman Comedy* (Ithaca: Cornell University Press, 1983); and Erich Segal, *Roman Laughter: The Comedy of Plautus*, 2nd ed. (Oxford: Oxford University Press, 1986). (Items cited in these notes in short title form only may be found in the Bibliography.)

2. *Hrotsvithae in sex comoedias suas praefatio*, in Jacques-Paul Migne, ed., *Patrologiae cursus completus. Series Latina*, 221 vols. (Paris: Migne, 1844–91), vol. 137, cols. 972D–973A.

3. E. K. Chambers, *The Medieval Stage*, 2 vols. (Oxford: Oxford University Press, 1903), 2:210.

4. Paul Grendler, *Schooling in Renaissance Italy* (Baltimore: The Johns Hopkins University Press, 1989), pp. 250–52 and L. D. Reynolds, *Texts and Transmission* (Oxford: Oxford University Press, 1983), pp. 412–20.

5. Jacob Burckhardt, in his *The Civilization of the Renaissance in Italy* (New York: Phaidon, 1965), discusses these festivals, especially on pp. 246–52.

6. Lily B. Campbell, *Scenes and Machines on the English Stage during the Renaissance: A Classical Revival* (Cambridge: Cambridge University Press, 1923; repr. New York: Barnes and Noble, 1960), pp. 11–12.

7. George R. Kernodle, *From Art to Theatre: Form and Convention During the Renaissance* (Chicago: University of Chicago Press, 1944), pp. 68–70.

8. Vitruvius, *De architectura*, 5.6.8.

9. On the similar dynamics of space in Latin New Comedy, cf. Segal, *Roman Comedy*, pp. 43–44.

10. L. *Vitruvii Pollionis ad Caesarem Augustum de Architectura liber primus (-decimus)*, ed. Joannes Sulpitius (Rome: Eucharius Silber, 1486), "Praefatio."

11. Cf. Anthony Grafton, *Alberti: Master Builder*, ch. 8. See also Erwin Panofsky, "Die Perspektive als 'symbolische Form'," *Vorträge der Bibliothek Warburg* 4 (1924–25): 258–330; reprinted in *Perspective as Symbolic Form*, tr. C. S. Wood (New York: Zone Books, 1997), pp. 38–41.

12. L. Vitruvii Pollionis, "Praefatio."

13. Alessandro Perosa in his 1983 edition of the text demonstrated (pp. 299–303) that it was a late fifteenth-century copyist, Francesco Negri, who provided act and scene divisions in accord with Donatus' programme.

14. For a full listing of Terence's metrical variations, see John Barsby, ed., *The Plays of Terence* (Cambridge: Harvard University Press, 2001), 2:369–75.

15. Pier Paolo Vergerio and Francesco Zabarella, *De arte metrica* (MS. Marc. lat. XIII, 41 [4729]), 3ᵛ.

16. Archimenides was probably modeled on Wilhelm Tacz, the imperial secretary while Piccolomini was at the Diet at Nuremberg, where the latter wrote the *Chrysis* (see note 1 in Notes to the Translation). He was forced to defend himself to Michael von Pfullendorff, the chief clerk of chancery to Frederick III (the emperor who crowned Piccolomini poet laureate in 1442). According to Enea Silvio, Wilhelm had attacked him for writing the comedy: "you scorn not only the poem but also the poet, and accuse me, who wrote the comedy, of being cheap, as if Terence and Plautus, who also wrote comedies, had not been praised." See Enea Silvio Piccolomini, *Opera quae extant omnia* (Basel, 1551), p. 586.

17. Quoted by Jon Pearson Perry, "A Fifteenth-Century Dialogue," p. 635. Cf. also Christopher S. Celenza, "Creating Canons in Fifteenth-Century Ferrara: Angelo Decembrio's *De politia litteraria*, 1.10," *Renaissance Quarterly* 57 (2004): 43–98.

18. For Tommaso Mezzo's use of his ancient models, see Braun's edition (1973), pp. 26–35.

HUMANIST COMEDIES

PAULUS

Prologus

Hanc dum poeta michi verecundus fabulam
tradidit recensendam, 'Iuvenis,' ait 'hec lusi,
iam plenior dabit sensum maturum etas',
veritus, opinor, ne se homines forte graves

5   levitatis arguant. Quos contra sentio,
siquis ita sentiat. Que sunt enim, rogo,
que plus ferant in vita levitates ponderis
quam nosce quantum sit inimica bonis
studiis rerum copia?

10   Date commodum aures michi atque animum intendite
quam comentus siet poeta fabulam,
dum non lugentium, sed negligentium
mores novos ratione corrigit veteri;
quantum momentum ad diluendas opes

15   in malis siet servis;
quam misere parentes fallat de natis amor.
Postremo satius esse sentit frustra se
laborare quam gratis ociosum agere: esse
servos infidos, sodales devios, parentes credulos.

PAULUS

CHARACTERS

Paulus, *a university student*
Herotes, *Paulus' hired servant and companion*
Stichus, *Paulus' slave*
Damma, *Paulus' servant*

Titus, *Paulus' aged tutor*
Nicolosa, *procuress*
Ursula, *courtesan*
Papis, *servant*

Scene: Bologna

Prologue

When the shamefaced poet handed me this play to be performed, he said: "When I was a young man I dallied in such things. Now that I'm older, age has given me a richer sense of what is appropriate." I think he was worried that serious men might perhaps blame him for this frivolity of his. Should anyone feel that way, my view is the opposite. After all, are there any frivolities in this life, I ask you, that have a more serious effect on our understanding of how inimical great wealth is to sound studies?

So lend an ear to me and pay close attention to the play that the poet has composed, in the course of which he uses an ancient genre of writing to condemn modern morals — not the morals of tragic figures, but of heedless ones.[1] He shows how strong the tendency is among wicked servants to destroy wealth, and how miserably love deceives parents when it comes to their children. Finally, the poet believes that it is more satisfying to work hard, even if the effort is vain, than to be lazy at someone else's expense; he also believes that servants are disloyal, friends devious, and parents easily taken in.

: I :

Paulus dominus, Herotes servus

20 *Pa.* Quis me? Quis est? Non iussi huic: 'Me
si quisquam mane velit, siet quivis,
negato domi'?

He. Nemo est quisquam, ipsemet
mensam solus pono; pauxillum adhuc securus
omnium dormi, dum paro.

Pa. Te perdat
25 Deus cum istoc tuo tripodum strepitu, qui me
ex periucundo sopore evigilasti! An nundum
in tertiam?

He. Nunc primum.

Pa. Deus
immortalis ac superi omnes! Quas michi delicias
tulit hic somnus, quos honores, quas inextimabiles
30 ac veras voluptates! Videbar ipse michi
coronatus iam emerita lauro in patriam
ivisse me, ac protinus sponsam virginem
generosam michi, que decore superaret solem.
Quis autem conventus ad me optimatium,
35 quis omnium concursus! Ego ipse videbar
consilia cuntis dare, iudicia regere,
interpretari leges veteres, leges constitui
autoritate mea novas. Quid multa?
Siquid exorbuissem amplius, rex eram!
40 Verum, tametsi hec sint insomnia,
non procul ab re tamen futura reor,
siquidem edisco clarusque fiam. Sed quid
infelix ago? Nulli natus usui, nulli
bonae rei datus nisi luxui et somno,

4

: I :

Paulus, master of the house; Herotes, slave

[*Paulus, a student at the university, lies abed until
the crash of a kettle awakens him.*]

Paulus. Who wants me? Who is it? [*Muttering to himself*] Didn't I 20
give orders to this fellow, if anyone comes looking for me in the
morning, no matter who he is, to say that I'm not at home?

Herotes. There's nobody there, it's just me setting the table. Don't
worry about anything; just go back to sleep for a bit while I'm
getting things ready.

Paulus. God damn you! You woke me up from a delightful sleep
with your clatter of pots and pans. Is it nine o'clock yet?[2] 25

Herotes. Just now. [*He leaves the room.*]

Paulus. By immortal God and all the heavenly host! What delightful things happened to me in this dream; what honors,
what unimaginable and genuine pleasures! I seemed to see my- 30
self home in my native country crowned with a well-deserved
laurel[3] and that I'd married without any delay a noble maiden
whose beauty outshone the sun. All the leading citizens of the
town came to me—what a crowd! Then I saw myself giving advice to them all, in charge of the law courts, interpreting old 35
laws and drawing up new ones on my own authority. In short,
if I'd swallowed any more power, I would've been king! But
even if these are only dreams, I don't think the future will be
much different if I study hard and become famous. 40

But what am I talking about, unlucky fellow that am? I was
born useless, the only thing I'm good for is self-indulgence and

45   quartum iam in studiis annum dego:
          vix totidem literas nactus sum!
          Omnia facio quam quapropter huc veni,
          dignus qui in ludum rursus ac ferulam eo:
          diem, numum roburque prodigo.
50   Verum, quoniam, ut aiunt, quiescentes
          sapere melius, hoc ipso in loco
          inertie mee nutritore
          conficiam de me: insistere ad summum tandem
          destino literis — certum est enim
55   nichil impossibile, difficile factu,
          quod sibi quis constituat faciundum —,
          herere, insudare, animum in libris ponere,
          dum doctus sum. Dinus, isque admodum
          tener, quam elegans biennio hoc evasit;
60   alter ille annum solum audivit literas
          iamque cum omnibus sedulo disputat.
          Sed copia est ea michi que inertiam nutriat:
          ego, si michi labore querendus esset
          victus, iam non in minimis connumerarer.
65   Sed efficiam profecto, ne me deinceps
          peniteat: in longam noctem
          vigilabo, noctem ad quartam
          ante diu exurgam, emittam
          hanc desidiosam iuventutem.
70   Vah, quantum preteriti mores subolent michi:
          studio, vigilia atque inedia
          veteres excastigabo errores,
          rennes domabo ieiunio! Hic itaque
          dies bene michi agendi principium sit:
75   quin protinus exurgo et propositum
          exequor? Heus tu, Herotes,
          infer ut quam primum lavem!

sleep. Already I've spent four years in school, but I've hardly ac-   45
quired a proportionate amount of learning! I do everything except what I came here for; I ought to return to grammar school
and the master's stick. I'm wasting time, money, and strength.
Well, then, since they say that calm minds have more wisdom,   50
in this very place that feeds my languor, I need to take myself in
hand and press on to accomplish at last my academic goals.
Certainly nothing is impossible or difficult to do if somebody   55
decides that he simply must do it. I just have to stick to it,
sweat it out, put my mind to my books until I become learned.
Look at Dinus,[4] who is quite a young chap: how cultivated he's
become in the last two years; then there's that other fellow who   60
has only been hearing lectures for a year and is already disput-
ing with everybody non-stop. It's my wealth that feeds my torpor; if I had to work for my keep, I wouldn't by now be classed
among the worst students. I really should get down to it so I   65
don't regret it later. I'll stay up late, get up at 4 A.M., and say
goodbye to this idle youth of mine.

Ah, these past habits of mine—how much they stink to me   70
now! By studying, late nights, and fasting I'll correct my old
mistakes, and I'll get control of my lower urges through absti-
nence. Let this day, then, be the beginning of my good behavior. Why not get up right now and follow through on my plan?   75
Ho, there, Herotes, bring some water so I can wash up as soon

Quisque dissuasor accesserit, hic michi
hostis siet, cui nec pace nec venia
80 unquam conciliari possit. Heus tu, Herotes,
infer quam primum ut lavem!

He.   Iubeo te
dies letum agere semper. Et quid his
Natalibus? Nichil ne? Cum ceteri
ferveant, nos frigebimus?

Pa.   Nescio quid
85 me vetet, quin ambos tibi oculos diruam,
omnium nequissime! Non sum ego, qui iam dudum,
ut me noris, qui iam dudum, neque qui hactenus . . .

He. (Profecto amens hic factus est, quanquam . . .)
Sed quid ita exarsisti? Quisnam offendit?

90 *Pa.* Quisnam? Ego me, ego me, qui iam diu
tempus omisi omne. Nunc vero, ut scias
quis sim: is sum ego, qui velim totis eniti
viribus in literas, idque nunc primum,
ceteraque respuere.

He.   Recte sane,
95 nam id ego iam dudum monere te constitueram,
et fecissem, nisi per te facturum sperassem.
Sed quamobrem tam sero?

Pa.   Non fit sero
quod bene aliquando fit. Ingenium
tale michi esse sentio, quo
100 facile amissa redimam.

He. Quam vero ob rem ita repente?

Pa. Hec iubeo ne queras, quia ita constitui.

He. (Sed ego pervertam omnia). Recte sane,
sed vide, ne, dum veram gloriam queras,
105 infamiam falso subeas. Si enim abstineas
ab his rebus, quas soles queque pars maior

as possible. Anybody who comes and tries to talk me out of my plan will make himself my enemy. I could never pardon or make peace with him. Hey you, Herotes, bring the water right away so I can wash up!   80

Herotes. [Enters] A very good morning to you, as always! And what are we doing this Christmas? Nothing at all? Shall we freeze while the rest are aglow?

Paulus. I don't know what keeps me from tearing out both your eyes, you utter scoundrel! I'm not the man you knew just a mo-   85
ment ago, who a moment ago . . . nor him who hitherto . . .
[Spluttering]

Herotes. [Aside] This man is certainly out of his head. That not-withstanding . . . [To Paulus] But what are you so mad about? Who, pray, offended you?

Paulus. Who, pray? It's I—I!—who have offended my own self,   90
because I've been wasting all my time for so long! But now—
just so you know who I am now—I am someone who would like to spend all my effort in study. This must come first; the rest I spit on.

Herotes. Quite right. I had decided some time ago to admonish   95
you about this, and should have done so had I not expected you would do it yourself. But why such resolution so late in the day?

Paulus. It's never too late to do the right thing. I feel I have the smarts to make up for lost time.   100

Herotes. But why this all of a sudden?

Paulus. Don't ask me. I've decided that's the way it will be.

Herotes. [Aside] But I'll undermine all this. [To Paulus] Quite right. But make sure that while you go in search of true glory you don't acquire a bad name you don't deserve. If you stay away from the festivities you normally engage in and which   105

hisce festis gerunt, non te recto studio deditum
dicent, sed aut inopia laborare aut
avaritia. Preterea nunquam tibi autor ero ego,
110 ut te excrucies. Modum in omnibus rebus
servari aiunt vestri philosophi. Non es tu
qui querendus sit ex studio numus —
servent Superi modo que domi sunt —
quem ve gravare possit impensa longior.
115 Ego, si detur optio michi, nolim plenus esse literarum:
ita raro summe litere cum summa prudentia coeunt.
Tu vero, quoniam abundans innata disciplina, quam
non dant scole, ubique clarus vel sine libris
eris.

Pa.   Quid si accedant litere et doctrina
multa?

120 He.   Quid, quod ita moriere ut quivis
indoctus, aut quod absit sensus post
multas literas?

Pa.   Ego vero velim, quantum fieri potest,
doctus esse.

He.   Haud dubie, sed his interea
diebus tete oblectare, quo possis
fortior rem aggredi.

125 Pa.   Faciam,
quoniam ita tibi videtur, sed postea
fac me iuves.

He.   Faciam sedulo
(Iam actum est, quanquam, etsi nichil admonuissem,
bidui aut ad summum tridui futurus
130 erat hic fervor. Somniavit profecto
aliquid, unde ita ferveret:
contraria omnia somnio diluentur).

Pa.   Sed heus tu, unde suberit numus?

most people observe this time of year, they'll say, not that you've devoted yourself to your proper studies, but that you're poor or stingy. Besides, I won't ever endorse any self-torture on your part. Our philosophers tell us that the mean should be observed in all things.[5] You don't have to worry about making a living from your studies — may the gods preserve the fortunes of your house! — nor is prolonged expense a burden to you. If I had the choice, I wouldn't stuff myself with literature, given that a high degree of literary skill rarely goes together with the highest degree of prudence. You overflow with the kind of innate knowledge schools don't provide: you'll be famous everywhere even without book-learning.

Paulus. But what if I add literature and great learning to my natural endowment?

Herotes. Why? So you can die just like any other ignoramus? So you can lose all common sense after acquiring all that booklearning?

Paulus. But I really want to be as learned as I can possibly be.

Herotes. I don't doubt it. But meanwhile, have some fun during the holidays so that you can dive into your studies with renewed vigor.

Paulus. I'll do it since you say so, but afterwards, you have to help me.

Herotes. I'll do so with all my heart. [*Aside*] This fever of academic ambition is already over with! However, even if I hadn't chided him at all, it would have lasted two or three days at most. He must have had a dream that got him infected this way: contrary humors all get discharged in dreams.

Paulus. But hold on, where will the money come from? My half-

Nam semiannua stips consumpta iam est.

135   Libri ex prioris anni contractis apud
creditorem sunt; fenoris
pauculum est, quod in diurnum
suppetat sumptum.

He.   Vah, quid
dubitas? Mutuum a quovis cape.

140 *Pa.*   Quis credat aut unde reddam?

He.   Credet? Ego iam, si velis, milia tibi
credi faxo. Abi iam protinus ad eum,
qui aures tuas quottidie obtundit,
dic te quam primum ad concurrentem iturum, nisi . . .

145   Dabit illico, crede michi. Id vero
dubium est, quod resarcire non possis.
Ad patrem illico scribes indigere te
libris aut priores consumptos incendio
cum rebus ceteris vel gravi te

150   morbo laborasse. Non deerunt nobis cause:
me, me notatorem face! Postremo, nisi det,
aut miliciam secuturum aut in extremam
barbariem, idest viciniam proximam,
iturum te minato. Tum proxime

155   senior parens obibit mortem,
quod emundum plurimi iam dudum fuerat.

Pa.   Ego vero, si unquam in manus veniat meas
administratio rerum, meo arbitrio utar
atque abutar; sed malo ob exiguum fenus

160   ad creditorem ire quam cuiquam ex mutuo
obnoxium me reddam. Abi igitur
et duos illos codices, qui soli apud me
sunt, vestesque ex scrinio collige, quoad
libras auri tres cogas; deinde in macellum
ito et in Ravennensem portam.

year allowance has already been eaten up. Thanks to my debts
from last term, I've pawned all my books, and there's only a lit-   135
tle bit left from the loan to pay my daily expenses.

Herotes. No problem. Just get a loan from somebody.

Paulus. Who'll give me credit and how am I going to repay him?   140

Herotes. Who'll give you credit? If you want, I can get you thou-
sands in credit right now. Go right away to the fellow who talks
your ears off every day, tell him you'll go immediately to his
competitor, unless! He'll give you the cash on the spot, believe   145
me. And anyway, it's not clear you couldn't pay it back. Write
to your father that you need new books, or that your old ones
were lost in a fire along with all your other effects, or that you're
suffering from some serious illness. We'll have all the excuses   150
we need; I'll be your witness. Finally, if he doesn't fork it over,
say that you're going to become a soldier or that you're going off
to some remote and barbarous place, while you really remain
nearby.[6] Then again, the old boy is going to die soon, anyway,   155
—something that should have been cleaned up a long time ago.

Paulus. Well, if I ever do get to manage my own affairs, I'll spend
and mispend my resources as I see fit, but given the small
amount we need, I'd rather go to a pawnbroker than incur any   160
fresh debt. So go get the two books I still have left and my
clothes from the closet; they should fetch three pounds; then go
to the market and the Ravenna gate.[7]

165 *He.*   Scio
quid velis.
Pa.   Hoc ipsum est quod nolo.
He. Qui scis quid rear?
Pa.   Quicquid
reris, id est quod nolo. Nunquam ego
ullius autor ero sententie primus?
170 Genus omne vestrum divinare semper sed falso
solet. Sed audi tandem michi:
ut bene curemur, stude.
He.   Hoc ego
dicebam.
Pa.   Hoc ego non iubeo tibi,
sed hoc ipsum te rogo, quoniam ita vis,
175 ne nos misere . . . Abi igitur: ego in hortulos
divertam, ut ex motu et frigore famem michi . . .

: II :

Stichus, Herotes servi; Paulus dominus

Sti. Here, scis quam fidelis rerum omnium siem.
Pa. Earum quippe, que non sunt, aut tibi
nequeas infidus esse.
Sti.   Nichil est opus,
180 ut amplius commendet me quisquam tibi.
Sed secreto me habe: vereor enim illum.
Pa. Quid rei est?
Sti.   Ego, dum suppellectilem
meam conficerem, preter cubiculum
tuum forte preterii atque intro aspexi.

Herotes. I know what *you* want.   165

Paulus. That's exactly what I don't want want.

Herotes. How do you know what I'm thinking?

Paulus. Whatever you're thinking, I don't want it. Don't I ever get
   to decide first? People like you are always guessing your master's   170
   thoughts, and guessing wrong. Just listen to me for a change,
   and try to see to it that we're well taken care of.

Herotes. That's just what I was starting to say.

Paulus. I'm not ordering you to do this, I'm asking you because
   you don't want us to spend the holidays in misery. So get going.   175
   I'll take a stroll in the gardens, so that between the walk and
   the cold, I'll work up an appetite.

: II :

Stichus, Herotes, slaves; Paulus, master

[*Paulus and Stichus walk together outside*]

Stichus. Master, you know how faithful I am in all matters of business.

Paulus. Well, you can hardly be unfaithful in business matters that
   don't exist.

Stichus. There's no further need for anyone to recommend me to
   you. But in confidence, I'm afraid of that man.   180

Paulus. What's the matter?

Stichus. While I was just minding my own business, I happened to
   go by your bedroom and look in. I saw Herotes rifling through

185   Vidi Herotem sedulo agitantem omnia,
            colligentem vestes atque omne ornamentum;
            recluserat scrinia omnia: veritus sum,
            ne furtum faceret.

     Pa.   Ut quid non
            conclamasti illico? Fortasse iam abierit.

190   *Sti.*   Timui, ut ne me exagitaret, ut solet.
            Atque id dico tibi: inhumane facis
            qui tantum illi de me sinas.

     Pa.   Ego vero non sinam postac. Sed quo pacto
            opinari hoc de illo potes, cuius michi

195   fides in omnibus rebus est perspecta?

     Sti.   Ego quodvis flagitium de eo facile
            credo, qui tam crudelis in me siet.
            Sed si quando auscultare michi voles . . .

     Pa.   Ne suspices igitur: ego iussi, ut pulverem
            vestibus excuteret.

200   *Sti.*   At vero
            et libros tuos illos precipuos coegerat.

     Pa.   Expurgare fortasse omnia voluit.
            Tu vero abi et para omnia,
            ut, cum voluero, cibus in promptu adsiet.

     He.   Stice!

     Sti.   Quis me vocat?

205   *He.*   Stice!

     Sti.   (Hei michi, Herotes est: audivit omnia, perii!)

     He.   Iners, ignave, neque respondes?
            Sursum ocius!

     Pa.   Abi ad eum!

     Sti.   Obsecro, mi here, ne me solum ad eum

210   dimittas: conficiet me atque extrangulabit.

     Pa.   Ne time: siquid voles, ad vocem adero.
            Deus bone, quam timidum est hoc genus hominum,

everything, gathering up your clothes and all your valuables; he   185
had opened all your chests. I was afraid he might be robbing
you.

Paulus. So why didn't you sound the alarm then and there? Perhaps he's already taken off.

Stichus. I was afraid that he might beat me up, as he often does.   190
And by the way, it's really cruel of you to let him treat me that
way.

Paulus. I won't after this. But how can you think such a thing
about Herotes, whose complete loyalty to me is so obvious?   195

Stichus. I can believe anything of a man who treats me with such
cruelty. But if you'll just listen to me . . .

Paulus. Well, you needn't be suspicious. I was the one who told
him to shake the dust out of my clothes.

Stichus. But he was gathering up even your most important books.   200

Paulus. Perhaps he just wanted to clean up everything. Now go get
everything ready, so the food will be ready when I want it.

Herotes. [*from inside*] Stichus!

Stichus. Who's calling me?

Herotes. Stichus!   205

Stichus. Oh, no! It's Herotes. He's heard everything. I'm finished!

Herotes. You lazy good-for-nothing, why don't you answer me?
Come up here right away!

Paulus. Get going.

Stichus. Please, dear master, don't let me alone with him. He's going to kill me! He'll strangle me!   210

Paulus. Don't worry, if you want anything, I'll be within earshot.
[*Stichus exits*]. Good God, how timid that kind of man is!

sive regio mundi sive fortassis
conditio servitutis imminuat animum!

215   Idem Ethiopibus evenit? Quam quidem opto,
ut habeam mecum unum — et habeo,
si me nichil preter vetustatem consumet —
in quem nichil velim ut Heroti liceat!
Cum enim preteriero, omnes me domine

220   spectabunt et mirabuntur qui sim,
qui Ethiopes Teucrosque servos habeam
empticios, cum ceteri non nisi
immundos Germanos, qui caules
sepo condiant et potent poculis oleum.

225   Sed quid est, quod audio? Quis tumultus,
quis clamor? Recte presagivit Sticus
subauditum se ab Herote. Sed adibo
ac sciam, egon ille ne domi presit.

: III :

Herotes, Stichus, Damma servi; Paulus dominus

He.   Nisi me huius tenuisset respectus
230   simulque quod in ignavos homines
manus meas conicere pudet, ita te
ego castigassem, ut semper mei
faxo memineris.

Sti.   Imo vero ita
ad summum concussisti me, carnifex
235   crudelissime, ut constare michimet nequeam,
neque te tenuit pudor nec etatis mee
reverentia.

Pa.   Iniquus es: Herotes,
dico tibi!

Maybe it's where they come from or the condition of slavery it- self that enfeebles their spirit.[8] I wonder if Ethiopians are like 215 that. I'd really like to have one as a slave — and I would have one, too, if I weren't being eaten up by things besides old age — a slave who wouldn't enjoy the same license that Herotes has with me. Then when I go by, all the ladies will look at me and 220 wonder who I am that I have Ethiopians and Turks as my chat- tels, while everybody else just has dirty Germans with their sauerkraut and beer. Now what's that I hear? What's all that 225 shouting and commotion? Stichus must have been right when he had a hunch Herotes overheard him. I'd better go and find out whether it's Herotes or I who am in charge of this house. [Enters]

:   III   :

Herotes, Stichus, Damma, slaves; Paulus, master

[Paulus has just entered]

Herotes. If respect for my master hadn't held me back, if I weren't 230 ashamed to lay my hands on a villain like you, I'd have given you such a thrashing that you'd remember it for the rest of your life.
Stichus. Actually, you thug, you've cuffed me so hard that I can't stand up straight; in fact, neither shame nor respect for my age 235 held you back.
Paulus. You're in the wrong — Herotes, I'm talking to you!

He.   Iam vero tu prius
iudicare vis quam me audias. Ego
240   cum facerem que tu iusseras et res
istas michi ac Damme subigerem, intervenit
iste clamitans: 'Quid agis, fur?
Res dominicas cum istoc consorte surripis?'

Sti.   Falsus es, iniquissime hominum!

He.   Damma, ita ne?

245 Da.   (Connixit: astruendum
est). Imo vero.

He.   Tum accurrit, ut
effrenis leo et diripere res tentat.
Quas cum leviter contraxisset, cecidit
ille vino, ut reor, plenus meque
accusat.

250 Pa.   Dixin crebro: 'Nichil tibi
cum istoc'? Tu non quiescis.

Sti.   Ita te
eradicet Deus, ut nichil michi hodie
ingestum est nichilque bibi nisi lacrimas,
quas colaphis expressisti michi; neque ego
255   quicquam conatus sum, sed quam primum
percuntatus sum: 'Quid agis? Quo defers?
Vide sis, ne non bene . . .', tu continuo
verbis, post verberibus es me aggressus.
Sed ita tu eum castigas et me: 'Tibi nichil
260   cum istoc!', et pateris eum uno momento
et domi tue esse. Ne subit, quod alumni
vice tibi sum datus, qui te tuaque curem?
Aliquando hec pater scibit! Non enim
is sine te hec ageret.

Pa.   Mirum, quod
265   te non iam sugillavit, qui tam omnibus

Herotes. Now you want to judge me before hearing me out. While   240
I was just doing your bidding, getting your stuff ready for me
and Damma to cart off, this character runs in shouting, "What
are you doing, you thief? Are you stealing the master's things,
you and your accomplice?"

Stichus. You're lying, you scoundrel!

Herotes. Damma, [*winking at Damma*], am I not right?

Dammas. [*Aside*] (He winked at me; I'd better pile on.) Indeed   245
he is.

Herotes. Then he runs up like a wild lion and tries to pull your
stuff away from us. But he has such a loose grip on it that he
falls over — drunk if you ask me — then blames *me*.

Paulus. [*To Stichus*] Haven't I told you again and again, "Don't
have anything to do with this man"? But you just can't keep   250
your mouth shut, can you?

Stichus. [*To Herotes*] God damn you, I've eaten nothing today, I've
drunk nothing but the tears your punches squeezed out of me.
I didn't try to stop you, I just asked you straight out, "What are   255
you doing? Where are you taking this stuff? Be careful with
that," but you attacked me right away with words and then with
whacks. [*To Paulus*] But you chide him and tell me, "Don't have
anything to do with this man." How can you allow him to stay
in your household for a single moment? Have you forgotten   260
that I was appointed your guardian, to look out for you and
your affairs? Your father is going to find out about this sooner
or later! If it weren't for you this man wouldn't be acting this
way.

Paulus. I'm surprised he hasn't beaten you to a pulp, you are such   265
a pain in the neck to everybody.

importunus sies.

Sti.   Itan tu ais?
Ego importunus sum, cum tibi
rebusque tuis consulo, quas luxu
lenociniisque consumis?

Pa.   Quid
ad te hoc?

270 Sti.   Scies, cum convenero
patrem.

Pa.   Abi iam, delire, et ne
me instiga!

Sti.   Omnibus furiis
ac vitiis omnibus instigatus iam es
cum tuo hoc artefice et ministro scelerum.

275 Pa. Heu, quid aberit, ne ab isto nudus
extremus vapulem, qui ita in me
audeat? Iam, ut scias, excrevi tutorem.

Sti. Sed non curatorem, si vel sexagenarius
sies.

Pa.   Ergo eum patiar, qui
280   vilissimus siet servus, nunc indignus
libertate, ita in me agat?

Sti. At non ita de me pater iudicavit
tuus, quando libertatem dedit. Videbimus
quid de te libero iudicet, de quo quidem
285   nichil dici potest nisi scelera omnia.

Pa. Nescio quid me teneat, ne tibi omne
mentum compilem.

Sti.   Compilas
patrem, quin me possis.

Pa.   Nisi eque
homines ac Deum verear, te protinus
e speculis precipitem do!

22

Stichus. How can you say that? I'm a pain in the neck, am I, when I take an interest in you and your property — the property you're wasting on hookers and high living?

Paulus. What's it to you?

Stichus. You'll find out when I've seen your father. 270

Paulus. Get out of here, now, you crazy old fool, and stop harassing me.

Stichus. You've already being harassed by all of your manias and vices, and this fellow is the architect and minister of all your crimes.

Paulus. Damn it, next this fellow is going to turn me over his knee 275 and spank me. How dare you! For your information, I'm no longer a minor.

Stichus. You may have outgrown a guardian, but you still need a keeper, and you'd need one even if you were sixty.

Paulus. So I'm supposed to put up with a slave when he treats me this way, a man who is the lowest of the low, now unfit to enjoy 280 free status?

Stichus. That wasn't what your father thought when he give me my freedom. You'll see what he thinks of you, despite your free status; the only thing that makes you remarkable is all your acts of wickedness. 285

Paulus. I don't know what keeps me from ripping the beard off your chin.

Stichus. You may rip off your father, but you won't rip anything off me.

Paulus. I'd throw you from the nearest tower if I didn't respect the laws of God and man.

290 *Sti.*   Nichil cure
michi, si modo in fide morior, pro qua
libertatem sum adeptus.

Pa.   Quin
tandem siles? Nisi, facio quamobrem me teque
post pigeat.

Sti.   Tu fac quodlubet.

295 Ego sileo, cum non audior; cum vero
audiar, non silebo.

: IV :

Stichus, Titus

Sti. Ita ne depravari quisquam malo consilio
potest, qui ad optima promptus siet,
ut recte dicas: 'Non est hic'? Fuit hic etate

300 prima indole tam preclara, tam suavi
et generoso more, ut omnes qui viderent,
parentes beatos predicarent multaque
presagirent, egoque multa de eo michi
promitterem, qui baiularem infantem.

305 Sed verum est quod dicunt, eos, qui bono
ingenio prediti sunt, ut valent cum sese
rectis applicant, eosdem malo suasore
corruptos deterrimos fieri. Sed omnia
semper in peius abeunt! Audivi maiores

310 natu, qui multa fide recenserent vidisse se
tam frugi, tam bene moratam iuventutem, ut
nichil supra aut dici aut existimari posset—
qui omnes maiores ut parentes vererentur,

Stichus. I could care less, so long as I die showing the same loyalty   290
    for which I was granted my freedom.

Paulus. Look, if you don't shut up, I'll do something we'll both be
    sorry for later.

Stichus. Do what you want. I shut up when I'm not listened to; if   295
    somebody is going to listen to me, then I'll speak. [*Exits*]

: IV :

Stichus, slave; Titus, Paulus' tutor

[*Stichus walks away from the house*]

Stichus. Is it possible for anyone with the potential for good to be
    so corrupted by evil counsel that you'd be right in saying,
    "That's not the same person"? Early in life this man was so
    gifted and had such a sweet and generous disposition that ev-   300
    erybody who saw him would declare that his parents were ex-
    tremely lucky, and they would predict great things of him. And
    I, too, who used to carry him around as a baby, believed he was
    very promising. But it's true what they say about those en-   305
    dowed with fine qualities, that they prosper when they hold fast
    to the straight and narrow, but become the worst of all when
    corrupted by an evil advisor.[9] Everything always goes from bad
    to worse! I have heard older men who would plausibly describe
    how they had known a younger generation so sober, so well   310
    mannered, that it would be impossible to imagine a better one.
    They respected all their elders as they did their parents, they'd
    stand up when their elders came in the room, wait on them,

assurgerent, servum facerent, comitarentur —,
315   tum vero diligentem, in ere acquirendo sedulam. Nunc vero
nescit hec desidiosa etas quam multo sudore
parentur bona, auscultare non vult senibus,
nec est quisquam ita minimus, qui non se prestare
Salomoni aut cuivis senum credat. O infauste
320   Sentio, quam nunc me miseret tui, qui iuvenis
terra marique omni periculo elaborasti, ut
res parares, quas iste nunc profunderet!
Clavo alice unico familiam omnem pascis,
deforme confectum et tertii generis panem
325   adhibes: hic vero prodigit atque ligurrit omnia.
Ac disceret quicquam, ut hoc remedio compensarentur
impense! Edidicit vero optime atque ebibit vitia
omnia atque omnem ignaviam. Raro in scolas,
idque ipsum non nisi pudore evictus; plenos eo
330   confert oculos, qui aut somnum proximum
aut studium multum demonstrent — utrum dubitat
nemo —; cum venit, librum obversat omnem
nec punctum invenit; assibilant omnes, ita
ut ineuntem me pudeat, quando intempestivus
335   advenit. Dehinc cum domum, execratur qui
tam diu garriat. Commensales adhibet,
post cibos sese oblectat cithara, post
somnos, hyeme etiam, invitat, deinde ad aleam venit,
post expatiandum est, deinde in collationem coit,
340   in cenam fere semper et lectum scortum adhibet.
Nec moriar, si non omnia patri! Quorum haud dubie
causa et fomentum extitit malorum hic nequam,
qui, dum gaudeat, dum similes sibi reddat,
nullam sibimet operam remittit. Convenit
345   cum istoc Damma: ille artifex, hic minister conficiendi
omnia. Mendacia sibi invicem mutuo reddunt,

dance attendance on them; and at the same time they would
work hard to make money. But nowadays this idle generation   315
has no idea how much you have to sweat to acquire the good
things in life, they don't want to obey their elders, and there's
not a one of them so third-rate that he doesn't think his wisdom surpasses Solomon's.

O Sentio, you unlucky man, I feel so sorry for you.[10] You en-   320
dured every danger on land and sea as a young man in order to
amass the wealth that this son of yours is now squandering!
You feed your whole family on a single dish of porridge; you eat
odds and ends of day-old bread, while your son soaks up and
squanders everything you have. If he'd just learn something to   325
pay you back for all your expenses! But the only lesson *he's*
learned is how to swallow every vice and every form of idleness.
He's rarely in class, and then only when overcome by shame,
and he comes with his eyes all puffy, showing that he's either been asleep or studying — and everyone knows which —   330
and when he does show up, he turns the books upside down
and can't find the right page.[11] Everybody hisses at him, so I'm
ashamed to see him come lumbering in when he gets there late.
After that, when he gets home, he curses anybody who talks   335
too long. He has friends over to eat and after the meal amuses
himself with his lute. Afterwards he takes a nap, even in winter,
then goes for a game of dice, then heads out for a stroll. After
that, he joins a dinner party and almost always takes a whore
with him to dinner and to bed. I'll die if I don't report all this   340
to his father.

There's no doubt that the spark behind all these misfortunes
is that scoundel, Herotes, who can relax and take it easy so long
as he's having a good time and being a bad influence on others.
Damma connives with him; Herotes makes the policy and
Damma acts as his minister. The two of them constantly tell   345
lies about each other and accuse the other so that they seem to

accusant sese plerunque, ut dissidere videantur,
utque magis faciant fidem, in pugnos interdum itur.
Hec michi primum iniuncta cura fuerat, ut coemerem,
350   conducerem, exolverem: hic autem nunquam cessavit
donec in se transtulit. Compilat undequaque
et in se subtrahit; lenones, aleones cognitos
omnes habet et imperium ut herus adducit atque
pro his omnibus pretium et amorem et dona refert:
355   ego pro fide pertusos oculos et fauces graves.
Sed heus tu unde venis, Tite? Non affuisti?

Ti.   Ego, cum adstudueram quod michi fas fuit, in ecclesiam
prodii et divinis rebus astiti. Sed quid est,
quod te lamentantem audio?

Sti.   Nunc tu ita
admonuisti: viden?

360 *Ti.*   Video hercle et
magnopere dolet id michi: sed quisnam tam audax?
Num herus?

Sti.   Ipsus quidem, quando patitur,
ut scelestus ille in me tantum audeat; sed tu
omnia ceco oculo obtusaque preteris aure, nec
365   unquam castigas: indigne facis admodum.

Ti.   Tu vero me accusas, quasi ego autor siem.
Crebro admonui: 'Quid agis, Paule? Non studes,
nichil fit a te boni: fuge hos socios!' Ille vero:
'Quiesce, nichil de istac re tibi; sine,
370   ut cibus proficiat tibi. Si hec displicent,
ne vide!' Itaque ego postea nichil. Sed iam ex hesterno
ieiunio famesco: itaque ad penu eo.
Tu tibi consule, qui sapis et potes.

Sti.   Quam preclara spes restituendi hunc in rectam!
375   Ceteri mali, hic preter literas nichil.
Sed ego, qua potero, vos hodie castigo:

at odds, and to make it look more convincing they even come to blows from time to time. In the beginning it was my responsibility to do the buying, hiring and paying of debts; but this fellow wouldn't rest until he had taken over all these duties himself. He's always pilfering and taking a cut for himself; he knows all the pimps and gamblers in town; he usurps the master's power and gets paid back for all his services with money, affection and presents. I get black eyes and swollen lips for my loyalty. [*Titus enters*] But hello, where did you come from, Titus? Where have you been?

Titus. Me? After I took care of a few chores, I went to church and heard mass. But what's all this you're bitching about?

Stichus. So now you're giving me advice? Take a look at this. [*He shows him his black eye*]

Titus. I do see it, by Hercules, and I'm really sorry; but who on earth had the audacity to do that? Surely not the master?

Stichus. Indeed he did, in that he allowed that impudent scoundrel Herotes to do as much. But you let it all go by with a blind eye and deaf ears. You never criticize him. It's really wrong for you to act that way.

Titus. You accuse me as if it were my fault. I've warned him again and again: "What are you doing, Paulus? You don't study, no good will come of this, get away from those companions of yours!" But he says, "Shut up, it's no concern of yours; let it go if you want to go on eating. If you don't like it, don't look!" So after that I said nothing. But now I'm hungry after yesterday's fast, so I'm off to the market. Take care of yourself; you're so wise and capable. [*Exits*]

Stichus. [*Sarcastically*] Well, there we have a fine hope of putting the master back on the straight and narrow! Everybody around

350

355

360

365

370

375

29

abibo et subigam aliquem, qui venisse
patrem nunciet. Ita deterrebo, subito ut
nesciant . . . Nichil refert, dum
380   corrigis, siquid mendacii pares.

: V :

Herotes servus, Nicolosa mater, Ursula filia

He.   Ita est sane: nescit ulli hominum convenire!
Tu vero, Damma, domum abi et hero ministra:
ego cetera, que iussit, exequar actutum.
Sed quid primum? An convivas adeo? An coemo
385   que opus est? Et recte quidem michi venit in mentem,
ut, quo sit huiuscemodi conventus ornatior,
convive singulo singulum scortum
adhibeam. Abibo igitur, ne preveniantur
a quoquam. Sed quo pacto huic nostro providebo,
390   cui iam subolent iste omnes?
Ah, video! In viciniam nuper venit quedam
cum matre, forma et etate integra,
que, ut videtur, questum paratura est,
etsi hactenus dissimulet. Nichil
395   tenere me iam potest, maxime cum et ipsi michi
sit opus: hoc aurum efficiet quicquid
volo, ut commonstravero. Quanquam est nemo
eorum, quos novi, famulantium,
qui non hero suo calce persolveret,
400   ego non ex his sum: malo enim quam minimum
cum gratia quam totum furto tollere. Sed
patent fores. Quis adest? Respondet nemo.
Quin introeo? Res est nostra! Sursum, ut opinor, sunt.

him is evil, but Titus' only virtue is his knowledge of letters. But today I'll fix you all, if I can: I'm going to go and get somebody to announce that his father has come. So what if you tell a few fibs while setting things to rights?[12]   380

: V :

Herotes, slave; Nicolosa, a procuress; Ursula, her daughter

[Outside Nicolosa's house]

Herotes. That's quite true: Stichus can't get along with anybody! Damma, you go home and tend to the master. [*Damma exits*]. I'll carry out his other orders forthwith. But what to do first? Should I round up some dinner-guests or buy what's needed? I have a good idea: a party of this sort would be much more im-   385 pressive if I supply each guest with his own tart. So I'd better go before somebody else beats me to it. But how am I going to take care of my dear master, who has already had a whiff of all the usual girls? Ah, I know! There recently moved into the   390 neighborhood with her mother a lovely, unspoiled young thing who is getting ready to enter the trade, I believe, though hitherto she's pretended otherwise. There's nothing to prevent me,   395 especially since I want her too. This gold will get me whatever I want, as I shall show. Although I've never known a slave who wouldn't pay his master back with a good kick, I'm not one of them; I prefer to skim off the tiniest bit and keep my master's   400 good will rather than steal the whole lot. But the door is standing open. Is anybody there? No one's answering. Why not go in? It's my business. They must be upstairs.

Ni.   Quis tu tam audax, qui in domum meam ingressus sies?
Foris iam protinus!

405 *He.*   Ingressus sum, ut
subspergerem.

Ni.   Spargeres hiccine?

He.   Quin imo, ut subligacula colligerem.

Ni.   Colligeres? Insanis ne et me vis insanam
reddere? Nescis quis hic habitet?

He.   Imo vero

410   scio, sed tu desine tantas voces et audi rem,
que, si sapias, prosit tibi.

Ni.   Dic atque abi
protinus, ne te quisquam hic solum videat.

He.   Nichil: ego sum frequens! Tu si vis, dico; si minus,
iube, ut abeam a te cum bona gratia et ne me
postea revoces.

415 *Ni.*   Iam vero dic quodlubet
quodque et te et nos conducat.

He.   Si eque
distribute forent opes ad mensuram
prudentie et ingenii, neque vos inopes
neque ego servirem. Verum, quoniam plerunque

420   inopia cogit ne faciamus quod vellemus
et quod deceret, compatior nostris
omnibus et, qua possum, consulo.
Gnatam habes ingenio bono, quantum dat
noscere indoles, preterea multa forma

425   et etate precipua. Omne ferme matrum,
que sapiunt minus, consilium summum est, ut
labore atque inedia quantulam cogant dotem:
siquam interea fortunam obtulerit Deus,
abnuunt. Id maximum est, ut gnatas matrimonio

430   collocent, et per plurimum in id, quod verebantur,

Nicolosa. Who do you think you are, entering my house like this? Get out of here at once!

Herotes. I came in to sow some wild oats.   405

Nicolosa. What, here?

Herotes. Or rather, I came on a panty-raid.

Nicolosa. You came on what? Are you out of your mind or are you trying to drive me out of mine? Don't you know who lives here?

Herotes. Indeed I do, but turn down the volume and listen to my offer. If you're smart, it may profit you.   410

Nicolosa. Speak, then get out quickly before someone sees you here alone.

Herotes. No problem; I'm a regular. Look, if you want me to, I'll make you an offer; if you don't, just tell me to go away in a friendly fashion and don't call me back later.

Nicolosa. Well, say what you want that's going to profit us both.   415

Herotes. If wealth was distributed evenly in proportion to wisdom and wit, you wouldn't be poor and I wouldn't be a slave. But since poverty generally prevents us from doing what we'd like   420 and getting what we deserve, I feel sorry for people like us and look out for them as far as I can. You have a nice daughter, as far as I can tell, a real beauty, and just the right age. Most   425 mothers are not all that smart: their chief thought is to work and starve to get together a little dowry, and if God offers them some piece of good fortune in the meantime, they turn it down. The best they can hope for is to marry off their daughters, and most of the time what they fear actually happens: a small   430

incidunt: nam tenuis dos inopem virum habet.
Que cum consumpta erit, hic abit, illa
cogitur vulgo questum facere. At non satius
fuerat cuipiam opulento, qui nolit
435   uxori sese obstringi, in domum et prolem
iungi? Id primum habent, quod domine sunt rei familiaris,
quibus serviatur; deinde, si liberos gignunt, solere
eos esse splendore patrum egregios; tum et id
nonnunquam, ut in nuptias ab his ipsis deducantur.
440   Viden quot commoda? Hoc omne dictum est,
quoniam reor et tibi et gnate fortunam datam,
que vos beare possit. Herus est michi generosus
inprimis ac dives, qui literarum huc gratia venit.
Quanquam et hoc ipsum ut reliqua a se modeste
445   exigat, is ad summum liberos optat.
Oblate sunt ei plurime, sed nulle vise
sibi sunt convenire. Ea, postquam est a se
visa, perplacuit, ac iussit, ut te convenirem.

Ni.   Absit a me, ut nunquam iniustis nuptiis gnata
cuiquam detur!

450 *He.*   Num dixi? Et tu quoque ex illis es!
Id ego tibi polliceor: si das — novi ego quam sit amans —,
omnem familiam nutriet; tu poteris minorem natu
filiam caste educare et ingenue.

Ni.   Ego istoc nunquam facerem, ut carnem meam
prodam.

455 *He.*   Ut lubet, sed scito michi plus
de rebus vestris constare quam tu ipsa fortassis reare.

Ni.   Quid? Nichil ne mali?

He.   Nichil hercle
nisi boni. Sed tamen iam apud vicinos
susurrari audio velle se viciniam purgatam esse.

460 *Ni.*   Vah, si purgatam velint, quas domi nutriunt

dowry gets them an impoverished husband. Once the dowry is used up, he's off, and she's forced to make her living on the street. Wouldn't it be better to fix her up with some rich man, who doesn't want to be tied up with a wife, in her own house, with her own children? First off, women like this are the mistresses of their household and have control of its resources; then, if they give birth to children, those children share in their fathers' distinction; then, sometimes, their paramours marry them. You see the advantages. I'm saying all this because I think you and your daughter have had a stroke of luck which could make you both very happy. I have a very well-born and rich master who has come to Bologna to study. He's not too demanding in that department as in others; what he really wants most of all is children. He's been offered lots of women, but none seemed to suit him. But when he saw your daughter, he really liked her a lot and told me to go meet you. 435 440 445

Nicolosa. Surely you're not suggesting that my daughter should be married to anyone unlawfully?

Herotes. Would I say such a thing? You must be one of *those* mothers too. I promise you this: if you give him your daughter — and I know how loving my master is — he'll support your whole family; you'll be able to raise your younger daughter chastely and honorably. 450

Nicolosa. I would never do such a thing and betray my own flesh and blood.

Herotes. As you wish; but you should know that I'm better informed about your affairs than perhaps you realize. 455

Nicolosa. What do you mean? You haven't heard anything bad?

Herotes. Nothing but good things, by Hercules. Still, I have heard some whispers from your neighbors that they want the neighborhood cleaned up.

Nicolosa. Bah! If they want it cleaned up, they should start by get- 460

uxores primum eiciant! Sed ego ista nichil metuo.
Mallem, ut ista essent vera que profers,
nam soletis omnes, da veniam, non tam
ut obsequamini quam ut illudatis mulieribus,

465   multa mentiri, quanquam tu minime ex illis videare.

He.   Egon mentiri? Sacrarium sum verorum,
sed ita quidem occlusum, ut prodire
nullum possit. Tu ergo propterea quod te fortasse
eluserint alii, ex illis me iudicas.

470 Ni. Nichil me alii: nichil enim secum ago.

He.   Quid tandem vis renunciem? Hoc tibi certo
polliceor: quod si placuerit, invenisti quod queris.

Ni.   Quid, si non placuerit? Non ergo meo cum dedecore
periculum faciam?

He.   Si remittet, quod quidem

475   ego non arbitror, magno donabit; sed id scio,
quod plurimum amat.

Ur.   At quis iste est,
qui tam misere amat? Nunquam istac preteriit
et neque aspexit nec dono quidem quicquam misit

He.   Nichil ego de te sum falsus: ea es quam quero,

480   at propter honestatem abstinet ne pretereat neve
aspectet; dona vero etiam plura quam velis habitura es
ab eo. Sed quid tandem?

Ni.   Ad me cras
redito.

He.   Nichil tibi his artibus opus est nobiscum;
ceteros ita exerce: mihi presenti est opus.

Ni.   Quid vis facio.

485 He.   Mirum quid dubites.
Post horam nonam iam iam — nam ea solent pauci
preterire — tu gnataque, quasi que templa visitastis,
ornate ⟨vos⟩ et lapillos adhibete digitis atque eo

ting rid of the wives they're supporting at home. I'm not afraid
of things like that. I'd like to believe your offer was made in
good faith: all of you men—begging your pardon—lie constantly, and not out of devotion to women but to make fools of
them. But you don't seem like one of that sort.   465

Herotes. I, lie? I am a positive shrine of truth, [*aside*] but shut so
tight that no truth can escape! Perhaps because other men have
deceived you, you judge me by their standard.

Nicolosa. Other men haven't done anything to me, and I've had
nothing to do with them.   470

Herotes. So what then do you want me to report? I promise you
this for sure: if he likes her, you've found what you're looking
for.

Nicolosa. What if he doesn't like her? Aren't I then risking a scandal?

Herotes. If he sends her back, which I don't think he will, he will
give her a large present. But I know this: he's very much in love.   475

Ursula. But who is this man who is dying of love? He never comes
by here and looks; he never sends any gifts.

Herotes. I'm being straight with you; she is the one I'm looking
for. It's his delicate sense of honor that keeps him from coming
by and taking a look. As for presents, she'll have more than she   480
can possibly want from him. So what do you say?

Nicolosa. Come back tomorrow.

Herotes. There's no need to practice your wiles on us; use them on
other men. I need to know now.

Nicolosa. I'll do what you want.

Herotes. I'm surprised you hesitated. Right after the ninth hour—   485
few people go by at that hour—you and your daughter get
dressed as though you were going to church, put rings on your

venite, ubi domus emicat altior. Viden?
Ego postico vos admittam.

490 *Ni.*   Satius est
in noctem.

He.   Herus nunc furit!

Ni.   Cum
emissa fuerit rabies, iam iam fastidiet.

He. Ad priores questiones non redis?

Ni. Ego iam facio quodlubet.

He.   Mea ope

495 ac consilio iam felix es: sed quid michi pro gratia
reddes?

Ni.   Quid, nisi quod nos resque nostre
tue sunt? Tu patronus et rector noster!

He. Recte ego, sed tu iunge dextram: iam tibi
plurimum boni faxo. Quis enim non recte consulat

500 huic faciei? Hui, quam floridas genas!

Ur. Sed tu desine!

Ni.   Vin tu una pransum?
Senties nos non misere vivere.

He.   Accede istuc:
ego, postquam vos in clientelam accepi, nichil pretermitto,
quin recte vobis consulo. Iam faxo

505 admonitione una, ut quidvis ab eo habeatur.
Quod si omnia pro vobis facio, num equum est,
ut michi quicquam retribuatis?

Ni.   Nam dixi, quicquid
nostrum est, tuum id esse!

He.   Nescis quantum herus
meo arbitrio, ne dicam consilio, faciat: quidvis

510 credere audebit, qui tantam pecuniam credat;
cuius iam faxo, si te unum admonuero, plurimam
partem feras.

fingers and come to the taller house sticking up over there — do you see it? I'll let you in the back door.

Nicolosa. It's better to do this at night.   490

Herotes. My master is mad with desire right now.

Nicolosa. When he's vented his madness, he'll immediately turn up his nose at her.

Herotes. You're not going back to that again, are you?

Nicolosa. I'm doing what you want.

Herotes. My help and advice has brought you good luck already, but what are you going to give me in return for my favor?   495

Nicolosa. What can we give you? We and all that we have is yours. You are our patron and our guide.

Herotes. That's right, I am. Let's shake on it. I've already done you a lot of good. [*To Ursula*] And who wouldn't look out for the interests of a pretty face like yours? Ooh, what lovely rosy cheeks!   500

Ursula. Oh, stop.

Nicolosa. Would you care to lunch with us? You'll see that we don't live at all badly.

Herotes. [*To Nicolosa*] Come over here. [*They confer off to one side*] Since I've accepted you into my clientele, I'll do everything I can to look out for your interests. I'll give you a piece of advice presently that'll get you whatever you want out of him. But if I   505 do all this for you, isn't it fair that you should pay me back with something?

Nicolosa. As I said, all that we have is yours.

Herotes. You don't know how much my master relies on my judgment, not to speak of my counsel. A man who would entrust   510 such a large sum to me will believe anything. If I can make just one recommendation to you, you'll walk off with the greater part of the sum I've already had from him.

Ni.   Iube igitur.

He.   Scis optime
quid velim.

Ni.   Imo vero nescio: dic tandem.

He.   Vin dicam?

Ni.   Dic.

He.   Cupio paulisper cum tua Ursula . . .

515 Ni.   Ah, iam tandem intelligo qui sies: huius rei
gratia sunt conficta hec omnia! Iam tandem abi!
Ego a te omnia habeo dum nichil volo.

He.   Quid ita?

Ni.   Ita ne compositus huc venisti, qui nobis
illuderes, qui nos ita falleres? Quovis

520   deduxisse iam poteras dum tibi omnia crederentur.

He.   Et fecissem hercle, si destinassem fallere;
nunc vero nichil nisi cum fide et gratia facio.
Quid enim, si aurum aut vestes aut quidvis
horum expostulassem, num dedisses?

Ni.   Utique.

525 He.   Nunc vero quid est, quod possit minus damnum
afferre aut facilius dari, quam quod semper
promptum quis habeat, quodque cum det
nichil minus habeat?

Ni.   Non est pro genere vestro
res istec: alias quere!

He.   Ne me despecta
530   propterea quod servio: est enim et genus et virtus
michi et quondam fortuna. Sed, ut in faciem tibi
dicam, sapis parum: si enim amicitias vultis
dominorum, servorum habeatis necesse est. Siquis preterea
sub noctem veniet aurum proferens, nichil tunc queretur

Nicolosa. So tell me what you want.

Herotes. You know perfectly well what I want.

Nicolosa. I certainly don't know what you want. Pray tell me.

Herotes. You want me to say it?

Nicolosa. Say it.

Herotes. I'd like to spend a little time with your Ursula . . .

Nicolosa. Oh, now I get it! I know your kind! That's why you've 515 made up all these lies. Get out of here. I'll get everything from you so long as I don't want anything.

Herotes. Why do you say that?

Nicolosa. You came here with the deliberate intention of deceiving us, of playing a trick on us, haven't you? So long as we trusted all your promises, you could wrap us around your little finger, was that your idea? 520

Herotes. I could have done that, by Hercules, if I'd planned to deceive you. But everything I'm now doing is done in good faith and friendship. What if I had asked you for gold or clothing or something like that, you wouldn't have given them to me, would you?

Nicolosa. Certainly not.

Herotes. Now what asset is less exposed to risk and can be given 525 away more easily than something which you always have ready to hand and which is not diminished in value by giving it away?

Nicolosa. Things like that are not for your kind; look somewhere else!

Herotes. Don't despise me just because I'm in service; in fact I am a man of good breeding and character and, once upon a time, 530 of ample fortune. But, if I may say it to your face, you aren't very smart. If you want the friendship of lords, you have to have that of their slaves too. Moreover, if someone came under cover of darkness and brought gold with him, you wouldn't be asking then whether he was a free man or a slave, master or ser-

535   liber servus ne, presit an famuletur:
    nemo status instrumenta exigat. Ego non plus vos
    habeo quam vos me.

Ni.   Hui, quam vereor, ne
    priora illa omnia minus sint vera!

He.   Superos omnes testor: plus quam vera omnia sunt.

540   Ego mentiri? Tandem cognosces quinam
    Herotes vir siet! Putas ne ego minori tibi
    commodo sum futurus quam herus? Ille numum
    dabit, ego quicquid erit penoris[1] in te conferam.

Ni.   Credon ego tibi? Est enim quoddam hominum genus,

545   quibus veritatem atque mendacium eque
    difficile est credere.

He.   Potes utique. Vin
    amplius in rem?

Ni.   Sed cedo, quid mones?

He.   Non facile quisquam a me hoc extorqueret —
    non enim decet heros fallere — sed dicam tibi:

550   fac simulet virginem; mirum enim quam optet
    carpere fructus primos: magno donabit!

Ni.   Sed non satius est primum ab eo aurum quod
    possumus tollere?

He.   Non publice sunt,
    que singulos numos volunt presentes?

555   Ostende te pecuniam negligere dum illi facias satis,
    et nichilo minus, cum eo veneris, magni res tuas facito,
    et cetera, que iussi prius.

Ni.   Sed quid nos
    tandem, mea Ursula? Heroti fac nostro
    commonstres domum; interea ego foco subservio.

vant; you wouldn't be demanding to see his manumission pa- 535
pers. I don't own you any more than you own me.

Nicolosa. I'm just so afraid that everything you said before wasn't
true.

Herotes. I swear by all the gods above that it was all true — more
than true. I, lie? You'll going to find out in the end just what 540
kind of a man Herotes really is! Do you think I'm going to be
of less use to you in future than my master? He'll give you
money; I'll give you whatever property he has that can be
pawned.

Nicolosa. Why should I trust you? There is, after all, a kind of
man whom it's hard to trust, indifferent to truth and falsehood. 545

Herotes. You can trust me entirely. Would you like an even better
deal?

Nicolosa. All right, what do you suggest?

Herotes. I wouldn't give this away to just anyone — it doesn't look
right to deceive one's master — but let me tell you: make out
that Ursula is a virgin. It's amazing how much he likes picking 550
fresh fruit. He'll give you a bundle for it!

Nicolosa. But wouldn't it be better to take what gold we can from
him?

Herotes. Isn't it the licensed prostitutes that want every cent up
front? No, show him that you don't care about money while
you're keeping him happy, and at the same time make a big deal 555
of your own resources when you go over there, and do all the
other things I told you to do earlier.

Nicolosa. Well, what are we waiting for, Ursula dear? Show our
Herotes over the house and I'll tend the hearth in the meantime.

: VI :

Paulus dominus; Damma, Herotes servi

560 Pa.   Iure siquidem obveniret michi, ut iste omnem
pecuniam asportasset, qui ita omnibus credo!
Damma, ubinam Herotem liquisti?

Da.   Apud forum.

Pa.   Quocum?

Da.   Solum.

Pa.   Quo tendebat?

Da.   Herebat quidem, cum me
565 dimitteret; sed cum abii, forte fio cuidam obvius,
qui verbis me impeteret; tenuit, respexi eum,
qui videbatur huc recta venire, etsi alio se
dixisset iturum.

He.   Pape, quam docta,
quam sagax sui muneris artifex virgo istec!
570 Que si ita se cum hero exerceat, periere
comenta omnia.

Pa.   Nec venit.

Da.   Non
ego quem viderim . . .

He.   Ter ego hodie
non minimum exolvi. Sed undenam tanta
me fames impetit? Verum est quod aiunt,
575 post Venerem esurire homines. Sed abibo
recta domum, ut famem hanc expleam.

Pa.   Maior hercle michi suspicio aborta est: nam si
alio divertisset, sperarem ad cetera, que
iussi, profectum; nunc vero, posteaquam nemo
580 eum vidit, furtim introgressus erit

: VI :

Paulus, master; Damma, Herotes, slaves

[*Paulus and Damma come out of Paulus' house*]

Paulus. It would serve me right if that man of mine had made   560
off with all my money, since I trusted him with everything.
Damma, where did you leave Herotes?

Damma. In the forum.

Paulus. With whom?

Damma. He was by himself.

Paulus. Where was he heading?

Damma. When he sent me off, he was just standing around, but
as soon as I left, by chance I happened to run into someone   565
who buttonholed me and held me up. So I looked back at
Herotes, who seemed to be coming right in this direction, even
though he said he was heading in a different one. [*Herotes leaves
Nicolosa's house, unnoticed by Paulus and Damma.*]

Herotes. [*To himself*] That was amazing, that girl really knew what
she was doing! What an artist! And so gifted! But if she services the master that way, all my schemes will go up in smoke.   570

Paulus. [*To Damma*] So he hasn't come yet?

Damma. Not that I saw.

Herotes. I've had it off no less than three times today! But how did
I get so hungry? It's true what they say: men get hungry after   575
sex. But I'll go right home and fill my belly.

Paulus. By Hercules, that makes me even more suspicious. If he'd
gone in the other direction, I might have hoped that he had set
off to do the rest of what I told him to do; but now, since no
one has seen him, he must have sneaked in, picked up his   580

        et res suas tulerit atque abierit.

        Aspice, Damma, num in cella sua siet.

He.   Moriar, nisi mulierem hanc ludam,

        que me inlusum nunc a sese extimat.

585   Nichil difficile est simpliciosas virgines

        fallere, que quidvis credant, aut etiam

        doctas matronas, que nichil extra familiarem rem

        suam sapiunt: summa vero laus est has callidas

        meretrices intervertere, que continuo

590   ac diuturno studio nichil intentant aliud,

        nisi ut fallant. Hec ipsa, cum in se primum,

        quando potuit, nunc vero in gnata studium

        suum exercet. Certum est experiri,

        illa ego ne callidiores sumus.

Da.   Occluse

        fores.

595 *Pa.*   Huic ego credidi! Non frustra sane

        tam instructus ad me hodie venit: preconceperat

        furtum ab hac urbe, aut hec ipsa experiri

        que me docuit perfidus ille hodie.

He.   Sed interea excogitabo aliquid: nunc propero,

600   ut famem expleam et illi desiderium impleam.

Pa.   Quis alius est? Quis est?

He.   Herotes est,

        omnis tue felicitatis autor.

Pa.   Ubinam

        tandiu?

He.   Ubinam? Quid enim me

        censes aut excogitare aut moliri aut

605   facere unquam, nisi quod tibi voluptati cedat?

Pa.   Quid queso hoc est?

He.   Dicam, sed sine, ut

        deponam inediam, quam pro te tuli.

things, and taken off. Damma, go see whether Herotes is in his room. [*Exits*]

Herotes. I'll die if I don't fool this woman, who now thinks she's fooled me. There's nothing really difficult about deceiving sim- 585
ple young girls, who believe whatever you want them to, or even experienced matrons, who know nothing except their own household affairs; but there is high renown to be won by swin-dling these shrewd courtesans, who make it their constant, 590
daily business to deceive others. This bawd practiced her tricks on her own behalf first, but now she works on behalf of her daughter. We're sure to find out whether she or I am the shrewder.

Damma. [*Returns from the house*]. The doors are locked.

Paulus. And I trusted this man! It must have been with no idle 595
purpose, then, that he came to me today with that ready-made plan: he had worked it out ahead of time to take the money and run, or to enjoy himself the very pleasures the blackguard was telling me to indulge in this morning.

Herotes. I'll cook something up in the meantime; now I'm hurry-ing off to satisfy my own desire for food and to inflame my master's desire for sex. [*Approaches Paulus*] 600

Paulus. Is someone else there? Who is it?

Herotes. It's Herotes, the man responsible for all your happiness.

Paulus. Where have you been all this time?

Herotes. Where have I been? What, do you think I ever make plans for and do things other than what conduces to your plea-sure? 605

Paulus. And what, pray, is it that you've been doing?

Herotes. I'll tell you, but let me first satisfy the appetite I've worked up in your service.

Pa.		Dic queso propere: ne me desiderio excrucia!
He.		Paravi tibi virginem speciosam.
Pa.		Virginem?
He.		Formosam admodum.

610 *Pa.* Quo pacto?
He. Quidnam efficiat numus?
Pa. Quantum dedisti?
He. Nichil preter spem.
Pa. O frater, frater mi,
nunquam a te sum liber: tantum debeo tibi! Sed
dic, queso, quonam effeceris modo atque ordine.

615 *He.* Facile satur et accipere et dare vacuo verba potest.
Id postac scies. Sed hic in specula morare:
siquam huc videris venientem, qualem dico,
me voca, nam iussi ut veniret protinus.

Pa. O mee delicie, sine quo ne unam possem

620 agere letus diem! Quam cuperem libens, ut
hic empticius meus tantum saperet!
Sed hoc est malignum genus hominum:
perpauca norunt eaque ipsa nolunt
vel negligunt. Hic vero conducticius omnes operas

625 ad hoc suas dat, ut michi ad votum subserviat,
idque preclare efficit. Quem si prece, spe, donis
tenere valeam, nunquam a me discessurus est
loci gentium. Sed nimium, anime mi, tardas,
nimium me excrucias!

630 Timebit, vereor, ac propterea tarda veniet:
sed ego solabor, lenibo ac demulcebo.
Dic, Herotes, quando se venturam pollicita est?

He. Iam iam cum matre aderit.
Pa. Expecto
et pendeo: istac ergo veniet?
He. Dextero

Paulus. Please tell me quickly: don't torture me with desire!

Herotes. I've fixed you up with a beautiful virgin.

Paulus. A virgin!

Herotes. A really beautiful one.

Paulus. How did you do that? 610

Herotes. Money can do anything.

Paulus. How much have you given her?

Herotes. Nothing except hope.

Paulus. O brother, my brother, I'll never be quit of you, I owe you so much! But tell me in detail, please, how on earth you accomplished this.

Herotes. The well-fed have an easy time of it when they converse 615 with the hungry. You'll find out later. Stay here on the lookout. If a girl such as I've described comes here, call me, since I've told her to come straightaway.

Paulus. You're a delightful fellow! Without you I wouldn't spend a single happy day! How I wish that this fellow here I bought [*in-* 620 *dicating Stichus*] was as smart as this! But he belongs to a nasty race of men: they know damn little and what they do know how to do they either don't want to do or they neglect to do. But the fellow I've hired out devotes all his energies to serving my wishes, and does an outstanding job.[13] If I can keep him by 625 entreaties and by giving him gifts and great expectations, he'll never leave me for anyone else on earth. But my darling, you're taking so long to get here! You're torturing me! I fear she's a timid girl, and that's why she's coming so late. I'll put her at her 630 ease, calm her down, caress her. Tell me, Herotes, when did she promise she'd come?

Herotes. She'll arrive with her mother any moment.

Paulus. I can hardly wait: where will she be coming from?

calle ex platea proxima.

635 *Pa.*   Nusquam igitur
ego deiciam oculos.

: VII :

Nicolosa, Paulus, Herotes

Ni.   Num satis videor amens, que me huic
credam, quem nunquam preterquam[2] hodie viderim?
Sed nunc falli facile, postac hercle non sepe
640   possum. Viam frustraverimus vel, siquid magis,
noctem, sed alius, qui non viderit iacturam istanc,
resarciet. Mea Ursula, abi et tete appara,
ut illoc eamus. Sed num satius est, ut ipsa vadam
prius sola et cum eo colloquar? Non carum fiet
645   quod tam facile emptum sit. Quid, si nunc
coegerit comites et conventum faciant, ut solent?
Spectare oportet omnia: adolescentes omnes sunt,
quibus omnia licent, multaque transmittunt impunita;
tum et supprimere res nesciunt. Si hoc fiat,
650   in propatulo res nostre sunt:
circumspicienda sunt igitur omnia. Audin tu?
Ego prius ad eum ibo, ut componam:
fortasse oblatus michi fuerit quem expilem.
Neminem hic video. Ille debuerat in foribus
655   hic adesse, qui me vocaret; ego priores amicos
convenire, qui domum norint: ego unum cognatum,
alium affinem, alium compatrem appellabo!

Pa.   Quid tandiu, Herotes, illas morari existimas?

Herotes. From the alley on the right coming from the next square.
Paulus. I'll watch it like a hawk. 635

: VII :

Nicolosa, Paulus, Herotes

[Nicolosa and Ursula prepare to leave for Paulus' house]

Nicolosa. I must surely be out of my mind to believe this man,
whom I've never seen before today! But, by Hercules, I won't
be taken in so easily again after this. We might waste the trip 640
over there; or worse, lose the whole night; but the other man,
who won't deem this a waste of time, will reimburse us. Ursula
dear, go fix yourself up so we can be on our way. But wouldn't it
be better for me to go over first and speak with him alone?
Things easily purchased are never dear. What if he's gotten his 645
friends together and they're having a party, as they usually do? I
need to consider everything. These fellows are all young men,
who can do anything they want and get away with anything;
furthermore, they don't know how to keep secrets. If this gets
out, our affairs will all be out in the open. So I'd better look the 650
situation over carefully. [*To Ursula, offstage*] Did you hear me?
I'm going over to Paulus first to arrange things. Perhaps he will
turn out to be someone I can pick clean. [*Nicolosa leaves and goes
to Paulus' house*] I don't see anyone here. The man who invited
me should have been at the door. I'll get together with some 655
old friends who might be acquainted with the household. I'll
call on my cousin, my in-law, and my godfather. [*She heads down
the street*]
Paulus. Herotes, why do you think they're taking so long to get
here?

He. Neminem vides?

Pa.   Neminem. Sed iam iam
660   preteriit anus, que hic plurimum spectaret
         ac penderet.

He.   Illa anus? Imo vero
         floridior virgo, que urbem hanc habeat.

Pa. Obsecro te, abi obviam illis.

He.   Iam primum
         aderunt.

Pa.   Cum ocius tum et fidentius
         te comite adventabunt.

665 *He.*   Eo igitur, quoniam lubet;
         sed siquid aderit loci, non frustra iero,
         quanquam iam nolim tot mihi precibus emptum dari,
         etsi quidvis potius quam numum do.

: [VIII] :

[*Herotes, Ursula, Paulus*]³

He. Salve, Ursula, veni: te herus anxius expectat.

670 *Ur.* Quid, non pro me mater venit? Sola enim iam dudum
         ad vos, ut et domum et tempus edisceret.

He. Illa vero iubet, ut mecum venias; nemo enim istac
         nunc solet. Sed tibi prius suavium do.
         Ah, quid ago? Interveniet fortasse mater atque omnia
675   perierint! Interveniat quivis, ego commodis meis

Herotes. You don't see anyone?

Paulus. No one. But an old lady just went by who was hanging around looking over the house for a long time.   660

Herotes. [*Herotes spots Ursula opening the door of her house. To himself he says*] She's an old woman? I'd say she's the rosiest virgin in town!

Paulus. Please, please, go out and meet them.

Herotes. They'll be here presently.

Paulus. It would be quicker and surer if you would accompany them.

Herotes. Then I'll go, since you wish it; [*aside*] but I won't have   665
gone in vain if an opportunity presents itself. Yet now I wouldn't want to be given something I purchased with so much wheedling, although I'd give anything so long as it's not money.

: [VIII] :

[*Herotes, Ursula, Paulus*]

[*At the doorway of the house belonging to Nicolosa and Ursula*]

Herotes. Hello, Ursula, come on; master is waiting for you anxiously.

Ursula. What? Didn't mother get there before me? She came   670
alone to you a short while ago to find out where the house was and the time of the assignation.

Herotes. She told you to come with me; the street is empty at this hour. But first let me give you a kiss. [*Aside*] What am I doing? The mother might break in on us and ruin everything! Oh, hell, if somebody wants to interrupt, let them! I'm concentrat-   675
ing here on what's good for number one. I'll have plenty of ex-

studeo: michi non desunt apud herum cause.

Pa. Iam vero omnes ego amiserim: nec iste redit
nec ille veniunt. Interposuit fortasse aliquis,
qui rem turbaverit: nunquam boni quicquam michi evenit,

680 quod non parte aliqua turbaretur!
Bellum nunc conserit Herotes: Herotes, enitere
manibus pedibusque atque elabora hoc michi, quod
cepisti! Quid enim in vanam me spem, si non
proficis, induxisti?

He.   Eamus ocius, nequid
suspicentur mali.

Ur.   Perii!

685 He.   Quam ego felix sum,
si hoc explere possim! Atat quam timui, ne illa esset mater!
Tu vero adverte et viam et domum, ut parenti
indices.

Pa.   Perii, solus redit! Imo vero, et vivo
et felix ante omnes sum homines, cui tanta

690 res sit oblata. Sed meminisse huius studeo,
quod visa sit aliquando michi fortasse: sed nunc et visa
et habita michi erit!

He.   Sequere me intro:
actum iam est.

Ur.   Quam sum felix, quod nemo
nos vidit preter eam senem, que fortasse

695 nichil trans nasum! Sed ubi est mater?

He. Sursum eamus!

Pa.   O mee delicie, o mee omnes
voluptates, anime mi, quanto ego te desiderio
expectavi iam dudum! Nichil timeas,
nichil a me speres mali: domi tue es,
tui nos omnes.

700 Ur.   Sed ubi est mater?

cuses to feed to master. [*Herotes and Ursula begin to make love, noisily*]

Paulus. Now everyone seems to have abandoned me; Herotes hasn't returned and the ladies haven't come either. Perhaps somebody has blocked them and messed things up; nothing good ever happens to me without something getting messed up! [*Paulus overhears the sound of the lovemaking*] Herotes has got- 680 ten into a fight! Herotes, fight as hard as you can, you have to deliver on this deal! Why raise false hopes in me if you're not going to get results?

Herotes. Let's get it over with quick, or people will think something bad is happening.

Ursula. [*Screaming*] I'm coming!

Herotes. I'll be lucky if I can come. [*An old woman stares at them,* 685 *then departs*] Oh my god, that really scared me, I thought it was your mother coming! You watch the street and the house and let me know if she's coming!

Paulus. I'm coming to the end of my tether![14] He's coming back alone! [*Paulus then catches sight of Ursula, coming along behind Herotes*] No, in fact, I'm coming to be the happiest of men, what a fabulous deal is coming my way! But I'm trying to re- 690 member—haven't I seen her somewhere before? But now I'll see her and hold her![15]

Herotes. [*To Ursula*] Follow me inside. It's all over with.

Ursula. I'm lucky no one saw us except that old lady who maybe can't see anything beyond her nose! But where's mother? 695

Herotes. Upstairs. Let's go. [*Paulus suddenly appears at the door*]

Paulus. O my darling, my joy, my heart, I've waited for you with such yearning—and for so long! Don't be afraid, I won't hurt you. Make yourself at home, we're all your friends.

Ursula. But where's mother? 700

He. In primis edibus, que garulam quondam
senem nequit a se divellere.
Vos huc intro! Ego eam protinus evoco.

: IX :

Herotes, Papis servi

He.   Postquam convivas invitavi non sane invitos
705   cenamque pro sententia opipare instruxi,
tandem in forum eo, ut me paulisper oblectem.
Sed quam tempestive Papim video: adeo, ut colloquar.
Salve, Papi!
Pap.   Et tu, Herotes, salve!
He.   Domi tue fui, ut herum in cenam vocarem. Quid agis?
Pap.   Nichil hercle.
710   *He.*   Nichil? Ego hercle nonnichil hodie . . .
Pap.   Scio te semper rerum aliquid moliri idque quam bonum.
He.   At, si scias!
Pap.   Quid, queso?
He.   Nunquam dicerem.
Pap.   Dic queso: quo enim pacto esse id tibi iucundum potest,
si solus scias?
He.   Non sum solus, sed nil ego
715   facio, nisi ut scias. Iamque longa fabula fiat,
si tibi velim omnia recensa facere, sed summam
complectar: nostin tu eam, que proxime
cum filia in plateam, que iuxta nos est,
mansum venit?

Herotes. She's down at the next house. She can't extricate herself from some babbling old woman. You two go inside! I'll call her at once.

: IX :

Herotes, Papis, slaves

[*Outside Paulus' house, some time later*]

Herotes. Having invited the dinner guests, who were happy to come, and having arranged for a splendid dinner to my liking, I've now finally come to the forum to amuse myself for a while. 705 But what good timing! I see Papis. I'll go over to him and have a chat. Hello, Papis!

Papis. And hello to you, Herotes!

Herotes. I was just at your house to invite your master to dinner. What are you up to?

Papis. Nothing, by Hercules.

Herotes. Nothing? By Hercules, I can't say *I've* done nothing to- 710 day!

Papis. I know that you've always got some scheme going, and usually something good.

Herotes. If you only knew!

Papis. What is it? Please tell me.

Herotes. I'll never tell.

Papis. Oh, please tell me: how can you enjoy it if you're the only one who knows?

Herotes. I'm not the only one, but it's no good to me unless you know too. It's a long story if you want the detailed account, but 715 to make a long story short: you know that woman who recently took the house right by us on the square with her daughter?

57

Pap.   Tertia ab angulo domo?

He.   Ea est.

720 Pap.   Vidi hercle adolescentem et facie
et habitu admodum liberali.

He.   Matrem induxi
spe, precibus, promissis, ut hero filiam prestaret,
idque tandem obtinui. Constituta est hora
qua diu ad nos veniret; sed, ut veneficii

725   metus abesset omnis, pregustavi. Is est enim mos michi,
quecunque ad herum veniat, ut tentem prius,
quid secum salis ferat.

Pap.   Eam tam formosam
habuisti?

He.   Ita ne mirum?

Pap.   Ego fortunas
has nunquam captare possum.

He.   Vos istec

730   non curatis. Cum ea igitur ad constitutum
non venit, redeo, domi reperio solam,
castigo iterum et apud nos matrem esse comminiscor,
que se vocet. Venit illa, in cubiculum induco,
matrem ivisse tunc primum ad vicinam subicio.

735   Illi sese intus oblectant. Sed hic tu maxime,
si dicam, risu crepes.

Pap.   Tu vero! Et quid est,
obsecro?

He.   Ego, quo magis gratiam facerem
hero, virginem illi esse hanc dixeram
atque ita admonueram matrem, ut edoceret

740   commode natam. Quod ego ratus simulque
metuens, ne nos interciperet mater venientes,
nichil edixeram. Cum igitur cubiculo inclusi sunt,
aurem ego foribus oculumque subicio,

Papis. The third one from the house on the corner?

Herotes. That's the one.

Papis. I saw the girl, by Hercules! She had the face and figure of a   720
real lady.

Herotes. I gave all sorts of promises and inducements to the
mother so she'd give her daughter to my master, and in the end
I got what I wanted. We set up a time for her to come to us
later, but to make sure the dish wasn't poisoned, I had a taste of
it first. That's my way: I check the seasoning first before any-   725
thing is brought to master.

Papis. So you've had that beautiful girl?

Herotes. Are you so surprised?

Papis. I never get that lucky.

Herotes. You never make the effort. So when she didn't arrive at   730
the appointed time, I go back to her house and find her home
alone, I bang her again, and then I tell her that her mother's
with us and wants her to come over. So she comes, I put her
in the master's bedroom, and that's when I tell her that her
mother is at a neighbor's house. The two of them get down to
it. But here's where you're going to fart from laughing.   735

Papis. Really? Why is that? Tell me!

Herotes. To make her really appeal to master, I had told him she
was a virgin and had advised the mother to this effect so she
could give the proper instructions to her daughter. Since I fig-   740
ured the mother had done this, and at the same time was afraid
the old girl might catch us while we were coming, as it were, I
didn't mention this to the girl. So when they shut themselves in
the bedroom, I put my ear and eye to the keyhole, and I hear

blanditias audio et sonantia oscula.
745 Illa propterea, ut puto, quod domi aliene erat,
verecundius agebat, sed tamen ita, ut ego
maturam semper meretricem, alii profecto
virginem nunquam crederent. Ad rem tandem
veniunt: nullo labore vique nulla opus fuit.
750 Ille continuo blanditias mulcentesque sermones
persequitur: 'Ne metue, mea Ursula,
nichil ego tibi mali facio, mea vita,
meum suavium, anime mi! Si patiare, dabo
aurea tibi serta vestemque stragulatam
755 et zonam quidem arte multa elaboratam.
Clamare noli — cum illa diceret nichil quidem —,
etiam paulisper adhuc suffer ut hactenus'.
Iamque fere operam suam implerat, cum demum
illa errorem agnovit et: 'Hei michi', inquit,
760 'ad quos veni, qui me ita excrucient?'
'Hui, iam tandem!' inquam vixque risum
compressum feci.
Pap.   Hahahe!
He. 'Absiste, cur me enecas? Hei michi, ubinam
est mater? Nunquam postac huc venio'.
765 Interea pulsari primes postes audio:
accurro, nequis forte interveniat.
Et ecce matrem illius anxiam, pavidam:
orat, siquid ego novi de filia.
Quid, putas, inquam? Nisi iam sese cum aliquo
770 oblectare et simul accuso maleque ab se
factum testor, que ita nos luserit.
'Sed non impune', inquam eamque a foribus repello.
Num tibi videor ita eas plexas a me, ut sunt
digne?
Pap.   Recte quidem, sed quo pacto

sweet nothings and kissing sounds. Meanwhile, the girl, I think because she's in a strange house, is acting a bit shy, but even so, 745 it looks to me like she's a trained courtesan, and nobody else would ever believe she was a virgin. Finally they got down to business, and it's not exactly a bloody victory. Yet he keeps up the sweet nothings and the pretty speeches: [*Imitating Paulus'* 750 *voice*] "Don't be afraid, dear Ursula, I'm not going to hurt you, my darling sweetheart dearest! If you'll just let me do this, I'll give you a gold headband and an embroidered dress and a pretty little belt. Don't scream!"—although she hasn't said a 755 thing—, "just hold on a little bit longer." Now he's just about finished his job when she finally sees her mistake and says, "Oh dear, what kind of people have I gotten mixed up with who torture me so?" "Whew, it's about time!" I say, and I could hardly 760 keep from laughing out loud.

Papis. Ha ha ha!

Herotes. "Stop, you're killing me! Oh dear, where is my mother? I'll never come here again!" Meanwhile, I hear someone knock- 765 ing on the front door. I run to keep anyone from interrupting, and lo and behold, it's the girl's mother, anxious and quivering with fear. She asks whether I have any news of her daughter. So what do you think I say? Just that her daughter is having a good time with some man, and at the same time I accuse her and denounce her wickedness in having played tricks on us. 770 "But not with impunity," I tell her, and I slam the door in her face. Don't you think I did a good job untying these knots?

Papis. Yes, indeed, but how did you excuse yourself to Ursula,

775   te ab ea, cui mentitus eras de matre,
         excusasti?

He.   Hunc ego hero laborem liqui;
         Dammam enim evocavi, in macellum ivimus,
         exhausimus omnia. Hanc ego cenam
         ad sententiam constitui: poteris tu adesse
780   cum hero, quanquam nichil nobis opus est familia.

Pap.   Ego vero, ut te iuvem . . .

He.   Cras ergo, ut patinas
         mundemus.

Pap.   Itan me ludis?

He.   Si poteris igitur, fac venias.

Pap.   Nisi obseraveris
         fores.

He.   Imo vero venias! Secretum enim
785   aliquid reponam pro nobis, non quidem,
         ut vos Tusci soletis, herbulas aceto,
         sale atque oleo conditas sed unctum quid:
         altilia et domestica et forensia ferinasque
         carnes congessi, tum et suillos lumbos.
790   Scin enim quam bene michi omnia ex sententia veniant?
         Errabat sus vicine ante fores perpinguis;
         tum ego perspecto: nemo aderat in via,
         escas passim expono, subsequitur atque
         introgressus est, occludo incautumque ad
795   occiput ferio ita ut ne minimum gruniret:
         tum adiutore Damma purgo setasque
         in privatum detrudo. Sus in manibus
         meis istis sub clavibus est. Huius statui
         plurima pars nostra ut sit.

Pap.   Recte igitur
         te sagacissimum dicunt!

800 *He.*   Nunquam preterit

when you'd lied to her about her mother?   775

Herotes. I left that job to my master. I called Damma and we went to the market and bought the place out. I have prepared this dinner to my liking; you might come with your master, even 780 though we don't need any household help.

Papis. I *could* help you . . .

Herotes. Come tomorrow, then; we'll do the dishes.

Papis. Are you kidding?

Herotes. Well then, make sure you come if you can.

Papis. If you haven't locked the doors!

Herotes. No, really, do come; I'll put something aside just for us. Not your usual Tuscan fare—salad seasoned with oil, vinegar 785 and salt—but something really juicy: a heap of fattened fowl, both home-grown and market, as well as game and pork loin. Do you know how all this worked out so well for me? An im- 790 mensely fat sow was wandering around the neighborhood in front of our doors. I looked around; there was no one in the street; I put out some bait here and there; it follows me and comes inside; I shut the door and whack the unwary beast on 795 the back of the head so sharply that it barely lets out a grunt. Then, with Damma's help I clean it and throw the hair down the toilet. The pig is in my hands now, under lock and key. I've ruled that the lion's share of it is ours.

Papis. People are right to say you're a very smart man!

Herotes. A day never passes that I don't dream up some new 800

dies, quin novi quid excudam. Cum
aliud nequeo, herum fallo moribusque nostris
erudio: quam mature ego confectum dabo!
Nescio enim quem Topum Lippum memorant,
qui servos egregie condiret; ego vero sum
Herotes, qui dominos male condiam.
Quot, putas, ab summis opibus ad infamie
hospitium compuli! Nullum est amplum
adeo regnum, quod non exile artibus
meis patrimonium faxo. Herum quendam
nactus sum, quem dum egregie salutarem,
dum assentirer omnia, quidvis ab eo extorsi:
eum tandem eo coegi, ut serviret;
quot ego libris venditis aut datis fenori
in militiam misi, quot abire nudos, ubi
sint incogniti, quot intra monasteriorum
claudier septa!—, alium, qui nichil penitus
audire vellet veri, cui cum facerem satis,
quanquam id reor michi natura datum, tam doctus
evasi, ut nichil possim verum dicere. Si verum
a me quicquam voles, contra semper ac dixeram
habeto, quoque magis deos adiuro, eo minus
iubeo credas: nobis enim, qui aliena
vivimus mercede, omnes comparande
sunt artes, quo magis dominis placeamus.
Sed quid vos? Nichil ne?

Pap.   Imo vero
preclare multa, sed non est is herus meus,
qui falli facile queat: alios fortasse
possum, eum vero minime. Sed multa una
gessimus: quisquis dux, alter est miles!
Cum enim non suppeterent ligna pridie —
nam in diem vivimus, ut aiunt—sepes omnes

scheme. When I can't do anything else, I trick master and teach him our ways. I'll finish him off soon enough! I don't know who this Lippo Topo is they keep talking about,[16] who used to get his slaves in a pickle; but I am Herotes, the man who pickles his masters. Do you have any idea how many I have driven from the heights of wealth to the poorhouse and infamy? There is no kingdom so bountiful that I can't reduce it to poverty using my wiles. I once had a certain master whom I always spoke to with great respect, agreeing with everything he said, but all the while I was robbing him blind. In the end, I forced him into servitude himself. How many masters have I bankrupted and sent off to the army, how many have left for parts unknown without the clothes on their backs; how many have I shut up tight inside the walls of monasteries! I had another master with no desire to hear the truth, and I satisfied him on this point (although I believe I have natural gifts in this line): I turned out to be so good at lying that I simply couldn't speak the truth. If you want the truth from me, always assume the opposite of what I've said. The more I swear by the gods, the less you should believe me. Yes, indeed, those of us who live on another man's money need to acquire all the skills that will help us better please our masters. What about you? Haven't you done anything to your master?

Papis. Oh, I've performed many splendid deeds, but my master is a hard sort of person to deceive; I could fool some other masters, but not him. However, the two of us have done many exploits together; one acts as a commander, another as a soldier. The other day, when we ran out of firewood — we live from day to day, as the expression goes — we tore down all the fences in the neighborhood under cover of darkness. We make a practice

805

810

815

820

825

830

vicinas noctu disiecimus; pistorias
conchas convehere domum solemus;
835   nemini sunt altilia vicino, que nocturnas
vigilias signent; omnes obseramus fores,
ut prodire nulli sub diem possint;
et si quando nos presidis militia noctu circumveniat,
tum lapidibus atque armis, tum simulatione,
840   tum fuga evadimus. Alea nemo plus
valet quam herus. Superiori affuit nocte
quidam mercator, numorum plenus, qui consereret una:
diuturna lis fuit et in longam noctem
contentio, tandem abrasum emisimus.

845 *He.* Sed quam post ea[4] liberalis in te atque in mensam est?
  Pap. In me quidem satis, in popinam vero, ut solet:
ipsi istoc opus est, ut mutet mores. Tu vero
nichil apud eum nichilque prestes, quod
non protinus reddat atque amplius eo quam
prestitum sit.

850 *He.*   Tarvisinus sum ego:
si me quisquam fallat, conscendere eum in celum
veto.

  Pap. At ille Tuscus, quocum siquis ludat,
non oportet luscum esse.

  He.   Id ipsum experiri vellem.

  Pap. Frustra id quidem aut certe cum damno
tuo. At, si lubet, heros mutemus!

855 *He.*   Ille vero
nunquam a se me dimitteret!

  Pap.   Crede mihi,
Herotes, quod et vulpes macellum habet.

  He.   Sed
oves plures.

  Pap. Qui fit, ut inique secum

of carrying home the baker's shells and no one in the neighborhood has any fattened roosters left to mark the watches of the 835 night. We lock all our doors so that no one can go out during the day, and whenever the police surround us at night, we escape them, sometimes by throwing rocks and fighting, sometimes by bluffing, sometimes by flight. My master is the best 840 dice-player there is. The other night a certain merchant showed up, loaded with money, and fought it out with master; the contest lasted all day and far into the night, but in the end we skinned him and sent him away.

Herotes. But apart from all that, how generous is he to you, and at 845 the table?

Papis. He's generous enough with me, but the food? Well, it's the usual story. He needs to change his ways in this department. But you can't get away with anything or get the better of him; if you try, he pays you back immediately and in spades.

Herotes. I'm from Treviso; if anyone cheats me, I'll make sure he 850 never gets into heaven.

Papis. But master is a Tuscan; if anyone fools around with him, they'd better have both their eyes.

Herotes. I'd like to put him to the test.

Papis. You'd be wasting your time, or most likely it would be your loss. But let's exchange masters if you like.

Herotes. But mine would never let me go! 855

Papis. Trust me, Herotes, even the fox ends up in the butcher-shop.

Herotes. But there are many more sheep there, aren't there?

Papis. Why is it that everybody complains with such ill humor

omnes actum de opibus querantur,
de prudentia nemo?

860   *He.*   Male sit, precor,
stulto, magis siquis eum se extimet. Nobis, ut
reor . . .

   Pap.   [*lac.*]⁵

   He.   Hoc ego tibi unum dico: Parum sapis;
tanti est unusquisque, quanti se facit.

about losing their money, but nobody complains about losing wisdom?

Herotes. The devil take all fools, especially if they figure out that they're fools. As far as we're concerned, I reckon [. . .][17]   860

Papis. [. . .]

Herotes. I'll tell you this one thing: you aren't very smart. The value of each person is what he makes of himself.[18] [*Exeunt*]

PHILODOXEOS FABULA

[Epistola dedicatoria]

1 Illustrissimo domino Leonello Estensi Leo Baptista Albertus.

2 Consuevere plerique scripta sua ad principes et viros illustres eam ob rem dedere, quod aut gratiam inire aut suis eo pacto rebus aliquam adicere auctoritatem studuerint. Mihi autem quam ob rem ad te principem illustrissimum nostram hanc fabulam deferri iuberem, horum nihil admonuit. Nam cum fratris tui Meliadusii, viri humanissimi et qui mihi optime semper studuerit, plane sim amicissimus, non eram quidem tam ineptus ut confiderem te magis fabulis moveri meis quam fratris tui amantissimi iudicio et voluntate, neque laudis cupiditate adducebar ut alio mallem quam ipso Meliadusio, cui sim carissimus, apud te uti interprete, tum et eorum institutum non approbabam, qui se aliorum suffragio quam propria virtute honestos fore cupiant: que etsi mihi virtus non tanta sit, ut non tua nobis si accesserit auctoritas plurimum sit adiumenti allatura. Tamen antiquius apud me fuit, cum multi amicissimi hanc a me fabulam peterent, unum te preferre, quem nostro dignissimum esse munere iudicarem. Et tibi quidem spero hanc eo futuram non ingratam, quo in dies intelliges me magis explicandi amoris, quo sum mirifice ob tuas virtutes in te preditus,

THE PLAY OF PHILODOXUS

[Dedicatory Letter]

Leon Battista Alberti to the most celebrated prince, Leonello 1
d'Este.[1]

Many men have been accustomed to dedicate their writings to 2
princes and other illustrious men because they strove to gain their
favor or because they wished thereby to have a degree of authority
conferred on those writings. In my case, however, neither of these
motives prompted me to have this play presented to you, our most
illustrious prince. Since I am obviously very close to your brother
Meliaduse,[2] the kindest of men and someone who has always been
zealous in my interest, I wasn't so foolish as to think that you
would be influenced more by my plays than by the judgment and
wishes of your beloved brother. Nor was I so drawn by the desire
for praise that I would prefer anyone else save Meliaduse himself,
to whom I am most dear, to act as my go-between with you, nor
moreover did I approve of the established practice of those who
desire to acquire honor through the recommendation of others
rather than through their own merit—although my merit is not so
great that it would not be considerably enhanced if your stamp of
approval were conferred on me. Nevertheless, it was more important to me, when many of my closest friends were seeking the dedication of this play from me, to prefer you alone, as I judged you to
be the man worthiest of my tribute. And I hope that for your part
the play will not be unwelcome, so that in the days to come you
will understand that I have sent you this play more as an expression of my love, with which I am wonderfully supplied thanks to

hanc tibi misisse fabulam quam ornandi mei. Tu igitur hanc perleges et me tuum esse voles. Vale.

Commentarium Philodoxeos fabule Leonis Baptiste Alberti

3 Hec fabula pertinet ad mores: docet enim studiosum atque industrium hominem non minus quam divitem et fortunatum posse gloriam adipisci. Idcirco titulus *Philodoxeos* fabule est: namque *philo* 'amo', *doxa* vero 'gloria' dicitur. Huius Doxe soror Phemia, quam eandem Latini proximo vocabulo 'famam' nuncupant; has quidem, quod Romam omnes historie fuisse glorie domicilium testentur, merito ambas esse matronas Romanas fingimus. Amicus amantis Phroneus, quem eundem 'sapientem ac prudentem' possumus appellare: nam quisquis glorie cupidus sit, hunc non imprudentem, sed admodum in rebus gerendis callidum esse oportet; Athenienses ambo, quod Athene artium bonarum et optimorum studiorum inventrices atque alumne fuerint. Tum Philodoxo adolescenti parentes Argos et Minerva, quorum alterum providentiam, alteram studium et industriam interpretamur. Tychie quidem, quam eandem nos fortunam nominamus, inconstanti et nulli coniugium servanti, quandoquidem illa istiusmodi maxime ingeniis delectatur adoptivum temerarium filium Thrasone et Autadia natum dedimus: Thraso autem audax et tumidus est, Autadia insolentia arrogantiaque dicitur. Servus Fortune Dynastes: hunc nos tyrannidem, potentiam vocamus, nam hec presertim quidem fortune subiecta est. Doxe vicinus Aphthonus, Tychie libertus, divitias et copias demonstrat, que proxime ad gloriam propagandam facultatem prestent. Sed quo libertum esse illum volui perque fallaciam edes eius ingredi, id plane docet ab industriis quoque divitias occupari, sed esse eas primo aggressu difficiles, tamen postea sese faciles prebere,

your virtues, than as a way of distinguishing myself. So do run your eyes over the play and claim me for your own. Farewell.

Commentary on the Play of Philodoxus by Leon Battista Alberti

This play deals with conduct, for it teaches the diligent and hard-working man no less than the rich and fortunate one how to attain glory. It is for that reason that the play is entitled "Philodoxus": for *philo* means "I love," and *doxa* means "glory."[3] The sister of Doxa[4] is Phemia, which is the same word as the cognate term "fame" in Latin. Appropriately, I represent both of these women as Roman matrons,[5] since all histories affirm that Rome is the home of glory. The friend of Philodoxus is Phroneus, which means the same as "wise and prudent man;" for whoever seeks glory must not be rash but wise and skillful in the conduct of his affairs. Both men are Athenians, because the inventors and nurslings of the liberal arts and the finest studies were in Athens. Argos and Minerva are the parents of this young man Philodoxus, the first of whom is construed as foresight, while his wife is understood to be study and diligence. We have given to Tychia, whose name means "fortune" in Latin — an inconstant and adulterous woman — a reckless adoptive son, since she delights chiefly in characters of this kind. The son was born to Thraso and Autadia; Thraso stands for audacity and overweening pride, Autadia for insolence and arrogance. The slave of Fortune is a man named Dynastes; this name refers to tyranny and power, for, indeed, power is especially subject to fortune. One of Doxa's neighbors is Aphthonus, the freedman of Tychia, who symbolizes wealth and abundance, which supplies proximately the ability to extend glory. Representing this man as a freed slave who enters into Tychia's household by trickery teaches clearly that riches are obtained by hard work too; that they are difficult at first, but afterwards offer themselves with ease, though they are untrustworthy and have learned to flee their hard possess-

verum esse infidas atque a duris possessoribus illico didicisse aufugere. Doxam[1] inquit palam atque publico velle cum amante colloqui: id affirmat veram gloriam fama comite affectare celebritatem atque odisse solitudinem. Chronos tempus est, eius filia Alethia, que apud Latinos Veritas nuncupatur; hec in tumultu presens omnia spectavit.

4   Doxa supremum fastigium conscenderat, quod ita prorsus evenit iis, qui non studio et industria adiutrice, sed temere procacitate quadam atque audacia quippiam etiam dignum gloria exequantur: namque hi non veram gloriam, sed fortune adminiculis famam usurpant. Alethie adservatrix Mnimia: hec est cognitio et memoria, que et Phronei uxor est. Nam si studium cesset, memoria res cognitu pretiosissimas denegat: idcirco antequam Doxa amanti adiungatur, memoria studio restituitur. Denique datur amatori legitima uxor, dum petulans Fortuna dari filio raptam orasset, quam sibi rem Tempus haud quidem concessit libere, at non denegavit tamen. Sunt et pleraque alia que salem habeant; ea brevitatis causa pretereo.

5   Itaque nostra, ut docui, fabula materiam habet non inelegantem neque quam ab adolescenti non maiori annis viginti editam quispiam doctus minime invidus despiciat; tum et ea eloquentia est, quam in hunc usque diem docti Latinis litteris omnes approbarint atque usque adeo esse antiqui alicuius scriptoris existimarint, ut fuerit nemo qui non hanc ipsam summa cum admiratione perlegerit, multi memorie mandarint, non pauci in ea sepius exscribenda plurimum opere consumpserint. Hic locus admonet ut recitem quonam pacto meam esse ignorarint.

6   Mortuo Laurentio Alberto patre meo, cum ipse apud Bononiam iuri pontificio operam darem, in ea disciplina enitebar ita

ors in a twinkling. It is said that Doxa openly and publicly wants to speak with her lover: this affirms that true glory, accompanied by good reputation, tries to win over the crowd and hates solitude. The character Chronos is Time, his daughter is Alethia,[6] which among the Latins is translated as Truth; she, present in the midst of blinding confusion, saw all things clearly.

Doxa had scaled the heights, which surely happens to those 4 who are unaided by zeal and hard work but who rashly, with a kind of abandon and audacity, go in search of something that is also deserving of glory; but these men usurp not true glory, but, with fortune's aid, merely the fame thereof. Mnimia is the protectress of Alethia: she represents knowledge and memory; she is also the wife of Phroneus. For if study should cease, memory refuses to know the most precious things. For that reason, before Doxa is joined to her lover, memory is reunited with study. In the end a proper wife is given to her lover even though a petulant Fortune has demanded that she be taken and given to her son, a matter which Tempus by no means allowed her freely, but didn't refuse nevertheless. There are many other devices that show wit, but for the sake of brevity I'll skip over them.

So, as I have informed you, our play has a subject that is not in- 5 elegant and one that no educated person (unless envious) would look upon with scorn just because it was written by a twenty-year-old youth. Then, too, it does have an eloquence to it, which until this very day all those schooled in Latin letters found themselves able to approve; and they used to judge the style to be that of some ancient writer, to the point where there was no one who hadn't perused it with the highest admiration; many committed it to memory; and not a few expended a good deal of energy copying it again and again. This topic reminds me that I should explain why they are unaware that the play is mine.

When my father Lorenzo degli Alberti died, it was at a time in 6 my life when I was studying canon law in Bologna.[7] I tried to excel

proficere ut meis essem carior et nostre domui ornamento. Fuere inter meos qui inhumaniter nostro iam iam surgenti et pene florescenti nomini vehementius inviderent, quos etsi iniustos et nimium duros in dies experirer, tamen neque odisse poteram neque non diligere, quippe qui illis omnia mecum licere arbitrarer. Tuli igitur illorum in me inhumanitatem animo non iniquo et magis officii et humanitatis quam iniuriarum memori, quoad ipse plane cepi intelligere omnes meos ad eorum gratiam et benivolentiam mihi conciliandam esse conatus irritos atque inutiles.

7   Idcirco hanc in eo quo tum eram constitutus merore incommodorum meorum et acerbitatis illorum, quibus ut essem carior omnes boni desiderabant, consolandi mei gratia fabulam scripsi, quam quidem inelimatam et penitus rudem familiaris quidam mei studiosissimus subripuit furtimque illam horis paucissimis quam celerrime transcripsit; ex quo factum est ut ad meas mendas scribendi quoque istius festinatione multa vitia adicerentur. Fecit tamen eius me invito copiam vulgo, apud quem librariorum imperitia nimirum omnino inconcinna reddita est: que enim inepte scripta aderant, ea quisque pro arbitrio interpretabatur. Neque defuere aliqui, nostri magis ingenii conscii quam amatores, qui quo meam esse suspicabantur, eo multa obscena interseruerint. Itaque puerilis et inelaborata corruptaque fabula, dum meam esse ignorarent, tanto fuit in pretio habita, ut nemo satis comicis delectari putaretur cui Philodoxeos parum esset familiaris.

8   Quam ego fabulam cum eo placere et passim a studiosis expeti, quo vetusta putaretur, intelligerem, rogantibus unde illam conges-

in that subject so that I would become dearer to my relatives and an ornament of our house. There were those in my family who developed a violent and unnatural hatred of the name I was now on the point of making for myself, and although I experienced their injustice and hard-heartedness day after day, I still couldn't hate them nor fail to love them, like someone who thought they should be denied nothing in matters relating to myself. Consequently, I suffered their inhumanity to me without prejudice, mindful more of duty and humanity than of their unjust actions, until the point where I began to understand clearly that all my attempts to reconcile myself to their good graces and good will were useless and wasted.

Hence, in this state of depression at my own troubles and at the 7 cruelty of those to whom all good men desired that I should be more dear, I wrote the play to console myself. While it was still in an unpolished and very rough state, a friend of mine who was extremely zealous on my behalf filched it and transcribed it rapidly in a few hours, whence it happened that to my own mistakes were added many faults owing to this man's haste in writing it.[8] Nevertheless, he circulated his copy against my will, and thanks to the ignorance of the booksellers it was of course turned into a dog's dinner. And once these inept writings became available, everybody began construing it each according to his own judgement. There was no lack of other men who were aware of my talent without being lovers of it, who inserted indecent bits into it in such a way that they would be regarded as my own. Thus, this juvenile and unfinished and error-ridden play of mine, although the public didn't know it, was mine, and was considered to be of such value that someone who didn't know the *Philodoxus* was considered to be someone who lacked appreciation of the comic poets.

Once I understood that the play was so liked and sought after 8 everywhere by the learned that it was believed to be an ancient work, I fooled the people who were asking from what source I'd

sissemus, per commentum persuasimus ex vetustissimo illam esse codice excerptam. Facile omnes adsentiri: nam et comicum dicendi genus et priscum quippiam redolebat neque difficile creditu erat adolescentem pontificiis scriptis occupatum me ab omni eloquentie laude abhorrere. Adde quod per hec tempora non eiusmodi vigere ingenia arbitrabantur. Tamen, ne meas lucubrationes perderem, adieci prohemium in quo et studia et etatem et reliqua hec de me omnia aspersa esse volui, ut, siquando libuisset, nostram liquido esse — quod fecimus — vindicaremus.

9   Denique annos decem vagata est, quoad e studiis pontificiis aureo anulo et flamine donatus excessi. Cum autem ad hec studia philosophie rediissem, hec fabula elimatior et honestior mea emendatione facta. Quod eam quasi postliminio recuperarim, invidia effecit ut minus placeat, et quam omnes etsi obscenam et incomptam cupiebant, eam nunc pauci sunt qui non vituperent. O tempora! Sed siqui sunt, qui nostrum ingenium et eloquentiam, quam pridem magnopere laudarant, modo reprehendant, ii profecto aut suum pristinum iudicium vituperant aut declarant quam sint natura invidi atque inconstantes. A quibus quidem, siquid leserint, satis pene ex eorum invidie stimulis sumpsimus; sin autem lesisse nequeunt, parvi eos possum facere, ubi me boni ob eorum improbitatem potius ament quam redarguant.

10   Nunc autem, o studiosi, qui vestram operam in colenda virtute, non in aliorum cursu interpellando ponitis, si officii est ingeniis huiusmodi, non inertibus neque desidiosis favere, vos precor atque obtestor, vestram imploro fidem et sanctissimam litterarum religionem. Defendite vestrum Leonem Baptistam Albertum studiosis omnium deditissimum; defendite, inquam, me ab invidorum

compiled it into believing it was excerpted from a very ancient manuscript. Everyone was easily convinced, for it smacked of the comic genre and of antiquity, nor was it hard to believe that I, a youth occupied with canon law, was quite incapable of acquiring any merit for eloquence. Moreover, comic wit was held not to be flourishing in these times. Nevertheless, so as not to lose all my hard work, I added an introduction in which I dropped some hints about my own studies and age and the rest of these personal details so that, if soever I pleased, I could lay a clear claim to the work—which I have done.[9]

Then the play wandered around for ten years until I had left 9 my canon law studies and had been granted the gold ring and had taken holy orders. When I returned to these philosophical pursuits, I polished the play and fixed it up so that it would be more decent. Once I had rescued it, as it were, from enemy hands, envy made it less liked, and the play everybody wanted when it was indecent and unkempt, almost everybody now made the target of their criticism. Such are the times! But anyone who now criticizes my talent and eloquence who formerly praised it to the skies is now certainly either criticizing his own earlier judgment or showing how envious and inconstant he is by nature. Indeed, the damage their envy has done, if any, has rather been a stimulus to me; and if they weren't able to harm me, I can hold them of little account, when thanks to their wickedness good men have loved me rather than held me in the wrong.

Now, you learned men, you who put your effort into cultivating 10 virtue and not into tripping other people up, if it is a matter of duty to show favor, not to the lazy and idle, but to talents of this kind, I beg you and call upon you as witnesses, I call upon your loyalty and holiest devotion to letters. Defend your Leon Battista Alberti, a man wholly devoted to the learned. Defend me, I say, from the carping of the envious so that, when leisure allows, I may be strengthened by your good expectations and approval and be

morsibus, ut, cum per otium licuerit, bona spe et vestra approbatione confirmatus possim pacato animo alia huiusmodi atque, non invita Minerva, longe in dies maiora edere, quibus et delectari et me amare vehementius possitis. Este felices.

Lepidi comici Philodoxios fabule
prologus incipit.
Lege feliciter.

11 Non diu preivit temporis postquam ebibi et nescio an abunde nimis: sed erit vobis indicio quod de bibundo[2] exanclarim quam longe limites, si apud vos loquar barbare. Nunc auscultate et iudicium date. Exoratum capi venio hanc unam singularem precibus e vobis ut impetrem gratiam, non ad vituperium in postremis dari, si preter vostram de nobis expectationem in negotium me ad scribundas fabulas miserim; quod si hoc sensero vostra pro facilitate e vobis posse, accipiam id pro summo, ut erit, opere pretio diffundamque quam hic suggero fabulam, usque adfluat in vulgo manus.

12 Hanc etenim si inter vos familiarem intellexero, animo institutionem ponam fortassis ad procreandas reliquas. Nunc sumite id vostra ex animi humanissimitate mihique etatique mee precibusque apud vos meis concedite, sinite ut exorem. Non quidem cupio, non peto in laudem trahi quod hac vigesima annorum meorum etate hanc ineptius scripserim fabulam; verum expecto haberi apud vos hoc persuasionis, non vacuum me scilicet, non ex undique incure meos obivisse annos.

13 Datisne admodum hoc gratie? Et datis, video. Ergo a me cupitis fabulam. Hercle, et bellula est: insunt qui ament, qui decipiant, qui construant festos. Certiores vos reddo: hec est fabula, Philodoxios hec dicitur fabula. Quid conspectatis ? Quid pendetis? Fa-

able with tranquil mind to give birth to other works of this kind, and even to greater ones, in accordance with my natural inclinations in the days to come. In this way you may take delight in them and feel a strong affection for their author. Be happy.

Here Begins the Prologue of the play Philodoxus
by the comic poet Lepidus.
Enjoy reading it!

It wasn't too long ago that I was drinking, and I'm inclined to 11 think probably too much; so you'll find some evidence here that I've gone way beyond my drinking limits if I should speak to you in the manner of a barbarian. But listen and then make your decision. I am persuaded by your prayers that I should seek favor for this one and only play, and that I won't be criticized hereafter if I should surprise your expectations of me and get myself into the business of writing plays. If I had felt you would have allowed it thanks to your easy temperament, I'd accept this one for the thing of high worth it will be, and distribute the play I put forward here, even let it slip into vulgar hands.

Indeed, if I find the play has joined your family, I shall perhaps 12 train myself to produce still others. Now receive it out of your super-kindness of spirit, and make allowances for me, my age and my prayers; let me win you over. I certainly don't desire, nor do I seek praise simply because I have foolishly written this play at the tender age of twenty; but I do hope to convince you that I am not brainless and that I haven't spent my years carelessly in every respect.

Will you do me this great favor? You will, I see. So then, you 13 want a play from me. By Hercules, it's a nice little thing: there are characters in it who love, some who deceive, others who make merry. Let me tell you: this is a play, and it's called "The Play of Philodoxus." What are you looking at? Why are you in suspense?

bule nomen est. Hem, iam nunc video: amplius me vobis notum voltis. Dixero: sum catus demens et inscitus sapiens. Hoc habetis iam nomen: Lepidus. Ha, ha, he, et vos lepidi estis! Ergo hanc tenete fabulam.

Argumentum

14 Philodoxus Atheniensis adolescens Doxiam Romanam civem amat perdite, atqui habet fide optima et singulari amicitia coniunctum Phroneum, quicum sua consilia conferat. Dat operam Phroneus amici causa ut Ditonum libertum, convicinum amate, benivolentia sibi advinciat. Homo fidem prestat rebus defuturum se nunquam. At interim Fortunius civis, insolens adolescens, Dynastis suasu hanc ipsam Doxiam cupere occipiens, lepidissima Phronei astutia depulsus est, quoad amans nonnihil verbis sese commendatum fecit mulieribus.

15   Denique irrisus Fortunius adolescens per vim edes ingreditur, Phimiam sororem Doxie rapit. Tandem Mnimia ancilla, cum virum suum Phroneum comperisset, atque Tychia, Fortunii mater, precibus exorarunt ut Chronos, excubiarum magister, omnia componeret: ex quo hic raptam tenuit, is vero amatam duxit.

This is the name of the play. Ah, now I see: you want me to tell you who I am. I will. I am a man who is madly shrewd and stupidly wise. Now you know what my name is: it's Lepidus. Ha, ha, he, you, too, are witty! So take possession of the play.

Argument

Philodoxus, a young Athenian, is desperately in love with Doxia, a 14
Roman citizen, while sharing with Phroneus a relationship of great trust and close friendship; with him he shares his deepest thoughts. For his friend's sake Phroneus devotes his efforts to placing the freedman Ditonus, a neighbor of his master's beloved, under obligation by acts of benevolence towards him. Ditonus pledges his trust that he'll never let him down. Meanwhile, however, a citizen named Fortunius, an insolent young man, also begins to desire this same woman Doxia, urged on by Dynastes; but through the extremely witty cunning of Phroneus Fortunius is kept away until the lover can find some words to recommend himself to the ladies.

Finally, young Fortunius, having been made a fool of, forceably 15
enters the home of Phimia, the sister of Doxia, and takes her by force. At last the maid-servant Mnimia, having established that Phroneus is her husband, and Tychia, the mother of Fortunius, prevail through their pleas upon Chronos, the commander of the watch, to re-establish order: as a result, Fortunius keeps the woman he has seized and Philodoxus marries his beloved.

Incipit Fabula Philodoxeos Leonis Baptiste Alberti.
Lege feliciter.

: I :

Phroneus

16 *Phron.* Et merito superis gratias habeo, quod me hoc etatis libere
atque ut volo sinunt degere. Quanto enim sum hoc felicior, qui
me huc dimisit! Nullis ego, ut ipse omnibus, afflictor curis,
quas forte, ut assolet, animo nunc denumerat suo: "Enim sic
debueram . . . hoc fecissem, recte institueram." Ergo id forte
dixerit: "Sane isthuc ipsum erit, at nolim . . . at malim . . . quin
veto . . . dii bene vertant!"

17   Merito ergo diis gratias, quoniam vivo ut volo, quod quidem
primum libertatis est munus. Atqui profecto graviter eius causa

The Play of Philodoxus by Leon Battista Alberti Begins.
Enjoy reading it!

CHARACTERS

Phroneus, *Philodoxus' companion*	Mnimia, *Doxia's duenna,*
Ditonus, *a wealthy freedman*	*long-lost wife of Phroneus*
Dynastes, *Fortunius' slave*	Alithia, *a maiden, daughter of*
Fortunius, *a young man, son of*	*Chronos*
Tychia	Chronos, *an old man,*
Philodoxus, *a young man*	*commander of the watch*
Doxia, *a maiden*	Tychia, *a matron, mother of*
Phimia, *a maiden, Doxia's sister*	*Fortunius*

Scene: Rome

: I :

Phroneus

[*A street in Rome fronted by the houses of Doxia and Ditonus*]

Phroneus. I am grateful to the gods, and rightly so, because they 16
allow me to spend this time of my life in freedom, doing as I
please. How much happier am I in this than the one who dis-
patched me here! I am carefree; he is harrassed by endless cares.
Perhaps he's counting them up in his mind even now, as he usually does: "I ought to have done it this way . . . had I done
that, I would have set things up right." Then again he might
have said this: "Surely it will have gotten to this point, but I
wouldn't . . . but I'd prefer . . . nay, I forbid it . . . may the gods
make it all come right!"

So it's right to thank the gods, since I live as I wish, which is 17
indeed the first gift of freedom. All the same, I'm really very

animo afficior: video namque ut perdite amet, ut timeat, ut ex-
pectet. Enim et quis hic est cruciatus, qui quidem animum et
trudat et scindat et agitet hominis? Curavi, mehercle, hoc tantum furoris ab egroto animo exstirpare, at nihil minus: malum
quidem hoc iam radices dedit nimias. Sed, proh deum, quid
hoc monstri est, hominem, quod alium amet, sibi ipsi admodum esse inimicum? Ne vero maiora procul dubio tormenta
sunt que amans ipse sibi afferat, quam que ab inimicis deve-
niant! Amantis animus nunquam tristi et cura et sollicitudine
vacuus est. Recte igitur mecum disceptare soleo qui maior furor
sit, an is, quo Mars agitat, an is, quo Venus inficit. Vehemens
in utramque partem mihi et anceps ratio est; sed illud constat,
hunc nostrum in dies magis fieri ex amore furibundum.

18   Et quam accurate, quam premeditate hoc me iupsit negotii
conficere! Hec dixit: "Nosti quod te diligo et nosti angiportum,
ubi operam omnem, diem omnem meque omnem contrito
consumoque miserum. Istuc ito ac, siquid videris sive quem
transeuntem, speculator. Ibi directo ad levam, quasi edibus
amate coadiunctum, ostium est semifractum abesum imbri, ubi
statua Plutonis constituta est. Edes ille multo mihi commodo
esse poterunt, dum in illius familiaritatem, qui inhabitat, nos
inserpias. Est ut hominem convenias teque amico et vite mee
amicum ac veluti vitam prestes. Hinc haud commoneo quicquam necdum impero: tute sapis et frugi es. Hominem ut
agnoscas, huc adverte: est fuscus, barba et capillo prolixus, clau-
dicans, cesius."

19   Itaque ille hec dixit; tum ipse abii, huc accessi, iterum atque
iterum bis quesivi pervolitans omnes vinarias tabernas, at nus-

worried about him: I see that that he loves her madly, that he's afraid and pines for her. And who is making the man suffer, who is pushing, shaking and breaking his heart? God knows I've tried to uproot this great madness from his sick heart, but without result: the roots of the evil have now sunk too deep. But, good god, what is this monster we call man who, because he loves another, becomes his own worst enemy? There's no doubt a lover brings greater torments on himself than those that come from his enemies! The mind of one in love is never free of depression and care and worry. Thus it is that I habitually debate with myself what the greater madness is: whether it is the one Mars sets in motion, or the one caused by Venus' infection. I could make a strong argument for either side; but one thing is obvious: this friend of ours is growing madder with love each day.

And how meticulously, with what forethought he ordered 18 me to perform this business for him! This is what he said to me: "You know that I love you and you know, too, the alleyway where I waste myself and all my time and effort, consuming myself in misery. Go there, and if you should see anything or see anyone passing by, act as my spy. Go straight to the left, to the alley adjacent to the house of my beloved; there's a door half broken by the force of a rainstorm, where the statue of Pluto is. That house could prove very useful to me, so long as you insinuate us into the friendship of the man who lives there. It's possible that you may meet the man, and offer yourself to him as a friend, and as a dear friend of mine. On this account I can hardly give you any advice, let alone a command: you'll look sharp and do the right thing. To recognize the man, note the following: he is swarthy, bearded and long-haired, he limps and is nearly blind."[10]

This is what Philodoxus told me; so then I left and came 19 here; again and twice again I've looked for the man, running

quam hominem. Hic ergo fessus operiar, dum fortassis redeat. Sed quis est, qui huc inter eundum interloquitur? Ipsus, enim vero ipsus est.

: II :

Ditonus, Phroneus

20   *Dit.* Iam, ut mihi persuasi fore, ita evenit. Nam quo studeo illis obsequi fenerariis, eo iterum studeo servitutem consequi. Durum sane genus hominum, qui quidem, ubi suum male sibi fraudent genium sibique victum discarpiunt pexime, quid censes aliis facturos, dum queant, fore? Neque enim illis sat est nostro opere cuncta, que sint ad rem domesticam et sumptum, suppeditarier, quin velint me iterum in servitutem redigere. Cecus sum, fateor; claudus, fateor: at non ita quin et viderim et abfugerim opportune.

21   Sed quis hic sedet homo? Fortene ex illis quispiam, me ut intercipiat miserum? Quis tu et qui hic? Audin? Quo te admoves? Hoc tibi edico, fieri libero iniuriam, que fiat mihi, homini omnium memori et vindici. Audin? Sum ipse Ditonus, fui Tychie famel: nunc eius ob gratiam, et quia bene de se meritus sum, quia cuncta facio eius ex voluntate et sententia, manu idcirco me in libertatem demissum. Audistin? Iam liber sum et te liberior libero, dum hanc habeo et libertatis patronam et iniuria⟨ru⟩m refugium: ne me proterve tetigeris! Hoc edico ut tuo tibi caveas dorso ac nequid tue confidas temeritati.

around through all the wineshops, with no luck at all. I'm exhausted, so I'll just conceal myself here and hope he shows up. But who is this man who is coming here and addressing me? It's the very man I seek; it is he.

: II :

Ditonus, Phroneus

Ditonus. So now it's happened, just as I told myself it would. I'm about as eager to oblige those moneylenders as I am to be a slave again. They're really a tough breed of men: when they cheat their own intelligence so badly and strip the sustenance from themselves to such ill effect, what do you think they would do to somebody else if they could? It's not enough for them that my efforts are relied upon to supply all my household's needs and expenses. No, these fellows want to reduce me to slavery again. Granted I'm lame, granted I'm blind, but not so much that I don't see and get away in time. [*Stepping forward*]

But who is this man sitting here? Maybe he's one of those moneylenders come to intercept my wretched self? Who are you and why are you here? Don't you hear me? [*Phroneus gets up and comes towards him*] Where do you think you're going? Let me put you on notice: an injury done to me is an injury done to a free man, and to one who remembers and avenges everything. Do you hear me? My name is Ditonus. I was the slave of Tychia, but now, thanks to her generosity and because I earned her gratitude, because I did everything for her willingly and satisfactorily, I was granted my freedom. Do you hear that? I am now a free man, freer than you are free, so long as I have her as patron of my liberty and as refuge for my injuries. So don't lay a hand on me! Let me put you on notice: you had better watch your own back and not take any foolish risks.

89

22   *Phron.* Proh deum, quam mihi provinciam delegavit! Non enim magis cupio quam timeam rem ex sententia posse succedere.

   Dit. Et hercle, preter viri boni officium agitis, dum ita infesti estis in me, qui studeam cunctis, et presertim vobis, meme in benivolentiam subdere. Num quidnam hoc e vobis meo benificio commeritus sum, ac si elaborarim saxa ut liquefacerem et lateres ut lotos redderem? Duri estis: obsequio apud vos benivolentia dissolvitur, non iungitur.

23   *Phron.* Volo ego te.

   Dit. Me? At me ne contingas, ne me comprehendas: erit hoc mihi pro vi et iniuria.

   Phron. At volo, inquam.

   Dit. At nolo, inquam. Hem, quid manum invehis? O populares, opem, opem afferte, accurrite, succurrite! Sine, inquam, ne me detentes!

24   *Phron.* Quin bono animo es?

   Dit. Quin et vos desinitis iteratis iniuriis me et timidum et suspectum reddere?

   Phron. Ausculta paucis: volo ego te scire me virum et tibi affectum esse.

   Dit. Quam ob rem? Quid in te admisi, ut ita detractes, ut male hoc mihi studeas misero?

25   *Phron.* Dico me erga te optimo affectum esse animo, non secus quam qui te unice diligunt.

   Dit. Neminem habeo in quem tuto fidendum arbitrer. Novi ego recte et etate et usu mores hominum: captari amicitias, ut ex amicitia quasi ex fundo fructus vel excipiant vel expectent, verbisque emi operas et operas vendi premiis. Haud quidem convenit te illi amicum esse, in quem dolos fingas.

Phroneus. [*Aside*] Good god, look at the field of action he's dele- 22
gated to me! I'm as afraid of succeeding in my plan as I am of
failing!

Ditonus. By Hercules, you are violating the duty of a good man by
being so hostile to me; I'm someone who tries to win everyone's
goodwill, especially that of you people. What have I done to
deserve this treatment from you, as if I were striving to melt
stone and return bricks for lotus-plants?[11] You are cruel; with
your kind, goodwill is destroyed by compliance, not secured by
it.

Phroneus. I want to speak with you. 23

Ditonus. Me? But don't touch me, don't shake my hand; I'll take
that as tantamount to violence and injury.

Phroneus. Still, I want to speak with you. [*He holds out his hand*]

Ditonus. But I don't want to talk to *you*. Hey — are you raising
your hand against me? Fellow-citizens,[12] help! Bring help! Run,
save me! Stop, I say, let go of me!

Phroneus. What, have you lost your mind? 24

Ditonus. And are you going to stop making me frightened and
suspicious with your repeated acts of outrage?

Phroneus. Just listen for a moment! I'd have you know that I'm a
man who is well disposed to you.

Ditonus. Why? What have I done to you that you manhandle me
this way; that you scheme against me, wretched fellow that I
am?

Phroneus. I'm telling you that I have the greatest good will towards 25
you, just like the people who have a special affection for you.

Ditonus. I have no one whom I think I can safely trust. From age
and experience I have a precise knowledge of the habits of men.
I know how friendships are sought out so that fruit can be
plucked from them, or hoped for, like apples from an orchard. I
know how services are purchased by words and sold for re-

Phron. Ah, bone vir! Ego, dum tua pro gratia liceat, volo tibi esse honori et commodo quam plurimo. Neque enim decet palam timere omnia, que ipse dubites, tum parum conducit semper in metu esse rerum earum, que casu non raro evenire soleant: nam

26   sepe incidit ut que heri sepius ac facile feceras, eadem hodie perquam raro possis. Spondeo tibi hac dextra fidem, diis testibus ac tua virtute, quam quidem velim fore amicitie nostre firmum perpetuumque vinculum.

27 *Dit.* Quis tu? Nostin me?

Phron. Ditonus es, amicorum amicis amicissimus. Ergo prebe operam, absecro, benivole te paucis ut alloquar.

Dit. Loquere.

Phrox. Audivi semper amicos et viros optimos, qui moribus et ingenio polleant, simplici et aperta amicitia adeundos esse; itaque aperto alloquar eo, quia te fidum et probum semper audiverim.

28   Adolescens hanc tuam convicinam amat Doxiam. Ea, ut opinor, haud egre id fert: neque enim invenustam neque interraro sese offert ceterisque in rebus, ut coniectura valeo, utitur amantium officio. Is, quod plus nimio hanc amet quodve plus satis honori inserviat suo, cuperet lares tuos sibi admodum esse familiares, ut inde absque plebe et fama oculos usque adeo depasceret suos.

29   Hoc solum et hanc ob rem illum et sua et meme tibi dedo et dedico, ut tuo pro iure tibi morigeri simus. Hanc facilem ob

wards. It hardly seems likely that you'd befriend a man on whom you would play tricks.

Phroneus. My good man! If you would just allow it, I would like to be a source of honor and the greatest advantage to you. It's not seemly to be openly afraid of everything you have hesitations about, and it's of little use to be always in a state of fear about things that commonly happen by chance. Indeed it often happens that the things you did yesterday often and with ease, you can only very rarely do today. I swear to you, with the gods and your virtue as my witnesses, how I would really like there to be a strong and lasting bond of friendship between us. 26

Ditonus. Who are you? Do you know me? 27

Phroneus. You are Ditonus, the most friendly of friends to his friends. Therefore, give me the chance, I beg you, to speak a few words of good will to you.

Ditonus. Speak.

Phroneus. I've always heard that friendly and virtuous men, those who carry weight for their character and talents, should approach one other in frank and straightforward friendship; so let me speak candidly, seeing that I have always heard that you were a man of integrity and good faith.

There is a young man who is in love with your neighbor, Doxia. She, or so I believe, welcomes his attentions, for she presents herself on numerous occasions in a not unattractive way, and in other matters, as I am able to infer, she fulfills the role expected of lovers. He, because he loves this woman to excess and dances attendance on her more than is consistent with his honor, wishes to make himself quite at home in your house, so that from it, free from vulgar rumor, he might feed his eyes on her to his heart's content. 28

For this reason alone and on this account I place that man, his possessions, and my own self entirely in your service, so as to oblige ourselves to you in return for your permission. For 29

rem amplam et promptam in amicitiam ius tibi prescripseris firmum atque perpetuum, unde utilitatis et presidii non minimum assequaris. Habemus namque, superum gratia nostroque ex labore et industria, cum benivolos tum familiares atque amicos nonnullos, quos re prospera et adversa nobis optimos et, uti deceat, frugi experti sumus, qui pro nobis et pro qui nos ament neque rebus neque, si deceat, vite parcant sue. Non erit ut in posterum eos illos fenerarios tibi inimicos quanti facias.

30　　Et cave hac in re hesites tuam erga nos facilitatem experiri. Fatis interdum res optime dantur, interdum attruduntur mortalibus, interdum tantum demonstrantur. Que monstrantur, nescio quo pacto ea nimio opere, nimis accurate petimus; que vero truduntur, omni quasi opera abnegamus.

31　　Tum erit, crede, hoc tuum benificium viro non indigno tibique posthac amicissimo pergratum. Volo omnia aperto alloqui. Is haud est civis Romanus, sed Atheniensis, summa ex familia, cui parentes Argos et Minerva. Accessit huc, ut rerum plurimarum visu fieret doctior, neque id tamen adeo ut se indignum hisce parentibus in res dederet. Sed nescio quo fato, cum hanc aspexit, illico amare occepit.

32　*Dit.* Estne is quem vidi isthac sub angiportu sepius inoperto capite, candido pallio? An vidin tecum?

Phron. Ipsus.

Dit. Et bone indolis, mehercle!

this easy service you will establish for yourself a fixed and perpetual right in a wide and active network of friends, from
which you will acquire no small amount of utility and protection. For thanks to the favor of the gods and our own effort and
industry, we have no few well-wishers, both family and friends,
who treat us well in good times and bad, and whose worth we
have tested, as is fitting. They are men who would not spare
their possessions and their own lives, if it were fitting to do so,
either for ourselves or for those who love us. In future you'll be
able to snap your fingers at those enemies of yours, the moneylenders.

And mind you don't hesitate to try out your access to us in   30
this regard. At times the fates grant us fine things, at times
mortal men can acquire them forceably themselves, but sometimes they are just available. For some reason we seek with too
much effort and concern the things that are available, but refuse
as though with all our might the things that require effort on
our part.

Then, believe me, this favor will be most welcome to a man   31
who is not unworthy and who will afterwards be extremely
friendly to you. I want to be perfectly frank with you. He is by
no means a Roman citizen, but an Athenian from a prominent
family, whose parents are Argos and Minerva. He has come
hither so that he might become more learned through seeing
the world, yet he has not done this to the point where he has
made himself in this matter unworthy of these fine parents. I
don't know by what fate it happened, but he fell in love with
this girl the moment he saw her.

Ditonus. Is he the fellow I see so often over there in the entrance   32
to the alley with uncovered head and a white cloak? Haven't I
seen him with you?

Phroneus. That's the man.

Ditonus. He's a fine fellow, by Hercules!

Phrox. Et macte virtutis!

Dit. Dii bene illi faxint, ut cupio, et tibi, ut vobis velis, quoniam digni estis eorum gratia et meo obsequio.

33 *Phron.* Ah, bone vir, cedo manum: hoc edepol neque iniuria de te persuadebamus! Ergo iube ad te ut veniat, tu ut virum agnoscas ipse tibique gratias agat, ut habet, pro tanto merito.

Dit. Velim maiora. Sic illi dicito, Ditonum, edes has et quid possim pro suis ut habeat. Sed estne hora ut edamus? Mecum eris in cena.

Phron. Semper sum tecum animo eroque alias corpore, ut iupseris. Iam bene vale.

: III :

Dynastes servus, Fortunius

34 *Dyn.* Sic se habet res: ut videris, non poterit secus quin meam in sententiam facile incidas.

Fort. Estne forma?

Dyn. Forma quidem et moribus, ut nihil addi, nihil optari amplius possit, ut vel formosiorem aut sane simillimam hanc Veneri diiudicem: decorum caput, venusta facies, aspectus hilaris, tum incessus modestus, denique habitudo, motus, verba, gestus eiusmodi sunt, quos in matrona et cive Romana laudes.

35 *Fort.* Nimis cupio hanc ipsam videre.

Dyn. Faxim, ad idque operam iam nunc paro.

Phroneus. Well done!

Ditonus. May the gods bless him as I wish they will, and you, as you would wish for yourself, since you are both worthy of their favor and my service.

Phroneus. Ah, my good man, you have my hand on it: by Pollux, 33 we have talked you into a fair deal. So ask Philodoxus to come to you so that you may get a good look at him and so that he may feel grateful and thank you as you deserve.

Ditonus. I would deserve even more of him. So do tell him that Ditonus, his house and his resources are at his disposal. But isn't it time to eat? You'll dine with me.

Phroneus. I am always with you in spirit and at some other time I'll be with you in body, as you bid. Now farewell. [*Exeunt*]

: III :

Dynastes, a slave; Fortunius

[*A street in Rome near Doxia's house*]

Dynastes. That's how the matter stands: as you'll see, it's impossi- 34 ble that you won't readily concur with my judgment.

Fortunius. She's a beauty, is she?

Dynastes. She is so beautiful and well-mannered that you couldn't add anything or wish for anything more. You'd think she was even more beautiful than Venus, or at least very like her. She has a charming head, a lovely face, a cheerful expression, as well as a modest carriage; her figure, movements, words, and gestures are of a kind that you'd praise in a Roman matron and citizen.

Fortunius. I'm dying to see her. 35

Dynastes. I'll fix it, and that's just what I'm working on this minute.

97

Fort. Quid ita?

Dyn. Quia has propinquas, ut vides, superbas edes ea inhabitat.

Fort. Et qui potero? Unde alloquar?

36 *Dyn.* Hoc scias velim: maturate atque attemperate omnia ut fiant opus est. Prebe te ut videat virum nec impudicum nec immundum nec lascivum primo, tum ut noscat et gestus et mores tuos, teque primo cum lubens, tum expectato ut videat; demum loquere, enarra: postrema hec munera ab his, qui amant, ut diiudicantur, ita sunt maxima, que, etsi perminima esse forte quis censeat, haud deceat tamen ea ab ignoto expetere. Curabimus igitur primo illam ut videas.

37 *Fort.* Tum hoc tu ex me non ignores velim, namque stat sententia. Non is ipse sum, qui unquam adduci possim, ut assiduo has porticus exarans operam et impensam ociose perdam.

Dyn. Demum tu qualem te philosophum prebes!

Fort. Profecto, quid vis? In me quam imperium femine queam perpeti?

Dyn. Non nosti, adolescens, ergo quid sit amor: tollit amor fastus omnes ex animo atque humilem reddit.

38 *Fort.* Utrumne hoc parum novi, gravissimo in merore versari eos qui hanc sibi amoris miseriam animo offirmant, quod facere plerosque video, ut liberi servitutem non inviti serviant? Equidem preter viri officium est non omnes odisse mulierculas porro, quibus tam diu sumus in gratiam amantes, quam diu nostra id coemunt dona, ut que Baccho et ioco ad superfluum

Fortunius. How so?

Dynastes. Because, as you see, she lives in these fine buildings nearby.

Fortunius. And how will I be able to see her? From where shall I speak to her?

Dynastes. I want you to understand something: everything needs 36 to be done at the right moment and in the fullness of time. Present yourself so that she doesn't see you as a shameless, dirty and lusty fellow first of all, then let her get to know your courteous ways and manners. At first she'll be willing to see you, then she'll look forward to it. Next, talk to her, tell her stories. Finally give her those gifts which lovers regard as the greatest of all; and although another person might think they were mere trinkets, it would nevertheless be highly improper to ask them of a man unknown to her. So we'll first see to it that you get to see her.

Fortunius. Then please don't you overlook this task I've set you, for 37 my decision is taken. I'm not a man who can ever be induced to plough endlessly up and down the porticos, calmly wasting expense and effort.

Dynastes. Now act like a philosopher!

Fortunius. Of course, what would you? How can I endure the power of this woman over me?

Dynastes. I conclude you don't know, young man, what love is: love removes all pride from the soul and makes a man humble.

Fortunius. Whether or not I know too little about it, don't I know 38 that men who fix in their own soul this misery of love, which I see most men do, involve themselves in the gravest suffering, so that free men willingly put themselves into slavery? Indeed it's really all a man can do not to hate all women, when we are accepted as lovers only so long as they purchase our gifts, so that the girl will deign to cast her eyes on us finally when she's filled

usque completa est, ea tandem in nos oculos dimoveat suos atque id quidem perparce, genus animantium peximum!

39 *Dyn.* Hoc quod dixti totum minus nihilo est. Habemus namque unde tuto conspicias et verba datatim commutes, dum lubeat.

Fort. Hem, forte id aliquid esset!

Dyn. Habeo virum qui olim conservus fuit, nunc mihi est amicus optimus, a quo facile queque, etsi grandia sint, impetrem. Is (viden isthanc statuam ostiariam?) edes illas possidet. Hominem conveniam, dicam velle ex eius horto . . . at aliquid dicam.

40 *Fort.* Et ego una tecum.

Dyn. Minime: volo enim te magnifaciat oretque, ut in gratiam se accipias tuam.

Fort. Lepidum caput! Ergo . . .

Dyn. Ergo deambulato. Ego ingrediar iam, cum fores patent.

Fort. Optume.

Dyn. Heus, heus! Et quis hic est? Et quid fores patent? At domesticus ipse sum, mihi semper patent: ingredior. Salvete, Lares.

: IV :

Philodoxus, Phroneus

41 *Phil.* Hec mihi commeatio pro triumpho est, totum iter hoc meum pre gaudio est. Nequeo ipsum me continere: quicquid video, iubeo salvere, ac si velim omnia hoc meo gaudio imparti-

up to the brim with wine and good cheer, and then only grudg-
ingly — they are the worst breed of animals!

Dynastes. What you've just said is totally worthless. You see, we 39
have a spot from which you can get a good look at her in safety
and take back your words, should you please.

Fortunius. [*He sees her*] Hmm, perhaps you have a point!

Dynastes. I know a man who once was a fellow-slave, who is now
my best friend, of whom I can readily ask anything, even big favors. The man owns that house over there — do you see the
statue in the niche? I'll meet with the man and tell him I'd like
from his garden to . . . well, I'll say something.

Fortunius. And I'll be there with you. 40

Dynastes. No, no; I want him to make much of you and beg you
to accept him into your favor.

Fortunius. What a clever fellow you are! Well then ...

Dynastes. So take a walk. I'll go in now while the door is open.
[*Enters*]

Fortunius. Good idea.

Dynastes. Hello there? Anybody home? Why are the doors open?
Well, I'm a domestic myself, so doors are always open to me:
I'll go in. Greetings, household gods!

: IV :

Philodoxus, Phroneus

[*Ditonus' house*]

Philodoxus. This passage of mine feels like a triumphal procession, 41
the whole way belongs to me for joy! I can't contain myself:
whatever I see I bid good day to, as if I wanted everything to
share in my joy. Be well — even if perchance you are treating me
rather unfairly — be well, O best of household gods, to whom it

rier. Salvete, etsi mihi satis iniusti forte sitis, salvete Lares optimi, quibus persepe liceat divam et videre et audire hanc. Salvete vos, superi, tuque, alme divum pater: gratias vobis habeo.
Et, mi frater, hoc tanto numnam exultas gaudio? Tibi etiam in-
gentes gratias—et utinam condignas exoptatasque!—pro tuo
hoc tanto facinore referam. Dixtin, certum hoc est inde eam audire ut possim?

42 *Phron.* Dixi audias, videas ut loco et tempore licuerit.

Phil. Proh deum, fortuna maximi te semper fecero, si semper!

Phron. Tace, obsecro.

Phil. Sic oportet animo morem ut suggeram meo, sinam pre gaudio sese ut diffundat decursitetque paululum.

Phron. Tace, tace, inquam: videre visus sum insolentem egredi ac
regredi frequentarium nescio quem ex amici edibus.

43 *Phil.* Hem, eccum hominem!

Phron. Huc accede post angulum aut columnam, ne nos videant.
Auscultabimus quid consiliorum congerant.

Phil. Hei mihi, quam male illico nostris rebus timeo!

Phron. Tace.

Phil. Hem, et Fortunium abhinc, dii, dii!

Phron. Tace.

: V :

Ditonus, Dynastes, Fortunius, Philodoxus, Phroneus

44 *Dit.* Ubi ipsus est?

Dyn. Iam nunc aderit. Sic decet amicos mutuo inter se convenire,
ut liberali animo et consulant et alternas operas referant, veluti
nos ipsi inter nos facimus: tibi nullum potuit rectius dari consi-

is permitted to see and hear this divine being so often! Be well, you gods above, and you, dear father of the gods; I give you all thanks. And, my brother, doesn't this great opportunity make you dance for joy? I owe you, too, enormous thanks—thanks that I hope are worthy and welcome!—in return for your help in this undertaking. Tell me, is it certain that I'll be able to hear Doxia from here?

Phroneus. I said you could; you can see that the time and the place will allow it. 42

Philodoxus. By god, I'll make you the luckiest man alive, ever!

Phroneus. Shh! I beg you.

Philodoxus. I must gratify my heart a little; let me allow it to overflow and run away a little out of happiness.

Phroneus. Shh, quiet, I say: I seem to see some unwonted visitor or other coming and going out of my friend's house. [*Sees Dynastes*]

Philodoxus. Ah, there's the man! 43

Phroneus. Come this way round the corner past the column, so they don't see us. We'll listen in on the plans they're making.

Philodoxus. Woe is me! Suddenly I'm terribly afraid for our plans!

Phroneus. Shh!

Philodoxus. O no! Gods, O gods, get Fortunius out of here!

Phroneus. Be quiet!

: V :

Ditonus, Dynastes, Fortunius, Philodoxus, Phroneus

Ditonus. So where is he? 44

Dynastes. He's coming now. It's fitting that friends get together, and in a spirit of freedom consult with each other and exchange plans, just as we do among ourselves; no better advice can be

lium. Sed eccum hominem. Salve, opportune advenis.

Fort. Salvete.

Dyn. Si scires quantum is cupiat se inter tibi familiares ut accipias, illi merito amicus fores.

Fort. Bene vos dii ament!

45 *Dyn.* Narravi parentes, mores, virtutes, probitatem ceteraque tua, ut potui, omnia.

Fort. Dii te ament!

Dit. Enarravit omnia sed, si lubet, dic, queso, qui vere fuere parentes tibi.

Fort. Thraso et Aphthadia.

Phil. Perii, ipsus est! Hic Fortunius Tychie filius est adoptivus, cui olim Ditonus fuit servus; inde iam ex ea domo mihi hoc preripietur commodi. Perii!

46 *Dit.* Te dudum aspiciens, tandem agnovi. At salve, iamne recolis, cum te parvulum gestabam e domo patris tui ad nostram?

Fort. Centies.

Dit. Quam eras fraudicolus! Semper in barbam et capillos duriter coniciebas manum.

Dyn. Semper te unice dilexit. Ut lepide applaudebat!

Fort. Ha, ha, he.

Dit. Huc advertite animo. Nunquam ego antea ex studio hanc conspexeram convicinam: nam me domi nisi interraro comperio et sat negotiorum habeo quibus me exerceam — ita dii in peximum omnia vertant illis fenerariis, qui tanta astutia fatigant me miseram in servitutem redigere! Verum nuper, cum domum redissem comessatum, accessit quidam exorans hanc eandem ob

given you than that. But here's the man. Greetings, you arrive just in time.

Fortunius. [*Enters*] Hello.

Dynastes. If you knew how much he wants you to include him in his household, you'd be his friend, and rightly so.

Fortunius. May the gods love you well!

Dynastes. I've told Ditonus about your parents, your character, your virtues, integrity, and all your other qualities, as best I could. 45

Fortunius. May the gods love you!

Ditonus. He did tell me everything, but if I may be so bold, tell me, please, who your parents really were.

Fortunius. Thraso and Aphthadia.

Philodoxus. [*Aside*] Damn, it's him! This Fortunius is the adopted son of Tychia, to whom Ditonus was once a slave; so now this advantage of mine will be taken out of the house. Damn!

Ditonus. Looking at you now for a while, I've finally recognized you. So, hello, do you remember now when I used to carry you as a small boy from your father's house to ours? 46

Fortunius. A hundred times.

Ditonus. And what a mischievous little fellow you were! You were always pulling hard at my beard and my hair.

Dynastes. He always had a special love for you. How amusingly he'd clap for you!

Fortunius. Ha, ha, he.

Ditonus. Pay attention here: I've never checked out the girl next door before with any care, since it's only rarely that I find myself at home. I have lots of business to keep me occupied — God damn those moneylenders who wear me out with their cunning, wretch that I am, trying to drive me into slavery! But recently, when I returned home sheared clean, a certain man begged me, for this very same reason, to open my house to him.

rem sibi edes ut paterent mee. Spondi operam; abiit amicum accersitum, cuius causa hoc impetravit gratie.

47 *Dyn.* Quis ille?

Dit. Atheniensis, cui parentes Argos et Minerva.

Dyn. Vidi hominem.

Dit. Post hoc accessi ad turrim et parvum per foramen vidi eam in superiori triclinio fidibus concinentem versus de laudibus Herculis serio et divum: ea, edepol, visa mihi est forma formosior Venere. Sed ad rem redeo: vos amo, tum nollem, si rediret.

48 *Dyn.* Recte habeo, caute id loqueris.

Fort. Ne vero timemus illos, qui nihil habent preter vitam, quam abs cruce precario possident?

Phil. Dii te malo divitent! Functus officio es, tum profecto verba blactis, ut dignus es, cui nihil proprium est, nisi lingua isthec fetida, pexima, que in deterius in dies convalescit.

49 *Phron.* Tace, in aurem consilia conferunt.

Fort. Minime eos metuo.

Dit. Nostin?

Dyn. Pulchre.

Fort. Quid dixti?

Dyn. Dixit illos se velle verbis oppletos et spe usque adeo delibutos abicere ab se.

Phil. Perii! Nullus amplius sperandi locus nobis relictus est. Tritum quidem proverbium: Integra cum fide tuta spes cohabitat; postea vero quam fides disrupta est, spes intereat necesse est.

50 *Phron.* Et tritum hoc est, quia quod tritum nimis est haud saporem habet. Tace, bono fac sis animo: quodque iter suum habet exitum.

Phil. Hei mihi!

I promised to do so; he left to summon his friend, for whose sake he requested this favor.

Dynastes. Who was that? 47

Ditonus. An Athenian who parents are Argo and Minerva.

Dynastes. I've seen him.

Ditonus. After this I went up to the tower[13] and through a small opening saw her in an upper dining room earnestly singing to the lyre verses in praise of Hercules and the gods: by Pollux, she seemed to me more beautiful than Venus. But to return to the issue at hand: it's you I love, so I should prefer that he not return.

Dynastes. I understand; you're speaking carefully. 48

Fortunius. Do we have anything to fear from those men, who own nothing but their lives, which they keep off the cross on sufference?

Philodoxus. [Aside] May the gods enrich you with evil! You've done your duty, then of course babbled away as befits you—you who own nothing but that foul, nasty tongue of yours, which grows sicker every day.

Phroneus. Quiet, now. They're whispering in each other's ears. 49

Fortunius. I don't fear them in the least.

Ditonus. Do you know them?

Dynastes. Very well.

Fortunius. What did you say?

Dynastes. He said he would load them down with words and rid himself of the men they'd imbued with so much hope.

Philodoxus. [Aside] Damn! There's nothing left to hope for. The proverb is a trite one: hope resides safely with integrity, but once faith is broken, hope necessarily dies too.

Phroneus. Yes, it is trite, since what's too trite has no flavor at all. 50 Quiet, now, and don't be discouraged; every journey comes to an end.

Philodoxus. Woe is me!

Phron. Tace, dum habeo argutam astutiam. Ha, ha, he, o dii, quid paro!

Phil. Quid agis? Qui ineptis? Cur te deturpas tam immunde luto? Dii testes, insanis!

Phron. Hem, quidnam? At lacernam . . .

Phil. Eia, insane, quid advolvis cruri?

Phron. Ut taceas atque videas; quod si intelliges licere, advola.

Phil. Quo is?

: VI :

Phroneus, Dynastes, Fortunius, Ditonus, Philodoxus

51 *Phron.* Hei mihi!

Dyn. Quis hic plorat?

Fort. Quid tibi vis, ebrie?

Phron. Sic opem expectabam ut dares!

Fort. Enim ut ebrius est: non se substinet.

Phron. O celum, o dii! Opem oro, o me miserum!

Dit. Surge, ne lacrima.

52 *Dyn.* Quid habes?

Phron. Habeo animam inter dentes et labia.

Dit. Porro loquere, quid hoc est?

Phron. Scies: querebam Philodoxum; dum itaque appropinquo — hei, doleo totus pre ictu!

Phil. Demiror quid nunc animo is fabricet suo.

Dyn. Quis percussit?

Phroneus. Quiet, I have a clever idea. Ha, ha, he, O gods, what a plan!

Philodoxus. What damn fool thing are you going to do? [*Phroneus begins to smear mud on himself*] Why are you befouling yourself in that filthy mud? As the gods are my witnesses, you're out of your mind!

Phroneus. Hmm, now what? Let's have your cloak.

Philodoxus. Hey, you crazy fellow, why are you wrapping it around your leg?

Phroneus. So that you shut up and watch, but if you know what's what, get out of here. [*Exits*]

Philodoxus. Where is he going?

: VI :

Phroneus, Dynastes, Fortunius, Ditonus, Philodoxus

Phroneus. [*Approaching Ditonus' house*] Woe is me!   51

Dynastes. Who is that crying out?

Fortunius. What do you want, drunkard?

Phroneus. I was hoping you'd give me some help.

Fortunius. He really is drunk: he can't even stand up.

Phroneus. O heavens, O gods! Help this poor wretch, I beg you!

Ditonus. Stand up, don't cry.

Dynastes. What are you suffering from?   52

Phroneus. I can hardly breathe!

Ditonus. Go on, speak, what is it?

Phroneus. You know: I was looking for Philodoxus; so when I approached him—ah me, I ache all over from the beating!

Philodoxus. [*Aside*] I'm absolutely amazed how he's making this up now out of his head.

Dynastes. Who beat you?

53 *Phron.* Dicam. Namque in foro legati ex Africa, bene re gesta, cum pompa nunc cum transirent, seduxi me ut eam ipsam pompam spectarem, quam tu quidem triumphum esse diceres: nam illic tibicines, currus, equi, leones, panthere, res denique mire atque innumerabiles, que videre longe opere pretium est. Interea putus caballum effrenum acriter virga et calcibus concussit. Nescio rem ut duxerit: hoc ipse aperto novi, crus mihi semifractum esse.

54 *Fort.* At qui legati?

    Phron. Peximi.

    Dyn. Ex Africa?

    Fort. Et sunt panthere?

    Phron. Utinam sic illis adsit perpetuum cordolium!

    Fort. Panthere? Proh dii, quam cuperem vidisse!

55 *Phron.* Nolim isthac lege, si te amo. Verum, si presto ieris, etiam videas. Mihi vero tam care cordi est ea vidisse, quam constitit ibi adfuisse.

    Dyn. Quo me trahis? Quo properas?

    Fort. Ehodum pantheras, equos, tibicines, pantheras ehodum!

    Dyn. Maiori etiam in re animo satis obsequar tuo. I pre, sequar.

    Fort. Quod nobis iter tenendum est ?

56 *Phron.* Recta te hac, recta versus forum. Namque aerem vocibus et tumultu opplent, ut procul audias.

    Fort. Sequere pantheras!

    Dit. Hercle, graviter fero tuum hunc casum.

Phroneus. I'll tell you. Well then, in the forum just now ambassa-   53
dors from Africa were passing by in a parade, having done some
great deed, and I was enticed into watching this parade, which
you call a triumph, because they had flute-players over there,
chariots, horses, lions, panthers, so many wonderful sights on
every side which seemed very much worth seeing. Meanwhile,
there was a young boy beating an unruly horse cruelly with a
riding crop and spurs. I don't know exactly what happened, but
this I do know for sure: my leg was nearly broken in two.

Fortunius. But how were the ambassadors?   54

Phroneus. Wicked.

Dynastes. From Africa?

Fortunius. And there are panthers?

Phroneus. Would that they suffered this endless pain!

Fortunius. Panthers? Good gods, how I'd like to see them!

Phroneus. I wouldn't want to on the terms you see here, Lord love   55
you. But if you go right now, you might see them, too. For my
part, seeing them was as dear and delightful as to be worth
what happened to me there.

Dynastes. Where are you dragging me? Where are you running off
to?

Fortunius. O my! Panthers, horses, flute-players . . . panthers, O
my!

Dynastes. Even in a more important matter I'd defer to your
wishes. Go ahead, I'll follow you.

Fortunius. How should we get there?

Phroneus. Go straight ahead on this side, then straight towards the   56
square. They're certainly filling the air with shouting and commotion, so you'll hear them from far off.

Fortunius. Follow the panthers!

Ditonus. By Hercules, I'm extremely upset at this accident of
yours.

Phron. Hui, quam dure pertractas! Perii! Mihi profecto nunquam hoc totum latus erit liberum.

Dit. Cave isthuc ita censeas, bono sis animo. Namque hic in tonstrina est Climarcus, et bovum et quadrupedum omnium atque hominum quoque suo pro officio medicus singularis.

57 *Phron.* Tibi amicus?

Dit. Maximus.

Phron. Quid stas, tibi dicon?

Phil. Men vocas?

Phron. Pol quidem!

Dit. Cui dicis?

Phron. Aggredere.

Dit. Dixtin mihi?

Phron. Enim: cur non pergis ad medicum? Intro, hei miser!

Dit. Quid intro? Nimirum homini huic ob dolorem mens delirat.

Phron. Hem, introducas medicum.

Dit. Quis introivit domum?

Phron. Te precor, hominem accersito.

Dit. Quis introivit hasce edes? Namque sensi dum attigit ostium.

Phron. Bone vir, adsis, precor. At quin abis?

58 *Dit.* Enimvero, quis istuc introivit? Heus, si fustem sumpsero! Heus, heus, te video!

Phron. Denique nemo homo istic est. At non te miseret mei! Vides quam afficiar dolore: abi, precor.

Dit. Eo sane, verum credideram . . .

Phron. Audi, prebe fustem.

Dit. Quam ob rem? Quin potius reside.

Phroneus. Oh, how hard you're treating me! I'm lost! No doubt this whole side will never heal.

Ditonus. Don't come to any conclusions about that — cheer up! This fellow in the barber-shop is surely Climarchus, a remarkable doctor whose speciality is cattle, quadrupeds of all kinds, and men too.[14]

Phroneus. He's a friend of yours? 57

Ditonus. A great friend.

Phroneus. [*Addressing Philodoxus*] Why are you standing there, am I speaking to you?

Philodoxus. Were you talking to me?

Phroneus. I did, by Pollux!

Ditonus. To whom are you speaking?

Phroneus. Come here.

Ditonus. Are you talking to me?

Phroneus. I am indeed: why aren't you going to fetch the doctor? [*To Philodoxus*] Inside, wretch!

Ditonus. Why inside? Doubtless the man's delirious with pain.

Phroneus. Um, I meant, bring the doctor inside.

Ditonus. [*Hearing the door open*] Who's going into my house?

Phroneus. I beg of you, go get the man.

Ditonus. Who's gone inside the building? I heard someone at the door.

Phroneus. Good sir, please come here. Or have you gone away?

Ditonus. Upon my word, who went inside? Look, if I pick up my 58 stick . . . ! Aha! I see you.

Phroneus. Really, there's no one there. Won't you take pity on me? You can see that I'm in great pain: please go.

Ditonus. All right, but I could have sworn . . .

Phroneus. Listen, give me your stick.

Ditonus. What for? You should really be sitting down.

Phron. Diis gratias! Non enim ero omnino miser. Ergo duc me, dum calet vulnus: nolo hic interim solus frigescere.

: VII :

Philodoxus, Doxia, Phimia

59 *Phil.* Non sine ingenio atque audacia fit magnum facinus. Mirabar quid ineptiarum ageret Phroneus, cum deformarat luto et gestu se ipsum. Dii perpetuum mihi hoc servent commodi! Dii secundent paria! Proh dii, quam e sententia res evenit! Introivi domum: ausculto, tempto, aggredior, contemplor, revertor. Interea visus audire sum vocem, uti erat, Doxie; adsum, obsecro operam, dum alloquar. Ea negat illic solitario in loco atque abscondito id licere, quod, siquid velim, iubet suas ad fores ut veniam: ibi se adfuturam. Sed quid dicam, miser? Unde exordium dicendi capiam? Ac quid, sic si dixerim: 'Amo, ardeo, morior. Tu id vides, tu cur hoc velis nescio. Ubi pietas, ubi misericordia, ubi animus ipse insignis huic tue pulchritudini condignus?' Vel dixerim: 'Si mihi unquam . . .'. At, at eccum eam. Hei mihi, quam totus discrucior animis pre gaudio, pre cura, pre metu!

60 *Dox.* Adsis, mi soror, dum alloquor, adsis precor: nolo hunc, qui sit in me honeste affectus, mea causa periclitarier. Cupio illi hac parva in re morigera esse: nam amanti curam levare maximam,

Phroneus. Thanks be to the gods! I won't be entirely reduced to misery. So take me while the wound is still fresh; I don't want to freeze here alone in the meantime.

: VII :

Philodoxus, Doxia, Phimia

[In front of Doxia's house]

Philodoxus. A great deed doesn't happen without ingenuity and 59 boldness. I wondered what foolery Phroneus was up to when he ruined his appearance with all that mud and posturing. May the gods let me keep the advantage! May they show favor to couples! Good gods, how agreeably everything has turned out! I entered the house; I listen, I feel my way around, I go ahead, I think about it, I return. Meanwhile, I seemed to hear a voice— Doxia's voice as it happened. I begged her attention while I addressed her. She said it wasn't allowed there in that solitary and hidden place, but that if I wanted something, she told me to come to the door; she'd be there. But what shall I say, wretch that I am? How should I start my speech? What if I say this: "I love you, I'm burning for you, I'm dying for you. You see it, but why you should want this I don't know. Where is the devotion, the mercy, the fine spirit that is worthy of this loveliness of yours?" Or should I say, "If I should ever . . ." But here she is. Ah me, how utterly tormented I am with joy, with anxiety, with fear!

Doxia. *[Enters]* Come here, my sister, come here, please, while I'm 60 talking. I don't want this man who is attracted to me in an honorable way put in any danger on my account. I want to comply with his wishes in this small matter: for to relieve the greatest anxiety of a lover, when you suffer no harm to your reputation,

115

ubi nullum fame suscipias incommodum, nusquam, ut puto, ignominiam afferet. Ergo hic adsis, soror! Sed eccum hominem: profecto, ut video, vel magis amat quam hactenus persuaserim. Philodoxe, dii te ament!

61 *Phil.* Et dii faxint ut me ames, ita uti condignum est, qui te plus velit quam se omni optimo perfrui! Dii faxint me ut ames, si id liberali officio honestoque animo opto atque oppeto!

Dox. Dii bene servent me honori meo, ut cupio et studui semper! Cedo, quid est, quod me velis? Loquere.

62 *Phil.* Nosti quod te iam diu amarim, sed forte non, ut se habet res, ita apud te notum est quam sollicito et quam firmo animo ipse erga te affectus fuerim. Namque, ut recte id videre potuisti, nimis honori tuo semper inserviebam et, ni fallor, eam ob rem forte persepius hoc tantum gratie abs te commeritus sum, verba mihi misero amanti dono ut dederes, quibus vitam hanc meam, que iam omnis inter suspiria et lacrimas diffusa est, reficeres et fugitivum cor, quod cura adustum sit, vite restitueres, que quidem omnia iam olim tuam in dicionem concesserunt. Hec enim, si cum non licuerit, tum non libuerit facere, non est quod percuncter; verum, ut gratias agam tanto pro hoc benificio tantoque tuo pro merito abs teque ut exorem, dum pro mea honestissima affectione in te mihi aliquid unquam debeat, ut huius te misereat vite et, postquam meo fato sic institutum est, tuus ut sim, malis me vivum, cum forte quantulum vobis emolumento esse possum, quam interemptum tua, ut ita dixerim, crudelitate: quod quidem neque laudi neque in partem ullam commodorum vobis accedet.

should never be a source of shame, I think. So come here, sister! But there is the very man. [*She sees Philodoxus*] And I see unquestionably that he is even more in love than I had hitherto believed. Philodoxus, may the gods love you!

Philodoxus. And may the gods cause you to love me, as is entirely   61
suitable in the case of a man who wants you more than anything in the world! May the gods bring your love to me, seeing that I desire and yearn for it with honorable intentions and gentlemanly respect for you.

Doxia. May the gods always well preserve my honor, as has ever been my desire and concern. I submit; what is it you'd have me do? Speak.

Philodoxus. You know that I've loved you for a very long time now,   62
but perhaps you don't know how the matter stands, how attentive and strong my feelings have been towards you. Certainly, as you've been able rightly to observe, I've always tried to devote myself very much to your honor and, unless I'm mistaken, perhaps because of my constant care for that honor I have earned from you at least this small favor, that you would deign to speak some words to me, your miserable lover, which might refresh this life of mine, which is already entirely poured out in sighs and tears, and also restore to life this fugitive heart, parched with anxiety; my life and my heart, indeed, have long since lain entirely under your dominion. It would be impossible for me to ask this if it were not proper as well as desirable; but I ask so as to give thanks for your great kindness and high merit, and so as to beg you, so long as I am owed anything in return for my most honorable feeling for you, that you take pity on this life of mine, and since my fate has laid down that I be yours, that you prefer me alive, and so possibly of some tiny service to you, than dead through your cruelty, an eventuality which can add neither to your honor nor benefit.

63 *Dox.* Quod me ames vidi et cognosco idque accipio animo neque
ingrato nequedum hoc iudico pre nunc male quicquam cordi
tuo e nobis nostra culpa advenisse.

Phil. Hoc fateor atque inde quam plurimum laudis et meriti merito commerite estis. Et nolim hec dixisse, si ea tibi egre sunt.
Sed, si pro tua pietate ac mirifica, ut nobilem animum decet, facilitate hoc abs te licet ut exorem, precor videndi te ut sepius
commodum sit et potestas.

64 *Phim.* Nescio ego quo pacto hoc vobis innatum sit amantibus, ut
nunquam sat sit, quod nimis sit.

Phil. Neque oppeto id nimis neque tum etiam id satis vestro sine
commodo velim nequedum rem factu difficilem, etsi mihi amplam et gratissimam, e vobis petii; neque amplius quicquam
dari opto, nisi ut meam hanc voluptatem et consuetionem
neque duro neque gravi feratis animo. Sinite deambulem, sinite
ut videam: hoc mihi ad voluptatem, hoc mihi ad vitam est. Hoc
mihi esse animi volui vobis dicier.

65 *Phim.* Dixti pulchre, sed gratam nobis rem ageres, istinc si ab-
duxeris te.

Phil. Quam ob rem?

Phim. Quia honori nostro conduceret.

Phil. Siquidem isthuc iupseris: nam et tu id recte nosti, quia semper satis honori dedi vestro idque ex animo atque studio.

Phim. Ergo abi: nam video quempiam inde ad nos.

Phil. Vale. Et tu vale meque memorie commendatum habe.

Doxia. I have seen and acknowledge that you love me and I do ac- 63
cept this not without gratitude, nor yet do I think that ere now
anything wrong came into your heart from us or through our
fault.

Philodoxus. I do confess it, and from this circumstance you de-
servedly deserve much praise and desert. I should not have said
these things if they distressed you. But if out of your goodness
and wonderful forbearance, so fitting for such a noble soul as
yours, you permit me to prevail upon you, I beg you to grant
me the advantage and opportunity of seeing you as often as I
can.

Phimia. For my part, I don't know why it should be in the nature 64
of you lovers that what is too much is never enough.

Philodoxus. I don't seek for what is too much, nor again would I
wish for it to be enough, unless it were to your advantage; nor
yet do I seek from you a thing difficult to perform—though for
my part it is a great and most welcome thing—nor, furthermore, do I wish to be granted anything except that you should
endure with neither a hard nor a heavy heart this pleasure of
mine, this intimacy with me. Allow me to walk about and see
you; this is my pleasure, this my life. To speak with you is my
dearest wish.

Phimia. You've spoken beautifully, but you'd be doing us a favor if 65
you'd get out of here.

Philodoxus. Why?

Phimia. Because that is what befits our honor.

Philodoxus. If this is what you wish; for you know it to be true
also that I have always sincerely and zealously respected your
honor.

Phimia. Then go; for I see somebody coming.

Philodoxus. Farewell. You be well too; think well of me. [*Walks
aside*]

: VIII :

Philodoxus

66 *Phil.* Equidem non inexperte hoc ipsum dici solet, cum primum qui mutuo se inter se ament ad loquendum coeunt, quia commutuent animas, illico dediscant loqui, siquidem id re nunc maxime expertus sum. Nam cum primum volui quicquam verborum exprimere, tum prius siquid aderat anime, prosiluit inter eius sinum, adeo ut et mei et verborum pene oblitus fuerim, miser. Debueram verba optima, verba precantia, verba collaudatoria, non que rixam aut odium, sed que prorsus benivolentiam et amorem excitarent atque nutrirent. Sic debueram: 'Ut solet aliis amor voluptas esse, mihi, non quod amo — nam nimis ardeo —, sed quod te amo voluptas et felicitas est. Nam venusta es, bella es et moribus atque omni virtute insignita, tum ceteris quidem in rebus egregie singularis. Sed quia me tanta in egritudine ob amorem constitutum video, ut mee interdum misere misereat vite, volui hoc a vobis gratie exorasse. Nam et nox et dies suum in me perverse officium peragunt; semper equidem meos inter oculos, semper animo, semper insita in meum hoc pectus ades. Multa mea causa vellem, longe tamen plura nolo, tue ne male afficiam honestati. Non sum meus, tuus sum, Doxia, tuus sum; tuum ergo ut recipias, tuum ut serves etiam atque etiam precor'.

67 Sed quin desino amplius ineptus esse? Quid, si isti, qui huc accedunt, me audissent? Et prope sunt et forte audivere ac videre omnia. Nimis incautus demum effectus sum, posteaquam occepi amare. Cuncta cum expavesco, nihil metuo, cumque me

: VIII :

Philodoxus

Philodoxus. There *is* after all something in the old saying, that   66
when people who love each other come together to talk, the
souls they share immediately make them forget how to speak—
an experience I've now had myself in the highest degree. For as
soon as I wanted to express anything in words, whatever was in
my heart leapt first into her bosom, so that, wretch that I am, I
nearly forgot both myself and my words. I owed her fine words,
words of entreaty, words of praise; words that would excite and
nourish her goodwill and love, not discord or hatred. This is
what I ought to have said: "It may very well be that for others
love is merely pleasure; for me it is not the fact that I love—
and indeed I'm passionately in love—but the fact that I love
you which brings pleasure and happiness. For you're charming, you're adorable, your character and virtues are remarkable,
you're utterly unique in every other respect as well. But since I
see myself in this love-sick condition, that you might from time
to time piteously take pity on my life, I wished to beg this favor
of you. For night and day have exchanged their proper roles for
me: indeed you are ever present to my eyes, always in my
thoughts, always planted in this heart of mine. I might allege
many things to further my cause, yet I shall restrain myself lest
I harm your honor. I'm not my own man; I'm yours, Doxia, I'm
yours; so take what is yours, protect what is yours, again and
again I beseech you."

But shouldn't I stop being a fool? What if those people who   67
came there had heard me? They are nearby; perhaps they heard
and saw everything. Being in love has made me far too incau-
tious. Though everything startles me I'm afraid of nothing, and
while everything makes me suspicious, my suspicions neverthe-

omnia suspiciosum reddant, fit tamen ut nulla ex parte me non negligentem atque supinum prestem: itaque solus amor curiosam hanc desidiam fovet. Ceterum, quid nunc mihi rerum agendum sit, incertum est. Tamen abnegandum otium est: ergo, postpositis rebus omnibus, nostrum fabricatorem fraudium conveniam Phroneum, ut narrem hec, quo tutius re, consilio et opere que in usum veniant conficiat. Sed quid hi servi mussant? Cupio hinc furtim auscultare.

: IX :

Ditonus libertus, Dynastes servus

68 *Dit.* Ego sic censeo, pro hac provincia te dignum legatum: nam tibi, quod veteranus interpres amantium sis, plane omnes mulierum mores notissimi sunt, ut, siquid incusarint recusarintve, illico confutes omnia.

Dyn. Ego secus censeo hanc tibi provinciam iure delegatam, cum et facundia longe plus valeas et, quia convicinus, multo id tutius potes.

Dit. Censen?

Dyn. Censeo.

Dit. Stat sententia?

Dyn. Stat.

Dit. Bene dii faveant! Et quid exordiar?

69 *Dyn.* Porro fabulas et muliebria: aut de ansere aut de gallo quere, aut pro cucurbitis semen exquire, aut denique siquid tale.

Dit. Scin quid meditabar? priusquam verba proferrem quicquam obsonarier. Nam digniora et multo pinguiora sese efferent verba

less make me wholly careless and passive; so it can only be love that fosters this curious idleness. But it's unclear what I should do about this state of affairs. Still, I must reject idleness, so let me put everything else aside and meet with Phroneus, our fabricator of frauds; let me tell him this so he can put his thoughts and energies to work cooking up some useful alternatives. But why are these slaves whispering? I want to listen secretly from this spot.

: IX :

Ditonus, a freedman; Dynastes, a slave

[On another part of the street]

Ditonus. It's my considered opinion that in this sphere of action 68
you are a worthy ambassador; for as a veteran lovers' go-between, you are extremely familiar with all the ways of women, and if they start making accusations or refusals, you can immediately refute all their arguments.

Dynastes. Actually, I think this is by right your own province, since your powers of eloquence are much greater and since, as a neighbor, you can do it in greater safely.

Ditonus. That's your considered view?

Dynastes. It is.

Ditonus. You won't budge?

Dynastes. No.

Ditonus. May the gods bless you! And how should I begin?

Dynastes. Just tell stories and stuff women are interested in: ask 69
about the goose and the cock, or see if they have some goardseed, anything like that.

Ditonus. Do you know what I've been thinking? Before I speak I should lay in some provisions. Words come out with so much

et, si nescis, plus centies hanc hodiernam interrupi cenam: non possum mei compos esse, ipse dum ieiunus presto.

Dyn. In amicorum causa multa solent, qui amant, perpeti atque permittere, que suam in rem non faciunt.

70 *Dit.* Vacua loqueris: mihi admodo ipse notus sum. Hoc est, quod te volo non ignorare: nihil in oratore magis detestandum est, quam ieiune atque incomposito, hoc est ventre loqui. Ipsi quidem calices plenam atque proclivem orationem effundunt.

Dyn. Bene, pulchre, probe! Verum, quod nunc temporis quasi superest optimi, convenit non vacuum nostro condigno opere prelaxarier. Turpis desidia est exoptatam occasionem per indiligentiam deserere. Agedum, ego post te adero, quod, siquid delires, quasi qui ad clavum sedeam, corrigam.

Dit. Itaque ingredior domum: sequere. At paululum vini . . .

Dyn. Ut lubet.

Dit. I tu pre, sequor.

: X :

Philodoxus, Phroneus

71 *Phil.* Servitus nulla libera est ac nulla libertas misera. Quidni? hinc est quod aiunt fidem esse deam atque supremi eteris incolam, quia in genere servorum, quod quidem inter mortales infimum est, nullam unquam comperies fidem. Atque ipse ne vero sum omnino plumbeus, bardus, qui hoc previderim coniectatim ac prescierim hosce res omnes meas seducere in proclivum neque quicquam opposuisse subtenaculi!

more dignity and richness, and—don't you know—lunch has been interrupted a hundred times; I can't be in command of myself as long as I'm ready to dry up.

Dynastes. Those who love each other are wont to endure and allow many things for ties of friendship which they wouldn't do in their own affairs.

Ditonus. You're talking gibberish: I know myself quite well. This is something I want you to be aware of: there's nothing more detestable in an orator than dry and awkward speech—speaking from the gut, in other words.[15] It's drinking cups that pour out full and forward speech.

Dynastes. Sure, beautiful, fine! But since the best time is almost past, it's important that we don't open up our cavity before doing our proper task. Idleness is shameful when one fails to take advantage of an opportunity through lack of diligence.

Ditonus. All right, I'll go home: follow me. But, just a drop of wine . . .

Dynastes. As you wish.

Ditonus. You go first, I'll follow you.

: X :

Philodoxus, Phroneus

[*Philodoxus alone*]

Philodoxus. No state of servitude is free and no freedom is wretched. Naturally. Hence they say loyalty is a goddess and dwells in the highest aether, since in the class of slaves, the lowest class of mortals, you never find any loyalty. And I'm not so altogether thick and stupid: I figured this out ahead of time, I foresaw that all my affairs would be dragged downward and there would be nothing to hold them up!

125

72   Enim oportuit sic dicier, hos istos esse infames servos; persuadere nequid audiant neve quid credant neve quid responsi dedant: infamiam esse infames non abhorrere. Hec tum oportuit dicier: namque norant nimis ut ipse amarem, pre me id ferebam, hei mihi! Nunquam denique hoc potuit mihi in tempore incidere in mentem, ut eas commonefactas redderem! Sed quid hoc malum est in amore? Nostrum semper, cum esset ex usu sapere, torpet ingenium, cum nihil prodest, homo nemo amante cautior est. Tum hoc in amore tormentum an est non maximum, quod quale amando sit nostrum admissum vitium sentimus nunquam, nisi cum reliquum aliud nihil est, preterquam ut dolere atque nos ipsos acerrimis exprobrationibus conficere multo possimus? Itaque ignarus amator continue peccat, gnarus perpetuo dolet.

73 *Phron.* Reviso quid agat noster Philodoxum. Sed eccum ante edes. O eho, bone vir, de legatis quam bene se res habent?

    Phil. Hem, huc ades: intermedie.

    Phron. Quin vel optume?

    Phil. Quia supervenerunt et legati et debacchati, malam in remque illis siet!

    Phron. Qui?

74 *Phil.* Enim, dum alloquebar hic ante edes, Ditonus et alter servus accedentes nostros sermones interrupere, ille abiere. Ego me seduxi, auscultavi; tum sic homines discrepabant: 'Quin tu, quia convicinus . . . muliebria oportet pro exordio . . .'. Ego sic facio coniecturam heluonem illum Fortunium, quem si vivo . . .

75 *Phron.* Atqui ausculta paucis. Eram ipse apud Climarcum medicum, tum interim se reducem offert Thrasis, minatur quod lu-

Indeed, I should have said it: these fellows here are infamous   72
slaves; they won't listen to any persuasion, they won't believe
anything, they won't give you any response: the infamous don't
shrink from infamy. Then I should have said it: indeed they
know all too well that I'm in love; I've been wearing it on my
sleeve, alas! In the end it could never have crossed my mind at
the right time to tell *them* about it! But why does love cause this
misfortune? Our mental powers always grow numb, although
wisdom comes from practice; when there is nothing to gain, no
man is more prudent than a lover. Is this, then, not love's greatest torment: that the sort of thing we allow in love we never feel
to be a vice, except when we have nothing else left but to grieve
and to level the bitterest recriminations against ourselves? Thus
the inexperienced lover sins continually, the experienced lover
grieves endlessly.

Phroneus. [*Approaching*] I'll go back and see what our Philodoxus is   73
doing. There he is in front of the house. Oh, say there, my
good man, how well do things stand concerning our envoys?

Philodoxus. Alas! Come here: so-so.

Phroneus. Why aren't they going very well?

Philodoxus. Because both the envoys and some raving lunatics
came on the scene, curse them!

Phroneus. How was that?

Philodoxus. Well, while I was speaking here in front of the house,   74
Ditonus and that other slave approached and interrupted our
conversations and the women left. I hid myself and listened; at
that point the men were having it out like this: No, *you*, because
you're her neighbor . . . you should start by talking about
women stuff . . ." So I draw the conclusion that that squanderer
Fortunius, whom while I am alive. . . .

Phroneus. Well, but just listen a little. I myself was with Climar-   75
chus, the doctor; meanwhile the son of Thraso offers to bring
me home, threatens to amuse me, then calls Ditonus over and

dos se fecerim, Ditonum mox advocat, tractant consilia, sta-
tuunt: 'Sic verbis meis dicito, ut dixi . . . et hoc quoque tum
dicito'. Hec illi: nihil vero amplius ex dictis eorum potui excer-
pere. Illico suspectare incipio oculis et animo atque eosdem huc
proficiscentes veluti ab insidiis longe prosequor.

Phil. Ergo quid hic censes?

Phron. Censeo . . . sic censeo, quia censent nos censere quod male
censeant.

: XI :

Fortunius, Phroneus, Philodoxus

76 *Fort.* Profecto in hominum vita nihil inprimis optimum a diis video dari mortalibus, quam ut nobis sic succedant bona, ut, siquid velis, id a te ipso exquiras. Bene me dii omnes amant, cum
mea me mater amat. Sum deus, cum nihil desit: habeo quidem
omnia cum diis communia, preter vitam; habeo voluptatem et
voluntatem, ut lubet; sum etate ad vires apta et venusta bellitudine; inter primos non postremus; suppeditant pecunie, benivo-
lentie, honores et omnia que virum optare fas est; adsunt preterea quam plurimi, qui me efferent laudibus, quibus et bene
possim facere quive semper student quam multa meam in utilitatem et voluptatem congerere atque accumulare. Siquidem
perpetua modo vita sit, ipse Apollo sum.

77   Enim ne videram, ne scieram, ne querebam quidem in hac
convicinia quicquam, at vero totum, quod insigne est, ultro

they put their heads together and decide: "Say it this way using my words, as I've told you . . . and then say this too." He responded, but I couldn't make out any more of their words. Immediately I start to suspect something from their eyes and attitude, and I follow them at a distance when they set out, as though from an ambush, for this place.

Philodoxus. So what do you think?

Phroneus. I think . . . this is what I think: that they think that we think what they think, with evil intent.

: XI :

Fortunius, Phroneus, Philodoxus

[*In front of Doxia's house*]

Fortunius. My observation is that in human life the gods certainly give mortals nothing so supremely excellent as the fact that good things come to us when we rely on ourselves to seek the things we want. All the gods love me well, since my mother loves me. I am a god, since I lack nothing: I have indeed every good thing the gods share, except life;[16] I have all the pleasure and good will I want; I'm at an age suitable to strength and agreeably handsome; I'm not the least among the best; I'm supplied with money, kindness, honors, and everything that it's right for a man to wish for. Besides, I have a great many people to shower me with praise, whom I can also benefit, or who are always trying to pile up as many things as possible for my use and pleasure. If only I had eternal life, I'd myself be Apollo. 76

In fact I have not laid eyes on, found out about, or sought for anything in this neighborhood, but they spontaneously offer me all that is fine. Moreover, they beg me to accept as gifts even 77

offerunt. Adde quod rogant delatum sane non minimum benificium dono ut accipiam. Ergo institui morem illis gerere: adibo
et quam pulchre recipiam Doxiam. Cum primum ingrediar domum, iupsero: 'Afferte subsellium'; cum accesserit, tandem paululum assurgam: 'Si vales et me amas', dixero, 'tractabo, amplectar, morsibus cunctam insignibo'. Sic par est omnes efficere
amantes: nam male agitata mulier bene diligit. Hec sunt munera et amoris pignora que, cum dolorem servent, tum multo in
memoriam amantem reducant atque retineant.

78 *Phron.* O ineptissime, etsi vera prefers, tamen quam insanis toto
capite!

Phil. Ha, ha, he, enimvero!

Fort. Quos hic vero arridere? Hercle, an denique ita sum vobis lu-
dus? Bene vertam in luctum, si cepero.

Phil. Favere et bona verba queso.

Fort. Et quid hic? Mene observas? Tu quoquene istic ades? Facite
ne vos hic posthac videam.

79 *Phron.* Hui, severum atque durum edictum!

Fort. Sic iubeo.

Phron. At parebitur sane, si obcluseris oculos.

Fort. Et hoc ad ludos etiam adminiculum datis? Quod si me irritaris, furcifer . . .

Phron. Enim quale supercilium!

Fort. . . . quod me si irritaris, faciam ut tuum illud crus e gremio
recipias, ut advoles ad Tibrim lotum et nectum una.

80 *Phron.* Equidem hoc iuro: nusquam facias ut curram, ni te sequar,
et videbor non claudus cum voluero, idque non sine maximo
tuo malo.

rather large services that are offered. So I have decided to comply with their wishes. I'll go over and, as prettily as possible, take Doxia. As soon as I enter her house, I shall bid her, "Bring me that stool." When she comes up, I'll in due course stand up for a little while and say to her, "If you are in good health and love me, I shall take your hand, embrace you, and mark your whole body with bites." It's a good idea for all lovers to do this, for a woman loves well when she's treated badly. These are gifts and tokens of love which, since they stay painful, remind her a great deal of her lover and keep him in her memory.

Phroneus. You are an utter fool. Even if what you say is true, there   78
is not an ounce of sense in your head!

Philodoxus. Ha, ha, he, you said it!

Fortunius. You are laughing at whom? By Hercules, am I really such a joke to you? If I get my hands on you, I'll turn your game to grief.

Philodoxus. Do us a favor and speak politely, please.

Fortunius. Why are you here? Are you keeping an eye on me? Are you also coming here? Just make sure that from now on I don't see you here again.

Phroneus. Whew! What a hard and stern edict!   79

Fortunius. I'm warning you.

Phroneus. And your order will surely be obeyed if only you will just close your eyes.

Fortunius. And this improves the game? But if you provoke me, gallows-bird . . .

Phroneus. My, what haughtiness!

Fortunius. . . . if you provoke me, I'll have you pulling that leg of yours out of your guts and running down to the Tiber to wash it off and drown at the same time.

Phroneus. I promise you this: you'll never make me run, unless it's   80
to chase you, and I won't seem lame when I want to, and this will mean big trouble for you. [*Leaving*]

Fort. Proh Iupiter, cur non me in iram solitam proveho? Et quidem non eris potis, Iupiter, quin hodie hunc mactem. Sed quid ago ineptus? Non convenit militem cum calone iurgari. Itaque tum ad istos pergam. Quis hic est? Ditone, heus! At ubi sunt isti confedusti bibones? Et nullus est: verum ingrediar.

: XII :

Mnimia, Phroneus, Philodoxus, Alithia

81 *Mni.* Hei mihi! Vix potis sum loqui pre timore, id quidem cum ceteras ob res, tum vel maxime huius virginis causa: narn inter tumultus virgo non sine pericolo aderat. Et, dii immortales, an uspiam hoc vidit aut audivit quispiam? Mehercle, mirum atque incredibile quempiam amare quam nunquam viderit, aut in ea re affectum esse, quam potissimum nesciat.

82 *Phron.* Accedo ut percuncter. Quid turbida es, mulier?

Mni. Ne vero vos ita erga hanc domum inhumanos habuistis!

Phil. Qui id? Nihil minus.

Mni. Ut audistis tantos tumultus, ut non illico opem attulistis, ut istic adstitistis conspectatores.

Phil. Hem, tumultus? Dic sodes.

83 *Mni.* Venit Thrasis . . .

Phil. Metuo.

Fortunius. By Jupiter, why am I not getting as angry as I usually do? Even you, Jupiter, will be powerless to prevent me from making a sacrifice of this fellow today. But why am I acting like a fool? It's not really fitting for a soldier to bandy words with a servant. So I'll just move on to these other people here. Who's this? Ditonus, hello there! But where are my bibulous allies? There's no one here: but I'll go in. [*Enters Doxia's house*].

: XII :

Mnimia, Phroneus, Philodoxus, Alithia

[*In front of Doxia's house*]

Mnimia. Oh, dear! I can barely speak because of my fear; I'm   81
afraid for other reasons, but most of all I'm afraid for this young girl. For she was present during the uproar and in danger. Immortal gods! Did no one see what happened or hear anything? By Hercules, it's surprising and unbelievable that someone was in love with a girl he'd never seen, and emotional regarding something he knew nothing at all about.

Phroneus. I'm here to see what's going on. Why are you so frantic,   82
woman?

Mnimia. You shouldn't behave in such a beastly way to this household!

Philodoxus. How's that? I've done no such thing.

Mnimia. Well, you heard all the uproar, yet you didn't immediately help us, but just stood there watching.

Philodoxus. What's that? There was an uproar? Tell me more, please.

Mnimia. The son of Thraso came . . .   83

Philodoxus. I'm frightened now.

Mni. . . . rupit . . .

Phron. Hem.

Mni. . . . introivit . . .

Phron. Malum.

Mni. . . . rapuit . . .

84 *Phil.* O me infelicissimum!

Mni. Nescio ego quid dicam, non sum mei recte compos nec valeo proloqui.

Phil. Porro, obsecro, narra.

Mni. Narro, at sinite me paululum animum resumere.

Phil. O diem acerbissimam! Doxiamne id monstrum rapuit, aut proterve illam aspicere me vivente ausus est?

85 *Mni.* Minime Doxiam.

Phron. Vel id ipsum, quicquid sit, ocius explica, ne in mora simus, siquid facto opus sit.

Mni. Breves quidem narrationes magnum non belle exponunt malum.

Phron. Bis nos excrucias, quod tristem et quod morosum nuntium afferas. Narra, obsecro.

86 *Mni.* Narro. Doxia Doxie soror Phimiaque Alithiaque, hec virgo, atque ego flores in horto et apium opera animi gratia spectabamus, dum is convicinus senex suo ex hortulo proximo, qui cratibus ab hortis Doxie conseptus est, nos quam plurime iubet salvere. 'Et quid fit?' inquit, 'Nunquamne a negotiis licebit vacare? Iuvat nempe interdum animum a labore ad voluptates honeste transferre, quod quidem facio ipse, qui, cum tempore et loco licet, omni studio et opera me omnibus ridiculum prebeo. Etenim isthuc duco esse officium prudentis, sapere inter philosophos, lascivire inter calices: namque omni loco omnique tem-

Mnimia. . . . broke in . . .

Phroneus. Oh, no.

Mnimia. . . . entered . . .

Phroneus. That's awful.

Mnimia. . . . seized her . . .

Philodoxus. How appalling! 84

Mnimia. I don't know what to say, I'm not thinking clearly and can barely speak.

Philodoxus. You must tell us more, I beg you.

Mnimia. I'll continue, just give me a moment to regain my composure.

Philodoxus. This is indeed a bitter day! Has that monster snatched Doxia, can he have dared look at her with shameless intent while I am alive?

Mnimia. Not Doxia. 85

Phroneus. Well, whatever it was, tell me quickly, so I don't lose time if action is required.

Mnimia. Brief tales are hardly suitable to great evils.

Phroneus. You're tormenting me twice, in that your news is sad and you're being difficult about telling it. Tell the story, for God's sake.

Mnimia. I'll tell you. Doxia, Doxia's sister Phimia, and Alithia, 86 this maiden, and I were enjoying ourselves looking at the flowers in the garden and the bees at their work, while our neighbor, an old man whose garden is next to ours and which is hedged in by wicker-work from Doxia's garden, greeted us with great courtesy. "How are things going?" he said. "We all need a break from work, don't we? It certainly helps to shift our attention occasionally from work to honest pleasures. I do that myself when time and place allow, and I devote myself energetically to playing the buffoon. For I believe it is the duty of a prudent man to be wise among philosophers and to relax among the wine-cups. For whoever at all times and places

pore quisquis vult se gravem, continentem ac tristem videri, meo iudicio ipsus est semper ineptus. Me vero, quod utrumque tempus moderari calleam, nemo in seriis rebus respuit, omnes in iocosis admittunt socium.

87 'Eam ob rem Fortunius Thrasis, adolescens omnium pulcherrimus, omnium liberalissimus, in sua quam hodie lautissimam apparavit cenam iussit summopere ut adessem, in qua quidem, ni fallor, habebo me pro censore triclinii, aut tum ero preses popine, aut in hirneis imperabo. Sed, dii boni, quales primo calices hauriam, denique, ubi satis fugaro sitim, quales iocosos in medium exercebo gestus! O Thrasim adolescentem dignum imperio, cum tanta liberalitate isthac, cantabo laudes tuas, quem omnes amant! Dispeream, si tibi ad integram felicitatem aliud quicquam quam moribus tuis et nobilitati consimilis coniunx deest! Felicissima tu quidem eris mulier, que huic bellissimo ac formosissimo adolescenti nupseris! Vehementer cupio, mi Doxia, hunc ipsum tibi fore coniugem, quin dabo operam ne te recuset.'

88 Nos illico inter nos hominem demirari cepimus. Tum ille enim: 'Thrasis, adesne?' inquit, 'Ehodum, parasti convivium nuptiale: tibi sponsa ne desit, hanc Doxiam accipias hortor coniugem'. Nos huiusmodi verbis perculse illico: 'Vale, consulto opus est', diximus et abfugimus in domum. Illi e vestigio abvulsis cratibus nos pavidas et trepidas sequuntur, confringunt, ingrediuntur, discursitant. Nos disgregamur; Doxia advolarat supra fastigium edium, ego procul omnes rumores hauriebam auribus ex abdito. Ceterum dic tu reliqua ut gesta sunt, mi Alithia, que coram omnia spectasti.

89 *Alith.* Quidnam? Illi, rapta Phimia, abiere.

wants to appear serious, self-controlled and severe in my judgment is always foolish. In my case, since I know how to regulate both work and play, no one rejects me in serious pursuits and everyone welcomes me as an associate in their amusements.

"That is why Fortunius, the son of Thraso, the handsomest 87 of young men and the most generous, bade me earnestly come to his house where today he has laid on a most sumptuous meal. At this banquet, if I mistake not, I shall be appointed the censor of the dining-room: either I shall be chief of the chow or general of the jugs. Good gods! the cups I shall drain! — then, when thirst has been routed, the slapstick jokes I'll perform in company! O son of Thraso, young man worthy of empire — such is your liberality — how I shall sing your praises, whom everybody loves! May I die if you go without a wife who is your match in good manners and nobility to complete your felicity! You'll be the happiest of women, you who shall wed this most handsome and appealing young man! I strongly desire, my Doxia, that he become your husband; indeed, I shall see to it that he doesn't refuse you."

We were immediately astonished among ourselves. For then 88 he said, "Son of Thraso, are you here? Hello, there, I see you've prepared a wedding feast: so that you won't be lacking a spouse I urge you to take Doxia as your wife." We were immediately knocked over by language like this. "Goodbye, we need to think about this!" we said, and fled into the house. They immediately pulled down the wicker lattices and followed us, terror-stricken and trembling as we were; they broke in, entered the house, and rushed about. We split up: Doxia flew to the roof-top; from a hiding-place I listened at a distance to all the noise. You tell what happened after that, Alithia, since you saw everything close up.

Alithia. What else is there to say? They seized Phimia and took 89 her with them.

Phron. Factum pexime!

Phil. Vosne tandem cetere valetis omnes?

Mni. Pulchre, ni hoc de Phimia egre siet, at . . .

Phil. Proh dii, que hominum petulantia, quis furor, que iniuria! Quam opto huic aliqua in re esse pro meritis, ut meretur, scelestissimo!

Mni. Itaque acta hec sunt, ut videtis. Nos eamus, virgo, ut hac de re certiorem reddamus patrem, hisce in edibus hoc esse admissum scelus.

Phil. Ergo tu, Phroneus, comitabere has. Ego accedam ad forum ut senem, si viderim, eum mox domum huc adducam.

: XIII :

Mnimia, Alithia, Phroneus

90 *Mni.* Enim quod datur fatis ferendum est. Diis nolentibus, quid est quod mortalibus liceat?

Alith. Nosne ergo ibimus domum?

Mni. Isthuc agimus. Sed, me misera, quam modo huiusmodi in animum redeunt multa ut, quod partim nollem, partim vellem, id ipsum tamen frustra optem!

91 *Phron.* Est hominum hec condicio, velle et nolle. At velle hoc et nolle in tempore quod ex usu sit, prope sapientum est; nolle autem que velle oporteat, at velle que minime possis, eorum est, qui sibi solis credant et cupiant. Tum olent scelesti semper suo scelere seque palam scelus trahit, parem ut parturiat penam. Non inulto hoc deos preterierit.

92 *Mni.* Non diffido sic futurum, ut autumas. Sed amplius meam incuso dementiam una et viri mei, a quo iam fere annis tribus habui discidium Athenis, quod repetenti a me anulos et aurea

Phroneus. What a wicked thing to do!

Philodoxus. But the rest of you are all right?

Mnimia. Fine, aside from our concern for Phimia, but . . .

Philodoxus. By the gods, the insolence of these men, how mad, how criminal! I really hope this utterly wicked man will somehow get what he deserves!

Mnimia. So as you see, that's what happened. Let us go, girl, to tell father about this, that a criminal act of wickedness has occurred in these dwellings.

Philodoxus. Phroneus, accompany these women. I'll go to the forum and will bring the old man home here directly, if I see him.

: XIII :

Mnimia, Alithia, Phroneus

Mnimia. Truly, what the fates have given must be borne. What is   90
there that is permitted to mortals against the will of the gods?

Alithia. Shall we then go home?

Mnimia. Yes, let's. But, poor me, how many things of this kind now come back to my thoughts! Part of them I would wish for, part of them I wouldn't, yet in both cases I would wish in vain.

Phroneus. This is the human condition: to will and to nill. Wise   91
men know how to will and to nill what is useful, and at the appropriate time; not to wish for the things one should wish for, while wishing for things you can't have, is for selfish and cynical types. Criminals always seem to give off a certain smell from the crime they commit and the crime pulls them into the open and so brings about the proper punishment. The gods will not let this crime go unavenged.

Mnimia. I trust it will be as you suppose. But I also blame myself   92
for my own madness together with that of my husband. I was separated from him now almost three years ago in Athens, be-

139

quedam signa parta suo labore, quas res apud me servandi causa posuerat, negavi. Feci ut solent fere omnes que sumus inepte mulieres, presertim si adsit forma. Fui enim pertinax, dum que sponte ipsa debebam tradere, ea virum precibus et blanditiis a me frustra exposcere gaudebam; quo factum est ut indignatus postridie abierit. Quod ni me in eum ita duram habuissem, plane degerem vitam neque vulgarem neque inopulentam ac minime aberrarem. Verum hec mihi eo in memoriam rediere, quod viro quoque meo id ipsum nomen Phroneo aderat.

93 *Phron.* Quidnam tu hac in urbe tibi vite delegisti, posteaquam virum ita repudiasti?

Mni. Ego vero semper totis viribus consectata sum vitam atque gentem, ut maxime quivi, honestissimam. Audiveram huc Romam meum accessisse virum. Tum ipsa quid agerem relicta sola? Eo frustra huc veni, ut fastu posito apud virum, cuicum et debeo et cupio, essem; quem quidem ubi nusquam inveni, cessi domum huius patris Alithie, cui nomen Chronos.

94 *Phron.* Novi sane hominem decrepitum, canum, gravem; atque idem est princeps excubiarum, si satis memini.

Mni. Ipsus est. Hanc habet filiam, quam ample diligat; hanc mee fidei commendavit regendam atque observandam. Ee deinde matrone, que huius virginis indole atque ingenio mirifice delectantur, mea opera cum huius virginis familia amicitiam contraxere; ex quo persepius una conferunt, postremo omni de re me participem faciunt: utor utraque familia familiariter, concredunt obsequuntur mihi.

95 *Phron.* Dic sodes, quod tibi nominis?

Mni. Mnimia.

Phron. Ne tu ergo prius voluisti, Mnimia, perdere anulos quam viro reddere?

cause I refused to give back to him when he asked for them the rings and and certain golden seals he had earned and deposited with me for safekeeping. I did what we foolish women almost all do, especially if we are also attractive. I was stubborn, for the things I should have returned willingly, I enjoyed having him beg from me in vain with pleas and flattery; that made him angry and he left the next day. But if I hadn't behaved so cruelly to him, I'd clearly be living a better and more comfortable life and wouldn't have gone wrong. But I was reminded of this because my husband's name, like yours, was Phroneus.

Phroneus. Why, pray, did you decide to spend your life in this city 93 after you had rejected your husband?

Mnimia. I have always made every effort, so far as I could, to pursue an honorable way of life and to live among people who are honorable. I had heard that my husband had come here to Rome. At that point, why should I be left behind alone? I vainly came here, so that I could put aside my pride and be with him whom I ought to be with and desired to be with; but when I failed to find him, I let a house from Alithia's father, a man named Chronos.

Phroneus. I know the man: bent with age, white-haired, grave; the 94 same man is commander of the watch, if I remember correctly.

Mnimia. He is. He has a daughter whom he adores; he commended her to my care and direction. Then there are those matrons who are wonderfully charmed by her good qualities and intelligence and who have through my efforts become friends with this girl's family; as a result they very often get together, and in the end made me part of all their doings: I am on friendly terms with both families, so they trust and respect me.

Phroneus. Please tell me, what's your name? 95

Mnimia. Mnimia.

Phroneus. Did you prefer, then, to destroy the rings rather than return them to your husband?

Mni. Me imprudentissimam! Neque tum negabam me redditu-
ram nequedum perdidi, sed ita ut fit mulierum more subinsani-
bam.

Phron. Demum amisisti anulos et virum?

96 *Mni.* Si mihi sic esset vir, ut sunt anuli, pluris tenerem anulos
quam instituerim. Satis illum perquirens expectavi, satis sum
functa meo officio; forte illos huic virgini dono dedero, cum satis perrexero in moram.

Phron. Sane isthuc fateor esse officium femine, certare simultate
atque pervicacia adversus eos, qui se ament, et odisse omnes,
quos nimium faciles atque obsequentes offenderint. Sed isthuc
cupio audire abs te: habesne anulos et aurea eadem signa?

97 *Mni.* Habeo, teneo servoque.

Phron. At salva omnia?

Mni. Ut nihil desit.

Phron. Cedo manum: nihil est quod eque cupiam.

Mni. Ah, mi vir, desine: hosce ego digitos, hosce anulos novi! Et
quam es non similis solito, quam denique difformis!

98 *Phron.* Istuc forte, ut aiunt, novos mores novos afferre vultus. At
tu, que dura olim ac difficilis videri solita es, quam nunc videre
facilis! Bene edepol gaudeo et optime est nos nobis compertos
esse. Da mihi te, ut amplectar.

Mni. Gaudeo, ac fiet quidem sacrificium diis tanto pro merito. Mi
vir, valuistin satis?

Phron. Satis.

99 *Mni.* Quid tibi cum illo adolescentulo?

Phron. Optima et aperta benivolentia, ampla et continua familiari-
tas, firma et simplex amicitia.

Mni. Et quid istic hesitabatis?

Mnimia. I was most unwise! At the time I neither denied that I would return them, nor yet did I lose them, but I behaved with a kind of borderline insanity, as women do.

Phroneus. So in the end you lost your rings and your husband?

Mnimia. If I had my husband, as I have the rings, I would attach 96
more importance to the rings than I do now. Searching everywhere for him I've waited long enough; I have done my duty long enough; perhaps I ought to offer these rings to this girl as a gift, since I've prolonged waiting for him long enough.

Phroneus. Certainly I agree that this is a woman's role, to contend and quarrel stubbornly against those who love them and to hate everyone they meet who is overly obliging and respectful. But I would like to hear your answer to this question: do you still have the rings and the same golden signets?

Mnimia. I have them, I hold onto them, and I keep them safe. 97

Phroneus. So they're all safe?

Mnimia. Not one is missing.

Phroneus. Let me give you my hand; there's nothing I want so much.

Mnimia. Ah, my husband, stop; I know these very fingers, these very rings! But how different you are from your usual self; you look terrible!

Phroneus. Perhaps it's true that, as they say, new habits bring 98
about new features. You too now look so obliging, when once you seemed so cruel and difficult. By Pollux, I'm really happy; it's wonderful that we've found each other. Let me embrace you.

Mnimia. I'm happy, too, and we must make sacrifice to the gods for so great a reward. My husband, are you well?

Phroneus. Well enough.

Mnimia. What is your relationship to that young man? 99

Phroneus. It's a relationship of fine and frank goodwill, of full and unbroken familiarity, of strong and straightforward friendship.

Mnimia. And why are you hanging around here?

Phron. Sane rogas quod cupio te ut scias. Is amat Doxiam hanc tuam perdite, quod, si utrisque consulendum est, nihil est quod magis approbem quam inter hosce fieri coniugium: est enim adolescens nobilis, doctus, prudens atque, ut vides, forma et indole egregia.

100 *Mni.* Prorsus amandus: omnia novi.

Phron. Quid? Annon Doxia hominem nonnihil diligit?

Mni. Nullam invenies usque adeo tristem atque algentem mulierem, que bellum amantem aspernetur.

Phron. Quid si innitare?

Mni. Possum quidem prodesse.

Phron. Idcirco precor, cum vales coniunctione apud has, tum id cures omni qua potes opera et industria, ut hoc coniugii fiat.

101 *Mni.* Mi vir, salve: geretur tibi mos. Ibo et virginem domi relinquam. Post illico conveniam Doxiam, conabor persuasione et precibus rem ex sententia ducere atqui, ut opinor, possum tibi bonam expectationem polliceri. Vale.

Phron. Ego Philodoxum requiram. Sed prius sub hac angiportu sordes istas et lutum abstergam meque pulchre comptum reddam.

: XIV :

Phroneus, Chronos, Philodoxus

102 *Phron.* Proh dii immortales, quantum habet virium dissuetudo, quam est efficax ad scindundas omnes bene obfirmatas vetustate amicitias! Equidem si fieri possit ut quispiam secum ipse

Phroneus. You're asking something I really want you to know. He loves this Doxia of yours desperately. If the interests of both parties are to be consulted, there is nothing I would approve more than for the two of them to be married. He is a noble young man, educated, prudent and, as you see, a youth of outstanding character and appearance.

Mnimia. Altogether worthy to be loved. I know all this.   100

Phroneus. What then? Does Doxia have some affection for the man, or not?

Mnimia. You won't find the woman so severe and cold that she would spurn so handsome a lover.

Phroneus. Will you lend some support?

Mnimia. I can indeed be of some use.

Phroneus. Well then, please, you are close to these women and have influence with them: do make every possible effort to bring about this marriage.

Mnimia. My husband, farewell. I'll gratify you in this matter. I   101 shall go and leave the girl at home. After that I'll immediately meet Doxia and I shall try by persuasion and pleas to bring the matter to the conclusion you desire. And I believe I can promise you a happy outcome. Farewell.

Phroneus. I shall look for Philodoxus. But first, down here in this alleyway I'll wipe off this dirt and mud and spruce myself up again.

: XIV :

Phroneus, Chronos, Philodoxus

[*A street in Rome*]

Phroneus. Gods above, how powerful absence is, how effective it is   102 in breaking up even strong and ancient friendships! Indeed, if it were possible that someone for a space of time could neither

aliquot temporis neque colloquium neque ulla in re consuefactionem habeat, fore prorsus existimo ut sese is aut breve aut nihil diligat.

Chron. Audivi, inquam, atqui omnia teneo. Mee dehinc erunt partes facere, que iure agenda videantur: iudicem decet iuri satisfacere inprimis, non homini.

103 *Phil.* Verum id actutum denique accurrendum censeo, ne novam aliquam turbam scelerosi innovent.

Chron. Forte hoc tibi persuades, quod me admodum gravem et morosum ac, veluti aiunt, depontam conspicias, ideo me cursu minime valere. Erras isthuc si putas: nam me hac ipsa etate complures valere cursu experti sunt. Sed ferme sic semper evenit ut, quod mature agimus, id nimium cupidis sero evenisse doleat; hi vero, quibus eadem res molesta futura est, nimis properasse incusent. Viden ut iam aliud agentes istic adsumus? Sed fessus sum, hic paululum considere certum est.

104 *Phil.* Perplacet. Sed eccum Phroneum hac eadem sub angiportu suas concinnantem plicas; accedam, ut hominem huc adducam.

⁚ XV ⁚

Phroneus, Philodoxus

105 *Phron.* Videon Philodoxus? Ipsus est. Videon senem? Ipsus est. Advolo, ut hominem onustum meo partim et suo faciam gaudio. Nam, ni me animum fallit, Mnimia rem conficiet ex sententia.

hold converse with himself or become a stranger to himself, I
think he would surely love himself either very little or not at all.

Chronos. I say, I have heard what you said and I agree with you totally. Hence, my role will be to accomplish what seems to be
necessary in the eyes of the law: it is only fitting for a judge to
satisfy the law first, and not the man.

Philodoxus. But I think help should be brought immediately, if it   103
comes to that, so that these criminals won't hatch some new
disturbance.

Chronos. Perhaps you convince yourself of this because you look
upon me as extremely severe and difficult and, as they say, a
disposable old man,[17] and so unable to move quickly. If you
think so, you're mistaken: many, many men have found out that
I'm able to move quickly despite my advanced age. But it nearly
always happens that what we do in good time pains those who
want it to happen by happening too late; while those to whom
the same action is unwelcome reproach us with acting too
quickly. You see how we've arrived while we were doing something else? But I'm tired, I must sit down here a moment.

Philodoxus. By all means. But, look, there's Phroneus in this same   104
alleyway straightening up his toga; I'll go over and bring the
man here.

: XV :

Phroneus, Philodoxus

[*In the alleyway*]

Phroneus. Do I see Philodoxus? It's the very man. Do I also see   105
the old man? It's him. I'll run over and load the man down
with my good news — and his. For, unless I'm deceiving myself,
Mnimia will settle the matter to our liking.

Phil. Nimirum hoc malum integrascit. Advolo ut percuncter. Proin tu, ne vero proterve aliquid denuo attentarunt in Doxiam petulantissimi? Porro, dic quidnam feras mali.

Phron. Bono sis animo, letissimum tibi affero nuntium.

106 *Phil.* Mehercle, preter spem isthuc: ita meme omnia undique extimescentem adversa hodierna fortuna Doxie effecit.

Phron. Ceterum quidem, tu vero ubinam offendisti tam extemplo patrem hunc virginis?

Phil. Advectabat se domum suam. Me superi, nunquam vidi hominem tardiorem!

Phron. Homo confectus etate et annorum plenus.

107 *Phil.* Quin immo se cursu validum predicat, dum se non secus dimovet ac si habeat calculos omnes ad unum usque pedibus dinumerare. Tum quidnam habes, quo me, cum a metu depulisti, in letitiam statuas?

Phron. Meministin quam sepius tecum explorarim tum fortunas, tum ineptias meas, qui tam levi indignatione actus fecerim ab uxore mea divortium, quam dictitabam: 'Si adesset!'? Nostin?

108 *Phil.* Pulchre.

Phron. Eam ipsam comperi.

Phil. Hem, at ubinam loci? Num valet?

Phron. Valet habetque anulos et signa aurea salva omnia atqui, quo magis congratulere, ea est premonstratrix eius virginis Alithie, huius senis filie.

109 *Phil.* An eadem ipsa est, quam modo abiens reliqui tecum, subruffam, litigiosam, aspero supercilio, tumidis oculis, naso gracili, mento preacuto, pusillam? Eia, Phroneus, pulchram nactus uxorem!

Phron. Mores condecent saltim forma si abest. Tum deformis coniunx non facile dictu est quam sit percommoda: solum virum

Philodoxus. This bad situation keeps getting worse. I'll just go over and investigate. So then, my man, have these insolent characters attempted some new outrage against Doxia? Give me the bad news straight out.

Phroneus. Cheer up, I'm bringing you the happiest of news.

Philodoxus. By Hercules, that's more than I'd hoped for; Doxia's 106 misfortune today makes me fear everything so.

Phroneus. Putting that aside, where on earth did you happen upon this father of the girl so quickly?

Philodoxus. He was trundling along home. Gods above, I never saw a slower-moving man!

Phroneus. The man has grown old and is full of years.

Philodoxus. In fact he claimed he could still get on well, though he 107 moves about as though he had to count each and every pebble at his feet. But what news do you have that will drive away my fear and bring me happiness?

Phroneus. Do you remember how very often I used to go over with you my ill fortune and my acts of folly, how a trivial outburst of anger drove me to divorce my wife, and how I used to repeat, "If only she were here!" Do you remember?

Philodoxus. Perfectly. 108

Phroneus. Well, I've found her.

Philodoxus. What's that? But where? She's all right, I trust?

Phroneus. She's fine and has kept safe the rings and all the golden signets and—this will make you happy—she is the duenna of the maiden Alithia, the daughter of this old man.

Philodoxus. Is she the same one you were with when I left you just 109 now, the reddish-haired woman, quarrelsome, frowning, with the swollen eyes and thin nose, that sharp-witted, tiny woman? It's extraordinary, Phroneus, you've found your lovely wife!

Phroneus. At least good behavior makes one seemly when beauty departs. But it's almost indescribable how very useful an ugly

non odit, cum a nullo diligatur deformis mulier, eundemque vacuum suspicione vigilantem facit.

110 *Phil.* Ne tu illam non noras primum? Aut quid veritus es, me coram ne in cachinum prorumperem?

Phron. Missa hec faciamus. Hoc est, quod te letitia oppleat: uxor
suscepit negotium de Doxia illa. Spero coniuge potiere, Mnimia
interprete.

Phil. O bellissimam ergo Mnimiam! O coniugem tibi amandissi-
mam!

Phron. Postremo hunc ad nos proficiscentem adeamus senem.

: XVI :

Chronos, Phroneus, Philodoxus

111 *Chron.* Nemo in cuiusvis amicorum malis satis diu ac suis misere-
tur aut dolet. Enim is, qui modo hac una qua accersivit me cura
adolescens excruciari visus est, tam repente mutato fronte nescio quid adveniens letissimum gestiat. Mihi prope animus lan-
guet, quod ad gnatam pendeam meam, tametsi virgini puelle
nihil eiusmodi suspicer.

Phron. Salvere Chronon iubemus.

Chrox. Et tune iis adfuisti rebus, cum fierent?

112 *Phron.* Modo audivi omnia una cum isthoc ab iis que adfuere
Mnimia et Alithia, quas tuam adduxi domum.

Chron. At filia satin valet?

wife can be: she won't hate her only man, since no man loves an ugly woman, and she frees a jealous man of suspicions.

Philodoxus. And you didn't recognize her at first? Or were you afraid I might burst out laughing when I came face-to-face with her? 110

Phroneus. Please, let's just drop this subject. What will fill you with happiness is this: my wife has taken up your business about Doxia. I am hopeful that she will become your wife with Mnimia as a go-between.

Philodoxus. O most beautiful Mnimia! O what a most loving wife she is to you!

Phroneus. Let's go at last, then, to meet this old man on his way towards us.

: XVI :

Chronos, Phroneus, Philodoxus

Chronos. No one shows pain or pity towards his friends' misfor- 111 tunes nearly as long as towards his own. Just look: the man who summoned me just now, the young man who seemed to be tor- mented with concern, now all of a sudden is coming up here with a wholly different attitude, exulting with joy. My heart al- most fails me with anxiety over my daughter, though I don't fear a similar disaster in her case; she's a chaste young girl.

Phroneus. Hello, Chronos.

Chronos. [*To Phroneus*] So did you also witness the events that took place?

Phroneus. I just heard everything, in company with this young 112 man here, from the eye-witnesses: Mnimia and Alithia, whom I've brought to your house.

Chronos. But is my daughter all right?

Phron. Ea domi, inquam, est tue salva.

Chron. Gaudeo. Verum quis impurus, improbus tantos tumultus ausus concivit?

Phron. Sane isthuc ignoro, tametsi constat Fortunium, Tychie filium, vi in edes irruisse, vi et iniuria domum affecisse.

113 *Chron.* Tu ergo illum ad nos citato lictor. Tu vero, Phroneus, iube dispesci istic omnes que adsunt in hisce edibus mulieres huc in publicum: namque hic equum est capitale facinus publice disquirere. Ego interim in hanc tabernam divertam, ut subscribam que ad annonam opus sunt; illico egrediar.

Phron. Abeo.

: XVII :

Tychia

114 *Tych.* Quam est omni in vita facilitas inprimis et grata is,[3] cum quibus vivas, et utilis his, qui isthac eadem virtute sciant uti! Difficilem omnes et noti et ignoti odere, facilem atque indulgentem nemo non diligit. Id quidem ipsum modo perdisci licet ex me, quod filium comiter ac benigne observo. Idem, queque agit, ultro me facit ut sciam: bene queque facit, palam probo et adiutrix sum; male ubi conatur aut permittit quicquam, illico surgenti incommodo rationem et modum obicio, quo futura mala coherceam atque reprimam. Magnum quodque malum minima habet principia: hec tollas, omnia sustuleris. Itaque his moribus instructus filius modo ad me lacrimans accessit: 'Mater', inquit, 'peccavi: hanc rapui civem. Stulte factum fateor. Tu

Phroneus. She's at your house, I say, safe and sound.

Chronos. I'm delighted to hear it. But what foul and wicked man dared raise such a uproar?

Phroneus. I don't really know the details, but it's evident that Fortunius, the son of Tychia, broke his way by force into the household, causing damage and using violence.

Chronos. Philodoxus, go as my lictor[18] and summon the man before us. But you, Phroneus, order that all the women who were present in this house be brought here to this public place: for it is just to investigate a capital crime here, in public. In the meantime, I'll turn into this tavern to sign off on what's needed for the grain supply.[19] I'll be back shortly.

Phroneus. I'm on my way.

113

: XVII :

Tychia

Tychia. How welcome is affability in every sphere of life to those with whom you live; how valuable it is to those who know how to practice this same virtue. A difficult person is hated both by those who know him and by those who don't, while an easy and indulgent person is loved by all. This truth may be well learned from my example, from the way I keep a kind and friendly eye on my son. Whatever he does, he keeps me informed about it, and voluntarily: I openly approve and help him when he acts well; if he sets about or allows some evil action, I immediately impose reason and restraint on the rising trouble in order to rein in future evils and keep them under control. Every great evil has small beginnings; if you take them away, you remove all the evils. So my son, imbued with this character, just now came to me crying: "Mother!" he said, "I have sinned: I have carried

114

rebus et fame et saluti nostre caveto.' Indolui ac plura tum verbis castigassem, sed visum est hoc tempus opportunius alio
quam in iurgiis consumere. Idcirco ad Doxiam pergere institui
nullasque conditiones recusabo, dum invidiam sedatam reddam; postea de corrigendo filio providebo. Sed eccum senem!
Iam non ero potis quicquam, ut institueram: mutandum consilium est.

: XVIII :

Chronos, Tychia, Phroneus

115 *Chron.* Alia me movet ratio, Caliloge, id ita ut istic conscriben-
dum putarem, tuum tamen ingenium et astutiam laudo. Verum
prebeto huc eosdem codicillos, ut relegam: nam summa negligentia est que scripseris non recognoscere, priusquam obcludas.
116 *Tych.* Me miseram, quid consilii captem? Hominem adeundum
censeo pervestigandumque quid in nos animi paret, quo prema-
ture sedem, siquid irarum insurgat adversum. Atque haud habeo quidem causam omnino iniquam aut prorsus inusitatam:
quis nescit omni in etate multa pretermittenda et tolleranda
esse? Amare ac ludere iuvenes, questui viros et rapinis inservire,
senes parcos et segniores esse decet. Verum hac in re, siquid est

off a female of the citizen class. I admit it was a stupid thing to do. You *must* take up the matter and have a care for my good name and my safety." I was deeply pained and I would have dressed him down at length, but it seemed more appropriate to spend the moment otherwise than in recrimination. So I decided to go to Doxia and agree to anything so long as I could lay her ill-will to rest; afterwards, I would see to punishing my son. But here's the old man! Now I won't be able to do what I had intended; I'll have to change my plan.

: XVIII :

Chronos, Tychia, Phroneus

[*In front of the tavern*]

Chronos. I find another explanation more convincing, Calilogus,[20] so I rather think this should be written there, but I commend your intelligence and penetration. Now bring those documents here so I can reread them: it's the height of negligence not to go over and correct what you've written before sealing the documents.

Tychia. Poor me, what plan should I adopt? I think I should go up to him and find out what he's planning against us, so as to nip it in the bud if his anger and hostility are mounting. The case I have to present is, after all, by no means unjust or unheard-of: who doesn't know that there are many things which must be overlooked and tolerated at every stage of life? It's fitting for young men to love and play; for men in their prime to be slaves to gain and plunder; and for old men to be stingy and sluggish. But in this matter involving my son, if there is anything I feel sorry for, it is only that his deed was done without my advice.

quod doleam, id solum illud est, quod me inconsulta hoc fecerit. Nam etsi cupio animi viribus et audacia valere eos, quos de-
lectos habeo quosve inter domesticos admitto meos, tamen alia
potius via — donis, fallacia — quam raptu suos amores explesset
mallem. Sed senem convenio, posthac ex tempore consilium capiam. Salvus sis, Chronos, quid opere hic est tibi cum tantis
syngraphis?

117 *Chron.* Hem, quasi id nescias, aut preter voluntatem tuam hec ac-
ciderint! Siccine oportuit in civem liberam?

Tych. Silicet paucis.

Chron. Nimis multa tibi licent, Tychia: rapitur, vivitur impudenter
ac superbe te annuente. Verum loquere.

Tych. Rescivi que hic gesta sint, fateor, que quidem, ubi conscia
me fuissent actitata, palam ea profiterer. Qua enim ex parte eadem se dederent, ut sanctum et equum iudicem vererer non video: nam si Phimia libera est, libere sane ac liberum sibi delegit
virum.

118 *Phron.* Revertor, edixi. Doxia sese adornat ut egrediatur.

Chron. Pexima es, pol femina es! Ergo tam liberas oportuit fieri
nuptias, confringere, turbare, asportare viribus et vi! Enimne
iupsi hominem accersiri scelestissimum? Siccine ludificabere?

Tych. Tamen ut iupseris fecero.

Chron. Iubeo.

Tych. Ehodum, bone vir, nostin filium?

Phron. Vidi hominem.

Tych. Noveris edes meas?

For although I do desire that those I hold dear or have taken into my home be strong of will and bold, I wish he had satisfied his amorous passions in another way—through gifts and deceit, for example—rather than by carrying her off by force. But I'll meet the old man, and afterwards improvise a plan. [*She addresses Chronos.*] Hello, Chronos; what are you doing with all those documents?

Chronos. What's that? As if you didn't know! As if what has happened was beyond your control! Was this any way to behave towards a woman of citizen status? 117

Tychia. If you'd just allow me a few words . . .

Chronos. You've already been allowed far too many words, Tychia: you have been condoning rape, impudent behavior and arrogance. But speak.

Tychia. I'm wise to what's happened here, I confess, and I admit openly that these deed were done with my knowledge. Insofar as the things seized have been surrendered, I don't see what I have to fear from a just and holy judge; for if Phimia is a free woman, she certainly is free to choose a free man for herself.[21]

Phroneus. I'm back; I've delivered the summons. Doxia is dressing up to go out. 118

Chronos. By Pollux, Tychia, you are the worst of women. So that's how weddings among free persons should be conducted, is it: by breaking and entering, causing uproars and carrying off women by force? Haven't I ordered this wickedest of men to be arraigned? Will you make a mockery of that?

Tychia. No; I'll carry out your orders.

Chronos. I do so order.

Tychia. [*To Phroneus*] Ho, there, my good man, do you know my son?

Phroneus. I've seen the man.

Tychia. Do you know where my house is?

Phron. Certius si mostraris.

119 *Tych.* Ergo adhibe huc animum: hac recta usque apud publicanos, tum verte ad levam usque ad pistrinum, demum conscende ad plateam; ibi ad dextram e conspectu videbis umbonem ad postes appensum, de more ubi hec inscripta sunt aureis litteris: NISI IAM FORTE. Ille sunt edes nostre: advocato gnatum. Intellextin?

Phron. Non auscultavi neque unquam comperirem. Iube ex his tuis quempiam.

Tych. Dii te perdant! Tu, Volipeda, accurre, iube Fortunium confestim huc advolare. Cessas.[4] Verum, heus, cum redieris, dicito te hominem nusquam comperisse.

: XIX :

Mnimia, Chronos, Alithia, Tychia

120 *Mni.* Perge, Alithia, huc mecum, ut viri mei iussa exequamur: tu quoque nonnihil proderis. Pol quidem, perquam cupio illi modesto adolescenti de amore suo commodi aliquid afferre! Doxiam conveniamus, animum qui nunc ei turbatus est primum sedabimus. Quid? Quod hec una causa nostrum iuvabit inceptum, nequis posthac audeat una iniuria duos, nuptam et maritum, ledere. In celibem atque viduam prona est cupidorum audacia. Sed quid, senem nostrum hic intueor? Huc adero. Salve, Chronos.

121 *Chron.* Ubi est nata?

Mni. Eccam. Adsis, Alithia.

Phroneus. I'll be a lot more certain if you point me in the right direction.

Tychia. Then pay attention: follow this road straight ahead until 119
you come to the house of the tax collectors, then turn left and head towards the bakery, then climb to the square; there you will see to the right of you a shield hung on a door, on which in the usual way are inscribed in golden letters the words: UNLESS ALREADY BY CHANCE. That's our house: summon my son. Understand?

Phroneus. I haven't heard a word you've said nor would I ever find it. Send one of your servants.

Tychia. God damn you! Volipeda,[22] you run off and bid Fortunius hurry here immediately. [*Aside, to Volipeda*] Stay a moment. Now when you come back, say: alas, you couldn't find the man.

: XIX :

Mnimia, Chronos, Alithia, Tychia

Mnimia. Come with me over here, Alithia; I want to carry out the 120
bidding of my husband, and you can help a bit, too. By Pollux, I really would like to be of service to that well-behaved young man in his love-affair! Let's meet Doxia and first put to rest that spirit of hers which is now so agitated. Why? Because this is one condition needed to achieve our purpose, which is to prevent anyone hereafter from harming with a single unjust act two people, a bride and her husband. Audacious and lustful men tend to go after unmarried women and widows. But hello: do I see our old man here? I'll go over there. [*To Chronos*] Hello, Chronos.

Chronos. Where is my daughter? 121

Minima. Here she is. Come here, Alithia.

Alith. Salve, pater.

Chron. Acta hec sunt, ut ferunt, abrupte fores, vi raptum?

Alith. Acta, mi pater.

Chron. Proh Iupiter, scelus detestandum!

Tych. Mea tu senem exoremus. Chronos, audi, obsecro.

Chron. Quid te audiam?

Tych. Non que nos obnoxias apud te loqui, sed que te mitem et humanissimum fas est audire.

Chron. Loquere.

122 *Tych.* Ni viderem hec, que paras, omnia huc tendere, mi Chronos, ut his, quibus illata videtur iniuria, par fiat, non esset quin vererer tuam in filium meum severitatem. Verum cum ipse cognoscas et ab homine adolescente et ab eo, qui flagranti amore affectus sit, et in eam mulierem hec esse acta, que non invita ab amato omnia hec possit perpeti, nonne erit abs tua iustitia alienum, ni huius unius peccati partim pietati in nos, partim humanitati tue concedas? Sine igitur te ut exorem; face in te coniecturam, finge in filiam sinistri quicquam: comprehendes quam perverse in parentes omnia redundant filiorum mala. Quid ais, Chronos? Tu item, Mnimia, obsecro, persuade, age!

123 *Mni.* Noli fodere latus hoc mihi amplius, mi Chronos! Redde te dignum solita et mansueta humanitate tua, sine ut exoret.

Chron. Quid est quod velitis fieri?

Tych. Velim mihi matri hoc ut fiat gratie, quam quidem si feceris, equam rem pariter et his omnibus gratam feceris.

Alithia. Hello, father.

Chronos. Did these things happen as reported, were the doors broken in and did a forceable seizure occur?

Alithia. They did, father.

Chronos. By Jupiter, what detestable crime!

Tychia. Let me appeal to the old man on my own account, Alithia. Chronos, hear me, I beg you.

Chronos. And what might I hear you say?

Tychia. Not what we are bound to say in your presence, but things that it is right for a mild and humane person such as yourself to hear.

Chronos. Speak, then.

Tychia. If I had not seen, my Chronos, that all your policies 122 tended in this direction — to be fair to victims of injustice — I should have been afraid of your severity towards my son. But since you recognize that these acts were committed by a young man — a young man burning with love — against a woman who might willingly have put up with all these acts had they come from a lover, will it not be foreign to your sense of justice if you do not, out of respect for us and out of your own humanity, overlook this one sin? Please allow me to persuade you; draw the conclusion for yourself; imagine something evil happening in the case of *your* daughter: you'll understand how perverse it is that all the wrongdoing of children should reflect upon their parents. What do you say, Chronos? You, too, Mnimia, persuade him, I beg you; go ahead!

Mnimia. Don't stab me in the side any more, my Chronos! Make 123 yourself worthy of your usual gentle humanity; let her persuade you.

Chronos. What do you want me to do?

Tychia. Please, grant me as a mother this favor — a favor which, if you grant it, will be just and at the same time welcome to everyone.

Mni. Mi Chronos, sponde, obsecro.

Chron. Quid tum?

Tych. Opto Phimiam filio fore coniugem meo.

Chron. Dum ea id non recuset.

Tych. Ergo dii te ament, dii perpetuo te conservent! Ibo domum, filium ut in nuptias traham.

124 *Chron.* Non vitupero isthuc consilium de Phimia, quandoquidem ea fama raptus iustis nuptiis deleatur. Quid tumne hic aliud agimus? Redibo ad forum, ut hos tabellarios cum syngraphis missos faciam. Tu, Mnimia, virginem commendatam habe.

: XX :

Philodoxus, Phroneus, Mnimia, Chronos, Doxia

125 *Phil.* Phroneus, si ob meam singularem in te observantiam commeritus sum abs te unquam, ut aut petere aut expectare possim quidpiam, nunc precor id omne, non quod debes tantum, sed quod potes, in amicissimi causa ut semper soles exhibeas. Ego Philodoxum tue dedico, tue commendo fidei.

Phron. Vah, quasi!

Phil. Minime. Sed quia nimis cupio, nimis ardeo, idcirco et precando sum nimius.

126 *Mni.* Mi vir, bono sis animo.

Chron. Quid conloquimini istic seducti? An improbatis quod de Phimia transegimus?

Mnimia. My Chronos, promise you will, I beg you.

Chronos. What is it then?[23]

Tychia. I want Phimia to be the wife of my son.

Chronos. I'll grant this as long as she doesn't herself refuse the offer.

Tychia. May the gods love you and keep you safe always! I shall go home and bring my son to the nuptials.

Chronos. I won't find fault with this plan concerning Phimia, see- 124 ing that the ill fame of a rape may be blotted out by proper nuptials. What else can we do? I'll return to the forum to send off these couriers with the documents. Mnimia, take charge of the young girl.

: XX :

Philodoxus, Phroneus, Mnimia, Chronos, Doxia

[*The street in front of Doxia's house*]

Philodoxus. Phroneus, if because of my special regard for you I 125 have ever merited anything from you, so that I might be able to seek or hope for anything at all, now I pray, in the cause of one so dear to you, that you will put all that at my disposal, as you always have, not because you owe me so much, but because you can. I consecrate Philodoxus to you, I commend him to your loyalty and good faith.

Phroneus. Oh, come off it!

Philodoxus. No, really. It's because my desire and ardor overflow all bounds that I'm so excessive in my entreaties.

Mnimia. My dear man, cheer up. 126

Chronos. What is that private conversation you're having over there? Are you condemning what we've decided about Phimia?

Mni. Minime. Verum hunc novo meum repertum virum alloquor.

Chron. Is ille tuus est?

Mni. Meus ipsus.

Chron. Gaudeo. Et quid est quod tractas? Siquid valeo, dicito.

127 *Mni.* Optime, dicam. Hic adolescens Atheniensis est; novi parentes eius, viros probos et primarios nostra in civitate. Is vellet,
mea et tua opera, hanc Doxiam sibi novam nuptam fieri. Ea, si
valeo coniectura, nec omnino id recusat. Credo, si isthuc ceptes,
nostra persuasione perfici ut utrisque pro expectatione ac desiderio satisfiat.

Chron. At dos convenitne?

Mni. Sat quidem secum apportat dotis huiusmodi, que modesta
et morigera est mulier.

Phil. Nusquam ad dotem hereo.

Chron. Ergo quidni modo isthuc agimus, Mnimia?

128 *Mni.* Maxime. Sed eccum Doxiam.

Dox. Phroneus properans verbis Chronos edixit ut exirem.

Mni. Huc, Doxia, anime mi, huc ad nos. Scin quid de Phimia te
absente confecerit Chronos? Prestare ratus est eam, uti res sua-
det, apud Fortunium coniugem dici, quam apud te vitiatam.
Idcirco petenti Fortunio despondit. Quid ais?

Dox. Quandoquidem in hunc locum adducta res est, ut meliora
expectare non liceat, minus quod adsit malorum eligere prudentis duco.

129 *Mni.* Non iniuria semper admirari vehementer soleo prudentiam
et humanissimam facilitatem tuam, cum cetera ob merita, tum

Mnimia. Not at all. I'm talking to my newly-rediscovered husband.

Chronos. He's your husband?

Mnimia. My very own.

Chronos. I'm happy for you. And what is it you're discussing? If I can do anything, tell me.

Mnimia. Excellent! I will tell you. This young man here is an 127 Athenian. I knew his parents, very decent people and pillars of the community. He would like, with my blessing and yours, for this woman Doxia to become his wife. If I'm right in my thinking, she is quite willing. If you'll set to work on this, I believe that with our persuasion the marriage can be brought to pass so as to satisfy the hopes and desires of them both.

Chronos. But has the dowry been arranged?

Mnimia. She brings with her enough dowry in this, that she is a gentle and obliging woman.

Philodoxus. I am not concerned about the dowry.

Chronos. Well, then, why not get on with it immediately, Mnimia?

Mnimia. By all means. Here's Doxia. 128

Doxia. Phroneus came hurrying to me and commanded me in Chronos' name to come.

Mnimia. Come here, Doxia, sweetheart, come here to us. Do you know what Chronos has arranged regarding Phimia in your absence? He has decided, as the circumstances suggested, that she would prefer to be called Fortunius' wife than your sluttish companion. So he betrothed her to Fortunius, who seeks her hand. What do you say about it?

Doxia. Seeing that the matter has come to this pass, and since there's no reason to expect any better results, I think it's prudent to choose the lesser of two evils.

Mnimia. I have always had good reason to admire your judgment 129 and your most kind and obliging nature in other meritorious actions of yours, but especially in this affair, because you didn't

vel maxime quod apud te his in rebus, que facto opus sint, nostris aut precibus aut longa persuasione minime indigeas, quod nosti quidem pro tuis commodis et honore tuendis quantam et curam et diligentiam capiamus. Narravi preterea quo in te animo Philodoxus affectus sit, quid exposcat. Consulebam senem: is approbat sententiam, ob quam te accersivit ut certiores nos redderes, quid tibi animi sit in nuptias.

130 *Dox.* Scio vos ea virtute preditos, ut possim tuto vobis et credula esse et morigera. Ego coniugem et quevis omnia vestra ex voluntate atque sententia accipiam ac recusabo quoad vobis id gratum et acceptum esse intelligam. Vestre sunt partes prospicere, quo me loci constituatis.

Phil. O dignam laude et amari cum isthac eloquentia atque mirifica modestia! Sed timeo hunc senem ne deficiat persuadendo.

131 *Chron.* Hoc velis scias, me non ex toto approbare virginem et eam quidem istius forme atque etatis diu domi sedere. Quod etsi plerumque fiat, tum quod non adsit cui digne connubat, tum quod in grandiorem familiam cupiant rem suam locare patres, non tamen id nunc abs te si fiat laudo, vel quia sola sis, quod sane est sinistra non vacuum suspicione, vel quia cetera omnia, que in connubiis deliberandi tarditatem solent afferre, longe cessent: nam neque dos neque affines neque mores ulla ex parte sese prebent, ut merito recuses nuptias. Dotem hic nullam petit, tum qualem maritum habitura sis spectas.

132 *Mni.* Pulcherrimum sane atqui, mehercle, dixti, Chronos, ut res est; quantove magis magisque cogito, tanto fit ut magis approbem quod faustum ac felix sit inter vos esse coniugium. Denique necesse est has fieri nuptias ac volo quidem fiant. Bene

need endless entreaties and arguments to do what needed to be done, and because you recognize how much care and effort we have expended for your benefit and honor. Moreover, I have explained Philodoxus' feelings about you, and what he asks of you. I consulted the old man: he approved the idea, and that is why he summoned you, so that you might let us know what your attitude is to the marriage.

Doxia. I know you are endowed with virtue, so that I can safely   130
trust and defer to you. I willingly and happily take you as my husband and any and all that is yours, and I shall demur only to the extent that I understand this to be welcome and pleasing to you. It is yours to plan what arrangements to make for me.

Philodoxus. O woman worthy of praise and love! What eloquence, linked with such marvelous propriety and deference! But I fear she may fail to persuade this old man.

Chronos. You should know that I do not completely approve of a   131
young woman, especially one of her beauty and age, staying in the home for a long time. Although this is commonly done, both because there is no spouse worthy of her and because fathers want to invest their substance in a grander family, I nevertheless don't approve of delay in your case, since you are alone — a state not free from suspicion of scandal — and because all the other conditions that are wont to cause delays in marriage negotiations are inapplicable: for neither dowry nor lineage nor good conduct offer any grounds for you to refuse the marriage. This man seeks no dowry from you; that should tell you what kind of husband you'll have.

Mnimia. By Hercules, Chronos, but you've stated perfectly the sit-   132
uation. The more I think about it, the more I'm convinced that it will be a fortunate and happy thing for there to be a marriage between the two of you. In sum, it is necessary that this marriage take place, and I certainly want it to take place. There is no fixed time for doing the right thing. Give her your hand, and

agendi tempus nullum prescriptum est. Cedo manum, et tu manum: hic tibi sit vir, hec tibi sit uxor. Voltis?

Phil. Volo.

Mni. Tuque id vis? Doxia annuit, ergo volt.

Dox. Volo.

Chron. Bene est.

133 *Phil.* Dii immortales, gratias vobis habeo quod in me propitii fueritis longe magis quam fuerim optare ausus. O me beatum!

Mni. Viden improbi alicuius peccatum quantas interdum bonis afferat voluptates?[5]

Phil. Exulto letitia. Plaudite, spectatores, hoc meo bono, plaudite. Tuque, tibicen, precine hymeneum: nos sequemur. Valete.

FINIS

you yours: let this man be your husband, let this woman be your wife. Do you both so wish?

Philodoxus. I do.

Mnimia. And do you also wish it? Doxia is nodding, so she wishes it.

Doxia. I do.

Chronos. Well done.

Philodoxus. Immortal gods, I give you thanks! You have been far 133 more propitious to me than I should have dared hope. What bliss!

Mnimia. Do you not see how the sin of some wicked person may from time to time bring pleasure to the good?

Philodoxus. I'm thrilled! Applaud, spectators, this good fortune of mine,[24] applaud. And, you, piper, play the marriage song: we shall follow you. Farewell.

THE END

PHILOGENIA ET EPIPHEBUS

Argumentum

Philogeniam cum amaret Epiphebus perdite, suasu et precibus eam noctu tandem domo abduxit et clam parentibus; cumque quereretur urbe tota, ad Euphonium traducta est, porro ad alium, ut lateret. Hoc ubi vidit Epiphebus Philogeniam apud se esse non posse diutius, hanc pro virgine Gobio dat uxorem, astu suo et Servie lene figmentis. Itaque disponsatur Philogenia et Gobius potitur ea uxore.

PHILOGENIA AND EPIPHEBUS

Argument

Since Epiphebus was desperately in love with Philogenia, using argument and entreaty he finally took her in the dead of night from her home without her parents' knowledge; and when the hunt for her embraced the whole city, she was taken to the house of Emphonius, then to another's house, to hide her. When Epiphebus realizes that he can no longer keep Philogenia with him, he gives the woman to Gobius to be his wife, passing her off as a virgin, using his own tricks as well as the play-acting of Servia, a procuress. Thus is Philogenia betrothed and thus does Gobius acquire her as a wife.[1]

CHARACTERS

Epiphebus, *a youth, lover of*
Nicomius, *a friend of Epiphebus*
Philogenia, *a maiden*
Cleopha, *Philogenia's mother*
Calistus, *Philogenia's father*
Emphonius, *a friend of*
    Epiphebus
Cariotus, *a slave of Emphonius*
Jubinus, *a friend of Epiphebus*

Zabinus, *Gobius's brother*
Gobius, *a peasant*
Servia, *a procuress*
Irtia, *a procuress*
Prodigius, *a priest*
Bitinus, *a peasant*
Salinus, *a music master*
Plancus, *a peasant*
Alphius, *an official of the state*

Scene: Pavia

: I :

Epiphebus, Nicomius

1 *Ep.* Vere hoc possum dicere, mi Nicomi, in amore me perditum et
miserum atque omnem etatem meam contrivisse, dum amori
operam dedi, utque uno verbo expediam: amavi frustra! Dii
boni, tanta ne duritia affectum quemquam ut amori non re-
spondeat? Id profecto vitium ingratum virginum tanquam per-
nitiosum legibus Persarum gravissimis merito plecti solent. Et
enim apud eos exploratissimum est quem alteri debere non sup-
puduerit, omnibus in rebus boni viri semper officium relinquere. Sed severius et durius, me Hercule, pena affici debent
qui sinceri amoris, quam qui pecunie debitores effecti sunt, si
nihil vereantur debitores naturae agnoscere quot debeant.

Nic. Quamobrem istec dicis?

Ep. Rogas? An clam te est ex animo me vicinam et hanc semper
amasse et item flagrantius nunc quam unquam?

Nic. Memini recte illud auditum sepe, sed non credidi adeo inca-
luisse te ut ais modo.

Ep. Quid igitur das consilii?

2 *Nic.* Ego ne ut animum impeditum expedias et calamitates istas,
solicitudines et cruciatus quos amor secum affert reicias et te
tibi vendices. Non enim decet omni tempore eundem esse; semel dum etas, locus et res postulant, non multum, vitio datur

: I :

Epiphebus, Nicomius

[*On a street in Pavia*]

Epiphebus. I can tell you truly, my Nicomius, that I am desper-   1
ately in love and miserable, and I've wasted my entire youth devoting myself to love. To put it in a nutshell, I have loved in
vain! Good gods, can there be anyone so hard-hearted that she
doesn't repay the debt of love? Indeed, the laws of the Persians
customarily punish this ungrateful vice of young girls as a pernicious thing, and rightly so. Indeed, among them there was
simply no doubt that the man who was not ashamed to leave
his debt to another unpaid was neglecting the duty of a man to
be good in all circumstances.[2] But, by Hercules, those who become debtors of sincere love should be punished even more se-
verely and harshly than monetary debtors, in cases where they
are unscrupulous about recognizing their debt to nature.

Nicomius. Why are you telling me these things?

Epiphebus. Can you ask? Has it escaped you that I have always
sincerely loved this girl who is a neighbor of mine and indeed
now more ardently than ever?

Nicomius. I well remember hearing this, and often, but I didn't
think you were so hot for her as you've just now said.

Epiphebus. What's your advice?

Nicomius. I think that you should free your mind from the bond-   2
age of love and that you should cast off the calamities, worries
and anxieties that love brings and reclaim your freedom and
self-control. For it's not fitting to be always the same.[3] It's al-
lowable to indulge a vice a single time, not a lot, when age, place
and circumstances require it. But wishing to spend your whole
life in sexual intrigues is indeed most shameful and criminal.

indulgere. Lascivos velle autem in eo ludo vitam universam degere turpissimum quidem et flagitiosissimum est. Quare heus, heus, expergiscere luxu et otio excedas impigre.

Ep. Probe dicis, si modo ut dicis, ita fieri facile posset.

3   *Nic.* Perge igitur ut cepisti, neque amplius me in hac re advoca. Difficile enim fit cuique quod non vult; quod vero firmiter et constanter quis voluerit, id quidem factu est facilimum. Ratione viris vivendum est, non autem pariter ut bellue appetitu duci debent. Hoc vir et bellua interest. Ea enim ad quodque delectabile sese accomodat; nos autem, qui cum diis animos communes habemus, uti ratione decet et huiusmodi motus ab honesto simul et utili penitus declinantes sub dicione nostra retinere, vicia cohibere ac virtutes fortiter amplecti.

4   *Ep.* Operam frustra sumis cum tua istac philosophia verbali; nunquam ita solutum animum et tam recte compositum habiturus sum, dum iuventutis annos degam, ut ista gravia stoycorum dicta michi persuaderi possint esse factu facilia. Ea autem predicare pulcrum est et sapientie singularis indicium[1] agendum est pingui Minerva, ut aiunt. Extreme profecto subtilitates franguntur denique. Quid rei militaris optimo duci conducet militibus rem factu perdificilem imperare quam existimet aut ab exordio nullum aggredi velle, aut in medio deserendam, aut in exitu precipitandam? Equabilia nature et ingenio quisque precipiat si pareri sibi postulat. Tibi dico, mi Nicomi, gratissimam rem michi facies si ea moneas que ad amorem, ad optata perducendum pertinent et me ad eam artem reddas calidiorem.

So, look, snap yourself out of this dissolute torpor and stop wasting your time in idleness.

Epiphebus. You're right. If only it were possible to do as you say so easily.

Nicomius. Then go on doing what you've been doing and don't   3
seek any more advice from me in this matter. It's difficult for any man to do what he doesn't want to do, but a goal a man pursues with firmness and constancy is achieved with great ease. Men must live their lives in accordance with reason; they shouldn't be dragged about by their appetites like beasts. That's the difference between man and beast. The beast fastens on whatever pleases him; we, however, who share the faculty of reason with the gods, ought to use our reason and hold in check inclinations of this kind that deflect us entirely from the honorable and the useful; it befits us to restrain vices and embrace virtues with courage.

Epiphebus. You're wasting your effort with this merely verbal phi-   4
losophy of yours; my mind is never going to be so free and well-ordered during my years of youth that these grave Stoic maxims could persuade me that they are easy to perform. They make fine material for a sermon, and it is a mark of singular wisdom for a dull-witted person to follow them. But such subtleties of reason always break down in the end. How is it profitable for the best of generals to order his troops to accomplish some really difficult objective which he knows is something they won't want to start doing, or will abandon in mid-course, or will throw away at the end? One should command things that are within the power and nature of people to do, if one expects to be obeyed. I tell you, my Nicomius, that you will be doing something I'd greatly appreciate if you'd give me advice about bringing to fruition my love and desires, if you'd make me more cunning in that art.

Nic. Exciderunt michi hec memoria vel, ut rectius loquar, nichil potui dediscere cum nil unquam dediserim. Tu tibi alium queras qui tue sententie sit equabilior.

5 *Ep.* Mane, mane, quo abis? Relictus sum. Quid nunc faciam miser? An hoc pacto me emori opportet et anichilari pedetintim. Atque rursus experiar si quo pacto moliri queant impresentiarum delitie mee et ad misericordiam reduci. Quamquam sepius hoc fecerim, fortassis tam diu copiam, tam diu concupiti amoris consequar. Non est desperandum prorsus; fortibus fortuna semper favit. Propterea omnes fere mulieres si frequentari divorticula et porticus perarari videant dies noctesque, et fores suas atque fenestras suspiriis obtundi, se cupi sinunt, denique volunt rogari, item exorari centies, ut mercature sue commertium carnis vendant et efficiant ut aliquando irate amatori suo possint obicere: 'Nunquam te deprecata sum, nec te quesitum veni'. Balistarii namque solent ab arcu plerumque sagittas centum emittere priusquam signum attigerint et forte fortuna exsultabit[2] unam que statim in metam statuetur. Sic mulieres, ut opinor et usitatum ab amatoris intelligo,[3] illaqueantur multis tandem modis et precibus, et momento magis quam mensibus; quamquam ego arbitrer novissima, si cui rem suam in portum deducant, ex prioribus vim illam ac potestatem maxima ex parte accepisse. Sed ut res iste sint, tantum hoc intelligo: nullum, aut ferme paucos, mulieres potiri posse nisi fuerit importunus aut insidiator continuus.

6 Agedum, postquam adventare noctem video, ibo hic et visam si hanc adoriri queam, que me tam diu innodatum habet et cru-

Nicomius. I have forgotten such matters or, to speak more accurately, I've had nothing to forget since I've never learned them in the first place. You should look for somebody whose sentiments are more like your own than mine are. [*Exits*]

Epiphebus. Wait, wait, where are you going? I've been abandoned. 5 What shall I do now, wretch that I am? Must I waste away and die little by little this way? Let me try again whether my darling can in some way be besieged and reduced to taking mercy on me. Although I've tried this many times already, perhaps at long last I shall have a chance with her; perhaps I'll get the love I want. I mustn't give up altogether; fortune always favors the brave.[4] On that account practically all women, if they see a man walking the streets and plowing up and down the porticos day and night, battering on their doors and windows with lover's sighs, will allow themselves to be desired, and in the end will want to be propositioned, then begged a hundred times to sell their merchandise — flesh — making it so that at some point they can throw it up angrily against their lover that "I never entreated you, I never came to seek you out." Cross-bowmen usually shoot more than a hundred arrows from the citadel before they hit the target and perhaps, by good fortune, one arrow will take wing from their bows which immediately sticks in the target. So it is with women, so I believe, and so I understand to be the case from the practice of lovers: women are ensnared in many ways and by many entreaties, but usually in a moment rather than after months — although if men manage at last to bring their affair into port, I rather think, they owe the final outcome in greatest part to the momentum generated by their previous efforts. However that may be, this one thing I know: that no one, or very few at most, can have their way with a woman without being importunate or an incessant plotter.

Come now, since I see night has come, I'll leave here and go 6 see if I can waylay this woman who has ensnared me and tor-

tiat. Diva Venus, michi pre[4] ceteris observata, faveas obsecro. Enitar quantum in me erit hanc tuis rebellem legibus in gregem tuum subducere. Dii bene vertant.

: II :

Philogenia

7   *Ph.* Epiphebus meus ubi nunc est? Ehy michi, quam cupio misera nunc ut redeat! Iratus edepol est, quod merito fortasis; namque quanti penderem eum nunquam ostendi, cum ab[5] me sepenumero velut lacrimans semper abiit, mortem expetens. Adeo ingrata hucusque in diem fui ut nunquam de me bene sperare potuerit. Miseram me, nunc demum sentio amorem in me concitari, quare dolorem ex eo non mediocrem capio. Nimis, nimis Epiphebo dura et aspera fui; sed id me facere compulit honestas, qua si virgo caret, est absque dote et extreme turpitudinis habetur et a mulieribus pudicis seposita. Dii boni, cur nobis partum dedicastis? Eam ob rem dumtaxat clause sunt nobis universe voluptates quas hec promiscui sexus copula secum trahit queque vitam iocundissimam et prolixiorem efficere

8   possunt. Vhe michi misere, incertum est quid agam: amore ardeo, parentes metuo, virginitas quoque, etatis nostre flos unicus et summum decus, non me sinit voluptati mee morem gerere. At tandem diutius ubi ferre nequero, omnes leges preteream et

tured me for so long. Goddess Venus, whom I revere above all other gods, aid me, I beseech you. I shall strive as far as in me lies to bring this rebel against your laws back into your flock. May the gods be propitious. [*Exits towards Philogenia's house*]

: II :

Philogenia

[*Alone in her house*]

Philogenia. Where is my Epiphebus now? I'm miserable with long- 7
ing for him to return! By Pollux, he must be angry with me, and perhaps he's right to be angry. I've never shown him how much I'm attached to him, when he on his side has often taken his leave of me as though in tears, as though he were suicidal. Up to now I've been so ungrateful that he could never have any hope regarding me. Wretch that I am, I now at last feel the flame of love catching fire within me, and it's causing me no lit- tle suffering. Too much, too much have I been hard and cruel to Epiphebus! But honor compelled me to act so. If a young girl loses her honor, she will have no dowry, she'll be considered a disgraced person and will be shunned by decent women. Good gods, why have you given the role of child-bearing to us women? Because of this one circumstance, we are shut off from all the pleasures which this joining of the two sexes brings with it and which can make one's life long and pleasant. Woe is me, 8
what shall I do? I'm burning with love, I'm afraid of my par- ents. And my virginity, the unique flower and highest ornament of my youth, won't allow me to indulge in the pleasure that is mine. Yet in the end, when I'm not able to bear it any longer, I'll ignore all laws and give free reign to the desires of my heart.

in omnem animi mei libitum prorumpam. Quid malum? Parentum negligentia peccandi michi causam affert. Quoad enim viro maturam virginem servare hedes opportet? Ad annos usque sedecim dici audio; ego vero vigesimum iam nacta sum meam in rem malam. Ego carne et ossibus nata sum ut cetere; michi propterea habitudo est corporis ad venerem aptissima, quare non possum non comoveri libidine. Atque peccatum hoc, quo nos ad id natura propensiores fecit, eo magis ignoscendum est; caritatem enim quandam in se habet, que virtus est ad humanum genus conciliandum necessaria et diis acceptissima. Nam hunc Epiphebum amo ut michi ex caro fiat carior, quod hac re tantum comprobare possum si mei copiam sibi fecero.

9   Sed quem deambulare huc sentio? Heya, ipsus est. Nam lapilli iactus aut screatus adventus huc[6] sui signa sunt. Quid moror? Ostendam tamen eandem esse me que fuerim iam dudum, quo sibi suavior sit fructus et sapidior quem labore maximo aquisierit.

: III :

Epiphebus, Philogenia

10 *Ep.* Salvete, parietes atque fores, vite mee futuri sepulcrum, nisi quid opis quispiam deus attullerit; hic manebo, sat scio, ad auroram usque rubescentem. Hec est mihi lex antiqua. Vhe mihi misero, quo reductus sum! Mea quidem vita, ut dici solet, in alearum ludo posita est. Sed quid audio? Hem, adest animi mei morbus perpetuus. O salve, anime mi, meum solamen unicum, meum corculum et mea suavitas. Tibi in manu est vivam an peream.

Why would that be wicked? It's my parents' negligence that affords me a chance to sin. Really, how long is it right to keep cloistered in the home a virgin who is ready for a man? Until she is sixteen, I hear it said; I'm already twenty, and it's killing me. I was born with flesh and blood like every other girl; my body is shaped for love, so I can't helped being excited by sexual desire. And the more nature has made us inclined to this sin, the more it must be forgiven; it's a sin that contains within itself a kind of charity, which is a virtue necessary for bringing harmony to the human race and one most pleasing to the gods. Indeed I love this Epiphebus; I want to make him ever dearer to me; and I can only demonstrate this desire if I give myself to him.

But whose footsteps do I hear? O my god, it's the very man. 9 Throwing pebbles and clearing his throat are the signals that he's coming here. Why hesitate? Still, let me pretend to be unchanged, the same as I was before: the fruit he'll pick with so much effort will be all the sweeter and tastier to him.

: III :

Epiphebus, Philogenia

[*Epiphebus in front of Philogenia's house*]

Epiphebus. [*To himself*] Greetings, walls and doors, the tomb of my 10 future life, unless some god grant me aid; here I shall remain, I'm sure, until dawn begins to redden the sky. This is my ancient rule. Woe is me, look at the miserable wretch I've become! My life, as they say, has become a game of dice. But what's that noise? Oh, it's the unending sickness of my heart. [*To Philogenia*] Greetings, O my soul, my only solace, my sweetheart and my delight. Whether I live or die is in your hands.

Ph. Hem, Epiphebe mi. Iterum ne repetis antiquam consuetudinem? Dixi tibi sepenumero ne redires amplius. Quere tibi aliam ne te hic frustra maceres. Vitam tibi tueare diutius quam possis; vigillare hoc pacto ad usque lucem si insueveris, vita profecto erit tibi brevissima ac intempestive senesces.

11 *Ep.* Tua istec omnis est culpa; ego animo lubenti amoris tui causa moriturus sum et ante omnia id optavi dudum. Sed quam egre laturi sint dii qui hec respiciunt, tecum animo fac cogites. Sunt equidem tibi metuendi si meo interitui opportuno causam dabis. Hei mihi, tu sola me salvum facere potes! Si te tantum amplectar respirabo atque post phenicem vivam. Nec me deseras, obsecro; aliter si facias, postremum propediem me videbis. Sattius est, mihi crede, ut me vivum amplexu tuo atque sinu foveas, quam anime tue immortali onus grave sim mortuus.

Ph. Facete dictum istuc est. Sed audi, Epiphebe mi, mei causa nolo moriare. Ymmo si mihi auscultabis, omnem tibi moriendi metum et periculum aufferam; denique tibi omnis erit dempta mollestia.

Ep. Hem, istuc volo, anime mi. Dic, queso.

12 *Ph.* Primum ut scias fratris loco te dilexi semper; ex adverso putabam te sincera fide amare me absque turpitudine ulla. Sed estis huiusmodi fere omnes; non amatis virgines nisi libidinem ut vestram expleant et rationem voluptatis vestre magis quam decus earum amatis.

Ep. Ha, mi Philogenia, non recte iudicas; bona venia negare hoc audeo.

Ph. Tace, tace.

Ep. Mitte me dicere.

Philogenia. Oh, it's my Epiphebus. You're back again to your old habits? I've told you many times not to come back again. Look for another girl; here you'll just wear yourself out in vain. You should take better care of yourself; if you go on staying up all night this way your life will be short and you'll be an old man before your time.

Epiphebus. All of this is your fault; I'm going to die — willingly! — out of love for you; that's what I've long wanted above all things. But be sure you realize how displeased the gods who watch over these matters will be. If you are the cause of my untimely death, you should fear their wrath. Alas, you alone can save my life. If I could only hold you in my arms, I'd breathe again and live longer than the phoenix. Don't abandon me, I beg of you; if you do, you will soon see the last of me. Believe me, it's far better that you hold me in your bosom while I live than that I die and become a heavy burden on your immortal soul.

Philogenia. Oh, you're just joking. But listen, my Epiphebus, I don't want you to die on my account. Indeed, if you'll just pay attention to me, I can get rid of all your peril, all your fear of death; and all your torment will at last be at an end.

Epiphebus. Oh, that's what I want! Please, tell me!

Philogenia. First of all, you should know that I have always loved you like a brother; and I've long believed that for your part you loved me sincerely and without any dishonorable motives. But you men, with few exceptions, are all alike; the only reason you make love to young girls is to satisfy your lust, and you love your own pleasure more than their honor.

Epiphebus. No, my Philogenia, you're mistaken; begging your pardon I must venture to contradict you.

Philogenia. Be quiet!

Epiphebus. Let me speak.

Ph. Non sino. Tu enim circumduceres me verbis argutis et calidis. Sat est si hec ut dixi iam apud seculum prius vera esse diffinita sunt et usu comprobata.

Ep. Vis me tibi falsum concedere? Concedo si prius abs te impetravero ut veritati primum sit locus; porro cum gratia, ut ne ex aliorum ingenio me iudices.

Ph. Ohe! Tu michi satis spectatus es. Turpe quidem esset te unum ab aliorum cetu[7] dissonare.

Ep. Me ennecas, hei michi! Sed saltem absolve quod michi policita es.

Ph. Quid? Ut miseratus tibi[8] finis sit et ne eiusmodi conflicteris malo?

Ep. Hem, istuc ipsum.

Ph. Fores istas perpetuo fuge, sicut Ditis[9] edes.

13 *Ep.* Hei mihi, quod dixisti! A cordolio me afficis, dum abitum hunc michi memoras. Ahi, ex tigride ne nata es? Tu me gladio iugula potius. Profecto si crederem id a te ex animo dici, ego ipse animam mihi erriperem. Num pietati, misericordie, humanitative apud te unquam locus erit? Et obsecro quam primum me perimas; illud facile perpeti possum; abire me hinc vivum et amantem perdite, id minime unquam ferre possem. Te obsecro, mi Philogenia, enneca me ut finem hiis erumpniis mors faciat. Amplius nequeo pati, neque hos labores, dolores et crutiatus tollerare. Video paulatim me resolvi, ut nix sole liquescit. Fer opem hiis rebus, obsecro, sine te exorari.

Ph. Quid igitur vis faciam, misera? Non ego te sanare unquam possem si quemadmodum dicis animo laboras. Diis dumtaxat ea medendi animis innata est potestas.

Ep. Ymo tu sola mihi salus esse potes et vite longeva productio et animi medella salutaris.

Philogenia. I won't. For you might just bring me around with your clever, sophistical talk. For me it's enough that what I've said has been found to be tried and true forever.

Epiphebus. Do you want me to agree to something false? I'll give in so long as I get you to agree, first, to respect the truth, then (by your leave) to not judge me by the attitudes of other men.

Philogenia. Oh, I've seen what you are like! The disgraceful thing would be to have you singing a different tune from the rest.

Epiphebus. You're killing me! But at least keep the promise you made me.

Philogenia. What promise? To put an end to your misery and stop you from struggling with misfortunes like this one?

Epiphebus. Exactly.

Philogenia. Well then, flee these portals as though they were the gates of Hell.

Epiphebus. Alas, what have you said? You're breaking my heart   13
when you remind me that I shall have to leave. You must have had a tiger for a father. You'd do better to cut my throat. If I really believed you meant this, I'd take my own life. Is there no place in your heart for pity, mercy or human kindness? Please, kill me as soon as you can: I could bear that easily. What I can never bear is that you should send me away alive and hopelessly in love. I beg of you, my Philogenia, kill me! That way, death may bring an end to these torments. I don't want to suffer anymore; I don't want to suffer these trials, pains and tortures any longer. Little by little I see myself dissolving, as snow melts in the sun. Bring me some comfort, I beg you; allow me to pay my addresses.

Philogenia. What do you want me to do, then, wretch that I am? I can never heal you if your heart suffers as you say. The power of healing hearts is reserved for the gods alone.

Epiphebus. No, only you can save me, only you can extend my life, only you can cure my heart!

Ph. Quonam pacto fare.

14 *Ep.* Dicam. Admitte me in edes quo tecum liberius ac tucius mihi que volo loqui liceat atque te complecti meo modo possim. Ubi me intromiseris, tum si dixeris 'abi', meam tibi astringo fidem, continuo e domo excedam. Da manum. Per ego deos tibi adiuro omnes perque divam Venerem, cuius imperio cuncta parent animantia et parere necesse habent, nil egressurum me mandata tua.

Ph. Epiphebe mi, ut aperte loquar, hoc sperare desine. Ego ne virum intromittam? Quid dixti? Quiesce. Num tibi atque soror cara sum?

Ep. Utique, mi Philogenia.

Ph. Id igitur consilii tu ne sorori dares.

Ep. Darem quidem, cur non? Quid mali facturus esset intromissus? Ah, mi Philogenia, non devorat amans delicias suas.

Ph. Epiphebe mi, non est tibi verbis mens consona. Verum, ut tibi rem omnem expediam, etsi maxime cuperem in edes te recipere, attamen id tam fieri potest quam celum ruere.

Ep. Quamobrem, mi Philogenia?

15 *Ph.* Quia parentes mei umbris advenientibus primum foribus obdunt pexulum, post non credentes pexulo, clavibus se tuciores reddunt et eas secum deferunt. Itaque nullo pacto tibi patere possent fores.

Ep. Occurram huic probe.

Ph. Quonam pacto?

Ep. Ex deambulatorio apud angiportum per scaligradium descendentem te,[10] mi Philogenia, meos in amplexus accipiam.

Ph. Me miseram, quod dixisti! Domo me noctu excedere me suades? Quid tum de me futurum esset?

Ep. Recte.

Philogenia. Tell me how.

Epiphebus. I'll tell you. Let me enter your house where I can say   14
what I want to say more freely and safely and where I can embrace you in my way. When you've let me in, then if you say,
"Get out," I give you my word I'll leave your home immediately.
Give me your hand. I swear to you by all the gods and by the
goddess Venus whose rule all living things obey and must obey,
that I will not overstep your orders.

Philogenia. My Epiphebus, let me be frank: forget about it. You
want me to allow a man into my home? What have you said?
Say no more. Am I not as dear to you as a sister?

Epiphebus. Absolutely, my Philogenia.

Philogenia. This isn't the advice you'd give your sister.

Epiphebus. Indeed I would, and why not? What harm would there
be in my coming inside? Ah, my Philogenia, a lover doesn't de-
vour his pleasures.

Philogenia. My Epiphebus, your intentions are not in harmony
with your words. But let me explain the whole thing to you.
Even if I had a great desire to let you in, it's as likely to happen
as it is for the skies to fall.

Epiphebus. But why, my Philogenia?

Philogenia. Because when evening falls my parents first put a bolt   15
on the doors, then, not trusting the bolt, secure the doors with
keys and take the keys away with them. So it really isn't possible to open the doors to you.

Epiphebus. I have a fine solution to this problem.

Philogenia. What's that?

Epiphebus. Just come down the stairway from the balcony next to
the alley and I'll take you into my arms.

Philogenia. O dear, what are you saying? You're urging me to run
away from my house in the dead of night? What will become of
me then?

Epiphebus. Everything will be fine.

Ph. Cave, istuc verbum nunquam ex te audiam. Missa hec face.

Ep. Quid missa?

Ph. Quam pridie mulierem in templo spectabas ita anxius, que tibi visa est facie splendidior.[11]

Ep. Quid hec ad rem nostram? Audi prius, si quod dixi tibi minus placet, exeundum est tibi per fenestrellam hanc demissam.

Ph. Tace, tace! Tue tantum parti consulis et pertinax; rem autem nostram parvi curas et floccipendis. Ehe, dic michi quis rumor esset populi si tibi essem morigera? Amabo ne me obtundas hac de re sepius.

16 *Ep.* Mi Philogenia, ausculta paucis rem istam. Profecto tam caute et accurate agemus ut soli dii, quos nihil latere potest, id rescituri sint. Parentes autem tui, cum te abesse domo comperint, clam omnibus id facient. Neque malum ab eis vereare. Parentes enim eiusmodi fere omnes sunt: interminatus filiis ne quid sceleris, flagitii, inhoneste commitant et eos observant quantum in ipsis est, quoniam recte sciunt non solum preceptis sed custodia magis et diligenti observantia filios cohiberi, cum iuventus omnis ad libidinem et ad animi oblectationes et ad ceteras voluptates a natura quodammodo procliva sit. Quo fit ut delicti adulescentes ac iuvenes mereantur veniam, non autem veterari senes, quos his voluptatibus abstinere etas illa merito cogit et imperat.

17   Sed, ut ad rem nostram pedem referamus, si quando forte superata parentum omni cura et vigillantia, filii, ut humanum est, quicquam flagitii impudentieve admiserunt, illud continuo

Philogenia. Look, I don't ever want to hear this kind of thing from you again. Forget about it!

Epiphebus. Why should I?

Philogenia. Yesterday you were watching a woman in church pretty intently; she must have seemed very beautiful to you.

Epiphebus. What does that have to do with us? Listen to me, if what I've just said doesn't suit you, escape then through this little window down here.

Philogenia. Quiet, stop it! You're only thinking of yourself, you stubborn man; you haven't given a thought to my situation. What would people say if I should agree to your proposal? Please don't keep insisting on this idea of yours any longer.

Epiphebus. My dearest Philogenia, just listen a little to my plan. 16 We'll do it so cautiously and carefully that only the gods, from whom nothing can be hidden, will get to know of it. When your parents discover that you've run away from home, they'll keep it secret from everyone. You have nothing to fear from them. Almost all parents are like this: they forbid their children with threats to do anything wicked, shameful, or dishonorable, and they keep an eye on them as much as they can, because they understand, correctly, that their children need to be controlled, not just by giving them rules, but even more by watching them carefully and guarding them, since every young person is in a sense naturally inclined to lust, to delightful passions and to other pleasures. It is for this reason that offending adolescents and youths deserve forgiveness, but not old men, whose age compels and demands that they abstain from youthful pleasures such as these.

But, to return to our situation, whenever it happens that 17 children overcome the surveillance and vigilance of their parents and, as is human, allow themselves to do some shameless or wicked act, their parents immediately, out of prudence, want to hide the indiscretion and try to prevent the reason for shame

sua prudentia occultari volunt neque causam sui dedecoris in publicum afferre student. Et hoc parentum est officium. Quare, mi Philogenia, nichil est quod vereare quando tempori occurramus celeriter, nec illud sinamus preterire nostris cum voluptatibus. Non est expectandum ut redeant utique bona fortune semel occasione prestita. Nunquam, crede mihi, culpabis hoc consilium si que fert adolescentia ea impigre, audacter et pertinenter carpas et usurpes. Nam id minus grave est habendum quod etas quasi iure suo quicquam exigit.

18 *Ph.* Me miseram, utinam modo hoc tuum sit salubre consilium! Si scirem a te sincera fide amari me mutuo, facile morem voluntati tue gererem. Sed estis vos omnes blandiloque moribus et verbis consimiles. Tantam enim vim habet in se eloquentia vestra ut non modo virgines teneras et ignaras rerum alliciatis, sed etiam lapides, ut aiunt, ex parietibus possitis evellere, et ubi vero abusi vestro modo puella fuistis et amor fugere cepit, quod fit brevi, ludibrio eas habetis, immemores amoris vestri causa virgines omnem honestatem et ruborem postputasse. Ah, pocius me tellus absorbeat quam istuc infortunium et calamitatem acerbissimam experiar! Desine iam orare me; aliter si facias, te michi neque amicum fidum neque benivolum esse rebor, sed hostem perfidum.

19 *Ep.* Ah, anime mi, quam iniquum est eadem sententia viros omnes dampnare! Etsi paucos admodum aut fere neminem id perpetrasse quidam predicent, ut amatrices suas impii et immanes relinquerint, attamen omni ex parte verum id non est quod modo dixti; omnes scilicet id facere. Credin tu, vite mee lux unica, usquam gentium posse me unum diem vivere si michi tam dura atque aspera unquam fors oblata sit, que me ab amplexu tuo disiungat? Ah, nullum certe unquam esset in vita michi suave aut salsum si, quod dicere abhominor, abs te dissociandus essem; tum nil esset michi preter mortem expetendum.

from being made public. This is what parents are supposed to do. So there's nothing to be afraid of, my Philogenia, if we make haste and not let this chance of enjoying the pleasures of love pass us by. One shouldn't expect that goods of fortune are ever going to return if we fail to take advantage of opportunities. Believe me, you'll never blame this advice of mine if you seize upon the pleasures of youth with energy and boldness. Any behavior that our time of life demands of us as though by right should not be regarded as a serious lapse of morals.

Philogenia. Oh dear, I just wish this advice of yours were sound! If 18 only I knew that you loved me back sincerely, I'd do what you ask in a heartbeat. But all you men are the same, with your winning ways and flattering words. Your eloquence has such innate power that you not only ensnare tender and ignorant girls, but you could even, as they say, tear stones from the walls. But once you've had your way with a girl and love starts to fade, which it does very quickly, you make a mockery of them, forgetting that it was for love of yourselves that these girls have put aside their honor and sense of shame. Oh, I'd rather the earth swallow me up than experience this misfortune, this bitterest of calamities! Now stop pestering me; if you don't, I won't consider you my faithful and benevolent friend but a treacherous enemy.

Epiphebus. Oh, sweetheart! It's so unfair of you to condemn all 19 men with the same sentence! Even though some people claim that one or two men have been so wicked and beastly as to abandon their lovers, it's still not entirely true what you were saying just now, that all men behave this way. Do you really believe, only light of my life, that I could ever, ever live a single day if so hard and bitter a fate befell me as to be separated from your embrace? Ah, there would certainly be nothing sweet or enjoyable left for me in life if—I can hardly speak the words!— I were forced to leave you. The only thing left for me would be

Atque, mi Philogenia, modo hera fortuna nos copulare vellit et copulatos esse sinat, ego neque cogitare unquam possem ut inter nos descidium eveniret. Credis tu potuisse me tot vigilias ferre, tot pernoctationes in via, tot estus, tot frigora, tot pluvias et ymbres, tot nives, tot labores, tot denique timores et pericula moriendi subire potuisse, si te amarem tepide ac vulgariter? Haud amor in te meus ad summum iam perductus unquam extingui aut remitti ulla ex parte posset, ut ex animo meo deleri[12] posset penitus! Non me tamen cruciari et perire funditus dies noctesque viderem. Pauculi quippe dies michi solis videndi sunt et restant si me deseris. Hei, michi sentio animam michi dolore nimio perfudi et a corpore exitum querere. Cernis michi qualis sit voltus? Desicari me paulatim vides, neque mei te miseret. Aha, obsecro, vitam hanc usui adhuc fortasse tuo futuram diutius tueare, postquam id tibi soli datum est. Si autem in rem magis est tuam ut moriar, ecce me; ubi vis paratus sum animam effundere.

20   *Ph.* Me miseram, redigis me ad insaniam et ad merorem maximum; nam nil cogitas quid me roges.

Ep. Heu, heu.

Ph. Lacrimas michi misere excussisti. Cohibeamus lacrimas ne usquam exaudiri possimus.

Ep. Hei miser, nequeo! Hei michi, sicne me mori opportet? O diva Venus tuque Cupido, qui me arcu et face tua feram hanc inesorabilem non modo amare sed insanire compullisti, succurrite pariter, obsecro!

Ph. Ve misere! Moriemur ambo una, postquam sic datum est fatis. Parere igitur necesse erit; hinc me precipitem dabo, aut ex tabulato superiori. Sine me! Cur retines?

to seek death. My dearest Philogenia, if Dame Fortune would let us come together and allow us to be joined, I couldn't ever imagine a rift between us. Do you think that I've suffered so many sleepless nights, that I could have borne so many endless nights in the street, so much heat and cold, so much rain and hail, so much snow, so much fatigue, and indeed so much fear and danger of death, if my love for you was some lukewarm and ordinary thing? There's no way that my love for you, now burning so intensely, could ever in any degree be snuffed out or diminished so as to be entirely blotted out from my soul. If that were so, I couldn't go on letting myself, day and night, suffer torture and total destruction. If you desert me, I shall have only a few days of sunlight left. Alas, I can feel my soul being poured out from excess of sorrow; I feel it trying to leave my body. Can't you see what my face looks like? You see me wasting away, but you don't feel any compassion for me. Ah, I beg of you, preserve this life of mine a little longer; it may still perhaps be of some use to you, since it is yours alone. But if you think it's better for you that I should die, look at me: I'm ready to breathe my last whenever you wish.

Philogenia. Oh dear, you're driving me mad, you're reducing me to 20 desperation. You're not thinking what it is you ask of me!

Epiphebus. Alas, alas! [He bursts into tears]

Philogenia. You've made me cry! We need to stop this weeping; we don't want to be overheard.

Epiphebus. I'm miserable, I can't stop myself! Alas, must I die this way? O goddess Venus and you Cupid, you who have compelled me with your bow and your torch not just to love this pitiless wild animal, but to act like a madman—both of you, help me, I beg you!

Philogenia. How unhappy I am, we shall both die together since the Fates have so decreed it. I must obey; I'll throw myself

Ep. Ymmo cave, mi Philogenia, si me salvum cupis.

Ph. Hey, unquam mihi utinam visus fores! Peritura sum funditus: hoc a me abiecit infelicitas.[13]

21 *Ep.* Anime mi, ne sis in necem meam tam pertinax. Tandem tu me ab orcho reducas in lucem, me tibi mancipium abducas quovis terrarum. Descende, mi Philogenia, descende! Labari usquam nec sinam scaligradium.

Ph. Hey mi, quid facio, misera! Ha, moriendum est mihi profecto insidiis tuis, Epiphebe.

Ep. Heya, mi Philogenia, mortem memoria ne repetas. Nam vita erit cum diis nobis perpetua et omnis felicitas nobis erit propria. Ha, nescis quot bona nobis in hunc diem cumullarunt dii! Gaudebis semper, mi Philogenia, et tecum melius actum est dices quam optare unquam ausa esses. Descende, inquam, mi Philogenia!

22 *Ph.* Dii, michi testes sitis hoc me tantum facere quod huius vite timeo. Inficiari tamen nequeo: flexit hiis tandem me lacrimis. Verum huius fletus, Epiphebe, facito ut memineris si quid adversi tui causa fortassis amori nostro, ut plerumque solet, acciderit.

Ep. Anime mi, ne metuas ut amori nostro intercedere unquam possit calamitas. Res omnis erit in vado atque unum diem sine te victurum me non esse certum habeas. Heya, anime mi, teneo ne te? O maxime animo exoptata meo, quis est hodie me fortunatior?

Ph. Ve michi misere, quid ego feci? Non sum apud me; obscurasti michi mentem et rationem.

23 *Ep.* Mi Philogenia, quid te maceras? Num ego sum tuus Epiphebus, qui te amat unice, qui te solam expetit, quoque cariorem

from here, or from the next floor up. Let me go! Why are you holding on to me?

Epiphebus. No, no, my Philogenia, not if you want to save me!

Philogenia. I wish I'd never seen you! It's all over for me. How wretched I am!

Epiphebus. Sweetheart, don't be so determined to kill me. Lead me   21
back from hell into the light at last, carry me away as your slave wherever you wish. Come down, my Philogenia, come down! I won't let the ladder slip!

Philogenia. Alas, what am I doing, wretch that I am! Ah, your tricks will be the death of me, Epiphebus!

Epiphebus. Ah, Philogenia, don't think about death! With the favor of the gods our life will be unending and all happiness will be ours. Ah, you don't know how many benefits the gods have laid in store for us today! You will always be happy, my Philogenia, and you will say that it's gone much better for you than you would have dared to wish. Come down, I tell you, my Philogenia!

Philogenia. Gods, bear witness that I am only doing this because   22
I'm afraid for the life of this man. Yet I can't deny this: it was his tears that moved me in the end. But make sure you remember these tears, Epiphebus, if thanks to you our love should encounter misfortunes, as often happens.

Epiphebus. My heart, don't be afraid! No calamity can ever hinder our love. Everything will come safely to quiet waters, and you may be sure that I shall not live one day longer without you. [*She comes down the stairs, into his arms*] O my darling, I can't believe I'm holding you at last! O, how I've longed for you! I'm the luckiest man in the world!

Philogenia. Woe is me, what have I done? I'm not myself. You've clouded my mind and my reason.

Epiphebus. My Philogenia, why do you torment yourself? Am I   23
not your Epiphebus, who loves only you, who desires only you,

habitura es neminem? Heya nunc digladiari possem me perpeti, postquam dii fautores et adiutores fuere, ut te meo amore amplecti possim. Mi Philogenia, sume atque refer suavia. Dii me perimant; ubi libuerit, contentus vitam excedam quando. Abeamus, nosque recludamus in cellulam, o mea respiratio, o sola spes.

Ph. I quolibet; ego te ad extremum usque diem vite sequar. Tu me amore ita inescasti, ut pocius vita quam te carere velim.

Ep. Te complectar in diem.[14]

Ph. Sine, pondus essem tibi maximum.

Ep. Mitte me. Nam est facile quod lubenti fit animo. Fero te. Hercule, arista leviorem!

Ph. Hey mihi, tibi cervicem et humeros nimis premam!

Ep. Tace, hic sunt edes nostre. Bono me augurio intus †ferro vel†[15] recipio. Veneri noctem hanc et ceteras dedicabimus, universos autem dies ad Epicurii sectam producemus.

: IV :

Cliopha, Calistus

24 *Cl.* Mi vir, sensi profecto nescio quid in edibus tumultuari.

Cal. Corripe te igitur e lecto et videas.

Cl. Faciam. Ad gnatam primum pergam. Heus, heus, Philogenia, hem quid est? Hostium pulso; nil enim obstat quin recta possim ingredi via. Quid, Philogenia, foribus pexulum non dedisti? Ubi es? Hem abiit; ve misera mihi! Quid viro nuntiabo? Caliste mi, accurre huc propere.

to whom you are dearer than anyone? I could take on the whole arena now that the gods have shown me their favor and help, now that I'm able to embrace you lovingly. Let's kiss, my Philogenia! The gods may strike me down as they please, I'll die happy! Let's go and shut ourselves in my little chamber, O my breath of life, O my only hope!

Philogenia. Go where you will; I shall follow you until the last day of my life. You have enticed me so with love that I'd rather be deprived of my life than of you.

Epiphebus. I'll take you in my arms every day. [*He picks her up*]

Philogenia. Put me down, I'm too heavy for you.

Epiphebus. No, let me do it. For a willing heart it's easy to do. I'll carry you. By Hercules, you're lighter than a feather!

Philogenia. Oh dear, I'm hurting your neck and shoulders!

Epiphebus. Quiet, we're home. We enter with good omen. We shall dedicate this night and all the others to come to Venus, but each day we shall spend on the model of the Epicurean sect. [*They enter Epiphebus' house*]

: IV :

Cliopha, Calistus

[*Inside the house of Philogenia*]

Cliopha. My husband, I'm sure I heard some kind of commotion 24 in the house.

Calistus. Then get up out of bed and go see.

Cliopha. I shall. First, I'll look in on our daughter. Hello, Philogenia? What's going on? I'm knocking on the door; there's nothing preventing me from walking right in. Philogenia, why haven't you bolted the door? Where are you? O no! She's gone!

Cal. Hem, quid est?

Cl. Philogenia nostra hedes est egressa.

Cal. Unde?

Cl. Nescio. Exploravi hostia, seras et omnes fenestras. Video omnia ordine esse quo statuta fuerant.

Cal. Unde igitur potuit exire?

Cl. Nescio, nisi forte ex deambulatorio in ultimis hedibus.

Cal. Eamus igitur visere.

Cl. Sequar.

Cal. Hem, Cliopha, hinc omne malum est, hinc abiit impurisima,
hic sunt vestigia.

Cl. Ve mihi! Quid igitur est faciundum, mi vir?

25 *Cal.* Dicam: primum cautio nobis sit, ne qua exeat. Si quis roget
ubi sit, quid faciat, egram simulemus, neque ullum sinamus vi-
sendi causa ad hanc accedere et id nobis in primis ab ypocrati-
cis traditum esse preceptum attestemur, propter genus morbi
et qualitatem malam. Interea perquiram diligenter et accurate,
omni denique indagine perscrutabor quo adducta esse possit;
quod si facile poterit unquam inveniri, bene est; alioquin, quid
mea, postquam officium nostrum fecimus? Dum apud nos pro
virgine sedit, monere eam et frequenter docere que usu facta essent, ut in dies doctior fieret et honeste vitam degere posset,
quantum quivimus; et ut paucis agam, postquam curam, omnem diligentiam, omne studium et operam in eam contullimus,
abeat in malam rem! Sumptu nos levabit et dote. Si fortasis
iniuria atroci nos affecisse arbitretur, filios nobis tantum expeta-

I'm so upset. What shall I say to my husband? My Calistus, come here at once.

Calistus. What is it?

Cliopha. Our Philogenia has left the house.

Calistus. How did she get out?

Cliopha. I don't know. I've checked the doors, the bars across the doors, and all the windows. I see that everything is in order, just the way it was left.

Calistus. So how could she have gotten out?

Cliopha. I don't know, unless perhaps she got out from the balcony on the top floor.

Calistus. Then let's go see.

Cliopha. I'll follow you.

Calistus. Oh Cliopha, that's where the trouble is, that's how that shameless girl got out: here are her footprints.

Cliopha. Woe is me! So what are we going to do, my husband?

Calistus. I'll tell you: first of all, we must be careful that the word doesn't get out. If anyone asks where she is or what she's doing, we must pretend that she's sick, and not allow anyone in to see her; and we'll cite in the first place a precept of the Hippocratic tradition, taking account of the type of disease and its malignant character. Meanwhile, I'll search everywhere for her with care, leaving no stone unturned, and I'll find out where she can have been taken. If she can be found easily, all is well; otherwise, what does it matter to me? As long as she lived under our roof as a maiden we did our duty to guide her; we constantly taught her how to behave, so that day by day she would become well-mannered and could live her life with honor. We did as much as we could. In a word, we lavished care, constant attention, and all our devotion and effort on her. So let her go to the devil! She'll relieve us of expense and the cost of a dowry. If she thinks perhaps she is inflicting some horrible offence on us, she should know that we parents only desire children to the extent

25

mus quantum digni sunt manendi aput parentes; abeundive
omnibus filiis potestas est libera, neque utitur me consule, qui
vult metu atque verberibus aput se filios persistere. Sed ut res
ista sit, nolo ob dementiam et effrenatam libidinem atque petu-
lantiam filie vitam ulla solicitudine aut angore mihi breviorem
efficere. Tu ittidem, mea Cliopha, facies, si mihi voles esse gratissima.

26 *Cl.* Ego ne misera, nunquam hec equo animo ferre potero, gnatam sic abiisse; neque id michi persuaderi unquam poterit,
filiam sponte id fecisse. Profecto nobis errepta est: novi indolem
eius et ingenium optimum huiusmodi aborere flagitia et quam
peccare erubescat. Religiosa et pudica, mi Caliste, nostra erat
Philogenia; sumper est verita quicquam se indignum admittere;
famam honoris semper tanti fecit, mi Caliste, ut forti animo
sumper contempserit omnis illecebras et voluptates. Hec neque[16] ego sola contemplata sum et admirata[17] quidem tantam in
virgine severitatem et continentiam. Quare, mi vir, si vera hec
resciri possent, extra noxam est virgo.

Cal. Vellem hoc ore magno depasisci.

27 *Cl.* Sic erit profecto. Virgo fortasis alicui audacissimo parumper,
ut fit, auscultavit; tum ille nimium temerarius et improbus,
manu violenta eam abduxit. Hoc minima mirum est. Nam hoc
idem multis etiam matronis quas pro sua pene incredibili virtute et sapientia deas appellare non dubitares, sepe contigit.

Cal. Tace, belua, quem audisti unquam ita fidentem sui et rationis
inopem et ieiunum ut audeat invitam mulierem domo trahere?
Non verisimile dicis; quare hoc missa. Ego ista probe caleo;

that they deserve to stay with us; all children should have the ability to leave. I don't approve of the man who wants to use blows and fear to keep his children around the house. But things being as they are, I don't want my life shortened by any anxiety or anguish due to the madness and unrestrained wantonness and petulance of my daughter. And you'll do me a great favor, my Cliopha, if you'll take the same attitude.

Cliopha. Poor me, I'll never be able to accept calmly that my 26 daughter has run off; nor can I ever be persuaded that Philogenia has done this all on her own. Doubtless she was stolen from us: I know that someone of her disposition and her fine character would shrink from this kind of wicked behavior; she'd be ashamed to sin this way. Our Philogenia, my Calistus, was a religious and chaste girl, always afraid to do anything unworthy of herself; she was so jealous of her honor, Calistus, that she always scorned temptations and pleasures with great strength of mind. And I'm not the only one who has observed and admired the girl's strictness and self-control. So, my husband, if we could only find out the truth, I'm sure our daughter would be found blameless.

Calistus. I wish she were being devoured by this shy reserve of hers.

Cliopha. She will be, surely. Possibly the girl heeded some shame- 27 less man just for a moment, as happens, then that rash and wicked fellow carried her off by force. This would be nothing to wonder at. The same sort of thing often happens even to many married women whom you wouldn't hesitate to call goddesses for their nearly incredible virtue and prudence.

Calistus. Shut up, you dumb animal! Have you ever heard of a man who is so confident of himself, so totally bereft of judgment, that he would dare drag a woman from her home without her consent? What you're saying is implausible, so let it go.

peccata pocius in eam quam in nos suo malo redeant. Sequere me.

Cl. Mi vir, non possum non graviter commoveri quod unica nata nunc, nec, ⟨ut⟩ decuit, nuptiis dedita, sic immerito ac incauta privata sum.

Cal. Huic rei modo finem facias. Desine modo; res ista ut pro meliori a diis accipienda est.

Cl. Ve michi misere! Nolem unquam matris nomen agnovisse!

28 *Cal.* Gratiam diis habes maximam, quod viscera post partum primum, qui nobis Philogeniam attulit, hexerunt tibi; idque proprie factum est ut huiusmodi malo nunquam amplius conflictari poteris.

Cl. Nescio quid dicam, nisi quod felix ut aiunt est tristicia nunquam filios genuisse. Orbari autem eis quoque modo, interitu, preda aut fuga, flebile quidem, durum et acerbum est.

Cal. Vulgo istec tradunt, sed aliter periti existimant qui de remediis utriusque fortune sum imbuti. Non edepol faciam.

Cl. Quid, mi vir?

Cal. Nostra[18] nunc animo obsequitur ventri,[19] obediens Bacco et Cereri indulget, concinit correisque gaudet in amore, tota est luxu perdita Venerique dedita. Nos ne dolorem nobis, angustias, merorem et cruciatum contra comparabimus? Non profecto, et nos vitam illarem queramus. Nobis reliquum hoc pauculum vite nostre degamus perpetua in leticia. Ita tibi impero.

Cl. Fiat ut vis, modo ut possim.

I know all about affairs like this; I just hope that her sins come down on her own head, and not on ours. Come with me.

Cliopha. My husband, I can't help feeling terribly upset that, through no fault of my own, I've been deprived of my only daughter in this way now, and not in the proper way, through marriage.

Calistus. You can forget about that ever happening. Stop crying now; we have to accept what's happened from the gods as all for the best.

Cliopha. Woe is me! I wish I had never acknowledged the name of mother!

Calistus. You should thank the gods that after your first birth, which brought us Philogenia, they made your womb barren; this happened precisely so you would never have to struggle again with another devil like her.

Cliopha. I don't know what to say except that it is a fortunate heartache, as they say, never to have borne children. To be deprived of them in any way, either by death, abduction or by their running away, is a hard and bitter thing, a truly lamentable thing.

Calistus. That's what most people say, but well-informed people think otherwise — the ones who have imbibed the remedies for good and ill fortune.[5] By Pollux, I'm not going to grieve that way.

Cliopha. Why not, my husband?

Calistus. Our daughter is now doing what her what her lower organs tell her to do, not her mind; she's a slave to Bacchus and Ceres, she's singing and dancing and enjoying her love-affair, completely given over to wantonness and Venus. Shall we, to the contrary, reap only suffering, penury, anguish and torment for ourselves? Let's try to spend the little of life that's left to us in unbroken happiness. I command you to do so.

Cliopha. I'll do as you wish, so far as I can.

Cal. Ego domum egrediar et ad forum ibo; fortassis inopinato casu certior factus redibo quo sit adducta. Vale.

Cl. I, mi vir, bonis auspiciis.

: V :

Emphonius, Jubinus

29 *Em.* Audivi rem admodum michi mollestam, Jubine.

Jub. Quid?

Em. Dum per forum iter haberem, aiebant ibi quamplures uno ore Epiphebum nostrum denuo rapuisse virginem.

Jub. Illud et iam pervenit ad aures meas et vix tum potui credere; tunc abs te reformatus sum, doleo quidem amici causa.

Em. Ibo igitur ad eum et admonebo ut, si res vera sit, ne eum imprudentem opprimant.

Jub. Recte facies.

Em. Ha, dii boni, quot mala fiunt pravis moribus!

Jub. Cur hec dicis?

Em. Quia plerumque incensi fimus libidine, iocosi adeo sumus ut nichil sani consilii mentibus nostris possit insedere. Ruimus, prosternimus cuncta impetu flagitioso; dum caremus libidine dumque optati nobis est penuria; in eo consequendo magis incendimus. Profecto, Jubine mi, istec nostra ad mulieres aviditas redigit nos insaniam.

Calistus. I'm going to leave the house and go to the forum; perhaps, unlikely as it is, I'll come back with information about where she's been taken. Farewell. [*Exits*]

Cliopha. Go, my husband, and good luck!

: V :

Emphonius, Jubinus

[*A street in town*]

Emphonius. I have heard something, Jubinus, that really upsets me.   29

Jubinus. What's that?

Emphonius. As I was taking a walk through the forum, a lot of people there were saying, as with one voice, that our friend Epiphebus has once again ravished a virgin.

Jubinus. I've already heard the same rumor and I could scarcely believe it, but now, hearing it again from you, I'm really sorry for our friend's sake.

Emphonius. I'll go then and warn him, so that, if the story is true, he won't be taken by surprise.

Jubinus. That's the right thing to do. [*They head for Epiphebus' house*]

Emphonius. Good gods, how many evils arise from corrupt habits!

Jubinus. Why do you say this?

Emphonius. Because generally when we we're inflamed with lust, we're so light-hearted about it that we lose all our common sense. We charge ahead, knocking over everything in our scandalous onrush; and during the time we're deprived of the object of our lust, we burn all the more in trying to get it. Without doubt, my Jubinus, this hunger of ours for women drives us insane.

30 *Jub.* Ego tibi acquiesco si plurimum temporis in ea re conteras; si vero tibi res succedat ex sententia et brevi curriculo, nil dulcius, nil utilius, nil denique gratius optari posset. Tum si vir sis, haberes quocum te oblectes animum; amplius vagari modo ad hanc, modo ad illam non sinis, ad id te aplicas, in eo permanes expletus: porro habes in quam, ut humanum est, libidinis stimulos evomas. Non abduceris tum a virtute et a studiis honestissimis, ut plerique solent, quorum cura, diligentia et opera tantum est in persequendis mulieribus. Nullam tamen unquam aut levitate sua aut infelicitate quadam nancisci possunt, cum hii dementes fiunt ea in re sumper occupati, que sibi a fortuna negata est. At si forte tandem concupite rei copiam consequantur, si viri sint et recordatio infinita pene contricti temporis in eorum mentem subeat, tum quicquid eis futurum dulce spes fuerat, exarcebatur maxime et adeo si[20] temporum curricula mortalium propria tantum esse cogitent, tum quelibet pupille tractatio here sibi constet maximo. Quare, mi Emphoni, hoc genus hominum in amore mihi miserum videtur et perditum et ab omni etate presenti venturave vituperationem et a superis penam expectare.

31 *Em.* O Jubine mi, ego de his loquor et ad hos a principio mea tendebat oratio; sed scin quamobrem plurimi temporis iacturam in amore paciantur?

Jub. Dixi quod infortunati quodammodo sunt.

Em. Ha, Jubine mi, alia est ratio probatissima.

Jub. Quenam?

Jubinus. I agree with you if you're talking about wasting a lot of 30
time chasing skirts; but if something comes along that you like
and can get with a short run around the track, well, then, nothing could be sweeter, more enjoyable and better for you. Then
again if you're a husband, you should have your heart's delight;
you won't allow yourself to chase after this one and that one
any more; you'll devote yourself to your marriage and stay satisfied with that — since you have, after all, somebody on whom to
vent your normal human libido. Then you won't be distracted
from virtue and honest employments, as often happens to those
who are totally obsessed with chasing women. Such men, however, never get anywhere with women, either because of their
own lack of gravitas or through some ill fortune. They go crazy,
being obsessed with the very thing Fortune denies them. But
if they do finally happen to achieve their desire, if they are
men and consider the infinite amount of time they've wasted,
whatever were their hopes for future pleasure, they're entirely
dashed. And should they come to see that time is the only
thing we mortals truly possess, they'll see that every time they
squeeze a tit it's costing them a patrimony. Hence, my dear
Emphonius, this kind of man seems to me wretched when it
comes to affairs of the heart — a damned soul, just waiting for
abuse from present and future ages and for punishment from
the gods.

Emphonius. My dear Jubinus, that's the kind of man I was talking 31
about; my speech was from the beginning directed against him.
But do you know why they let themselves waste so much time
in love-affairs?

Jubinus. I told you: because in some way or other they are victims
of fortune.

Emphonius. Ah, my Jubinus, the most plausible reason is something else.

Jubinus. What reason is that?

Em. Dicam. Nos[21] ipsi quidem damno nobis[22] sumus.

Jub. Cur?

32 *Em.* Sine me: ita sumus incontinentes fere ut bruta. Cum in templo cernimus mulieres auro et gemis ornatas, vestitu splendidas, facie expolitas, alter alterum propellit ut anteat reliquos et se ut stipes[23] illis pro termino statuto antestet. Hoc fieri videt superba mulier et fatua sui visandi causam delirat; item magis pro gaudio videt tot avidas provocationes oculorum, tot ad se protendi procaces vultus, vix patitur se opertam[24] se vestibus esse. Tum aput sese et amanti misero contumax et ingrata, sic secum meditatur: 'Multi me sibi expetunt; amore igitur non carebo. Unum tantum ex omnibus mihi deligam, sed non ita repente; prius consulam'. Quo fit ut, dum deliberandi sibi secum tempus postulet, nequeat unquam diffinire, cum se credat a multis amari et optari vehementer, ut illis sepe contigit quibus dubium prandium apponitur. Itaque vere et ex animo amanti cum sit opus remedio, huiusmodi facilitate iuvenili prava et incontinentia detestanda deducitur ad fatum atque nec fame tunc nec tempori parens mulierem insequitur, illudentem insidias et retia que in amore pendula, omnium cursus exuperat et querellis et lacrimis amantium cantu risuque respondet.

33 *Jub.* Quid igitur presidii tu his statues?

Em. Audies, mea est sic ratio; ea quidem optima si modo omnes integre et pariter ea observarent.

Emphonius. I shall tell you. We ourselves are the cause of our own ruin.

Jubinus. Why do you say that?

Emphonius. If I may say so, we are almost as intemperate as the 32
brutes. When we see women in church, adorned in gold and
gems, splendidly dressed, all made up, each of us pushes forward to get ahead of the others, then poses in front of the ladies like we're setting up a boundary marker. The vain woman
sees this happening, and the silly thing is ecstatic at being ogled
this way; and it only adds to her enjoyment to see so many eager, flirtatious eyes, so many impudent faces turned her way;
she can hardly bear being covered by her clothes. Then, return-
ing to herself, she shows herself unyielding and ungrateful to
her wretched lover, reasoning within herself like this: "Lots of
men want me, so I can have a love-affair whenever I want. I
should choose one man from all these, but not so fast: let me
think about it first." Thus it happens that she takes her time
making up her mind and isn't able to come to a decision, as she
thinks that she is loved and desired by many men. It's like what
often happens to people who are served many dishes at dinner
and don't know where to start.[6] Thus the true and sincere lover,
who needs a cure for his love, is led to his fate by the girl's perverse and juvenile frivolity, her deplorable lack of self-control,
and he dances attendance on the woman, taking no account of
his reputation or the time he's wasting, while she makes a joke
of the traps and nets that are set for her in love, outpacing all
her lovers in the race, and answering their complaints and tears
with song and laughter.

Jubinus. So what defenses would you erect against women like 33
these?

Emphonius. Listen, here's my advice, and it would be the best solution to the problem, if only everybody without exception would
follow it completely.

Jub. Quenam? Cupio hodie his in rebus abs te fieri doctior.

Em. Non est opus tibi monitore. Sed sine pervenire me quo volo.

Jub. Perge.

34 *Em.* Mulieri si obviam factus fueris, lumina retorqueas, eam videre nole ostendas, fitque tibi contemptui. Denique omnibus omnes idem faciant. Profecto tum disperate et furentes, iracundia atque libidine confecte, procul dubio amore insanient; rotabunt sese undique ut sibi viros reconcilient et in gratiam eorum se restituant. Tunc fiet mutatio: prosequentur nos quocumque, tendent nobis insidias et laqueos, capient nos per fora, per vicos, per theatra, denique per deorum templa et ubi nos offenderint, pro fausta preda nos intercipient. Quid tibi videtur?

35 *Jub.* Emphoni, istec vera sunt! Corrupti sunt animi libidine et ebrietate omni, quare hec impetrari nunquam possent.

Em. Sic quoque ego opinor, sed mihi conveniendus est Epiphebus. Tu, quid est tibi negotii?

Jub. Paulum quoddam. Nam audio merces meas adventas esse, quamobrem nunc ad portum pergam. Attamen si quid me vis, relictis omnibus, ecce me tibi.

Em. Ymo perge et rem tuam age diligenter.

Jub. Vale ergo.

Em. Tu quoque.

Jubinus. What is it? I want to take advantage of your experience in these matters.

Emphonius. You don't need a counselor. But let me get to my point.

Jubinus. Go ahead.

Emphonius. Whenever you meet a woman, avert your eyes, show 34 that you don't want to look at her, and scorn her. Every man should do the same to every woman he meets. Surely it will then follow that women, desperate and furious, consumed with anger and lust, will beyond doubt go insane with love; they'll turn somersaults to ingratiate themselves with men again and restore themselves to our good graces. Then everything will change: they'll follow *us* wherever we go, they'll lay traps and snares for *us*, they'll accost *us* in the marketplaces, in the streets, in the theaters, and even in the temples of the gods. And when they meet up with us they'll snatch us up like manna from on high. What do you think?

Jubinus. Emphonius, you are absolutely right. But men's minds are 35 so corrupted by lust and drunkenness of every kind that you could never ask them to do this.

Emphonius. I think so too, but I must go to meet Epiphebus. Do you have any business to attend to?

Jubinus. Just a bit. I hear that my goods have arrived, so I'll go down to the port now. However, if you need me for anything, I'll drop everything and come.

Emphonius. No, go attend to your business.

Jubinus. Farewell, then.

Emphonius. You too. [*They depart in separate directions*]

: VI :

Epiphebus, Philogenia, Emphonius, Cariotus

36 *Ep.* Philogenia, animi mei lux perpetua, constitui me hodie equalem conventurum esse. Ibo ad eum, mox ad te revertar.

Ph. Ehi michi, ne me diu solam relinquas.

Ep. Adero, inquam, hic continuo.

Em. Heus, heus Epiphebe!

Ep. Intus.

Em. Si aperias veniam.

Ep. Fores insulta pedibus et patebunt.

Em. Sic factum. Dii tibi afferant qualem diem expetis.

Ep. Tibi autem salutem, lucrum et amoris tui copiam. Quo is tam
mane?

Em. Ad te.

Ep. Quid est?

37 *Em.* Uno verbo expediam. Rumor est virginem Calisti domo te
excepisse vi, quare nuntiatum tibi venio ne aput te eam momento teneas. Nam confestim hic aderunt commilitones et sa-
thelites presidis qui hedes istas perquirent diligenter. Vhe tibi si
aput te quicquam amplius hec maneat.

Ep. Hey mihi, postquam res in publicum producta est peccatum
meum ellatum foras[25] negare non audeo. Sed quid facturus
sim[26] consule amabo ac mature.

Em. Exorna eam virili veste et post me iube veniat et aput me tecum erit ittidem.

: VI :

Epiphebus, Philogenia, Emphonius, Cariotus

[*In Epiphebus' house*]

Epiphebus. Philogenia, the perpetual light of my heart, today I've 36
decided to meet a friend, a fellow my age. I'll go meet him,
then come right back to you.

Philogenia. Oh dear, don't leave me alone for too long. [*Retires to
the bedroom*]

Epiphebus. As I said, I'll be back right away.

Emphonius. [*Outside the house*] Hello, there, Epiphebus!

Epiphebus. I'm inside.

Emphonius. I'll come in if you open up.

Epiphebus. Just kick the door with your feet and it will open.

Emphonius. Done. [*He comes inside*] May the gods bring you the
kind of day you want.

Epiphebus. May you have health, wealth, and your lover's love.
Where are you off to so early this morning?

Emphonius. To see you.

Epiphebus. Why is that?

Emphonius. I'll explain briefly. There is a rumor going around that 37
you've carried off a maiden by force from Calisto's house, so I
came to tell you not to keep her with you for a moment longer.
The police and the governor's bodyguards will be here shortly
to inspect this house. There will be trouble if she stays with you
a second longer.

Epiphebus. Well, I don't dare deny it, since the matter's been made
public and my sin has been dragged out of the house. Please,
quick, tell me what I should do!

Emphonius. Dress her in men's clothes and tell her to follow me;
tell her that you'll join her at my place.

Ep. Recte dicis; eo propere ad eam. Philogenia, indue paulum hoc citissime et me sequere.

Ph. Sequor quamobrem?

38 *Ep.* Nunc non est narrandi locus. Sic opus est, Philogenia mi, sequere Emphonium quoquo ibit; te sibi comendo simul et vitam meam. Is in via tibi rem narrabit ordine et quare sic fieri oporteat.

Ph. Ve mihi misere! Abeunti michi e domo mens, futuri mali prescia, dixit hec.

Em. Ne metuas, Philogenia. Nescis quod dicis; nundum rem rescivisti.

Ph. Hoc unum scio, me miseram esse.

Em. Ha, Philogenia, nil est mali, mihi crede, sed opus est aput me maneas per aliquot dies. Interea res ista refrixerit. Nunc te queritant; quare si restitisses aput Epiphebum tuum haud latere potuisses. Nam universas eius hedes statim vestigabunt.

Ph. Hey mihi, non eo me redire post licebit!

Em. Certe, sed sequere me intus.

Ph. Sequor.

Em. Cariote, heus, heus, ubi es?

Car. Here mi, adsum.

39 *Em.* Fac paratum sit et maturius quam soles. Ego, Philogenia, transieram ad forum, ut hunc tuum Epiphebum adducam. Tu interea frontem illarem, ea⟨m⟩ si cares, summas. Mutuo modo respira. Omnem tibi et Epiphebo metum hoc pacto demptum feci. Vale.

Ph. Obsecro, quam primum vos domum recipite; nimis enim crutior in solitudine.[27]

Epiphebus. A good idea; I'll go to her right now. [*He calls to her in the bedroom*] Philogenia, put this on as fast as possible and follow me.

Philogenia. Follow you? Why?

Epiphebus. We don't have time to talk right now. Philogenia mine, 38 you've got to follow Emphonius wherever he goes. I entrust you — and my own life — to him. He'll tell you the whole story on the way and why we have to do this.

Philogenia. Woe is me! When I left my home I had a premonition in my heart that told me something bad was going to happen.

Emphonius. Don't be afraid, Philogenia. You don't know what you're saying; you haven't found out what's happening yet. [*They depart for Emphonius' house*]

Philogenia. I know one thing: I'm terribly unhappy.

Emphonius. Oh, Philogenia, there is nothing wrong, believe me, but you need to stay with me for a few days. In the meantime, things will cool down. Right now they're hunting for you, so if you'd stayed at your Epiphebus's house, you couldn't have remained hidden. They're going to search every inch of his house immediately.

Philogenia. Oh dear, so I won't be able to go back there!

Emphonius. Sure you will: but follow me inside. [*They enter Emphonius' house*]

Philogenia. I'm coming

Emphonius. Hey, Cariotus, where are you?

Cariotus. Here I am, master.

Emphonius. Get things ready, and be quicker about it than you 39 usually are. Philogenia, I'm going over to the forum to bring your Epiphebus here. Meanwhile, stop frowning and smile. Take a deep breath. Thanks to my plan, you and Epiphebus have nothing to fear. Goodbye.

Philogenia. Please, please, come home as soon as you can; the torture is too much when I'm alone.

Em. Ymmo nichil aliud est querendum deinceps nisi quemadmodum leti vivamus. Quare dum detur fruare risu et gaudio. Est
enim solicitudo et animi tristicia potissimum salutis inimica.

Ph. Abi cito et redeatis ambo.

Em. Abeo.[28]

: VII :

Philogenia

40 *Ph.* Ve miseram, quam subito nos offendit calamitas! Ha, fors fortuna saltem sinisses nos triduum hoc perpeditum in letitia degere! Quot incomoda mortalibus affert hec tua varietas! Vellem
pocius nunquam te nobis facilem prebuisses. Turpis exitus retro
fedat principia. Hey mihi, vix licuit amplecti et salutare Epiphebum meum; vereor ne diutius una vitam producturi sumus,
tum ne me deserat. Quod si fit, per solas terras errabo, demens
et devia. Hei mihi, quid mecum queror? Peritura sum funditus. Ante oculos omnia posita futura video: luctum, infamiam,
cruciatum, denique mortem. Utinam me preripiat;[29] invisus utinam mihi foret Epiphebus! Hey mihi, non opportet me tantum
pietati concedere ut lacrimis et conflictis verbis fidem darem;
exaudiri haud decet inhonesta rogantes. Hec amicitie prima lex
traditur.

41 Verum quantum intelligere possum, amor iste perfluens ex
impetu concitato libidinis, ex ratione nihil, ut exitum tristem
secum ferat subitoque frigeat necesse est, quod quidem magis

Emphonius. No, no, the only thing we have to figure out from now on is how to live in happiness. So smile and be happy while you can! Worry and depression are the greatest enemies of good health. [*Exits*]

Philogenia. Go quickly; may you both come back to me.

Emphonius. I'm going.

: VII :

Philogenia

Philogenia. Woe is me! How suddenly misfortune befalls us! Ah,   40
Fors Fortuna,[7] at least you allowed us to spend these three con-
tinuous days in bliss! How many misfortunes your fickleness
causes for mortals! I wish you hadn't been so indulgent towards
us. A shameful outcome casts a dark shadow backwards on the
beginnings of an action. Alas, I've barely been allowed to embrace and bid farewell to my Epiphebus; I fear we won't be able
to continue our life together any longer; I fear he'll desert me. If
that happens, I shall wander the lonely lands, mad and lost.
Alas, why this lament? I'm going to be utterly ruined. I see my
whole future before my eyes: sorrow, infamy, anguish, and finally death. If only Fortune had taken me before my time, if
only Epiphebus were hateful to me! Then, alas, I shouldn't have
abandoned my sense of duty so as to trust his tears and his con-
tradictory statements; it's not right to heed people who ask for
dishonorable things. This is traditionally the first law of friendship.

But, so far as I can understand, this love that springs from a   41
sudden excitation of lust, not from reason, is bound to have an
unhappy outcome and to grow cold suddenly, and this is more
the man's fault than the woman's. For even if a woman happens
to take a longer time at the start before she gives in to her lover,

fit viri culpa quam mulieris. Mulier enim si forte prolixa sit in
principiis antequam amatori obsequatur, attamen ubi decrevit
amare, flagrantius et stabilius quam vir amat et in amore eum
exuperat. Vir enim, ubi potitus est muliere propter quam se de-
perire dudum ostenderat, secum sic cogitat: 'Hoc meo arbitratu
et iussu sumper erit; ad aliam aucupemus' et pro munere pal-
mario sibi ducit si plures, ut aiunt, in codice descripsit. Mulier
enim, cum intelligat nil esse sibi deterius atque fame honorive
suo magis adversum quam amorem suum pluribus impertiri et
his in rebus mercaturam velud quamdam negociari, ei quem a
se dignum amari iudicavit, cuiusque voluntati se semel dedica-
vit, suum amorem illibatum incorruptumque conservat. Hem,
porro mulieri suo pro merito hec a viro refertur gratia? Ubi expletus est et viscera sibi omni voluptate complacita refarcivit,
eam aspernatur et deserit.

42   Ve mihi misere, recte mihi in mentem hec venerant! Sed isthuc factura eram: hoc scilicet fatale fuit. Quam sepe evenit ut
in re quappiam libratis undique ratiunculis tuis deteriorem in
partem sciens accipias. Ha dii, quot effrenatos et sui oblitos
amor fecit, quot dedit precipites, quot cecavit ratione, quot denique crudeliter interemit! Hey mihi, video me ad extreme turpitudinis et miserie terminos reductam esse. Nam nil preter
mortem expeto. Heu, heu, absolvam rem lacrimis. Heu misere
mulieres, adversis flere in rebus solum nobis hoc est remedium
et sumper recursus ad lacrimas. Hey mihi, facta si fieri possent
infecta, semotus nunc omnis esset a me dolor et cruciatus. Merito hoc mihi evenit, fateor. Nam que istec fuit inscitia, noctu

nevertheless, once she decides to love him, she loves more passionately and more constantly than the man and outdoes him in love. The man, indeed, once he's gotten control over the woman, whom previously he had made a show of loving desperately, thinks to himself: "She'll always be in my power and under my orders; let's go hunting for another woman," and he thinks he's a conquering hero, as they say, if he keeps a list of his many girlfriends in his little black book. For once she realizes that nothing is worse for her and more harmful to her reputation and her honor than to share her love with many men and to make, as it were, a business of love, the woman will keep her love pure and uncorrupted for the man whom she has judged to be worthy of her love and to whose will she has given herself once and for all. But does the man then go ahead and thank her in accordance with her deserts? No! When he's satisfied himself and stuffed himself to his liking with every pleasure of the flesh, he despises her and deserts her.

Woe is me, I was right to think this was coming! But I knew 42 I would do it anyway; it was fated to be. How often it happens that you knowingly make the wrong choice after carefully weighing and considering something from every angle. God, how many people has love caused to loosen the reins and forget themselves! How many has it pushed over the brink, how many have had their reason darkened, how many have died cruel deaths! Alas, I see myself dragged to the extremity of shame and misery! I've nothing left to hope for but death. Ah, let me find release in tears. Alas for us women, to weep in times of suffering is our only remedy; our refuge is always in tears. Oh, if it were possible to undo what has been done, I would now be released from all suffering and torment. I got what I deserved, I admit it. What an ignorant thing to do, to leave home in the middle of the night, abandoning my parents without even a goodbye. Certainly I could have taken my pleasures at home, as

domo excedere et parentes sine salute relinquere! Nam me poteram domi oblectare, quemadmodum scio fecisse alias virgines et equales meas. O meliflua Epiphebi verba et suavia plusquam dici queat, quo me adduxistis? Persuasit tandem mihi fraude sua et caliditate quod voluit Epiphebus. O pestiferum genus hominum et supra venenum omne letale! O mentes verbis sumper dissone! O homines callidos! Quis non crederet Epiphebum, cum mihi dabat emori pro dolore animamque sibi precordiis excerpi? Aha, falaces viri, et vestra cum merce verborum mulieribus, si sapiant, aborrendi. Qualem escam et pernitiem verbis ingeritis!

43   Sed quid ego nunc mecum frustra fabulor? Reintegrari res nequit amplius, neque ulla ex parte restitui. De futuris igitur est habenda deliberatio. Ut vulgo traditum est, aqua qualis fluit excipitur. In hac re disperata forsan deus quispiam inspirabit auxilium; quod enim ab homine nequit impetrari, solet a diis implorari. Res nostra est huiusmodi. Succurrite dii, igitur; opem ferte, si quid vos humana movent. Peccasse a me fateor, tum mea tum aliena culpa. Veniam date; omnis enim pene innocentes esse statuistis penitentia. Et si id neque merita sim, attamen misericordia sinite vos flecti. Ad vexillum vestre clementie confugio. Obsecro mihi sitis presidio; hi⟨n⟩c vobis faventibus et quantum eniti potero, peccandi finem faciam. Sat est verborum. Quo fortuna trahat atque retrahat eundum est. Sed quoad Epiphebum meum opperibor?[30] Dii ad me faciant eum celeriter reducere.

I know other girls my age have done. What have you brought me to, Epiphebus, with your honeyed and indescribably sweet words? The man talked me into doing what he wanted with his clever deceits. How deadlier than poison is the pestilent human race! How perpetually at odds are its words with its real intentions! How crafty men are! Who wouldn't have believed Epiphebus when he claimed he was dying of distress and ready to tear his soul from his breast? Oh, you men are deceitful, and women, if they are wise, should refuse your merchandise of pretty words. What kind of pernicious bait is it that you dangle on your words?

But why am I wasting time talking to myself? The situation 43 is beyond repair, in whole or in part. So I have to think about the future. As the proverb says, it's all water under the bridge. In this desperate situation, perhaps some god will point out a means of help; what can't be obtained from man is generally sought from the gods. That is my plight. So come to my aid, gods! If any human needs move you, help me! I confess that I have sinned, both through my own fault and that of another. Grant me your pardon—for you've laid it down that penitence restores someone almost entirely to innocence. Even if I don't deserve it, be merciful! I take refuge under the banner of your clemency. I beg you for your protection. From this day forward, with your blessing and my own sincere efforts, I shall put an end to this sinful way of life. But enough talking. Where fortune drags us, up or down, I must follow. But how long must I wait for my Epiphebus? May the gods bring him swiftly back to me!

: VIII :

Epiphebus, Emphonius, Philogenia

44 *Ep.* Postquam hoc ittidem tibi placere, Emphoni mi, sentio, accingar. Media luce rus ibo et rogabo Gobium, de quo modo verba fecimus, uxorem ne velit Philogeniam meam. Narrabo non serio, sed quantum opus erit sciri que ad rem perficiendam pertinebunt, calide attingam.

Em. Atqui ita opus est ut aput te sis; res ista, nisi tractetur astu, in irritum evadet. Verum si hec ad effectum reddas, quemadmodum optamus, animo lubentiori, cetere deinceps virgines sui nobis copiam facient, cum intelligant nos amatrices nostras, quibus satis abundeque potiti sumus, viris colocare. Hec res quoque apud omnes pia atque sancta censebitur et effertur laudibus. Preterea huic misere dolorem, quo nunc maxime tabescit, plurimum levabis et pudorem temerarium opinione comuni sibi restitues. Profecto istuc si proficies, rumor omnis et confabulatio statim extinguetur et has ambages vulgo precides[31] taciturnitate; demum omnia istec sedabuntur.

45 *Ep.* Ita credo. Eamus igitur propere ad Philogeniam.

Em. Perge.

Ph. Audivi ne meum Epiphebum? Et certe is est. Epiphebe mi, mea voluptas et meum suavium, quam amori nostro Fortuna invidet!

Ep. Anime mi, ne metuas, res secundabunt ex sententia. Consilium nobis superi profecto dedere, quo tu mecum reviviscas et gaudeas perpetuo.

: VIII :

Epiphebus, Emphonius, Philogenia

[*The two friends approach Emphonius' house*]

Epiphebus. Since I understand that you like my plan, my dear   44
Emphonius, I'll get started on it. At noon, I'll go into the country and ask Gobius — the man we were just talking about —
whether he wants take my Philogenia as his wife. I won't tell
him the whole story; I'll just touch artfully on what he needs to
know to see the matter accomplished.

Emphonius. You'll need to keep your wits about you; the plan will
fail unless it's handled with cunning. But if you bring it off happily, as we hope, afterwards other girls will let us have our way
with them, too, as they'll know we can find husbands for our
girlfriends once we've satisfied ourselves with them. Everyone
will think your plan is pious and holy, too, and praise it to the
skies. Moreover, you'll greatly relieve this poor girl's suffering
that's wearing her down, and you'll restore her damaged reputation in public opinion. Certainly if you bring this off, all the ru-
mor-mongering and chitchat will be turned off at once, and
you'll cut short in silence all the distorted accounts that are
making the rounds, and everything will finally blow over.

Epiphebus. I think so, too; so let's go to Philogenia.   45

Emphonius. Come on. [*They enter Emphonius' house*]

Philogenia. Is that my Epiphebus? Yes, it certainly is! My darling
Epiphebus, my pleasure and my sweetness, how jealous Fortune
is of our love!

Epiphebus. My heart, don't be afraid, everything is going to turn
out the way we want. The gods above have given us a plan, I'm
certain, which will bring you back to life and make us happy together forever.

Ph. Ita sit velim et deos obsecro, sed quonam pacto me moneas.

Ep. Paucis agam, si vis.

Ph. Ita, queso; quid est?

Ep. Virum tibi dare decrevimus.

Ph. Virum?

Ep. Quocum una honeste et iucunde vitam agere tibi liceat.

Ph. Virum! Ehy mihi, disperi[32] misera!

Ep. Mane, prius ausculta rem omnem, nec me intervertas. Dotem nos opulentam tibi dabimus.

Ph. Hey michi, te malo quam dotes omnes. Tu michi dos eris amplissima atque ditissima.

Ep. Mane, mane, meliorem animum ad te recipe; tu non[33] es aput te.

Ph. Ego ne? ehy mihi!

46 *Ep.* Audi, si⟨c⟩ res, ut ex me audies, tractabitur. Postquam haud est diis placitum vel Fortune Male, quam pocius accusare licet quam deos, ut mecum esse non possis — et id quamobrem fieri nequeat intelligere te recte arbitror — inveni tibi virum et dotem. Tace, sine me commode orationi finem facere. Aput virum tuum vives summa cum laude et pudicitie corona donaberis[34] ut relique nupte que bene cum viris suis conveniunt. Nec tamen hac re nostre voluptates commoventur. Tu enim imitari disces quod mulieres bene ac provide factitarunt sumperque tucius amatore suo potite sunt, que[35] nuptui tradite sunt. Nam tum nil metuunt principio si gravide fiant; viri partum omnes predicant. Et id legislatoris auctoritate comprobatum est, ut quibus in laribus quisque natus sit, ab eisdem cognomen accipiat. Itaque latiores habenas consecuntur colloquendi, ridendi, inneundi et yocandi, cum his quos diligunt. Tu ittidem facies: in urbem venies sepius, ad forum poma, nuces, passiculas, olera,

Philogenia. I hope that will be so and I pray the gods it will be: but tell me how.

Epiphebus. I can explain it in just a few words, if you want.

Philogenia. Yes, please; what is it?

Epiphebus. We've decided to give you a husband.

Philogenia. A husband?

Epiphebus. Someone you can live with pleasantly and in decency.

Philogenia. A husband! Oh no! I'm wretched, without hope!

Epiphebus. Wait. Don't interrupt until you hear the whole plan. We'll give you a rich dowry.

Philogenia. Oh dear, I'd rather have you than all the dowries in the world! You are the greatest and richest dowry I could have.

Epiphebus. Wait, wait. Get ahold of yourself; you're not thinking straight.

Philogenia. I'm not? Oh dear!

Epiphebus. Listen to me, I'll tell you how the plan will work out. 46 Since the gods have decided (or rather Ill Fortune, whom it's better to accuse than the gods) that you can't live with me — and I think you understand why that's impossible — I've found a husband for you and a dowry. Now quiet down, let me finish my speech. You'll live irreproachably with your husband and win the crown of purity like other brides who get along well with their husbands. But this won't affect our pleasures. You'll learn to imitate what respectable, discreet women do; married women can always take a lover in greater safety. For they have nothing to be afraid of if they get pregnant; they all just claim that the child is their husband's. Their claim is buttressed by the authority of the lawgiver, in that every child takes his family name from the house where he's born. Married women have freer rein to talk, laugh, flirt and joke with the men they love. You'll do the same: you'll come into the city quite often, carrying with you fruits for the market: nuts, dried grapes, vegetables, olives, chestnuts, and other such things. As soon as I see

olivas, castaneas et cetera huiusmodi tecum ferres. Cum primum te videamus, interpellabimus de commercio; vendes scilicet. Tum aderit parasitus noster, in quem nulla inhonesti potest cadere suspicio. Is prodoctus probe inquiet:[36] 'Mulier, post me corbam hanc deferas; in proximo site sunt hedes nostre'. Tu, ut alie solent, venies cum parasito nostro. Hic tum oblectabimus; preterita[37] memorabimus. Crede mihi, hoc pacto nulla unquam amori nostro intercidere poterit calamitas. Noli adversari, obsecro, huic rei; si sic feceris, amor noster, qui nos tam cupide conciliavit, manebit cum soliditate sempiternus. Quid ais, mi Philogenia?

47   *Ph.* Ego ne adversus animi tui libidinem nil conari unquam ausa essem. Si hoc in rem nostram putas, ecce me, factura sum quod voles; tibi me et vitam meam in fidem tutellamque tuam comendo. Age ut lubet tibi. Rursus dico, quicquid iusseris faciam, et si minus gratum mihi imperaveris.

  Ep. Eya, mi Philogenia; nil unquam preter bonum et equum tibi precipiam. Nunc mihi videre sapere et me amare, cum sinis me tibi prospicere, et consilium meum vis ipsa re comprobare. Mea igitur manebis perpetuo.

  Ph. Ita cupio, misera.

  Em. Bono animo sis, Philogenia. Oppido te dii respiciunt.

48   *Ep.* Emphoni mi, rus ego statim ibo. Tu interea aput Philogeniam assiste, concinite quicquid, donec hoc agam negotii. Tu, mea Philogenia, vale et mitte solicitudinem omnem et deos deprecare, ut nobis hanc rem secundent felicitentque.

  Ph. Abi, anime mi et meum decus, in deorum fidem. Si modo non pernoctes foris, hoc placet.

you, I'll stop you for some business, and you'll sell me something, say. Then I'll send my agent, who can't be suspected of any dishonorable intentions. Instructed by me, he'll say with perfect propriety: "Woman, please follow me and bring your basket; our house is close by." You'll come with our agent, like all the women do. Then we'll enjoy ourselves here and remember our old times together. Believe me, this way, no calamity can ever sunder our love. I beg of you: don't resist this plan. If you do as I ask, our love, which has united us with such passion, will remain steadfast for ever. What do you say, my darling Philogenia?

Philogenia. I would never dare put up resistance to your passions. 47 If you think this plan is to our advantage, look, I'll go ahead and do what you want. I entrust myself and my life to your loyalty and protection. Do what you like. I'll say it again: I'll do whatever you command me, even if you order me to do something disagreeable.

Epiphebus. O my Philogenia, I would never instruct you to do something that wasn't good and fair. Now it looks like you've seen reason and that you love me, since you're letting me look out for your future and you're willing to take my advice in this matter. This way, you'll be mine forever.

Philogenia. That is what I want, wretch that I am.

Emphonius. Cheer up, Philogenia. The gods are looking out for you in every way.

Epiphebus. My dear Emphonius, I shall go at once to the country. 48 Meanwhile, stay with Philogenia, and sing a song together while I conduct the negotiations. Farewell, my Philogenia; banish every anxious thought and pray to the gods that they favor this plan of ours and make us happy.

Philogenia. Go, my sweetheart, my fine young man, and trust in the gods. I'd like it if you didn't have to spend the night away from home.

Ep. Id ne vereare; nunquam mihi gratum fuit ruri pernoctare. Oblecta te interim quantum potes et bene vale.

Ph. Tu quoque, occele mi. Redditum ad nos maturare in memoria habeas.

Ep. Habeto. Vale, Emphoni.

Em. I fortunatus et validus.

: IX :

Philogenia, Emphonius

49 *Ph.* Quid credis, Emphoni?

Em. Quid me rogas?

Ph. Animum qualem mihi futurum existimes, si meus Epiphebus tam ab humano sit alienus ut amare me desinat? Ab amplexu in primis me queritat removere. Id mihi ferendum est equo animo, cum facti necessitas id cogat; quamquam nil unquam gravius in vita mea senserim. Porro autem, si a me suum animum ob⟨a⟩lienaverit penitus, quid mihi spei reliquum est quin acerbe peritura sim? Quid ais, Emphoni?

Em. Abi, ne cogites que nunquam possent contingere.

Ph. Utinam, sed quod non, fare.

Em. Meministi cantilenam veterem? Ex vero venerando[38] derivetur.

Ph. Quam ais cantilenam?

50 *Em.* Hanc scilicet: 'Qui vere diligit et corde sincero, id nunquam potest dediscere. Amor a nobilitate si derivetur, stabilis manet perpetuo et ex animo nunquam excidit'. Cetera missa facio, ne nimis in verbis sim. Observabit Epiphebus tuus hec amoris

Epiphebus. Don't be afraid; I've never enjoyed spending the night in the country. In the meantime, amuse yourself as best you can, and farewell.

Philogenia. Fare you well too, my darling. Remember, come back as soon as possible!

Epiphebus. I'll remember. Farewell, Emphonius. [*Exits*]

Emphonius. Go with courage and good fortune.

: IX :

Philogenia, Emphonius

Philogenia. What do you think, Emphonius?   49

Emphonius. What are you asking me?

Philogenia. What sort of attitude do you think I should adopt if my Epiphebus is so beastly as to stop loving me? He's already begun trying to keep me at arm's length. I should bear this calmly, since the necessity of the case compels me to, although it's the deepest wound I've ever felt in my life. Yet if his affections should become alienated from me, what hope would I have left beyond an early and bitter death? What do you say, Emphonius?

Emphonius. Come now, don't worry about things that might never happen.

Philogenia. I hope they don't, but tell me why they won't.

Emphonius. Remember the old song? It expresses a venerable truth.

Philogenia. What song are you talking about?

Emphonius. The one that says: "He who loves truly and with heart 50
sincere, can never unlearn love. If love springs from the noble heart it remains forever constant and will never depart from the soul."[8] I'll omit the rest for the sake of brevity. Your Epiphebus will treasure this monument of love carved in his heart forever

monumenta in corde sculpta perpetuo et te cum vita simul amare desinet. Neque scio si mortuus non amet te. Si enim animorum immortalitati datur ut, que[39] iuncti corporis cognoverint, separati remi⟨ni⟩sci possint, non dubito quin ubi mortem obieritis, ambo copulandi sitis ut una maiestatem deorum et orbes sidereos mundique machinam universam contemplemini. Sic futurum est, tibi persuade.

Ph. Me miseram, bene ita dixti ut mihi maximam partem calamitatum mearum substulleris.

Em. Sed parendum est quidem Epiphebo, qui abiens ut concinemus imperavit.

Ph. Age ut libet.

Em. Ego accipio. Note grandes erunt mee dumtaxat, tu acutis et superacutis utere et ex multis simul adiunctis consonis et dissonis armonias efficias.

Ph. Hac in re bona fide utar.

: X :

Epiphebus, Zabinus, Gobius

51 *Ep.* Dii boni, quantum ad felicitatem michi esse putabo adiectum, si quemadmodum cupio res ista secundabit! Confingam omnia probe. Ubi in rem tuam sit, Epiphebe, ne vereare fallere aut mentiri. At si de falso postea arguaris, pro clipeo vultum obicias audacter, nec pudeat aut id refellas aut id ioco te fecisse dicas. At quid[40] si res gravis sit quam dolis in quempiam obtrudis? Ferrat ille equo animo si velit, cum tu plus tibi commodi quam sibi incommodi ea re comparaveris. Si clamitet indigne et impu-

and will only stop loving you when his life ends. And I'm not sure he'll stop loving you even then. For if souls are immortal and can remember in their disembodied state what they knew in the body, I've no doubt that when you die, you'll both be united in contemplation of the majesty of the gods, the starry spheres, and the universal movement of the earth. This is the way it will be; convince yourself of it.

Philogenia. Oh dear, you've spoken so well that you've freed me from most of my afflictions.

Emphonius. But really, we should do as Epiphebus bade us do when he left: let's sing a song together.

Philogenia. As you wish.

Emphonius. I'll begin. I'll take the low notes and you take the higher notes; you can make a melody by adding at the same time consonant and dissonant tones.

Philogenia. I'll do my best.

: X :

Epiphebus, Zabinus, Gobius

[*On a farm near Epiphebus' country estate*]

Epiphebus. [*To himself*] Good gods, if this plan will only succeed as 51 I want, how much more happiness I shall have! I'll make a fine fiction of it all. When it's in your interest, Epiphebus, don't be afraid to deceive and lie. If you're accused of lying afterwards, just brazen it out, and don't be ashamed to rebut the charge or say you did it as a joke. So what if it's a serious burden that you're palming off on someone with your deceitful tricks? Let him resign himself if he wants to — it will be more helpful to you than it will be harmful to him. If he shouts that your be-

denter factum, surdo tibi fac narret fabulam. Ubi clamitando defessus erit, mutescit tandem. Sed qui rescierint num te culpent? Credis et flagitiosum et improbum dicant? Ohe, aliquis fortasse bonis insuetus detrahere damnabit id prave factum; non autem id omnes credent. Vah, in re omni si sumper velis fame parcere et omnia que feceris uno ore laudari,[41] res tua male se habebit. Utilitatem ego plerumque honestati et rumori plebis anteponendam censeo, quamquam sit in *Officiis* traditum alterum sine altero esse non posse. Sed video ne quos mihi optabam dari? Et certe ipsi sunt. Adibo.

52 *Za.* Sarmenta illa illinc auferri bis iam pueris iussi; quod si tercio iussero, vapulabunt.

Go. Noli irasci, nunc redibunt et ea quovis exportabunt. Sed miror cur iste plante nil pullulent, nec ista vitis in ulmo adducta rite capita sua potest extendere. Ei namque, ut opinor, impedimento sunt ramusculi.

Za. Eos igitur abscide.

Go. Faciam ut iubes. Qualem nobis baccum dabit hec vitis propagatio, si adoleverit ut spero.

Za. Diligenter igitur cura, ne quid eis noceat.

Go. Aliud manda. Ego tantum in his oblectabo me; nam caritudo potus preterita, cum mihi in mentem venit, terret adeo me, ut nequeam collendis in vitibus satiari. Sed quemdam audio in umeto nostro cursitare. Hem, si satis cerno Epiphebus est. Et certe ipsus est.

Ep. Salvete.

Go. Salvus quoque sis.

havior has been low and shameful, stop your ears and let him tell his tale. He'll finally shut up when he gets tired of shouting. Do you think the people who find out will blame you? Do you think they'll call you a contemptible blackguard? Oh, there will be some detractor, perhaps, unused to the ways of fine gentlemen, who will condemn it as a depraved act, but not everyone will believe it. Bah, if you want to save your reputation in everything all the time and have everything you do receive a chorus of praise, your affairs will end up badly. My view is that utility should be put before honor and the chatter of common folk—whatever Cicero's view in the *De officiis* may be, that you can't have the one without the other.[9] But look, it's just the people I was hoping to meet; it's them. I'll go over to them.

Zabinus. I've told the boys twice now to clear off that underbrush;   52 if I have to tell them a third time, they'll get a beating.

Gobius. Don't be angry, they'll come back now and take it anywhere you want. But I'm surprised that these seedlings aren't sprouting and that these vines haven't been trained onto the elm so they can grow their buds properly. I think the little branches are blocking them.[10]

Zabinus. Then prune them.

Gobius. I'll do so as you say. Planting this vineyard will give us a nice little wine, if they grow as I hope

Zabinus. Be careful, then, not to harm them.

Gobius. You don't need to tell me. I love working in the vineyard above all things. In fact, when I think of the shortage of drink we've had in the past, I get so scared that I can't get enough of pruning these vines. But I hear somebody running around in our vineyard. Ah, if I'm not mistaken, it's Epiphebus. Yes, it's certainly he.

Epiphebus. Greetings.

Gobius. Greetings to you, too.

Za. O salve Epiphebe. Quid tibi est hiis regionibus negocii?

53 *Ep.* Nichil, sed deambulandi causa urbem egressus fueram primo; dumque eo imprudens cogitando, ut fit, tandem me sensi abesse longius ab urbe et propinquior vobis. Ego tam mecum: 'Zabinum atque Gobium volo saltem salutare'. Itaque veni vos visere.

Za. Bene fecisti, Epiphebe. Nam si otii nobis quicquam daretur, tecum in urbe sepenumero essemus. Sed vidistin opera nostra atque sata?

Ep. Vidi et modo ea contemplabar. Ita me dii ament, hunc agellum coluistis mirum in modum. Heya, pergite ut cepistis; nam hoc pacto implebitur vobis orea et cellaria.

Za. Diis gratia quod nil nobis est gratius quam curare ut agellus iste melior efficiatur in dies, oliveta componere, cetera viridaria ordine conservare.

Ep. Bene facitis. Sed audite paucis: cultus ruralis, ut vos optime noscere arbitror, hominum copiam exigit.

Za. Sic est.

54 *Ep.* Vos pro virili satis agitis, tu Zabine cum uxore tua et cum Gobio fratre. Sed si aperte[42] dicendum est, nequibitis tamen huic predio suppetere. Quamobrem ego mecum meditabar rem vobis utilem et honestam et cuique optabilem.

Za. Quid est expedi.

Ep. Uxorem Gobio ut daremus.

Za. Vellem quidem bonam et opulentam sibi dare, vel pocius duas.

Ep. Quid ais, Gobi?

Go. Ego iam dudum id desidero.

Zabinus. Oh, hello, Epiphebus. What business do you have in these parts?

Epiphebus. None, really. I had just left the city and was out for a walk, and while I was daydreaming, as happens, I realized I had ended up rather far from the city and quite close to you. So I said to myself, "I'll go say hello to Zabinus and Gobius at least." So I've come to see you.

Zabinus. You did well, Epiphebus. If we had more free time, we'd be with you more often in the city. But do you see what we've been building and planting?

Epiphebus. I did see; I was just looking at it. By the gods, you've done a marvelous job with this little plot of land. Just continue the way you've started and you'll fill up your granaries and cellars.

Zabinus. Thanks be to the gods, because there's nothing we like more than taking care of this little plot and making it better every day: laying out olive groves, keeping the other gardens in good order.

Epiphebus. You've done well. But listen, agriculture requires a lot of men, as I'm sure you know very well.

Zabinus. Yes, it does.

Epiphebus. You do as much as you can, Zabinus, with your wife and with your brother Gobius. But if I may speak frankly, you're not going to be able to keep up this piece of land. So I've been thinking of a plan you'll find useful and honorable, one that anyone would wish for.

Zabinus. Explain what you have in mind.

Epiphebus. My idea is to get a wife for Gobius.

Zabinus. I'd like to give him a fine, rich wife too, maybe even two of them.

Epiphebus. What do you say, Gobius?

Gobius. I've wanted this for a long time now.

Ep. Mane, mane. Ad manum tibi habeo ydoneam et quam vere optares.

Go. Dotis quantum, ut rei domestice prius consulamus?

Ep. Mi Gobbi, ordinem pervertis in uxore diligenda. Fortassis rogasti sana ne sit an insana?

Go. Ego prius attigi quod mihi maiorem (ut aiunt) affert pruriginem.

55 *Ep.* Non recte rogasti, Gobi. Quatuor in muliere querenda sunt, cum nubere vult: primum quam sapiat, quam honesta et pudica sit; porro quam formosa; tertio, unde origines habeat et que affinitas; postremo heris quantum ferrat secum. Tu a novissimis accepisti: caude frena ponere. Sed hoc tibi responsum habeas: dos ampla est.

Go. Nil adhuc intelligo. Rem apertius fare.

Ep. Primum tu responde michi: dotis quantum vis tibi dari, cetera modo complaceant?

Go. Roga fratrem, cuius consilio maritus fieri volo.

Ep. Recte dicis, nam maior est natu et, pace tua dixerim, his rebus peritior; quare secum facilius conveniam. Dic tu, Zabine, quantum vobis dari vultis.

Za. Epiphebe, prius ex te scire volo vel cupio, mulier ista unde sit et cuius. Post istuc veniemus.

Ep. Placet istuc principio. Ut dillucide vobis rem expediam, virgo ista annos sedecim vix nata est, succiplena et valida, omnibus laboribus assueta.

Za. Atque aput nos sic opportet.

Epiphebus. Well, just hold on, then. I've got somebody available who's perfect for you and whom you'll find really attractive.

Gobius. How big a dowry does she have? Let's put the interests of the household first.

Epiphebus. My dear Gobius, you've got this business of loving a wife backwards. But perhaps you're asking whether she was healthy or unhealthy?

Gobius. I was scratching my biggest itch first, as they say.

Epiphebus. You're asking your questions in the wrong order, 55 Gobius. One should inquire about four things when you want to marry a woman. First, is she prudent, honest and well-behaved? Second, is she pretty? Third, who are her ancestors and relations? And finally, how big an inheritance does she bring with her? You've started from the last question: you're putting the bridle on the horse's tail. But here's the answer to your question: she has a large dowry.

Gobius. I still don't understand. Tell me more clearly what you mean.

Epiphebus. First, tell me this: how much of a dowry are you looking for, assuming the rest is to your liking?

Gobius. Ask my brother; I want to be married with his advice.

Epiphebus. You're right, for your elder brother, if I may say so, has more experience in these matters, so I'll come to an agreement more easily with him. You tell me, Zabinus, how much are you two looking for?

Zabinus. Epiphebus, first of all I really want to know where this woman comes from and whose daughter she is. Then we can go on.

Epiphebus. This is an excellent start. Let me explain the thing to you clearly: the girl is just sixteen, she's juicy and in good health, and she's used to work of every kind.

Zabinus. In our house, she'll need to be.

56 *Ep.* Anus quedam, mihi matertera eam educavit a parvula; ex oppido Castigii eam abduxit. Modo cum sit matura viro et esse periculum intelligam si diutius virgo domi innupta maneat, ne, ut humanum est,[43] animum ad libidinem possit flectere, studeo eam viro copulare. Quare prima luce vos in urbe recipietis et virgo, si, ut spero, vobis erit forma et etate complacita, despondebitur. Nam scio dote omni contenti eritis.

Za. Mi Epiphebe, certiores redde quid dotis.

Ep. Ymo tu dotem postula.

Za. Ego decem aureos postulo.

Ep. Ne metue, dabuntur tibi, ego spondeo.

Za. Item lectulum cum ornamentis accessoriis.

Ep. Habetis.

Za. Item palium ut secum ferrat virgo, ut id aurum aput nos absolutum maneat.

Ep. Et hoc dabitur tibi. Satin hec sunt tibi?

Za. Satis, nisi quod Gobius velit. Res enim sua agitur.

Go. Ego nil preter uxorem volo.

Za. Modo vellet uxorem in cubiculum sibi sua sine opera ductam esse.

57 *Ep.* Quid mirum? Et tu fortassis istuc etatis idem cupiebas? Et hoc adolescentibus commune vitium, ut cum muliere prius ad rem quam ad verba se conferre velint et omnes moras ferunt graviter. Tum et minus miror si gaudere adeo accipit, nam uxoris sponsio et ductio, dignitatis adeptio et e vinculis liberatio maximam letitiam et gaudium pro ceteris rebus solent afferre. Quid ais[44] modo, Gobi?

Go. Epiphebe mi, animo mihi nil insedere potest tristitie.

Epiphebus. An old aunt of mine raised her from the time she was a 56
little girl, and she's recently brought her from the town of
Casteggio.[11] She's now ready for a husband, and as I know
there is some danger, should she remain at home an unwed virgin, that she might turn her thoughts to the pleasures of the
flesh, as is only human, I'm eager for her to have a husband. So
come in to the city at dawn tomorrow, and if the girl is to your
liking in beauty and age, as I hope, we'll fix the engagement. I'm
sure you'll be entirely satisfied with the dowry.

Zabinus. My dear Epiphebus, let us know what the dowry is.

Epiphebus. No, no — you tell me how much you want.

Zabinus. I want ten gold pieces.

Epiphebus. Don't worry, you'll get them, I promise.

Zabinus. And a bed with all the fancy accessories.

Epiphebus. It's yours.

Zabinus. Plus, the girl should bring her own cloak with her, so we
don't have to touch the money.

Epiphebus. You'll have that too. Is that enough for you?

Zabinus. Yes, unless Gobius wants something. It's his business, after all.

Gobius. I just want a wife.

Zabinus. He just wants a wife brought into the bedroom without
any effort on his part.

Epiphebus. That's no surprise. You probably wanted the same thing 57
at his age. This is a common vice with young men; they want to
get down to business with a woman before talking to her, and
they're annoyed at any delays. But it's not so surprising that he's
so happy: engagement and marriage to a wife, finding a position
in life, and being freed from jail are usually thought of as the
things that bring the most happiness and joy, beyond all other
things. What do you say now, Gobius?

Gobius. My dear Epiphebus, I couldn't be happier.

Ep. Et quidem sapienter. Sed, Gobi mi, cum videris Philogeniam. . . .

Go. Nomen placet.

Ep. Vix eris aput te pro gaudio. Crede michi, est facie egregia et
venusta, bonisque morata moribus. Heya Gobi, dabo tibi puel-
lulam bellam, lepedulam, facetam et lactiniam, tam tenellam ut
eam ungue scinderes. Et mihi quid gratie?

58 *Go.* Ego profecto primum edum qui de grege nostro nascetur, tibi
dono dabo.

Ep. Vide quid agas; perliberalis es nimium.

Go. Sic erit.

Ep. Ego gratias habeo et cum dabis referam. Quid restat amplius?

Go. Nichil.

Ep. Crastina die vos in urbem expectabo. Ibi bonis auspiciis bona
conficientur.

Za. Veniemus scilicet.

Go. Nox ista etas mihi videbitur.

Za. Abi, puer importune, ad ne ante mensem ista uxore satura-
bere ut quocumque aspicias, uxores decem tibi videantur cer-
nere.

Go. Sine me; hoc tantum mihi cure sit.

59 *Ep.* Iam advesperascit; tempus monet ut in urbem me recipiam.
Valete et parate vos illares in nuptiis. Tu autem, Gobi, exorna
te, parumper expolies. Ego enim, cum aput Philogeniam fuero,
de te continuo predicabo atque sapientiam, formam et valitudi-
nem tuam laudabo.

Go. Ha, parce tamen et minus quam verum sit, ut cum me viderit
se plus lucri fecisse existimet quam animo conceperit.

Ep. Mitte me. Ego ista probe caleo.

Za. Abi sospes.

Epiphebus. And you are wise to be so. But, my Gobius, when you get a look at Philogenia . . .

Gobius. Nice name.

Epiphebus. . . . you'll be beside yourself with joy. Believe me, she's unusually good-looking, a delightful girl, very well-behaved. Really, Gobius, I am about to give you a real doll, a pleasant little thing with a great sense of humor, white as milk, so soft you could cut her with your fingernail. So what favor are you going to do me?

Gobius. I'm going to make you a present of the first kid that's born 58 in our flock.

Epiphebus. Careful; don't be too generous.

Gobius. It's already decided.

Epiphebus. Thank you. I'll reciprocate. Is there anything else?

Gobius. Nothing.

Epiphebus. Then I'll expect you tomorrow in the city. If the auspices are good, we'll bring this good business to a conclusion.

Zabinus. We'll be there, you can count on it.

Gobius. This night will seem like an age to me.

Zabinus. Be quiet, you impatient lad; before a month is up you'll be so fed up with this wife that wherever you look, you'll swear you see ten wives.

Gobius. Let me alone; it's my business.

Epiphebus. It's getting dark already; I have to be getting back to the 59 city. Farewell and get ready to enjoy yourself at the nuptials. Gobius, make sure you dress properly and try to clean yourself up. When I see Philogenia, I'll give her a long sermon about you and praise your wisdom, beauty and sound health.

Gobius. Oh, don't lay it on too thick: tell her less than the truth, so that when she sees me she'll think she's made a better bargain than she'd imagined.

Epiphebus. Leave it to me. I know all about things like this.

Zabinus. Keep safe!

Go. Et fortunatus.

Ep. Profecto res ista, ut opinor, diis faventibus in portum traduce-
tur. Agrestem hunc hominem coniciam in nuptias, sed hoc est
opere precium pro virgine dari mulierem huic frustro carnis oc-
culato. Nunc quam primum in urbem venero. Serviam lenam
adoribor et huic rei magistram efficiam. Perdocta est probe; iam
diu simulare et dissimulare didicit peregregius atque struere fal-
latias et ridicula figmenta.

60 *Za.* Gobi, postquam uxorem cras ducturus es, id convictis necessitudine nobis indicare officium est, ut parati sint in nuptiis
utque suo consilio etiam ista res agatur. Abi dum, tu illis nuncia
cras in urbe nobiscum ut veniant.

Go. Sic faciam. Tu interea paratum sit fac.

Za. Cum veneris, poteris discumbere et sorbilare.

Go. Eo igitur.

Za. Heus, heus pueri, mensam tendile et parate omnia!

: XI :

Servia, Irtia, Epiphebus

61 *Ser.* Credin tu, Irtia, questum nostrum in dies augeri posse, si per-
gamus facere quemadmodum occepimus?

Ir. Quamobrem hec dicis?

Ser. Quamobrem, rogas! Quare perliberales nimium sumus.
Nostre salutis inimica quidem est liberalitas; nullius fidei credas
pollicitationi promissionive unde non est acquiescendum. Tu-

Gobius. And good luck!

Epiphebus. [*Aside*] I think this ship is really going to come into port, with the gods' blessing. I'll push this country-boy into marriage, but it's worth it to pass off as a virgin an experienced woman to this hunk of flesh with two eyes in front. I've got to get to the city as soon as possible. I'll go see the procuress Servia and put her in charge of the business. She has lots of experience, and learned a long time ago to pretend and cover things up in the most amazing way; to think up tricks and ridiculous imaginary situations. [*Exits*]

Zabinus. Gobius, since you're getting married tomorrow, it's our 60 duty to talk to our friends here so that they may prepare for the nuptials and so that this matter may be done with their advice. So go tell them to come with us into the city tomorrow.

Gobius. I'll do it. Meanwhile, you get everything ready.

Zabinus. When you get back, you can relax and have something to drink.

Gobius. I'm on my way.

Zabinus. Hey, you boys! Set the table and get everything ready!

: XI :

Servia, Irtia, Epiphebus

[*At the brothel of Servia and Irtia*]

Servia. Irtia, do you really think we can increase our profit day af- 61 ter day if we keep on doing what we've been doing?

Irtia. Why are you saying this?

Servia. Why, you ask? Because we are much too generous. Liberality is the enemy of our well-being; you don't need to provide services to anyone whose promises and offers are untrustwor-

tum est sermone proverbium fidei spiritum non appenditur. Profecto deinceps hinc nullus abibit qui non relinquat aput nos sui memoriam, aut aurum aut pignera.

62 *Ir.* Recte facies; istuc quidem volui tibi dicere. Abeunt hinc isti iuvenes ingrati, petulantes et superbi: nos irrident postea, si gratis voluptatem suam expleverint; aut nos[45] inutiles aut non, semper odio summo nos prosecuntur. Quare lege nostra utamur: cum aurum accepimus, tum gratias habeamus. Merces enim remissa aut dono data vitam profecto facit breviorem; nec mihi mollestum est quod senescam[46] sed quod erudiri nunc accipio. Heya, qui volet veniat; nisi expilatus et explumatus usque ad cutem domum redeat, alio me nomine appelles.

Ep. Sed video optime quam volebam; hem, item alteram que mihi non minus est opportuna. Eas adibo. Salvete iuvenum salus et regimen et reipublice maximum solamen et necessarium!

Ser. Et tu quoque lepedule, salve.

Ir. Bonam in rem hic adductus sis. Quid est negotii?

Ep. Nimis propere postulas; sine paululum ad me spiritum revocare, post narrabo ordine cur ad vos ventum sit et quod a vobis velim.

Ser. Recte dicis.[47]

63 *Ep.* Mi Servia, relictis preambulis que vulgariter ab impetrare volentibus premitti solent, res hec ad vos venire me compellit, quam brevi vos explicabo. Virginem amavi quandam atque maximo labore, summis vigiliis infinitisque periculis tandem ea potitus sum. Aput me eandem accepi clam suis parentibus; tum quesita est urbe tota. Ego in suspicionem adductus sum presidi.

thy. A reliable proverb says that a trusting spirit doesn't get paid. Certainly nobody should be getting out of here from now on who doesn't leave behind with us some memento of himself, either gold or guarantees.

Irtia. Well done! In fact, that's just what I wanted to say to you. 62 These young men who leave here are ungrateful, willful and proud: they make fun of us afterwards if they've gotten their pleasure for free, and they go on despising us whether we're useless to them or not. So let's apply our rule: we'll show gratitude once we have our gold. The woman who relaxes her grip on her merchandise or gives it away is just shortening her life; and what annoys me is not getting old but the thought that I'm only now learning my craft. Well, let him come who will, but don't call me Irtia if he doesn't go back home thoroughly plucked and skinned like a chicken!

Epiphebus. [*Aside*] Now that one is just what I'm looking for, and the other one will be no less useful. I'll accost them. [*To the women*]: Good day to you, saviors and governors of youth, you who are the greatest and indispensable solace of our state!

Servia. And good day to you too, my little charmer.

Irtia. You've come here for a good reason, no doubt. What's your business?

Epiphebus. You're going too fast; let me catch my breath, and I'll tell you in proper order why I've come to you and what I want.

Servia. Give it to us straight.

Epiphebus. My dear Servia, leaving aside the long preamble which 63 people who want to ask for something commonly begin with, this is the business that compels me to come to you. I can explain it to you briefly. I fell in love with a certain maiden and finally got my way with her after the greatest trouble, long vigils and infinite perils. I brought her to my house without her parents' knowledge, and then there was a search for her through the whole city. I came under suspicion with the governor.

Ubi hoc intellexi, cum salute scilicet nostra aput me diutius residere non posse, eam ad equalem traduxi. Latuit tum complures dies; porro, ubi rescitum id fuit, ad alium est traducta, item ad alium. Hoc itaque pacto plurimi, ut fit et vos quoque scire arbitror, in ea se oblectaverunt.

Ser. Perge.

64　*Ep.* Ubi ego vidi virginem hanc pernoctare opportere modo aput hunc, modo aput illum et pluribus usui turpiter esse, mecum ipse cogitavi eam ab hac turpitudine penitus removere, postquam mei causa pudoris terminos excesserat.

Ser. Epiphebe mi, piam et sanctam rem aggressus es et quanquam id arti nostre minime conducat, attamen nequeo summa cum virtute quid efficeris quin collaudem. Sed perge.

Ep. Ausculta ergo. In suburbiis scis esse michi predia.

Ser. Credo.

Ep. His agrum contiguum collit homo quidam, agrestis, truculentus et in dumis assuetus, cuique sumper in opere vita fuit. Huic est frater minor, qui sine uxore vixit hactenus; hunc adii. Denique, ut paucis utar verbis meis, effici ut vellit hanc pro uxore sibi dari. Ego autem sibi finxi virginem hanc a parvula educatam esse aput meam materteram et nunc velle eam nuptui dare. Tu vero scis mihi nec esse materteram nec amitam, nec genus aliquid mulierum. Quamobrem ad te confugio, mea Servia, et obsecro ut hac in re michi sis fautrix et adiutrix, si modo quicquam de te sperare licet.

Ser. Vere cupio. Tu instrue qui factura sim.

65　*Ep.* Recte dicis. Domum meam perge cum Irtia. Tu simulabis mihi materteram esse et virginem educasse parvulam. Tu autem

When I found this out, since the girl couldn't stay with me any longer without endangering us both, I took her to the house of a friend my age. She hid there for several days; then, when that hiding place was found out she was taken to another friend, then to yet another. In this way a lot of men amused themselves at her expense, as usually happens, and I imagine you also know something about that.

Servia. Go on.

Epiphebus. When I saw that this girl was obliged spend her nights 64 now with this one, now with that one, and had been used shamefully by a number of men, I decided to get her out of this disgraceful situation, as it had been my fault that she violated the norms of common decency.

Servia. My dear Epiphebus, you've undertaken a pious and holy cause, and I can't but praise your virtuous deeds, even if they tend little to the profit to our profession. But go on.

Epiphebus. Then listen. You are aware that I have estates in the country nearby?

Servia. I believe so.

Epiphebus. There's a man who farms the field next to mine, a rough, gruff fellow used to living among the brambles, a real workhorse. He has a younger brother who hasn't married yet; it's him I approached. To make a long story short, I finally induced him to take my girl as his wife. I pretended that she was a girl who had been raised by my aunt since she was a little girl, and that my aunt now wanted to marry her off. You know that I don't have any aunts on either side or female relatives like that. So I've had recourse to you, dear Servia; I'm begging you to help and support me in this situation, supposing I have any right to expect something of you.

Servia. I'll gladly help. Tell me, what should I do?

Epiphebus. Right. Come to my house with Irtia. You will pretend 65 that you are my aunt and that you've raised the girl from child-

247

Irtia, virginis te necessariam dices. Res componetur ita calide vestra auctoritate, prudentia, consilio et industria ut melius neque pulcrius quicquam optare possem. Vestris postea pro meritis vobis erit merces dignissima et priusquam rem istam aggrediamini, vos absolvam et explebo ex sententia.

Ser. Epiphebe mi, hic tibi adsumus, tuo arbitratu obtemperature dudum. Rebus tuis fuimus use tam familiariter et liberaliter et tuum ingenium ita novimus ut non vereamur abs te sine munere unquam abire posse.

Ep. At quidem, prius quam ad rem hanc attingam, me vobis gratum esse cognoscetis. Sed properate domum meam; nam hii rustici babillones hic aderunt fortassis de improviso. Interea virginem instruite, monete quid actura sit et eius animum flectatis ad nuptias.

Ser. Abi deambulatum et animo obsequare. Rem istam nobis mitte; quo cupis eo cuncta producemus integerrime. Nos ad eam pergimus. Tu tibi quid vis carpe solatis.

Ep. Ite cum diis optimis.

Ser. Heus, Epiphebe, nomen virginis quod est, ut sciam salutare?

Ep. Philogenia.

Ser. Sat est.

: XII :

Servia, Irtia, Philogenia

66 *Ser.* Eamus Irtia, Epiphebus noster tantum de rebus est meritus ut nullum in nos sibi beneficium claudi merito possit. Cum putas hoc iubet† Inter tot enim facinora que nobis faventibus et

hood. You, Irtia, will say that you're one of the girl's relations.
With your strong support, prudence, wise counsel and hard
work the matter will be settled more prettily and better than I
could have ever hoped. You'll have a fine reward for your services, and before you begin, I'll pay my debts to you and satisfy
you as you desire.

Servia. My dear Epiphebus, we're here for you, we'll do whatever
you command. We've had the liberal and friendly use of your
resources in the past and we know your character; we have no
fear that you would leave us without some reward.

Epiphebus. Indeed, before we start in on the plan, you'll get a taste
of my gratitude. But hurry to my house; these rustic simpletons
will be there any minute. Meanwhile, clue the girl in, tell her
what she's going to do and talk her round to the marriage.

Servia. Go take a walk and enjoy yourself; leave everything to us.
We'll bring the whole thing off exactly as you wish. We'll go see
her. You just have a good time.

Epiphebus. Go, and may the gods be with you!

Servia. Oh, one thing, Epiphebus: what's the name of the girl, so I
can address her?

Epiphebus. Philogenia.

Servia. That's all I needed to know.

: XII :

Servia, Irtia, Philogenia

[Servia and Irtia approach Epiphebus' house]

Servia. Let's go, Irtia, our Epiphebus has earned so much of our   66
consideration that we can hardly in justice deny him any service
we can perform. Making him happy is also a pious duty.[12]
Among the many wicked deeds that are perpetrated daily with

249

iuvantibus cottidie perpetrantur, aliquando debet esse locus virtuti et misericordie. Preterea intermissione nulla si male sumper
agas, quis deus hoc ferre poterit? Nobis plerumque reconciliari
deos traditum est, si de milibus unum pure,[48] pie, sancte et incorrupte designaverimus.

Ir. Propera confabulando, nec me detineas in via.

Ser. Ha, queso, ne sis irata; sanguinem suavem plurimum ad te
valere sinas. Heus, heus!

Ph. Quis tu que pepulisti fores?

Ser. Servia, Epiphebo gratissima et Irtia Epiphebi de grege primaria.

Ph. Vos intro ferte pedes.

Ser. Salve multum, Philogenia!

Ir. Philogenia, salve!

Ph. Et dii vos felicitent et vobis optata afferant.

67 *Ser.* Epiphebus nos hic venire iussit. Ait se tibi virum hodie daturum. Et quare rem omnem tenere te arbitror, desinam.

Ph. Scio et me tedet, sed postquam diis sic placet, Epiphebi mei
non adversabor libidini. Hei michi, non est a superis datum ut
Epiphebum meum amplexibus mihi liceat perfovere perpetuo.
Dii me in his rebus adversis donent fortitudinem, et omnem
procellam et fortune vim superare me faciant animi magnitudine et pacientia.

Ser. Mea Philogenia, sumper dii fuere bonis presidio et iuste deprecantibus, quare bono sis animo. Sed istuc est sapere, mi Philogenia, si que preter spem et equum eveniunt, fortiter feras, et

our help and encouragement, there ought to be room at some
point for an act of virtue and mercy. If you are always doing
wicked things without intermission, what god is going to put
up with it? There's a tradition that you can reconcile yourself
with the gods if you can point to just one out of a thousand
acts that has been done from the purest motives, with piety and
holiness.

Irtia. Pick up the pace a bit while you're talking; don't hold me up.

Servia. Oh please, don't get angry; bad blood isn't good for you.
Hello! Hello! [*Knocking*]

Philogenia. Who's knocking on my door?

Servia. Servia, a very dear friend of Epiphebus, and Irtia, one of
Epiphebus' closest companions.

Philogenia. Come in.

Servia. Hello, hello, Philogenia!

Irtia. Hello, Philogenia!

Philogenia. May the gods grant you happiness and bring you what
you desire.

Servia. Epiphebus told us to come here. He said that today you 67
are to be given a husband. As I imagine you are already acquainted with the plan, I'll say no more.

Philogenia. I know the plan and it sickens me, but since it has so
pleased the gods, I won't oppose the desires of my Epiphebus.
Alas, it was not granted by the gods that I should make my
nest forever in Epiphebus' arms. But may the gods give me
strength in these hard circumstances; may they allow me to
overcome every storm and blow of fortune with patience and
strength of character.

Servia. My dear Philogenia, the gods always take care of the good
and those who call upon them in a just cause, so be of good
cheer. But this is wisdom, Philogenia: whenever something
unhoped-for and unjust happens, bear it bravely, and if necessary, adapt your mind to it without calling on the support of

ubi quando opus sit, animum sine deorum suffragio flexeris. Heya, non sumper decet a diis auxilium implorari, cum nobis rationem cum virtute dedere atque nobis infundere animos, qui possunt omnem fortune metum et tempestatem evadere seque ipsos cohibere et sensibus dominari. Sed si tu quoque feceris ut morate mulieres scite quoque provideque facere solent, semper gaudebis Epiphebo.

Ph. Tu consules; ego obsequar.

68 *Ser.* Sic volo, ut commodati[49] simus temporibus. Nunc censeo, mi Philogenia, ut animum prepares ad nuptias; prius autem, ut a maioribus institutum est, adhibis nostri vicinatus pontificem, cui errata tua pariter et debita sponte fateberis.

Ph. Age, fiat.

Ser. Eamus. I pre, Philogenia.

Ph. Eo.

Ser. Sequere, Irtia.

Ir. Sequor.

Ser. At tu, Irtia, precurre ut eum moneas ut paratus sit audire Philogeniam.

Ir. Fiat.

Ser. Mi Philogenia, tecum repete memoria quicquid peccaveris. Id ne vereare pontifici propalare. Sic opus est. Ubi animam peccatis levaris,[50] levius corpus efficies et omnia bonis auspiciis secundabunt.

Ph. Recte consulis. Faciam.

the gods. Yes, it's not always fitting to ask the gods' help: they have given us reason and the practice of virtue, pouring into us the rational souls that can escape from every threat of fortune and every tempest, that can exercise control over ourselves and can master our senses. But if you will just do what other fine ladies commonly do, and act with intelligence and foresight, you'll be able to enjoy Epiphebus' love forever.

Philogenia. Tell me what to do; I'll obey.

Servia. I want us to be ready for all contingencies. I think now, 68
Philogenia, that you you should prepare your heart for this marriage; but first, in accordance with ancestral usage, you should seek out our local priest and confess freely your venial and mortal sins.

Philogenia. All right, come on.

Servia. Let's go. You go first, Philogenia. [*They depart for the church*]

Philogenia. I'm going.

Servia. Follow, Irtia.

Irtia. I'm following.

Servia. On second thought, Irtia, you run ahead and tell the priest to get ready to hear Philogenia's confession.

Irtia. All right. [*Runs ahead*]

Servia. My Philogenia, try to remember all your sins. Don't be afraid to make a clean breast of everything to the priest. It's necessary. When you lighten your soul of sins, you make your body lighter too, and you'll have the gods on your side in everything.

Philogenia. That's good advice. I'll do it.

: XIII :

Irtia, Prodigius sacerdos, Servia, Philogenia

69   *Ir.* Hem, hic adsunt tibi, Prodigii, viden?

    Pr. Video et paratus sum. Recipiam me in templum. Tu iube ad me veniat.

    Ir. Faciam; huc properate.

    Ser. Quantum quominus† importuna est hec mulier.

    Ph. Idem michi videtur.

    Ir. Prodigius expectat intus. Philogenia, ad eum ambula.

    Ph. Ambulo. Dii, quorum sub imperio sunt omnia, quique benigne respicitis mortales, obsecro mihi mentem meliorem date, quo possim sumper maiestatem vestram cultu vero, caste et incorrupte contemplari. Salve, pontifex, iura deorum observans ac distribuens, adsum hic tibi, tum ex animo, tum inconsulte prava peccatrix.

70   *Pr.* Principio[51] deo flectas genua, Philogenia. Diis eris acceptissima si te peccasse peniteat.

    Ph. Certe penitet.

    Pr. Hic recte vivendi modus est, velle se diis expurgare. Primum responde. Estne animus tibi in eandem vitam item denuo recadere?

    Ph. Non profecto.

    Pr. Probe dicis. Sed credin mandatis iuris pontificis?

    Ph. Credo.

: XIII :

Irtia; Prodigius, priest; Servia; Philogenia

[In front of the church]

Irtia. Look, do you see them coming, Prodigius?   69

Prodigius. I see them and I'm ready. I'll go into the church. Tell
  them to come to me.

Irtia. I shall. Quick, get inside!

Servia. [*Walking behind with Philogenia*] That woman is a pain in
  the neck.

Philogenia. I think so too.

Irtia. [*Going back to Philogenia*] Prodigius is waiting for you inside.
  Philogenia, go to him.

Philogenia. I shall. [*Enters*] O gods, who rule all things and who
  look down on us mortals with kindly eye, please give me a
  better frame of mind, so that I may always gaze upon your majesty with true reverence, chastity and purity. Hello, father, you
  who bind and loose in accordance with the laws of the gods,
  I've come to you as one who has sinned gravely, sometimes con-
  sciously, sometimes unconsciously.

Prodigius. First of all, kneel down before God, Philogenia. You'll   70
  be most acceptable to the gods if you repent of your sins.

Philogenia. I am certainly sorry for them.

Prodigius. This is the right measure of a well-conducted life, the
  wish to purge oneself of sin before the gods. Do you have any
  intention of falling back into the same life of sin hereafter?

Philogenia. Certainly not.

Prodigius. Good. But do you believe in the commands of canon
  law?

Philogenia. I do.

Pr. Et Christiane secte fidem universam approbas?

Ph. Et id quidem approbo.

Pr. Optime. Re atque verbis, quantum quisti, fuit ne aput te misericordie locus?

Ph. Fuit.

Pr. Contempsistin unquam miseros?

Ph. Nunquam.

Pr. Fuistin equalibus adversa?

Ph. Nemini.

Pr. Indegentibus subvenisti ubi quando opporteret?

Ph. Subveni.

Pr. Avaritia ne te criminari merito quisquam potest? Nam id mulierum nimis naturale est.

Ph. Non, Prodigii, nec enim unquam habui, itaque tenax aut parca nichil esse potui.

71 *Pr.* Mirum est profecto et placet. Sed hactenus nullum peccandi genus in te fuisse reperio. Veneri autem quantum indulsisti?

Ph. Hei mihi, heu, heu!

Pr. Cohibe lacrimas. Ne vereare rem aperte fare; si quid peccatum erit, a nobis delebitur.

Ph. Mi pater, plurimi mei copiam turpiter habuere.

Pr. Et id ne factum est voluntate tua?

Ph. Istud quidem minime, sed blandiciis calidis capta sum atque domo educta sum, misera, nimium credula, ut sumus omnes adulescentule. Quare me opportuit multorum libidini inservire.

Pr. Id ergo peccatum non est. Nam omnis actio, ut[52] viciosa vel virtuosa dici possit, voluntaria sit opportet. Quamobrem, si nunc ad id turpitudinis te non voluntas sed necessitas impulit, te innocentem esse dico.

Prodigius. And do you accept the whole faith of the Christian sect?

Philogenia. Yes, I assent to it.

Prodigius. Excellent. Have you had occasion to practice acts of mercy, in word and deed, as far as lay in your power?

Philogenia. I have.

Prodigius. Have you ever scorned the wretched?

Philogenia. Never.

Prodigius. Have you ever been hostile to your neighbor?

Philogenia. No.

Prodigius. Have you helped the needy whenever necessary?

Philogenia. I have.

Prodigius. Can anyone justly blame you for avarice? That's a vice that's all too natural with women.

Philogenia. No, Prodigius, I've never had any property, so I couldn't be stingy with it or grasping.

Prodigius. That's really amazing; I'm pleased. So far I've found no 71 sin of any kind in you. But how much have you indulged in sex?

Philogenia. Alas, alas! [*She begins to cry*]

Prodigius. Don't cry. Don't be afraid to tell me all about it; if there is sin, we'll absolve you of it.

Philogenia. My father, many men have had sex with me.

Prodigius. And this happened of your own free will?

Philogenia. Oh, no, not at all! I was seduced by clever flattery and abducted from my home, wretch that I am; I was naïve, as all of us young girls are. That's why I had to service the lust of so many men.

Prodigius. This, then, is no sin. For any action to be called virtuous or vicious, it has to be voluntary. So if it wasn't your own will but necessity that forced on you this shameful act, I say that you are innocent.

Ph. Heya, diis igitur gratias ago, quod sumper absque noxa libidinem meam explevi.

72 *Pr.* Ira ne damnari potes?

Ph. Minime, neque scio irasci.

Pr. Equidem id facies tibi mansueta indicat. Bene facis, nam homines ira cecat ratione et eos ad brutorum genus deducit. Ventri autem quantum es dedita?

Ph. Nichil. Plus namque amo villes quam delicatas epulas.

Pr. Mi Philogenia, id quidem insulsum est. Mi Philogenia, malo ova quam fabas, amigdolas quam cicera, edum quam succulum, item pullum quam yrondinem, perdicem quam anserem. Dampnatur dumtaxat qui ingluviunt, devorant et sorbillant plusquam eorum calor naturalis queat digerere et qui plus impense faciunt in commesationibus quam redditus eorum possunt suppetere. Horum ebrietates, crapule, compotationes, eluationes tantum culpantur, non eorum convivia et vitaciones qui ex malis bona fercula diligunt et ex grossis tenuia cum utraque posita habeant et pari sumptu. Sed quid invideri ne cuiquam dici potes?

Ph. Non profecto.

73 *Pr.* Invidia crimen est pessimum et innate complexionis alteratio et humidi radicalis sensuum consumptio, nulla cum voluptate sed cum tristitia et dolore perpetuo. Quare cavendum est omnibus ne afficiantur invidia. Sed quam ocio libenter indulges?

Ph. Nunquam mihi placere potuit inhertem sedere, quamquam si ceteri labores desint mihi, huc illuc cursito, ne tempus ullum exercitio vacare possit.

Pr. Istuc satis placet. Postremo postquam te comperi satis sinceram et vacuam esse crimine, te hortor et impero sic facere pergas ut cepisti.

Philogenia. [*Aside*] Well, thank God I was always able to satisfy my passion without doing anything wrong!

Prodigius. Can you be found guilty of anger? 72

Philogenia. No, no; I don't know how to be angry.

Prodigius. Indeed, your gentle face shows this to be true. You do well, for anger blinds men's reason and brings them down to the level of animals. Have you committed gluttony?

Philogenia. No; I prefer ordinary food to fine dining.

Prodigius. Now my dear Philogenia, that is really quite silly. I myself, Philogenia, prefer eggs to beans, almonds to chick-peas, goat to ham, chicken to swallow, partridge to goose. The only people guilty of gluttony are those who gorge themselves or guzzle more than their natural heat can digest and those who spend more on the table than their income can support. It's their drunken routs, their hangovers, their drinking parties and their debauchery that are at fault, not dinner parties as such, or the fastidious habits of people who choose good dishes instead of bad ones, and delicate foods instead of gross fare, when both kinds are available and cost the same. But have you envied anyone?

Philogenia. Certainly not.

Prodigius. Envy is the worst of sins. It's caused by a change in our 73 natural complexion and the depletion of the basic humidity of our sense organs, bringing no pleasure but endless depression and suffering. So everyone must be careful not to be affected by envy. But what about sloth — have you ever indulged in that sin?

Philogenia. I never could like people who sat around doing nothing. If I have nothing else to do, I rush around hither and thither to keep myself busy.

Prodigius. Very good. Lastly, since I find you quite pure of heart and free from serious sin, I encourage and command you to go on acting the same way.

Ph. Factura sum, scilicet diis faventibus.

Pr. In gratiam deorum igitur te restituo ea potestate que michi a primario pontifice tributa est. Abi dum, et hinc[53] peccandi finem facias et animum affirmes viro tuo convenire et morem ei geras in omnibus, si modo recta precipiat. Ira si precinctus fuerit, clamorem eius, convicia, contumelias, tacita paciener excipias; diligentiam, curam, laborem omnem in re familiari conservanda adhibeas.

Ph. Recte mones.

Pr. Abi dum, cum diis optimis.

Ph. Vale cum religione tua bonam in rem.

: XIV :

Irtia, Servia, Philogenia

74 *Ir.* Heus, Servia, quam mature Prodigius noster Philogeniam absolvit.

Ser. Ubi ea est?

Ir. Ex adverso respice.

Ser. Video. Certe Prodigius non est in verbis multus, sed brevissimus; tantum ad rem quod pertinet rogat. Non autem lubenter confabullatur ut ordinis sui plerique solent.

Ph. Salvete matrone, sexus nostri decus!

Ser. Onus maximum te abiecisse existimo.

Ph. Sic est profecto; et timui male ab exordio ne mihi satisfactionem perdificilem et onerosam nimis indiceret. Sed omnibus me flagitiis et noxiis absolute liberavit; astinendum mihi tamen deinceps mandavit.

Philogenia. I shall, if the gods are willing.

Prodigius. Therefore, by the power vested in me by the supreme pontiff, I restore you to the grace of the gods. Go and sin no more. Resolve to obey your husband and defer to him in all things, provided his commands are just. If he is predisposed to anger, receive his shouting, abuse and insults with silence and patience; apply all your energy, concern and effort to taking care of the family and its property.

Philogenia. That's good advice.

Prodigius. Then go with the protection of the gods.

Prodigius. Farewell, and may you be rewarded for your piety.

: XIV :

Irtia, Servia, Philogenia

[*Outside the church*]

Irtia. Oh Servia, look how quickly our Prodigius has absolved   74
Philogenia.

Servia. Where is she?

Irtia. Look over there.

Servia. I see her. Prodigius is certainly not a man of many words; he gets to the point very quickly. He doesn't chatter on as so many of his profession do.

Philogenia. Greetings, matrons, the honor of our sex.

Servia. I think you've lifted a great weight from your shoulders.

Philogenia. Yes, indeed. I was so afraid at first that he'd give me a really hard penance that would be too heavy for me. But he absolved me completely of my sins and wrongdoing and then just told me to go and sin no more.

261

Ser. Benigne tecum actum esse potes dicere. Eamus igitur domum propere ne denuo abesse te vir tuus, si forte advenerit, comperiat.

Ph. Recte dicis. Eamus.

Ser. Sequere, Irtia.

Ir. Sequor.

: XV :

Zabinus, Gobius, Bitinus, Salinus, Plancus,
Epiphebus, Servia, Irtia, Philogenia, Alphius

75 *Za.* Gobi, postquam adventus noster, sic passitando, ad hedes Epiphebi fit propior, illarem te fac, exporge frontem.

Go. Ego fortasse tristis?

Bi. Mitte eum; irridet nebulo.

Go. Irrideat quantum velit. Ego novam uxorem, etate florida, cum parentibus, nummis et quos cudi nuper dicas, ducturus sum. Ipse autem sua gaudeat veterima, cum papille protense sunt usque ad genua, sine here ullo. Quid tu ais?

Bi. Rationem optimam tu predicas et idem ego summe optarem quod hodie tibi futurum est; et cum isthuc etatis essem, mihi cupiebam uxorem, relictis omnibus, qua tum meo modo oblectare atque tranquilitate et ocio frui possem. Quamquam enim prius quam uxorem haberem, amori operam darem, nunquam ex eo tantum voluptatis capiebam quantum[54] mihi plus meroris denique contingeret. Id quamobrem dicam?

Go. Ita obsecro.

76 *Bi.* Ego semper, relicta diis muliere dedicata, nupta atque vidua, virgines amavi, que vehementius amant quam omnes relique

Servia. You could say you've gotten off lightly. Now let's hurry
home so that your husband won't find you missing, if by chance
he's arrived already.

Philogenia. You're right. Let's go.

Servia. Irtia, follow along.

Irtia. I'm following. [*Exeunt*]

: XV :

Zabinus, Gobius, Bitinus, Salinus, Plancus,
Epiphebus, Servia, Irtia, Philogenia, Alphius

[*The rustics approach Epiphebus' house in the city*]

Zabinus. Gobius, since with every step we're getting closer to   75
Epiphebus' house, cheer up and put a smile on your face.

Gobius. Do I seem depressed?

Bitinus. Let him be; the rascal is making fun of you.

Gobius. Let him mock me as much as he wants. I'm about to
marry a virgin bride in the flower of youth, with families ties
and money fresh from the mint. He has the pleasure of an ancient hag without any dowry, whose breasts hang down to her
knees. What do you say to that?

Bitinus. You make an excellent case, and if I were you, I'd be yearning for the same thing that you have before you today. When I
was your age, I longed for a wife for just one reason: so that I
could enjoy myself with her after my fashion and get some
peace and quiet. I spent a lot of effort on love affairs before I
was married, but I never took enough pleasure in them to equal
the suffering I had in the end. May I tell you why?

Gobius. Please do.

Bitinus. I never paid attention to nuns, married women or wid-   76
ows; I always loved young girls, who love more passionately

263

hec, quia sunt in amore novitie et molles, ut sicut facile ymaginem mollibus ceris potes imprimere, ita eas in amore tuo quibus volueris institutis tibi liceat effingere. Mihi furate sunt corculum, verum fateor; non adeo docte sunt ut he, quas ut modo paulo ante memoravi; quare non eque amorem ad optimum finem commode, sapienter et celeriter queunt perducere. Sepe enim volunt ubi tu nescis et imparatus es; ubi autem tibi commodum tempus datur et occasio aptissima, tum aut mutate sunt aut nequeunt aut fortassis imprudentes quandoque, libidine flagrantes, ruunt precipites ut te intromittant; tum tu complexando, ipsa vero luctando — vel quod forte rubore suffusa sit vel quod consilium intromittendi momento post dampnarit — exauditi eritis. Aut si fortasse parum sibi prospexerit amoris impatiens, latebunt insidie que tum patefient. Inde tumultus ingens in hedes oritur. Tum ira, dolor, cruciatus anime ipsius, denique langor et extinctio nos consequitur, ubi amor noster magis observatur in dies, nec[55] tangere, conloqui [vide] aut videre nobis ullo pacto permisum[56] sit. Que mors[57] ista est crudelior et terribilior?

77　　　Vidue, nupte, quamvis astu maiore rem pertractare scirent, attamen mihi nunquam digne vise sunt in quas amorem meum intenderem, tum quod plerumque nos aliciunt in alio amore occupate, tum quod ad nostram consuetudinem eas referre velle, moribus alienis assuetas, non nisi magno ingenio et singulari cura potest impetrari. Ego autem in amore primum esse puto morum similitudinem, que ad idem velle et idem nole nos annectit. Preterea nisi viris aut amatoribus qui primi vidue aut nupte amorem abstullerunt sigillatim responsum sit a nobis, egre clam ferunt, aut eos sumper contumeliose nobis obiciunt.

than the others, since they are new to love and plastic. Just as you can easily impress an image on soft wax, so you can mold them to love you in any way you want. I confess they stole my little heart; they are not so expert as the kind of women I just mentioned, so they are not equally skilled at bringing a love affair to full fruition in a convenient, prudent and swift way. Often they want you when you're unaware of it and unprepared; but when you think that the time and place are perfect, they change their minds or can't. Or sometimes, imprudently, they rush headlong to let you in, burning with passion; then, while you're putting your arms around her, she starts to fight back—either because she happens to feel ashamed or because she's regretted her decision to let you in a moment later—and you are overheard. Or maybe she is a little too impatient in love and doesn't take precautions, so that traps are laid, then sprung. Then an enormous uproar breaks out in the house. Then, when our love is placed under daily surveillance, and we are not allowed to have contact, talk or see each other in any way, then anger, suffering, mental torment and finally depression and death follow. What death could be crueler or more terrible?

Widows and married women, though they know how to 77 conduct an affair more cleverly, have nevertheless always seemed to me not worth chasing, first because they generally set about ensnaring us while carrying on with somebody else; then because it's impossible to get them to adapt themselves to our ways when they're used to somebody else's ways, unless you are extremely clever and careful. My belief is that the principal basis for love is shared habits, being bound together by the same likes and dislikes. Moreover, unless we match, like a seal in wax, the husbands or lovers who first stole their love, these widows and married women become secretly bitter or are always throwing this in our faces with contempt.

78   Ego itaque in puellas teneras etate, sincere mentis, incorrupte fidei et suavis ingenii sumper amorem meum contulli: has deperii; hec incommoda tum mihi enarrem sepe, que modo paulo ante recensui. Quas ob res animum ad uxorem adieci, quacum mihi pacem eternam comparem atque frugaliorem vitam quam extitisset prius exegerim[58] et quacum meam, ubi opus esset, libidinem explerem sine fame aut salutis periculo, queque mihi harum quas dixi miseriarum finis esset et remedium. Tu ittidem fecisti nunc, quare vitam tibi letam et iucundam certe futuram tibi predico.

   Go. Sic ego opinor quoque. Sed ecce fores; tu, Sabine, i pre.

   Za. Vos me sequimini.

   Sal. Perge, sequemur.

   Pl. Et ego lubens primum canere accipiam. Tu Saline, emitte spiritum in fistulam ut festivi videamur, neque frustra huc advenisse.

   Sal. Fiat.

79 *Za.* Heus heus, intus me recipiam?

   Ser. Ohe, bonam in rem adducti sitis.

   Za. Hera, verbis omnium salve.

   Go. Salva sponsa?

   Ser. Salvus ne sponsus?

   Go. Atque letus est et validus.

   Ser. Virgo autem tua mesta est et admodum dolore gravi afficitur.

   Go. Quamobrem?

   Ser. Quia eunichum esse te audivit.

   Za. Hahahe!

   Go. Egon eunichus? Re ipsa reperiet.

   Ser. Ego autem nunquam id credidi. Sed huc ascendite; hic omnis res conficitur.

   Za. Eamus.

That's why I've always bestowed my love on young girls with   78
unspoiled minds, unsullied loyalties and sweet tempers. I've
loved them desperately, though I would often then tell myself
the tale of the misfortunes I just now listed. That's why I married a wife: I could get lasting peace with her; I could lead a less
expensive life than I had led before; and I could satisfy my desires with her when I needed to without endangering my life or
reputation. She has been the end of and the remedy for the all
miseries I've described. And now you have made the same decision, and I predict your future life will doubtless be happy and
pleasant.

Gobius. That's what I think too. But here is the door. You go first,
    Zabinus.

Zabinus. All of you follow me.

Salinus. Go ahead, we'll follow.

Plancus. I shall have the pleasure of being the first to take up a
    song. Salinus, play your bagpipes so that we look festive and
    like we have some reason to be here.

Salinus. Here goes.

Zabinus. Hello, there, may I step inside? [They enter the house]   79

Servia. Oh, you are very welcome!

Zabinus. Mistress, greetings in the name of us all!

Gobius. The bride is well?

Servia. Is the husband well?

Gobius. He is happy and in good health.

Servia. Your girl, however, is depressed and sorrowful

Gobius. Why's that?

Servia. Because she's heard that you're a eunuch.

Zabinus. Ha ha ha!

Gobius. Me, a eunuch? She'll soon find out the facts!

Servia. Personally, I've never believed a word of it. But just come
    upstairs; everything is settled here.

Zabinus. Let's go.

Bi. Tu, Gobi, i mecum una.

Go. Eo. Vos ceteri post nos.

80 *Ep.* Heus heus, salvete, vos dudum hic expectavi.

Za. Eo. Et tu hic es, Epiphebe. Tam diu tacitus?

Go. Mi Epiphebe, salve.

Ep. Et tu quoque, quem Philogenia felix novum est factura maritum.

Ser. Accedite ad Philogeniam.

Go. Recte dicis.

Bi. Hem, Gobi, mercaturam profecto egregiam negociatus es!
Virgo hec est forma luculenta et recte comprehensa. Tu adeo
deinceps eris apud te ut tibi pendulas palis nullus audeat attingere.

Go. Ha, num me noris?

Za. Ha, tristis, nuptam parumper attingas.

Ser. Eho, ad me, Gobi!

Go. Adsum ubi vis.

Ser. Hanc prope assiste, eam roga quam amet te.

Go. Philogenia, ut vales?

Ser. Responde, Philogenia, ne vereare. Tuus hic manebit perpetuo; responde, inquam.

Ph. Tuo arbitratu.

81 *Ser.* Misera, non audet te nomine appellare, Gobi mi. Virginem
hanc a parvula educavi mihi, neque apud me erga eam defuit
quicquam preter matris nomen. Ego, quantum in me fuit, curavi ut omni officio muliebri perdocta esset probe.[59] Hanc ego
tibi, si aperte dicendum est, haud lubenter trado. Vellem, si honeste fieri posset, sumper eam apud me vivere. Sed quia forma,
etas, locus et consuetudo aliter suadent, est a me Philogenia se-
greganda et tradenda nuptui. Tibi autem ante omnes (qui qui-

Bitinus. Gobius, come with me.

Gobius. I'm coming. The rest of you follow us.

Epiphebus. Hello, there, greetings to you! I've been waiting for you 80 quite a while.

Zabinus. I'm coming. And here you are too, Epiphebus! Why didn't you say something sooner?

Gobius. My dear Epiphebus, your very good health!

Epiphebus. And yours too. Philogenia is going to be happy with her new husband.

Servia. Go see Philogenia.

Gobius. Well said!

Bitinus. Hey, Gobius, what a deal you've made! This girl is gorgeous, really well put together. From now on you'll be so full of yourself that no one will dare touch the hem of your cloak!

Gobius. Ha, did you think you knew me?

Zabinus. Hey, don't be churlish, go see your bride for a second.

Servia. Come over here to me, Gobius!

Gobius. I'll go where you want.

Servia. Stand next to this woman, and ask her if she loves you.

Gobius. Philogenia, are you all right?

Servia. Answer, Philogenia, don't be afraid. This man will be yours forever; answer, I say.

Philogenia. [*In a small voice*] As you wish.

Servia. Poor girl, she doesn't dare address you by name, Gobius. I 81 have raised this maiden from childhood and I've been a mother to her in all but name. I've done as much as I could to see her well trained in all her womanly duties. To be frank, I'm a little reluctant to hand her over to you. I'd like — if it were possible to do so decently — to keep her with me always. But as her beauty, age, position and the common practice of our times argue otherwise, I have to separate myself from Philogenia and give her away in marriage. I willingly made the decision to join her with you before all the others (and there were many men who

269

dem multi fuere magnopere eam exposcentes sibi) lubens copulare eam decrevi propter tuas virtutes singulares admodum ut in homine agricola et negocioso cui vita tantum sit in opere. Tu mihi certe frugalissimus esse iudicatus es, cum intellexerim te continentem ruri esse parcum et sobrium atque labori non parcere, sed absque inhertia querendis opibus inhiare, ut res tua domestica sufferre queat et sumptus cottidianos et emergentes tollerare. Hem, hec est viri virtus summis cum laudibus efferenda; quare hanc meam tibi virginem trado et comendo tue fidei. Habebis profecto, mi Gobi, quacum iuventutem tuam oblectes; maxime omnibus in rebus tibi erit morigera et obsequens, atque si quando, ut evenire solet, merore aut tristicia confectus eris, eam tibi lenibit Philogenia, te hortabitur et consolabitur. Nunc primum disces vivere, michi crede, Gobi.

82 *Go.* Quid opus est verbis? Bene sane invicem conveniemus dum modo rationem et curam pro virilli rei familiaris primam apud se habeat, et me ante omnia explere cogitet. Accipio ex te Philogeniam et lubens.

Ser. Que mandabis, Gobi, curabit diligentissime, nec ulla erit in ea mora, ubi apud se tibi rem gratam intelliget.

Go. Missa hec.

Ir. Heus tu, Gobi, hanc mihi summa coiunctam necessitudine duces uxorem, non cognita prius affinitate?

Go. Id quidem volo, sed fare unde tibi sit affinis Philogenia, ut ego tecum affinitatem servare possim.

Ir. Dicam. Ex fratre nata est meo.

Go. Hoc placet maxime.

83 *Ir.* Ea ubi patre caruit, apud matrem mansit parvula. Mater, ubi paulatim amorem primi coniugis ex animo delerit, cuiusque avi-

begged to have her for themselves) because of your truly remarkable virtues as a hard-working farmer and man of business. I judged you to be a man of great frugality, when I learned
that you kept yourself in the country in a thrifty and sober way,
and that you worked hard and made an effort to save your pen-
nies so that you could support your household and bear the
burden of your daily expenses and extraordinary outlays. That's
why I'm giving my girl to you and am entrusting her to your
good faith. You'll have a girl, my dear Gobius, with whom you
can enjoy the delights of youth; she'll be obliging and obedient
to you in all things; and if you are ever struck with moments of
sorrow or sadness, as is wont to happen, Philogenia will as-
suage your hurts, encourage and console you. You will learn
how to live now for the first time, believe me, Gobius.

Gobius. You don't need to tell me. We'll get along just fine so long 82
as she makes her first duty the management and care of our
household, and remembers above all to keep me satisfied. I accept Philogenia from you with pleasure.

Servia. She'll take very good care of whatever you entrust to her,
Gobius, and she won't hold back when she understands that
there is something within her power that will make you happy.

Gobius. That's settled, then.

Irtia. Oh Gobius, are you going to make a wife of this girl who is
so close to me without making the acquaintance of her relations
first?

Gobius. I do want to do that, but tell me how Philogenia is related
to you, so that I can keep up the bond of affection with you.

Irtia. I'll tell you: she's my brother's daughter.

Gobius. I'm pleased to hear it.

Irtia. When she lost her father, the poor girl remained with her 83
mother. After her love for her first husband faded little by little
from her heart, her mother found that her passions had not
been quenched by her first husband, and so took a second one.

ditas primo viro lassari non potuit, ad secundum se transtulit. Tum hec Servia a nobis, virgini propinquis, tandem impetravit cum gratia ut eam educaret. Educavit pro sua; in ea se oblectavit; hanc ut decuit modo pro uxore tibi tradidit. Et una adiutrix fui ut esset tua; quare, mi Gobi, hanc inter nos affinitatem perpetuam esse volo.

Go. Et ego quoque, mea Irtia. Profecto nil mihi gratius posset contingere quam uxorem habere magis affinitate multa sociatam quam fortunatam et, ut aiunt, auro et gemmis ornatam.

Ir. Est mihi, Gobi, sermo tuus honestissimus et mature gravitatis. Tibi dii bene faciant.

Go. Et tibi quoque.

Ser. Hic evocate Alphium, qui sponsalibus publice prefectus; is ea verba facturus est, Gobi, que his in rebus haberi solent.

Ep. Adest hic tibi dudum.

Al. Hic sum, vobis paratissimus.

Ir. Rebus brevibus expedias.

Al. Faciam. Huc te deflectas paululum, Gobi.

Go. Ecce me!

Al. Tenuit vetus consuetudo atque moderna custodit, digitos anulis ornari. Ubi anulus?

Go. Hic tibi est.

84 Al. Sat habeo. Bonis igitur auspiciis a summo Iove capere initium statuo, a quo ratio omnis, mos gentibus, et ipsa natura quodammodo exordiendum esse persuasit. Bone Iupiter et tu pronuba Iuno, diveque Iminee mortalibus gratissime et tu Talassi adolescens, gratiose favete, obsecro, ut felix et fortunatum sit hoc coniugium. Nuptias vero iussu et imperio celebramus ut sobolis legitima fiat procreatio et fornicandi, strupandi, mecandi et incestuandi dempta sit occasio. Nuptias profecto qui

Then at length Servia here kindly asked us, her relatives, if she might have her and bring her up. Servia raised her like her own child and took delight in her; and has now, as was fitting, given her to you to be your wife. I was Servia's one helper in giving her to you. So, my dear Gobius, I want there to be an eternal bond between us.

Gobius. And I want that too, my dear Irtia. Certainly nothing more pleasant could happen to me than to have a wife who is recommended more by her extensive family than by her fortune — by mere gold and by jewels, as they say.

Irtia. Gobius, your words do you great honor and show the weight of maturity. May the gods bless you.

Gobius. And you as well.

Servia. Summon Alphius, the official in charge of marriages; he will pronounce the words, Gobius, proper to the occasion.

Epiphebus. He has already been here for some time.

Alphius. I'm here, and most ready to be of service.

Irtia. Please get through the business quickly

Alphius. I will. Turn this way slightly, Gobius.

Gobius. I'm here!

Alphius. The ancients had a custom, preserved to this day, of adorning fingers with rings. Where is the ring?

Gobius. Here you are.

Alphius. That's fine. I shall open the ceremony invoking the good   84
auspices of high Jove, being persuaded to begin with his name by reason, custom and in a certain sense Nature herself. Good Jupiter, and you, Juno, companion of brides, and divine Hymenaeus, most favorable to mortals, and you, young Thalassius[13] — show us your gracious favor, I pray, that this marriage may be fortunate and happy. We celebrate marriage with the order and command to procreate legitimate offspring and to remove all occasion of fornication, shameful intercourse, adultery and incest. The marriage that is preserved holy and

sancte incorrupteque servaverint, diis erunt acceptissimi; quod
ut isti facturi sint, vos supplices exoramus. Tu itaque, Gobi, responde: estne Philogenia tibi primum complacita et tibi visa
digna que tecum simul vitam agat et suum diem claudat extremum?

Go. Certe inquam.

85 *Al.* Tu, Philogenia, Gobium ne dignum existimas quo mulier fieri
velis? Tacet. Hic quidem mos mihi non placet. Scio te magis
cupere Gobium quam ullum qui vivat usque gentium, utque[60]
vix istud abs te videar impetrare cum gratia, rogabo te iterum.
Post me mutum dices? Philogenia, nunquam Gobium ne dignum putas quo mulier fieri velis?

Ser. Responde!

Ph. Ita.

Al. Ohe, diis gratias habeo! Accede huc Gobi; efferas anullum.

Go. Hic est.

Al. Eum digito anullari imponas.

Go. Fiat.

Al. Et ei modo da suaviter, ut pacem tibi cum ea concilies.

Go. Tametsi nullus moneat, id faciam lubens.

Ep. Aha, impudens! Verum[61] ignosco ego, ut aiunt, quid amor va-
leat; nescio, quod nundum animum induxi habere uxorem.

Ser. Tu, Saline, cane fistula et hii correas agent, nisi quod aliud[62]
est agendum.

Al. Quid de dote? Ne quid spopondit Epiphebus tu servabis inte-
gerime, Servia?

Ser. Istuc certe factura sum.

Go. Placet!

uncorrupted shall be most acceptable to the gods; and we pray
you on bended knee that these young people will so preserve
it. — Now Gobius, answer me: is Philogenia pleasing to you before all women and is she worthy in your eyes to live together
with you until death do you part?

Gobius. Yes indeed!

Alphius. And you, Philogenia, do you count Gobius worthy so   85
that you wish to be made his wife? [*A long pause*] She's silent. I
really don't like this behavior. I know you want Gobius more
than any living man, but I don't want to seem to be begging you
for an answer. So I'll ask you again. Are you going to mutter
behind my back? [*Louder*] Philogenia, do you count Gobius
worthy so that you wish to be made his wife?

Servia. Answer him!

Philogenia. Yes.

Alphius. Well, thanks be to the gods! Step forward, Gobius; bring
the ring.

Gobius. Here it is.

Alphius. Put it on her finger.

Gobius. Right.

Alphius. And now give her a nice kiss so that you may be united
one to the other in peace.

Gobius. I'd do it with pleasure, even if nobody told me to. [*Kisses
Philogenia*]

Epiphebus. You cheeky devil! But I have to make allowances for
what they call the power of love; I don't know it myself, because
I haven't yet convinced myself to take a wife.

Servia. Salinus, play a song with your pipe and let these people do
a dance — unless there is some other business?

Alphius. What about the dowry? You'll keep in full the promise
Epiphebus made, Servia?

Servia. I shall certainly do so.

Gobius. Good!

86 *Al.* Igitur correis gaudete, psallite, concinite et quoad vobis datur
iocundi sitis. De futuris dubius est eventus, nec in iocunditate
vite sitis avaris consimiles, qui sumper ingenium suum fraudant
et numis parcunt, ut in futuris necessitatibus sibi oppitulari
queant; quos tamen mors prius opprimit quam advenerit, suo
tamen iudicio, necessitas. Hec vobis dico: vivite leti dum fata sinunt.

Bi. Bene imperat; et nos tue sententie aquiescendum putamus.

Ep. Heus, Alphi, accede huc.

Al. Quid vis?

Ep. In celulam hanc recludamus.

Al. Sequor.

87 *Ep.* O mi Alphi, quam preclare res et memorabiles iste sunt. Dii
sumus, si modo vita sit perpetua. Potiti sumus illa virgine sine
ulla infamia. O felicem et faustum hunc diem! O preclarum
munus a diis datum! Profecto erat omnis voluptas dolori et soli-
citudini admixta, nisi a nobis virgo hec unde erat egressa, ad
honestatem scilicet, perducta foret. Age, age, hic agrestis masti-
gia et nebulo pociatur ut libet, quamquam, mehercule, si velis
rationem veram exequi, non sit dignus pedem eius attingere. Ita
venusta est bellitudine, gracili habitudine atque in universum
formosissima, tum et comitati lepida atque omni genere virtutis
ornata, ut mea sententia facile vulgus omne mulierum anteat.
Sed hoc quodammodo fatale dici potest, ut omnia iniqua forte
comperiantur. Hec enim pulcherrima et mulier perdocta turpis-
simo et rudi coniuncta est. Sed ferret equo animo si volet.

Alphius. Now dance and enjoy yourselves, play, sing, and make   86
merry as you can. What happens tomorrow is uncertain, but in
your celebration don't be like greedy men who always cheat
their own desires and hoard their money so that they can be
protected against future necessities; for death comes before they
make the judgment that any necessity stands at their doors. I
tell you this: live and be happy while the fates allow.

Bitinus. That's a fine command, and we believe we ought to follow
your advice!

Epiphebus. Hey, Alphius, come over here.

Alphius. What do you want?

Epiphebus. Let's shut ourselves inside this little room.

Alphius. I'll follow you. [*They leave the others and go into an empty
chamber*]

Epiphebus. My dear Alphius, this whole affair has been so splen-   87
did, so memorable![14] We'd be gods if we only had eternal life.
We've had our way with this girl without loss to our reputation.
What a happy, lucky day! What a wonderful gift the gods have
given! All my pleasure had been mixed with trouble and worry
until we were able to put this girl's feet back on the path of
honor. Well, well, this country bumpkin and rascal may have
his way with her as he pleases, although in strict justice—by
Hercules!—he doesn't deserve to touch a hair of her head.
She's so stunningly beautiful, elegantly simple in her carriage
and absolutely lovely in every way; she's such a charming companion, adorned with virtues of every kind, that in my view she
easily surpasses the common run of women. But one might say
that, in a certain way, there is a fatal tendency, perhaps, for all
things to find their opposites. An example is this beautiful and
very well-brought-up woman who has been joined to this crude
and repulsive fellow. But she'll make the best of it if she puts
her mind to it.

88 *Al.* Abi sic, insciens! Nil hoc sibi fortunatius evenire poterat: is sibi est maritus babillo, inhers, sompniculosus et, ut ita dicam, hominis quoddam simulacrum. Quare tucius et sine periculo magis adhuc nobiscum victitabit quovis eum suavi verbo capiet. Explebit enim officia et inde[63] triduano post eum ad laborem domo extrudet, ubi se defatigabit usque ad frigora, bibet usque ad lacrimas, domum defessus redibit; eum sompnus opprimet nec excitabitur a crepusculo usque ad meridiem. Tu, quid facturus sis, satis intelligis.

Ep. Intelligo et gaudeo sepenumero. Tum in urbem veniet ut eam monui.

Al. Et isthuc quidem facilius. Tu autem cum ea operam dabis ut admittar[64] ad cognatam, uxorem Zabini. Nam Zabinus, huius Gobii babillonis frater, commensator et sorbillator est maximus; simili morbo cum Gobio laborabit. Ipsi dormient ociose; nos fictilia miscebimus et queque suo loco reponemus.

Ep. Probe dicis; nil amplius loquimur; eamus propere ad eos. Iter parant rus ut audio.

: XVI :

Gobius, Epiphebus, Zabinus, Servia, Philogenia, Irtia, Salinus

89 *Go.* Iam iam tempus eundi. Iam advesperascit.

Ep. Quo tam cito?

Za. Epiphebe, domo abeuntes nos reddituros statim diximus, quare convivas nostros admirari nolo cur tantum detineamur in via.

Alphius. Get out of here, you don't know what you're talking 88
about! This is the luckiest possible outcome for her. She has a
simpleton for a husband, a blockhead, a sleepwalker, a mere
mockery of a man, so to speak. So she'll still be able to live it up
with us, but more safely than before, as she'll have him hanging
on her every sweet little word. She'll fulfill her duties and three
days later she'll boot him out of the house and off to work,
where he'll wear himself out till he's numb and drink till he
cries, until he comes home exhausted. He'll sleep like a dead
man till noon the next day. And you know perfectly well what
you're going to do.

Epiphebus. I do indeed, and it makes me happy whenever I think
of it, which I do often. Then she'll come to the city as I've told
her to do.

Alphius. This plan is even easier. You arrange with her to have her
sister-in-law, Zabinus' wife, take me as her lover. Zabinus, the
brother of this bumpkin Gobius, eats like a horse and drinks
like a fish. He'll find himself in the same state as Gobius.
While the two of them are snoring, we'll mix up the pottery
and then put everything back in its place.

Epiphebus. That's a great idea; but enough talk. We have to get
back to the others; it sounds like they're getting ready to go
back to the country.

: XVI :

Gobius, Epiphebus, Zabinus, Servia, Philogenia, Irtia, Salinus

Gobius. It's time to go now. It's already getting dark. 89
Epiphebus. Why leave so soon?
Zabinus. Epiphebus, when we left we said we'd come back at once;
and I don't want our dinner-guests to wonder what's detained
us so long on the road.

Ep. Ut libet, si pur⟨e⟩ eundi vobis stat sententia. Nolo mei causa vos in mora diutius esse.

Ser. Accede igitur huc, Philogenia.

Ph. Heu, heu, me miseram! Te ne visura sum amplius, mea mater.

Ser. Fletu abstine. Ibi manebis triduo; post huc revertaris volo. Abi sospes, tu illaris. Tibi eam dedo, Gobi, hanc ames, hanc expeties dies ac noctes, tibi unicum solamen et refugium.

Go. Haud aliter faciam; crede mihi, laudabis.

90 *Ir.* Sine te amplectar, mea Philogenia. Bono sis animo; dii te solam respiciunt. Qui tibi diem istum cumularunt beneficiis, quando summa cum dote virum nacta es frugalissimum et cui luce te cariorem futuram scio. Eya, spiritum revoca cum diis optimis.

Ph. Vale, mea Irtia. Atqui peritura sum nisi te videro.

Ir. Abi, scis sospes; me videbis propediem quantum voles.

Go. Eamus!

Ser. I, Philogenia mi, et accura sapiens mulier ut sis.

Ph. Enitar id quantum potero. Mea mater, vale.

Ser. Et tu, mea spes unica, cum Gobio tuo.

Go. Et tu vale, Servia, et tu, Irtia.

Ir. Sis felix coiunx et fortunatus.

91 *Go.* Hanc vobis restituam illexam, a vobis ut accepi, quare ne metuat quicquam.

Ser. Heu, tu quidem[65] eunichum[66] eris quem esse te advenienti tibi diximus! Et credam, nisi viri officium feceris.

Go. Hem, intelligo; tu partes attigisti quas nec cogitaram. Valete omnes.

Ser. Et vos quoque.

Epiphebus. As you wish, if you're really determined to go. I wouldn't want you to be late on my account.

Servia. Come here, Philogenia.

Philogenia. Oh, oh, I'm so unhappy! I won't see you anymore, dear mother.

Servia. Don't cry. You'll stay there for three days; after that, I want you to come back here. Have a safe journey and be happy. I give her to you, Gobius; love and desire her day and night; let her be your only comfort and refuge.

Gobius. I'll do exactly as you say, and believe me, I'll win your approval.

Irtia. Let me embrace you, dear Philogenia. Cheer up, the gods 90 are taking special care of you! They've heaped blessings on you this day; just think of your fine dowry and this husband of the soberest habits you managed to get! I know he'll become dearer to you than the day. Take heart, and the gods be with you!

Philogenia. Farewell, my Irtia. I'll die if I don't get to see you again.

Irtia. Go, you know you'll be fine; you'll see me soon, as much as you want.

Gobius. Let's get going!

Servia. Go, Philogenia, and take care to be a prudent wife.

Philogenia. I shall try as hard as I can. Farewell, dear mother.

Servia. You too, my only hope; go with your Gobius.

Gobius. And fare you well too, Servia, and you, Irtia.

Irtia. May you be a happy and fortunate husband!

Gobius. I'll bring her back to you safe and sound, just as you gave 91 her to me; so don't worry about anything.

Servia. Oh, in that case you really will be the eunuch I said you were when you came in! And I'll believe it too, unless you do your duty as a husband.

Gobius. I get it. But you've put your finger on something that's never entered my head! Goodbye, everyone!

Servia. And goodbye to you too.

Go. Saline, i pre et fistulam insufles.
Sal. Fiat. Turlurututu. Vos valete et plaudite.

Alphius retesui.

Deo gratias amen.

Expleta fuit comedia illius ardui et splendidissimi ingenii domini Ugolini de Parma legum scolaris.

Gobius. Salinus, go on ahead and pipe us a tune.

Salinus. Right! Turlurututu. [*To the audience*] Farewell, all, and clap your hands.

Alphius recited the text.

Thanks be to God. Amen.

The comedy of that towering and most splendid of wits, Master Ugolino of Parma, scholar of the law, is finished.

CHRYSIS

: I :

Dyophanes, Theobolus

Dyo. Edepol nulla, opinor, est ratio prior,
quod emuli nimium clero sunt populi:
nam commoditates nobis invident bonas.
Soli miseri carent invidia viri;
5   quisquis beatus est, huic livor est comes.
Nobis divitie sunt, opes, delicie,
ad esum nati tantum et ad potum sumus,
dormire possumus et satis quiescere;
vivimus nobis, alii vivunt aliis.
10   Nulli pulcra est quam nobis gratior Venus;
non, ut alii, stabilem uxorem ducimus,
que, si stomacosa sit, habenda est tamen;
nova in dies connubia, himeneos novos
celebramus: si placet amor, revertimur;
15   ubi displicet, alio flectimus iter.

ENEA SILVIO PICCOLOMINI

CHRYSIS

CHARACTERS[1]

Dyophanes, *a priest*

Theobolus, *a priest*

Chrysis, *a courtesan*

Sedulius, *a young man*

Lybiphanes, *his friend*

Pythias, *a matron*

Charinus, *a young man*

Archimenides, *a lover*

Antiphila, *a courtesan*

Canthara, *a procuress*

Artrax, *a cook*

Cassina, *a courtesan*

Congrio, *a slave*

Scene: Basel

: I :

Dyophanes, Theobolus

[Approaching Canthara's brothel]

Dyophanes. By Pollux, the leading reason, in my view, why ordinary people envy the clergy is that they are jealous of our comforts. Only poor wretches are exempt from envy, while envy is a constant companion of the man who's happy. We have wealth, 5 resources, luxuries; we are born but to eat and drink; we can sleep and relax as much as we want. We live for ourselves; others live for others. Beautiful Venus is more favorable to us than to anyone else. We don't have to take a permanent wife, as others must, who, if she's irritable, still has to be put up with. We 10 celebrate new marriages everyday, new nuptials; if a lover suits our fancy, we return to her; if we don't care for her, we simply change course and go off in another direction. After putting a 15

Ex mille cum periculum fecimus, eam
que cordi fuit stabili prosequimur fide.

Theo. Michi sic videtur. Sed quali iam nos putas
usuros nocte? Dum subagitabis tuam,

20 egon, adherentem pectori meo meam
tenens, dabo suavium et labrum mordicus
stringam et niveas milies premam papillas?
Vah, quotiens inter sua crura tibias
innectam meas! Sed hoc molestum est mihi . . .

Dyo. Quid istuc est?

25 *Theo.* 'Antiqua est palla mea; novam
faxo ut habeam: quatuor michi da minas.
Baltheum nullum est mihi etiam; adiuva ut habeam'.
Hec vox mihi semper sonat in auribus.
Talentum impertitus sum, sed quo plus do, magis

30 expetit: 'Hoc indigeo, hoc prebe, hoc volo.
Es quidem nullum in crumena superest mea;
despoliandus est quisquis indigens mei
advenerit. Ligari amantis marsupium
nequit'. Nil satis est meretricibus malis.

35 Sed unum singraphum quam facimus hodie
persolvet cenam; tum post, aliud aliam.
At iam in angiportu, ubi manendum est, sumus.
Nichil tumulti audio. Vereor . . . vereor
huc ne frustra venerimus. Sed pulta hostium.

40 *Dyo.* Ah, nescis publicam custodes ad ianuam
e proximo?

Theo. Ergo fac signum, ut veniat anus.
At ego expectando crucior miserrime;
nil mora peius, nil expectationibus.
Mane, mane! Observat nos ianitor, quem pii
omnes dii perdant!

45 *Dyo.* Tace parum, et signum dabo.

thousand to the test, we remain faithful only to the one that's in our heart.

Theobolus. I agree. But how do you think we'll spend the night? While you go for a gallop on your girl, what will I be doing? I'll hold mine tightly to my heart, and kiss her and bite her on the 20 lips and caress a thousand times her snowy breasts. Oh, how many times shall I entwine my legs with hers! But there is something that bothers me.

Dyophanes. What's that?

Theobolus. [*He imitates his girlfriend's voice*] "My cloak is out of fash- 25 ion; I have to have a new one: give me four minas. I don't even have a belt: help me get one." This is the voice that always rings in my ears. I've given her one talent,[2] but the more I give her, the more she demands: "I need this, give me that, I want that 30 too. I haven't a penny left in my purse! Whoever comes to see me but hasn't the ready cash had better resign himself to being stripped naked. A lover's purse shouldn't be tied up tight." Nothing is enough for these unscrupulous courtesans. But one loan we take out today will pay for dinner tonight; then tomor- 35 row a second will pay for another dinner. But we're now in the alley where we have to wait. I don't hear a sound. I'm scared. I fear we've come here for nothing. Knock on the door.

Dyophanes. Shh! Can't you see that the guards of the city gate are 40 close by?

Theobolus. Then give the sign so that the old woman opens up. Waiting like this is absolute torture. There's nothing worse than delays and having to wait. Stop, stop! The porter sees us. May all the holy gods send him straight to hell!

Dyophanes. Keep your voice down, and I'll give the sign. 45

: II :

Chrysis meretrix, Sedulius amator, Lybiphanes familiaris

Chry. Cur hac noctu non es mecum? Quo nunc properas?
  Mane, amabo! Dormito hic, ut nudi simul
  in amplexu simus. Cur mihi suppetias
  quasi gravastellus das?
Sedu.   Ne noceam tibi.
Chry. Ohe! Ne noceas, ais?
50 Sedu.   Aio: balneum
  quis tibi persolvit, aut tu cur hodie
  preter morem lavisti? Tete illic habeat,
  argentum qui dedit. Nam qui dat, ipsus parum
  iniurius, si tibi lucrum auferat, siet.
55 Chry. Parvi me pensitas et me facis nihili,
  qui rivalibus me quam tibi vis potius.
  At at . . .
Sedu.   Quid 'at at'? Tui causa facio,
  ne dantes abigam, qui prebeo perparum.
Chry. Hem! Dantes! Quasi me plurimi nunc habeant,
  quod tu solus et unus, vel . . .
60 Sedu.   Aha, 'vel'! Scio:
  nemo nisi ego te unus, vel centum alii!
Chry.Expetessunt plures, paucis datur frui.
  Sic me dii amassint, ut preter te vix duo
  consueverint mihi. Nunc, ut mundior tibi
65   advenirem, lavi. Tibin sum morigera?
  Anime mi, mane, mane! Noli irascier.
Ly. Ut blanda est meretrix! Iam tendit insidias.

: II :

Chrysis, a prostitute; Sedulius, a lover; Lybiphanes, his friend

[*In the house of Chrysis*]

Chrysis. Why won't you stay with me tonight? Where are you rushing off to now? Please stay! Sleep here, so we can lie naked in each other's arms. Why are you giving me money like some old coot?

Sedulius. So as not to get you into trouble.

Chrysis. Oh! Get me in trouble, you say?

Sedulius. That's right. Who paid for your bath? And why have you   50
bathed yourself more than usual today? Let the fellow who gave you the money have you. It's only fair for the man who paid you to have the profit of his bargain.

Chrysis. You must think little of me and set little value on me, if   55
you're wishing me on rivals rather than on yourself. But . . . but . . .

Sedulius. What's this "but . . . but . . ."? I'm doing this for your sake, so as not to drive away your paying customers, since I can offer you so little.

Chrysis. Really? Paying customers? As if there were many men enjoying my favors! But it's you who are my one and only, except perhaps . . .

Sedulius. Aha! "Perhaps"! I know—I'm the only one, except "per-   60
haps" a hundred others!

Chrysis. There are lots of men chasing me, but only a few get to enjoy my favors. So help me god, besides you, I have had scarcely two other lovers. I took a bath just now so I'd be nice and clean for you. Aren't I always trying to please you? Stay,   65
sweetheart, stay with me! Don't be angry.

Lybiphanes. [*Aside*] These courtesans are so flattering and manipu-

289

Viden ut amplectitur, quasi amatrix probe?
Non michi has induceres sicophantias;
70 aurum his verbis ut veneris studes, pessuma!
Novi ego mores meretricis; namque, cum
pauper est, arridet et quidvis facit.
Amare assimilat, non amat, quando lacrimas
ut lubet vortit atque ut volt: obediunt
75 meretrici lacrime. At istic sese putat
alterum Ganimedem aut Parin coli alterum.
Nosce te, Seduli: istuc etatis hominem
non amat mulier; si quid das, amat.
Aliam vitam et mores iam debes alios
80 istac etate induere; nam vesperus adest.

Sedu. Sic est, nec me quod dicis latet. Nugas scio
istarum.

Ly.   Quid igitur heres? Quid hic agis?
Nulla hic habenda est mora, postquam Venus iacet.
Quin imus et aliis cedimus?

Sedu.   Animo
85 gerundus mos est; lubet ridere cum ioco.
Scortis ut scortis utor: simulant, simulo;
fingo me captum nec sum; par pari refero.

Ly. At istuc, hercle, magni plenum est discriminis.
Urit amor pusillatim clamque ingreditur,
90 et iocos scimus in seria mutarier.
Vide, sis: nam, si ardere incepisses, spoliis
te direptionique para, quasi sies
captivus. Tigris est, non mulier, meretrix;
cum amari scit, petit, capit, spoliat, rapit.

95 *Sedu.* Desine, scio. Quid, malum, in fornice venis
philosophari? Leno hic, non Cato, loquitur.

Ly. Decet ubique bene loqui atque facere.
Non veto scortari, sed scortari nimium.

lative! She's already spreading her nets. Do you see how she embraces him as though she were sincere in her love? Tricks like that wouldn't fool me! You're going for his money with talk like that, you bitch! I know what courtesans are like. When 70 she's poor, she smiles and does whatever you want. She pretends to love, but doesn't love. She turns tears on and off like a spigot; a courtesan sheds tears on command. Meanwhile, this fellow thinks he's another Ganymede or another Paris. Know 75 thyself, Sedulius.³ A woman doesn't love a man your age; she loves you when you give her money. You should be living a different kind of life with different mores at your age; you're in your sunset years. 80

Sedulius. You're right; I'm quite well aware of what you're saying. I know the games these women play.

Lybiphanes. Then what are you hesitating for? What are you doing here? There's no point in waiting around, now that you've had your fill of Venus. Why don't we get out of here and leave her to others?

Sedulius. Well, I need to entertain myself too. I like laughing and joking; I use whores for what they are; they pretend, I pretend; 85 I act like I'm in love when I'm not; I give them tit for tat.

Lybiphanes. By Hercules! That way lies tremendous risk. Love's sparks catch fire little by little and enter your heart without your realizing it; and we know how jokes can turn into something serious. Be careful! If you start to catch fire, prepare your- 90 self to be despoiled and picked clean like a prisoner. A courtesan is a tiger, not a woman; once she knows you're in love, she'll plead with you, take from you, despoil and steal from you.

Sedulius. Relax, I know all this. Why are you coming to a whore- 95 house to philosophize, damn it? It's not Cato who gives speeches here; it's the pimp.⁴

Lybiphanes. One should act well and speak honestly everywhere. I didn't tell you not to go whoring, just not to do it to excess.

Chry. Quid vos inter vos his murmurationibus
100   concertatis? Adesto, Seduli, propera.
Sedu. Adsum.
Chry.   Sequere me huc intro.
Sedu.   Sequor lubens.

: III :

Lybiphanes, Pythias

Ly.   Illi iam intus secundas agunt nuptias.
      Perlepida est istec tua soror, Pythias.
      Sed ubinam illam invenisti? Quo balneo
105   lavit? Estne, ut opinor, quod Theobolus
      stipem dederit? Nam ille hanc noctem redemit pretio.
      Dic, amabo. Soli sumus, nusquam effluet.
      Tum te hic agnoscam et coniacebimus simul.
Py.   Quis tibi istec dixit?
Ly.   Qui scit: ipsus hodie
      in foro Theobolus.
110 *Py.*   Rem omnem, ut est, tenes.
      Ego, ut adventastis huc, rapio pallam,
      in balneas curro festina, Chrysim voco.
      'Heus, Chrysis!' inquam 'Chrysis, frater adest domi,
      peregre reversus. Quid stas? An nondum venis?'
115   Ille, qui argentum dederat, rubet illico,
      post pavet. 'Hem, mea Chrysis, hoccine' ait
      'te facere? Insalutatum me deserere?'
      Illa 'Bonum animum' inquit 'habe: redeam,
      ad cenam veniam ubi decretum est. Vale'.
Ly.   Dixin ego? Sed quid Cassina?
120 *Py.*   Etiam redit.

Chrysis. What are you two arguing about under your breath?
Come here, Sedulius, quick!   100
Sedulius. I'm coming.
Chrysis. Come inside with me.
Sedulius. Gladly.

:   III   :

Lybiphanes, Pythias

[*Inside Canthara's brothel*]

Lybiphanes. Those two are celebrating their second nuptials inside.
That sister of yours, Pythias, is very charming, isn't she, but
where did you find her? Where did she bathe? Is it true, as I
think, that Theobolus paid for it? He was paying for tonight   105
with her bath-ticket. Tell me, please. We're alone, the secret
won't leak out. Then we'll lie down together and make love.
Pythias. Who told you about this?
Lybiphanes. Someone who knows: Theobolus himself told me today in the forum.
Pythias. Then you know the facts of the story. When you arrived,   110
I grabbed a cloak and ran straight into the bath and called
Chrysis. "Hey, Chrysis! I say, Chrysis, your brother's home
from abroad. What are you staying here for? Aren't you coming
yet?" That man who had given her the money first turns red,   115
then gets frightened. "Oh, my Chrysis"; he says, "How can you
do this? Are you going to leave me without even a greeting?"
And she said, "Don't worry, I'll be back. I'll meet you at dinner
at the place we decided on. Farewell."
Lybiphanes. I knew it! But what about Cassina?
Pythias. She came back too; Charinus ran into her and escorted   120

Charinus obviam fuit, qui illam domum
perduxit. Nunc reor ambos permolere.
Sed nos, quid agimus? Cur non coimus etiam?

Ly. Pone puellum.

Py.   Iam dormit. Ah, vir veniet!

125 *Ly.* Ne dubita. Cadum hunc exhaurire prius
sententia est; nam fauces omnes arent. Bibe.

Py. Bene admones; nam potus eque atque coitus
sapiunt michi. Istec si absint, nolim vivere.
Sed infelix est omnis nupta, que imperium
fert viri.

130 *Ly.*   Infelicior istic, qui femine
subiectus est. Emori velim quam nubere.

Py. At nullum fidelem invenias virum sue
coniugi.

Ly.   Nec ullam marito feminam.
Casta est quam nemo rogat, nemo stimulat.

135 Oculo potius solo quam solo viro
contenta est mulier: indomitum est animal,
nullis regendum frenis nullisque monitis.
Tolerabile est, si quis inscius colla dat
maritali capistro semel tantum; sed hic

140 qui, liber factus, novis se iugis implicat,
tam excusari potest quam qui bis naufragium
pertulit, primo non sat admonitus malo.
Scite, mehercule, canones eos abigunt
sacerdotio qui secundas in nuptias

145 migrant: namque stultis sunt stultiores quidem
indignique templis ministrare biiuges.
Coniugis maritus est vile mancipium,
servitutem malam quod servit et pessimam.
Is sapit qui vobis sic utitur ut ego:

150 tu michi vas tuum das, ego tibi meum

her home. Now, I think, the two of them are screwing. But what about us? Why don't we have sex, too?

Lybiphanes. Put our little boy to bed.[5]

Pythias. He's already asleep. Oh look, there's a man coming!

Lybiphanes. No doubt! But I vote for finishing off this jug of wine first, as our throats are dry. Bottoms up! 125

Pythias. Sound advice; it's smart to drink and have sex if you ask me. If they didn't exist, I wouldn't want to go on living. Every married woman who is under her husband's thumb is unhappy.

Lybiphanes. But the man who's subject to a woman is even more unhappy. I'd rather die than be married. 130

Pythias. You'll never find a married man who's faithful to his spouse.

Lybiphanes. Nor a wife faithful to her husband. The only chaste woman is the woman whom no one wants and who isn't sexy. A woman is as happy having one man as she would be having one eye. She's an untamed animal, ungovernable by any restraints or advice. It's tolerable if an inexperienced man puts his head in the marital noose just once. But a man who's been set free and puts his head under the yoke a second time is as inexcusable as the man who has been shipwrecked twice, having learned nothing from the first disaster. Canon law is wise, by Hercules, to exclude men from the priesthood who drift into second marriages.[6] For men with two yokes on their necks are dumber than dumb, and unworthy of serving in temples. A husband is a vile slave to his wife; the grievous servitude he suffers is the worst. The wise man is he who uses courtesans as I do. You give me your pot to use, and I give you mine. I'm exactly as in- 150

utendum; tantum tibi obligor quantum tu michi.
Popisma ut emisimus, liberi ambo sumus.

Py.   Nimis sciolus es, postquam bibisti satis!
Sed veni, mi columbe, mi passerule,
mi turtur, mi galle! Quid agis?

155 Ly.   Hem, venio.

: IV :

Charinus

Char. O stultas hominum mentes et vanas nimis!
O mortalium ceca pectora! O Furie
Eumenides, quid vexatis humanum genus?
Quo sapientiorem se quisque iudicat,

160   eo stultior est. Vidi plures in foro
nuper propter Armeniacos ire anxios;
illos namque invasisse dolent imperium
et occidisse quosdam Suicenses truces.
Hostem volunt alii externum propulsarier

165   ulciscique suos. Tum post quidam togati
non capio quid divisionis flebile
inter pontifices aiunt esse maxumos.
Ego sapientis verbum mente teneo:
curas post tergum decet inanes mittier.

170   Ut in cavea certant pulli gallinacii
esce causa, quibus cras est decretum mori,
sic propter imperium contendunt homines,
quod quam diu tenere debeant nesciunt.
At ubi carendum sit, imperio prius

175   quam cibo malim carere. Quid refert mea,
Gallus an Teutonicus uter imperet?
Stulta est cura que nichil parturit commodi.

debted to you as you to me. After we've both gotten off, we're both free.

Pythias. You're a real know-it-all when you've been drinking! But come, my dove, my little sparrow, my turtle-dove, my barnyard cock. Get to it!

Lybiphanes. Oh, I'm coming.   155

: IV :

Charinus

[Alone, in front of his house]

Charinus. O how foolish and vain are the minds of men! O how blind are their hearts! O you Furies, O Eumenides, why do you vex the human race so?[7] The wiser every man thinks himself to be, the more foolish he is. I've seen numbers of people just now going about the forum moaning about the Armagnacchi; they're   160 lamenting that the latter have invaded the Empire and killed some ferocious Swiss soldiers.[8] Some people want to drive the Armagnacchi out and revenge their dead comrades. Then there are some gentlemen of the toga who say there is some kind of   165 awful dissension between pontiffs.[9] For my part, I keep in mind that saying of the wise: that useless worries are best put behind you. Just as chickens who are destined to be slaughtered tomorrow fight among themselves for feed in the henhouse, so men   170 contend for empire when they have no idea how long they'll be permitted to hold it. If I'm going to give up something, I'd sooner give up an empire than my dinner. What does it matter to me whether a Frenchman or a German rules? It's foolish to   175 worry about things that bring no benefit. There's nothing better

Nil animo melius placido et libero;
nec regnum nec honor cum quiete convenit.
180   Qui, paucis contentus, ad naturam sibi
instituit vitam nec studet honoribus,
istic, me iudice, sapit; hunc ego sequor,
huic me parem prepare; que sunt, divitias
effundo, non quero novas. Qui me sequitur,
185   illic sibi curet. Nil post obitum volo.
Nemo funera faxit mortuo nec mihi
sarchophagum statuat. Quid gloria vanius
sepulchrali? Seu me vermes edant vel aves,
tantumdum facio, dummodo vivens edam
190   et bibam quod placet, dummodo letus meus
sit animus. Hoc ago curoque sedulo.
Nunc ex balneo Cassinam accersivi meam
et ad me iussi ut veniret. Quamvis alius
argentum dederat, sibi ut esset mundior,
195   ast ego primitias habeo. Ter Venus
restincta est illinc, euax! quo lubet modo.

: V :

Archimenides amator, Antiphila meretrix, Canthara lena

Ar.   Tu sola hic es? Ubinam alie, Anthiphila?
      Ubi alii?
An.   Sola, et anus hec. Sole sumus;
      sed aderunt, ut autumo, quam citissime;
200   cena iam cocta est, et vinum affertur vetus.
Can.   At istuc primum esse oportuit, Anthiphila!
      Viden ut arent fauces? Pulmone nichil

than a tranquil and free mind; neither power nor glory are compatible with tranquility. The wise man is he who is content with few things and leads his life according to nature without 180 pursuing honors; and I follow and model myself on the wise man.[10] I only spend what money I have; I don't seek for more. The next generation can look after itself. After I'm dead I won't want for anything. No one will hold a grand funeral or erect a 185 tomb for me. What glory is vainer than a glorious tomb? It's all the same to me whether I'm eaten by worms or birds, so long as I can eat and drink as I please while I'm alive; so long as my heart is serene. It's this that I care about and work for. Now I've 190 summoned my Cassina from the bath and bade her come to me. Even if somebody else gave her the money for her bath, I'll get the first pick of the garden. I've had it off with her three 195 times —hooray— in just the way I like.

ː V ː

Archimenides, a lover; Antiphila, a prostitute;
Canthara, an aged procuress

[*Canthara's brothel*]

Archimenides. Are you alone here, Antiphila? Where are the other women? Where are the other men?

Antiphila. Yes, we're alone, I and this old woman. But the others will be back, I'm sure, as soon as possible. Dinner is ready and a vintage wine has been set out. 200

Canthara. The wine should come first, Antiphila. Don't you see

est meo siccius. Proh, vix queo spuere,
vix loqui! O vinum! Heu vinum! Cur, vinum, taces?
205 Non vereor vera loqui: sum multibiba,
merobiba, non limphibiba aut medobiba,[1]
neque cervisiam bibo neque siceram:
Theucris hec largior et Boemis pocula.
Quasi lagena sum, ubi vinum solet Chium
210 condi. Quid opus verbis? Sum vinosissima,
et fluvium, si vini siet, recipiam . . . Ah,
flos veteris vini meis naribus
obiectus est! Nunc eius amor me cupidam
letificat. Ubi, ubi est? Euax, est me prope!
215 Ar. Eccum, accipe vitrum. Pota, festiva, bibe!
Esto michi propitia, suscipe phialam.
Can. Canthara mihi est nomen: ex cantharo bibam.
Ah, habeo! Salve, anime mi, Liberi lepos!
Ut veteris, vetusti vini sum cupida!
220 Nam omnium unguentum odos pre tuo nausea est.
Tu mihi cinamomum, tu rosa, tu crocus,
tu cassia es. Nam ubi tu profusus fueris,
illic ego me sepultam, hercule, pervelim.
Ut dulcis nasum odos obsecutus es meum,
225 da vicissim meo gutturi gaudium.
Accede, Bacche! Tete ipsum expeto tangere,
tuos liquores peramo. Sitio, bibam!
Vah, quam molliter, quam percurrit arterias
suaviter! Iam venas omnes letarier
230 sentio; cor salit, redeunt iam spiritus.
Hoc est vivere, hoc agere est hominis!
Ar. Bella potatrix! Viden ut pulcre ingurgitat?
Eapse merum sic condidicit bibere;
aliis aquam, ut bibant, dat mulieribus.
235 Sed ubi tu nunc es, libello Venereo

how parched my throat is? Nothing's drier than my gullet. Good God! I can hardly spit or talk. O wine, dear wine! Why don't you talk to me, wine? I'm not afraid to tell the truth: I'm a wine-bibber. I drink it neat:[11] I don't drink wine mixed with water, I don't drink it mixed with honey, I don't drink cider or beer. I leave those tipples to the Turks and Bohemians. I'm like a wine-flask, a wine-cellar for Chian wine. In short, I'm a positive sponge when it comes to wine: if there were a river made of wine I'd drink it! Ah! I can smell the bouquet of a vintage wine! [*Purblind, she feels her way towards the bottle*] My love for it fills my greedy heart with joy. Where is it, where? Hurray! It's right here!

Archimenides. Here, take the whole bottle. Drink, celebrate, down the hatch! Cheers! Lift your glass.

Canthara. Canthara is my name, and it's from a cantharus[12] that I drink. [*She finds the cantharus*] Ah, I have you! Hail, my soul, delight of Liber![13] I'm greedy for old, for ancient wines! Next to your fragrance all other perfumes stink. You are my cinnamon, my rose, my saffron, my marjoram. I want to dig my grave on the ground where you are spilled, by Hercules! Your sweet scent has gratified my sense of smell, now let it pleasure my palate! Come hither, Bacchus! I long to touch you, I'm besotted with your juices. I thirst; let me drink! Ah, how softly, how sweetly it courses through my arteries! How it cheers all my veins! My heart leaps up; my spirits are now restored! This is what it means to live! This is what it means to be human!

Archimenides. You beautiful drunk! Do you see how beautifully she gulps it down? She's mastered the art of drinking wine neat; she gives the water to the other women to drink. But where are you now, you who have served me with a summons from Venus? Look, I present myself to the court; are you appearing against me?[14]

205

210

215

220

225

230

235

que me citasti? Ecce, me sisto; contrane ades?

An. Adsum; nam, si absim, nichil mihi recusem mali.

Ar. Anime mi, non est consentaneum procul
amantem abesse. Retine me, amplectere.

240 *An.* Hoc etiam est quamobrem cupio vivere,
quia te ipsum video, teneo, potior.

Can. Enimvero quis non istos iam nunc arguat?
Bonum est parum amare sane, insane non bonum est;
verum totum insane amare, hoc isti faciunt.

245 *Ar.* Sibi habeant regna reges et divitias,
sibi honores, sibi virtutes, pugnas sibi,
sibi prelia, sibi quodlibet, dum mihi
abstineant invidere, sibique habeat
quod suum est quisque; tu mihi semper, Anthiphila,

250 ut nunc placeas teque perpetuo fruar.

Can. Vos istec missa facite; post repetite,
cum accubabitis. Iam cenare nos et bibere
tempus est. Sed forum crepitum et cardinum
visa sum audire. Apage te, iam veniunt.

: VI :

Dyophanes et Theobolus amantes; Canthera lena

255 *Dyo.* Nimirum fallimur, decepti sumus!
Silentium magnum est hic in edibus.
Sed eccam Cantharam. Salve, Canthara.

Can. Salvete, mea vindemia, messis mea!
Quin ascenditis, aucupium meum?

Theo. Ha he he!

Can.   Quid rides?

Antiphila. I am; if I didn't, I would be admitting my guilt.

Archimenides. Sweetheart, it's not right for a lover to stand so far away. Hold me, embrace me!

Antiphila. This is what gives me reason to live: to see you, hold   240
you, make love to you.

Canthara. [*Aside*] Upon my word! Who wouldn't scold them for the way they are acting now? A little healthy lovemaking is a good thing, unhealthy love isn't; but the kind of billing and cooing these two are getting up to is positively sickening.

Archimenides. Let kings have their kingdoms and their riches, their   245
honors, virtues, battles and wars, whatever they wish, so long as they don't envy me; to each his own. May you delight me always as you delight me now, Antiphila, and may I enjoy you forever.   250

Canthara. Stop all this mush, you two. Save it for later when you're in bed. Right now, it's time for us to eat and drink. But if I'm not mistaken, I hear the hinges of the door creaking open. Be off with you! They're coming!

: VI :

Dyophanes, Theobolus, lovers; Canthara, a procuress

[*The vestibule of the brothel*]

Dyophanes. Obviously we've been tricked, we've been made fools   255
of! This house is dead quiet. But here's Canthara. Hello, Canthara.

Canthara. Welcome, my vintage, my harvest. Why don't you come up, my fine-feathered fowl?

Theobolus. Ha, ha, he!

Canthara. What are you laughing at?

Theo.		Te rideo.
260	*Can.*	Cur?

Theo. Quia veridica es, remque, ut est, ais.
    Nam, nisi nos simus, fame pereas.
Can. Siti perire possum, non fame.
    Sed vide, quia non bene dixi aucupium
265   vos esse? Sed questus quem facio
    similis est aucupii. In aucupio
    hec sunt: auceps, area, cibus, aves
    Hec domus est area, cibus est meretrix,
    ego sum auceps ac vos estis aves.
270   Qui bene salutati consuescitis
    et, compellati blanditer saviis,
    attractu papillarum et oratione venustula,
    tamquam aves deprendimini retibus.
Dyo. Nunquam melius dici verum vidi prius.
275   Sed ubi esca est nostra et nostri calamitas
    fundi? Perii, Theobole, nil video.
    Interii miser! Quid iam dicam aut faciam?
Can. At iam aderunt.
Dyo.   Istuc 'iam' annus erit!
Can. Imo mox venient.
Dyo.   'Mox' more Gallico,
280   quod annis quatuor et decem perficitur.
    Heu me miserum! Argentum ut aliis lavaret dedi.
    Siccine fit, Cassina? Siccine me trahis
    promerentem optime? Hoccine premium
    bene merenti reddis? At malo cum tuo,
285   perlecebre, pernicies, exitium!
    Nam mare non mare est ut tu es mare.
    Ingrata atque irrita sunt omnia
    que dedi aut, pol, feci bene! At posthac tibi
    male quod potero facere faciam.

Theobolus. I'm laughing at you.

Canthara. Why? 260

Theobolus. Because you speak with the mouth of truth; you tell it
as it is. Indeed, if it weren't for us, you'd die of starvation.

Canthara. I can die of thirst but not hunger. But look, wasn't I
right when I called you my fowl? My line of work is just like
fowling. In hunting for birds you have four things: a hunter, a 265
clearing, bait and birds. This house is the clearing; the bait is
the courtesan; I'm the hunter; and you are the birds. You feel at
home here and start to haunt the place; you're driven towards 270
us with sweet kisses, sweet little speeches, breasts for caressing,
then we take you like birds in our nets.

Dyophanes. I've never heard the truth spoken so well before!
But where is our bait, the scourge of our estates? Damn it, 275
Theobolus, I don't see anything! I'm so depressed I'm going to
die. What's left to say, what's left to do?

Canthara. They'll be here presently.

Dyophanes. This "presently" of yours is going to be a year.

Canthara. No, really, they'll be here soon.

Dyophanes. "Soon," *à la mode française*, in other words, fourteen
years! I'm so depressed! I gave her money so she could bathe 280
and be beautiful for other men! Isn't this what's happened,
Cassina? Is this how you treat me, somebody who deserves the
best? Is this my reward for treating you so well? Well, the hell
with you, my little decoy, my ruin, my destruction! You're as 285
dangerous and destructive as the high seas! By Pollux, does it
count for nothing, all that I've given you, all that I've done for
you? But from now on I'm going to treat you as badly as I can.

290 Ego, pol, te ulciscar ut digna es utque meres
de me, ut que sis nunc et que fueris scias.
Redigam te unde orta es, ad egestatis terminos;
que, priusquam te adii, pane sordido
vitam oblectabas et in panis inopia.

295 Nunc, quia est melius, me, cuius opera est, fugitas,
meque ignoras, mala, qui vestibus
te nudam operui. Sed reddam iam te ex fera
mansuetam, si vivo, et humilem fame.

Theo. Vin meum experiri consilium?
Dyo.   Quid est?
Theo. Sine eas venire.
300 Dyo.   Si venerint tamen.
Theo. At venient, hercle! Rimate stabula
postquam fuerint omnia et omnes viculos
percurrerint, venient squalide, sordide,
inmunde, fimo ac stercore fetide.

305 Dicent rem seriam sese fecisse domi,
sed odos teter indicabit scelus.
Venient, quia nemo cubilibus
dignatur eas; nec ipsi qui fricant equos,
postquam restinctus ignis est, retinent eas.

310 Colluvies primitus omnis hominum
fexque populi debet saturarier;
tum, culinarum peruncte abdomine
eruptatoque vino in nostros madide
migrabunt amplexus; et quo nunc coquos

315 ac muliones ore et sandapilas,
histriones et mimos et tibicines
exosculantur, eodem nobis savium
oppegisse volent. Tum nos hic in angulis
spernentes eas sedebimus, nec bibere

320 aut comedere, nec condormire quoque

306

By Pollux, I'll take my revenge on you as you deserve and as   290
your treatment of me merits — you'll find out the difference between what you were to me before and what you are now! I'll
send you back to the life of destitution I rescued you from. Before I came, you were happy with a dirty crust of bread, when
you had bread at all. Now, when things are better you run away   295
from the man who made things better for you. You ignore
me — me! — you bitch, the man who dressed you from head to
toe! But if I survive, I'll tame you, you wild beast! Hunger will
make you humble again!

Theobolus. Would you like a word of advice?

Dyophanes. What is it?

Theobolus. Just wait until they arrive.

Dyophanes. If they arrive at all.   300

Theobolus. They'll be here, by Hercules. After they've stuck their
heads into every stable[15] and peddled themselves down every
alley in town, they'll be back, filthy, sweaty, caked in mire
and stinking of dung. They'll claim that they had some heavy
housework to do, but their foul odor will reveal the nasty truth.   305
They'll be back because no one thinks they're worth taking to
bed; not even the stable-boy who rubs down the horses, once
his fire has been put out, will keep them around. They have to
satisfy first the dregs of humanity, the lowest of the low; then,   310
their bellies smeared with kitchen-grease and soaking in wine-
vomit, they'll wander into our embraces; and after they've bestowed wet kisses on cooks and mule-drivers and gravediggers   315
and actors and trumpet-players, they'll want to plant kisses on
us with the same mouths. When that happens we'll just sit
here in the corner and scorn them; we won't deign to drink or
eat with them, or sleep with them either. This way, we can tor-   320

307

dignabimur. Hoc eas cruciatu nimis
afficiemus, ulciscemurque iniurias.

Dyo. Si nos amarent, tunc istoc utier
modo liceret; sed ille nos nihili
pendunt.

325 *Theo.*   Dum quod damus amant iam diu!
Nos amittant, facileque iniurias
illis damus.

Dyo.   At istuc nobis multo egrius ·
quam illis erit, si neque loqui neque tangere
licet.

Theo.   Quid ais, ridiculum capitulum?

330 *Dyo.* Male ulcisci qui plus sibi quam hosti nocet.
Carere cena et potu queo, cubatu non queo.
Ego in sinu mee dormire volo,
vel si caprum oleat.

Theo.   Si sic devincier
sinis teque captivum prebes, iam funditus

335 occidisti. Nam te fixum sentiet
aput se clavo Cupidinis nec redimi
posse, nec tibi parcet; nam meretrix,
cum amanti parcit, sibi non retur parcere.
Actum est, ilicet, et conclamatum est: rapiet

340 actutum quicquid est usquam tibi gentium.
In frena te stringet, sellam coget ut feras,
quasi mule dorso insedebit tuo.
Heu, quibus te miserum lacerabit modis
tua Celeno! Nam quem meretricis amor

345 urget, is, nisi amorem dissimulat,
perditior est perditis in lacu Stigis.

Dyo. Quid igitur faciam?

Theo.   Ut simules te nichil
curare hanc.

ment them without mercy and avenge ourselves for our injuries.

Dyophanes. If they really loved us, we could deal with them this way, but the fact is they don't give a damn about us.

Theobolus. What they've loved for a long time now is the stuff 325 we've given them. Just by taking them off the payroll, we'll do them a lot of damage.

Dyophanes. But if we can't talk to them or touch them, it's going to hurt us much more than it will them.

Theobolus. What are you talking about, you pinhead?

Dyophanes. It's poor revenge when you hurt yourself more than 330 your enemy. I can deprive myself of food and drink, but not sex. I want to sleep in the arms of my Cassina, even if she does smell like a goat.

Theobolus. If you let yourself be beaten that way and become her prisoner, you're ruined already. She'll know she's got you locked 335 up with Cupid's key; you can't ransom yourself and she won't show you any mercy; for when a courtesan shows mercy to a lover, she has no mercy on herself. Forget it, it's all over but the shouting. In a minute she'll have you stripped of all you're 340 worth. She'll be pulling the reins, she'll make you carry the saddle and will ride you like a mule. Alas, how many ways is this Celaeno of yours going to tear you limb from limb, you poor fellow![16] A man in love with a whore who doesn't know how to 345 conceal it is more damned than the damned in Hell.

Dyophanes. So what should I do?

Theobolus. Pretend you don't care about her at all.

Dyo.   At neque istec quicquam magis
me faciet.

Theo.   Faciet.

Dyo.   Qui? Si ego renuo?

350 Theo. Nosco mulierum mores et ingenia;
nam que velis nolunt, que nolis volunt.

Dyo. Si sic admones, parebo.

Theo.   Sic facto est opus.
Sed heus, tu!

Dyo.   Quid vis?

Theo.   Non tamen prohibeo
hanc illis exprobrarier contumeliam,
at verbis.

355 Dyo.   Verbis constantibus, mordacibus.
Sed quid iam nunc illic clamitat coquus?

: VII :

Artrax coquus

Obsonium coctum est; iam cena deperit.
Iam disquamavi pisces; congros, murenulas
exdorsuavi, iam faxo exossata sient.

360   Pulli gallinacii et pigargi bulliunt.
Oricem veru tenet et leporem.
Clunes apri optumo more condiam.
Ardee quoque due atque merule decem
asse sunt istic cum duobus pavonibus.

365   Perdices dum vivo iam plus mille memini
coxisse, sed his nunquam meliores puto.
Vah, cena bona, uncta, sapida, lepida!
Ipsus mihi, dum narro, salivam moveo.

Dyophanes. But that's not going to make her treat me better.

Theobolus. Oh yes it will.

Dyophanes. How's that going to happen, if I reject her?

Theobolus. I know how women act and think: whatever you want, 350
they don't want, and vice versa.

Dyophanes. If this is your advice, I'll follow it.

Theobolus. You really must. But see here.

Dyophanes. What?

Theobolus. I'm not saying you shouldn't lay into her — I mean with
words.

Dyophanes. With firm, biting words! But what's all that shouting 355
from the cook? [*Noise from the kitchen*]

: VII :

Artrax, a cook

[*The kitchen in the brothel*]

The main course is cooked and dinner is already being ruined.
I've scaled the fish; I've filleted the conger-eels and baby eels:
they'll be all meaty now. The chickens and hens are on the boil. 360
A baby goat and a rabbit are turning on the spit. I shall season
well this loin of boar. There are two herons and ten blackbirds
roasted, along with a couple of peacocks. I can remember cooking a thousand patridges in my life, but none better than these, 365
I think. Yes, it's a fine dinner — succulent, tasty, and inviting.

Sed huius quid si crus alterum voro gruis?
370   Facile hoc genus avis dicam monopedum,
que semper in pratis uno consistit pede.
Vah, comedant isti frigidum, ego calidum!

: VIII :

Charinus et Sedulius amantes, Lybiphanes familiaris

Char. Nil amor est aput homines nisi
dura carnificina, aspera et teterrima.
375   Hoc ego in me sentio, qui omnes homines
supero animi cruciabilitatibus.
Iactor, vorsor, agitor, stimulor, crucior
in amoris rota; miser exanimor.
Feror, differor, distrahor, diripior,
380   ita meo nulla mens est animo,
ita ingenium omne perdidi meum.
Quod lubet non lubet iam id continuo,
ita me amor lapsum animo ludificat;
fugat, agit, appetit, raptat, retinet;
385   quod dat non dat, deludit, quod suasit modo
iam dissuadet, quod dissuasit mox imperitat.
Ubi sum, ibi non sum; ubi non sum, illic est animus;
ut maris fluctus huc et illuc trahor;
iam mihi nulla abest perdito pernicies.
390 *Sedu.* Quid hic secum duriter amorem culpitat?
Edepol, qui amat, si eget, miseris
erumnis afficitur! Adibo atque alloquar.
Salve, Charine. Quid est?
Char.   Hem, Seduli, quid est

My mouth is watering just describing it. It won't matter if I just gobble a second leg of crane. It will be easy to tell them that this species of bird is a monoped, given that they're always standing on one leg in the meadows. Bah, let them eat the food cold; I'm eating mine hot!   370

: VIII :

Charinus, Sedulius, lovers; Lybiphanes, servant

[*In front of Canthara's brothel*]

Charinus. [*To himself*] For men, love is nothing but merciless torture, savage and horrible. I feel this in my own case, I who exceed all mankind in the mental agonies I suffer. I've been led on, turned around, shaken, stirred, and flayed alive on love's wheel. I'm dying of misery. I have been so drawn and quartered by this love that the capacity to think has deserted my soul; I've lost my wits entirely. Love makes such a mockery of my shattered reason that my likes and dislikes change continually. Love puts me to flight, drives me away; it wants me, it grabs me and holds me fast; it gives with one hand and takes away with the other; it dupes me, it urges a course of action that only just now it had disfavored, and what it had disfavored it now commands. I'm not where I am; my heart is where I'm not. I'm tossed hither and yon like the waves of the sea; in my doomed state, I'm prey to every disaster there is.   375   380   385

Sedulius. [*Aside*] Why is this fellow talking to himself, blaming Love with such severity? By Pollux, everyone who loves suffers afflictions when deprived of his lover. I'll go over and talk to him. Hello, Charinus. What's wrong?   390

Charinus. Oh, Sedulius, you want to know what's wrong? I'm

313

rogas? Exedor, maceror et exenteror;

395 amando miser perii, occidi, interii!

Sedu. Absurde facis, qui te sic angas animi;
in re mala animo iuvat utier bono.

Char. Consule quid agam.

Sedu.   Morbum patefacito.

Char. Mea Cassina et tua Chrysis dormient

400 aput Cantharam lenam in edicula.

Sedu. Scio.

Char.   Scis et taces?

Sedu.   Scio et taceo.

Nam scortum fortunati est oppidi simile,
quod rem non servat sine multis viris.
Nubere vult meretrix quotidie

405 novis maritis. Nupsit hodie mihi,
hac noctu nubat ut aliis decet.
Nunquam vidua cubare vult domi;
nam, si non nubit sepe, fame perit.
Num tibi sat est horis compluribus

410 in eius amplexu iacuisse quam amas?
Da locum aliis, queso: nihil diminuent!
Que nunc est hec, etiam cras eadem
ad te redibit.

Char.   Hau! Hau! Frustra tecum loquor.
Quid tu, Lybiphanes, michi nunc ais?

415 *Ly.* Eum qui amat hominem miserrimum.

Char. Imo, ecastor, qui pendet multo est miserior!
Sed consule, obsecro atque reobsecro, mihi.

Ly. Si mihi auscultas, excudi iam consilium.
Scio Dyophanem atque Theobolum

420 nunc his succensere, quia tardiuscule
cenatum vadunt. Monebo has meretriculas,
illorum ut temnant iras atque irrideant;

eaten up, I'm exhausted, I'm eviscerated; wretch that I am, I'm
finished, dead and buried—all because of Love!   395

Sedulius. It's absurd for you to torment yourself so. It's better to
keep a cheerful attitude in unfortunate circumstances.

Charinus. Tell me what I should do.

Sedulius. Explain your affliction to me.

Charinus. My Cassina and your Chrysis will be sleeping at
Canthara's brothel.   400

Sedulius. I know.

Charinus. You know, but you say nothing?

Sedulius. Exactly. Look, a prostitute is like a prosperous town that
needs many men to preserve its flourishing state. A courtesan
wants to marry new husbands on a daily basis. Today she mar-   405
ried me; tonight it's fine for her to marry some other men. She
never wants to go home to her bed as a widow; if she doesn't
take frequent husbands, she'll die of hunger. Isn't it enough for
you to have lain for so many long hours in the arms of the
woman you love? Give others their chance, please: they're not   410
going to eat her up! The girl will come back to you tomorrow
the same as she is today.[17]

Charinus. For God's sake! It's a waste of time talking to you. So
what are you telling me, Lybiphanes?

Lybiphanes. I'm saying that someone in love is bound to be the 415
most miserable of men.

Charinus. No, no, by Castor: somebody hanging from a gibbet is
much worse off! But I beg of you, I implore you: tell me what
to do!

Lybiphanes. If you'll just listen to me, I already have a plan. I know
that Dyophanes and Theobolus are angry with the girls because
they arrived a bit late for dinner tonight. I'll tell these little tarts 420
to pay no attention to their lovers' anger and make fun of it;

nam sic eos ludificabunt magis.
Tum rixam miscebunt seseque divident.
425 Vos in insidiis ibidem presto eritis,
ut, his abeuntibus, ingrediamini.
Char. At si lena faveat; nam me nescit ea.
Ly. Cedo argentum; cuius est ymagine
signatum?
Char. Cesaris.
Ly. At hec novit Cesarem,
430 et te lubentius quam Lubentiam
agnoscet; nam crumena illorum est vacua,
et tua nova est et plena plenior.
Idem est lene amator quod piscis quidem:
nam piscis nequam est nisi sit recens;
435 is habet sucum, is suavitatem,
quovis pacto coquas atque condias.
En, quam leta erit te piscem advenisse novum!
Sed eccas euntes. Nisi te tenes, eo.
Char. I, frugi servule; iam nos sequimur.

: IX :

Charinus

440 *Char.* Hoc quod iste facit servi faciunt boni,
qui neque more neque molestie imperium
habent herile sibi. Nam qui ex sententia
servire postulat hero, hunc in herum
matura, in se sera condecet capessere.
445 Et qui servus amare cognoscit dominum,
is retinere ad salutem herum, vel si tacet,
debet, ut istic occipissit modo.

that way, the girls will make even bigger fools of them. They'll
then provoke a quarrel and create a rift. Meanwhile, we'll be
lying in wait, ready to go in the moment Dyophanes and   425
Theobolus leave.

Charinus. It will work if the old bawd will help, but she doesn't
know me.

Lybiphanes. Take this coin: whose image do you see on it?

Charinus. Caesar's.

Lybiphanes. Well, she knows Caesar very well, and she'll make the
pleasure of your acquaintance more readily than that of the   430
goddess Pleasure herself. After all, their purse is empty, while
yours is brand new and overflowing. For a madam like that, a
lover is like a fish: a fish is no good unless it's fresh; fresh fish is
juicy and sweet, however you cook it and season it. You'll see   435
how happy she'll be to have a fresh fish like you in her net! But
look, they're coming. Go before they catch you.

Charinus. Go ahead, my fine young servant! I'm following you.

: IX :

Charinus

Charinus. Good slaves do what this one here does; he regards the   440
command of his master as something to be done quickly and
without complaint. For the man who wishes to serve his master
sincerely needs to attend to the master's business early and his
own late. And the slave who knows his master is in love ought   445
to uphold his master's interests, even if his master says nothing,

Nam, quamvis dissimulat Sedulius,
non tamen ardet minus; quod servulus
450   agnoscit callidus. Ideo, quasi mihi
salutem procurassit, vel illi consulit.
Namque erubescit hic amorem faterier,
quia meretrix est quod amat. Ego
nil mihi dedecoris existumo fore,
455   si quod palam est venale nummis emo.
Nemo me ire publica prohibet via,
dum ne per agrum clausum faciam semitam.
Si nuptis abstineo, vidua, virgine,
nemo me scortum amare prohibet aut vetat.

: X :

Chrysis et Cassina meretrices

460 *Chry.* Recte, ut opinor, Lybiphanes ait:
acerbis quam blandis retinetur artius
amator verbis, quom captus est semel.
At eant hi quo velint, abeant, fugiant;
an forma nostra est que vendi nequeat?
465   Satis hos emunximus; nam sanguinem
elicias oppido, si premas amplius.
Quod si procos redamassimus novos,
de pleno melius promeremus ubere.
Volt placere novus amator statim,
470   volt posci, volt dare, volt effundere,
volt placere sese lene, volt mihi,
volt pedisseque, volt catulo meo,
auroque gravem porrigit manum.
Subblanditur semper amator novos,

just as Lybiphanes here is doing. Sedulius, even though he pretends otherwise, is no less in love than I am, and that clever little slave of his knows it. So he consults his master's interests 450 while appearing to look out for mine. Sedulius, in fact, is ashamed to confess his love because it's a courtesan that he loves. As for me, I don't think there's anything dishonorable if I buy what is lying out openly for sale. Nobody is going to pre- 455 vent me from going down the public road so long as I don't stray into a fenced-off field. If I stay away from married women, widows, and virgins, no one will prevent me or forbid me to love a whore.

: X :

Chrysis, Cassina, prostitutes

[*Approaching Canthara's brothel*]

Chrysis. I think Lybiphanes was right to say it: once a lover is 460 caught in our trap, he's kept there more securely with bitter than with sweet words. But let them go where they want, let them leave; let them fly; our beauty will always find buyers. We've wiped the noses of these two enough already; if you squeezed any harder you might positively draw blood. But if we 465 were to become attached to new suitors, we might suck better from a full teat. A brand-new lover wants to please you right away, he wants to be asked, he wants to give, he wants to be generous, he wants to ingratiate himself with the madam, with 470 me, with my maid, and with my pet puppy; and when he holds out his hand, it's heavy with gold. A new lover is always fawn-

475   antiquus semper inclamitat. Decet
         ad suum quemque questum esse callidum.
Cas.   Ita est ut dicis. Ego istuc sedulo,
         sic me dii servassint, adnitor facere.
         Nemo mihi plus mense amator sapit;
480   semper nove kalende amores novos
         afferunt michi.
Chry.   Nimis amas solide!
         Nam nonas et ydus celebrare nuptiis
         convenit recentibus; vel, ut ego
         institui vitam, cum novo sole novos
485   concubinos querere. Sed eccam in hostio
         Cantharam.
Cas.   Ipsa est, an non?
Chry.   Ipsissima est.

: XI :

Canthara lena, Chrysis meretrix

Can.   Quis tantum auri vel argenti in loculis
         servassit suis quantum nos, que sine
         prediis vivimus, largimur foras?
490   Argento solem et lunam et aquam et diem
         et noctem non emimus aut tenebras;
         cetera que volo Gallica mercor fide.
         A pistore cum panem petierim,
         vel cum vinum posco ex cenopolio
495   aut ex macello piscem, agnum vel edum,
         vacua redeo nisi es dederim.
         Itidem amatores ex me sentiunt:
         nemo huc intrat nisi dat argentum prius.

ing on you; an old one is always shouting abuse. Fittingly,   475
they're both wily at getting what they want.

Cassina. You're right. So help me God, that's just what I keep trying to do. No lover tastes good to me for more than a month;
the Kalends of each month always brings me new lovers.   480

Chrysis. You are far too constant in your love! It's really a better
idea to celebrate fresh nuptials on the Nones and Ides — or to
follow my way of life and seek new bed-mates every morning.
But look, Canthara is on the doorstep.   485

Cassina. Is it really Canthara?

Chrysis. Indeed it is.

:   XI   :

Canthara, procuress; Chrysis, courtesan

[*The vestibule of the brothel*]

Canthara. [*To herself*] Is there anyone who keeps as much gold and
silver in his strongbox as we, who live without landed property
to support us, squander abroad? We don't buy the sun and the   490
moon and the water or the shadows of the night with silver, but
everything else I want I have to buy on French credit.[18] When I
shop for bread from the baker or wine from the wine-seller, or
fish, lamb, or goat from the butcher I return empty-handed un-   495
less I've paid cash. Johns hear the same thing from me: nobody
sets foot in this house without paying in cash first. I can't eat

Non pascor verbis, credo quod video.
500   Illi iam suum dederunt symbolum,
et mihi quod equum fuit. Si tamen duo
adveniant novi, qui argentum novum
afferant, non recusabo pandere
posticum, ut intrent domum clanculum.
505   Sed quisnam est qui Vulcanum in cornu gerit?
Chrysin video. Salve, Chrysis mea.

Chry. Salvam hercle gaudeo te esse, Canthara.
Quid nostri homines?

Can.   Subtristes accubant.

Chry. Duc nos supra; iam faxo ut sint hilares.

510 *Can.* Ite, pascua mea et feraces vinee!

: XII :

Chrysis et Cassina meretrices, Theobolus et Dyophanes amantes

Chry. Salvere iubeo amatores optumos;
salvete, qui fidem facitis maxumi!
Ducite ex animo curam et hilares
hac noctu, fidi amantes, gaudio
515   operam date. Salvete, animuli,
vite nostre, festivitates mere.
Quid agitis, voluptates et festi dies?
Quid agitis, passeres, columbi, lepores?
Facessat meror. Quid aiunt? Proh, tacent!

520 *Cas.* Indignis qui bene dicit, is dicit male.
Potin tacere, cum sic ipsi tacent?

Chry. Indigna digna habenda sunt, que facit amor.

words, and I only believe what I can see. Those two have already paid their quota, with a fair share to me. But if two new   500
clients show up carrying more money, I wouldn't refuse to open
the back door and let them in the house on the sly. But who is
the person carrying the lantern? It's Chrysis. Hello, dear Chrysis!   505
Chrysis. By Hercules, I'm glad to see you're well, Canthara. What
are our men up to?
Canthara. They're lying down, sulking.
Chrysis. Take us upstairs. I'll try to cheer them up.
Canthara. Go, my pastures, my fertile vineyard!   510

: XII :

Chrysis, Cassina, prostitutes; Theobolus, Dyophanes, lovers

[*The bedroom*]

Chrysis. Hello and welcome, best of lovers; welcome, most faithful
of friends! Banish your cares and be glad this night, faithful
lovers; devote yourselves to pleasure. Welcome, sweethearts,   515
you who fill our lives with joy and feasting! What are you up to,
you who are the source of our delights, you who are our holidays? What are you doing, little sparrows, sweet doves, little
bunny-rabbits? [*To Cassina*] They're still sulking. What's that
they're saying? Oh for God's sake, they've shut their mouths.
Cassina. The person who speaks fine words to the unworthy is   520
wasting her breath. Couldn't you just give them the same silent
treatment they're giving you?
Chrysis. Unworthy actions caused by Love should be regarded as
worthy.

Cas. Mitte has, precor, statuas marmoreas.
Nemo plane sua intelligit bona
525   nisi, cum in potestate habuit, perdidit.
Chry. Noli obloqui, nec mirere quod silent:
decet verecundos esse adolescentulos!
Istec barba vix annos est tonsa bis decem.
Theo. Viden ut magna ingenia in occulto latent?
530   Nasci te virum, Chrysis, par fuerat!
Proh, verum est quod dicitur: mulieres duas
peiores esse quam unam. Sic experior!
Ite, meretricum genus pessimum,
que quasi musceque culicesque et pulices
535   omnibus estis damno atque molestie,
bono usui nulli! Nec quisquam hominum
vobiscum frugi consistere potest.
Qui consistit, culpant eum ceteri,
ipsumque remque fidemque dicunt perdere.
540   An satis peccasse fuit, nisi ultro etiam
irrisum nos veniretis, meretricule?
Cas. Quid nos peccavimus aut fecimus mali?
Venire diximus, ventum est. Pueri
non faxint que facitis. An nos aves
545   creditis, que volatu quo petitis
actutum percurramus? Exquirite alias!
Dyo. En audaciam muliebrem: viden
in manifesto ut se excusant scelere?
Cas. Nulla tam parvi est mulier pretii
550   que, si culpam in sese nullam admiserit,
nomen non velit suum retinere bonum.
Sed nichil ego vos demiror modo,
nam hec inter amandum sepe interveniunt.
Incidunt voluptates atque miserie,
555   intervenit ira, redit rursus gratia.

Cassina. Please, just forget about these marble statues. No one
truly understands the good things he has until he loses them.   525
Chrysis. Don't interrupt me. And don't wonder that they're so
quiet. Little boys *should* be restrained and meek; this lot must
be about twenty, their beards have hardly been cut.
Theobolus. Don't you see that men of great talent flourish in the
shadows? You should have been born a man, Chrysis. By God,   530
what they say is true: two women are worse than one. I know
this from experience. Go to hell, you courtesans, you evil breed!
You're just like flies, gnats and fleas, a dead loss and an annoy-
ance to everyone and useful to no one. No man can afford to   535
get involved with you. The man who does so is faulted by everybody else; they say he's ruined himself, his property, and his
reputation. Wasn't it enough to have mistreated us, without   540
coming here to make fun of us into the bargain, you little sluts?
Cassina. How have we mistreated you or done you harm? We said
we'd be here: we're here. Even little boys don't behave as you
two do. Do you think we're birds who will fly where you want   545
instantly? If that's what you think, find some other women!
Dyophanes. The impudence of that woman! Do you see how they
try to justify themselves for a manifest act of wickedness?
Cassina. There is no woman of such little worth that she won't try
to clear her good name when she's done nothing wrong. But I'm   550
not surprised at the way you two are acting; these little tiffs often happen in the course of love affairs. Pleasures and miseries
come and go, hot words are spoken, then you're reconciled to
each other again. And if you do happen to have a fight, then   555

At ire si que forte interveniunt,
si reventum in gratiam post fuerit,
bis tanto crescit amor quam perprius fuit.
Consulto agitis, ut maior voluptas siet,

560   in nostram cum remeaveritis gratiam.

    Dyo. Vestram nos redeamus in gratiam?
Ite in malam crucem ut estis merite, lupe!
Subicite vos quibus placet lenonibus,
que nulla non taberna prostatis hodie.

565 *Cas.* Per Iovem iuro et matrem familias
Iunonem et, quam vereri me decet, Venerem:
nemo me hodie extra te unum tetigit.

    Dyo. Vera istec velim.

    Cas.   Vera dico.

    Dyo.   Mulier es,
audacter iuras atque falsum iuras sciens.

570 *Cas.* Dii me omnes, nisi sum veridica, perdiunt!

    Dyo. At vos neque deos creditis neque deas
usquam esse, et animas cum corporibus
extingui putatis, scelestissime!
Verum, ut tu, Cassina, meam sententiam

575   et quid animi geram erga te scias,
ita me dii deeque superi et inferi
et medioxumi et Iuno regina
et Iovis supremi Pallas filia,
ac me Saturnus ipsius patruus

580   atque Ops opulenta illius avia
servassint et amassint diutius,
ut ego te, pessuma, dum vixero,
nec tangam posthac unquam nec alloquar,
quamvis per annos vivam Nestoreos.

585 *Cas.* Hei mihi, iam perimus, Chrysis! Quid agimus?
Amatores bellos amisimus, teneros.

make up afterwards, your lovemaking is twice as passionate as it was before. You two are doing this on purpose to increase your pleasure after you've returned to our good graces.   560

Dyophanes. Return to your good graces? Go to the hell you deserve, you she-wolves. Go spread your legs for the ruffians you like; after today you'll be on sale in every tavern in the town.

Cassina. I swear by Jove and mother Juno and Venus, whom I 565 should honor,[19] no one has laid a hand on me today besides you.

Dyophanes. Would that this were true!

Cassina. I'm telling you the truth.

Dyophanes. You're a woman. You'll swear with reckless abandon, in the full knowledge that you're perjuring yourself.

Cassina. May the gods strike me dead if I'm not telling the truth. 570

Dyophanes. But you don't believe the gods and goddesses ever existed, and you deny the immortality of the soul, you wicked creatures! But just so you know what I think, Cassina, and how 575 I feel about you, I swear by all gods and goddesses above, below, and in the middle regions of the earth, by Queen Juno and Athena, daughter of high Jove, and by Saturn his uncle and by Ops the wealthy, his grandmother; I swear, as I hope these 580 gods may succor me and love me in future, that I shall never again touch you nor speak to you, you dregs of womankind, so long as I live, even if I should live for Nestor's years.

Cassina. [Sarcastically] O woe is me! We're lost, Chrysis, what 585 should we do? We've lost two handsome, young lovers. Where

Ubinam gentium reperire similes
quimus? Proh, iam deserte, iam sumus vidue.
Heu, iam pullas oportet nos vestes emere!
590   At his saltem pretium emundis duint.
Chry. Sed meus hic amator me non relinquet, scio.
Theo. Quia reliqui, et dedi te tuis stabulis.
Abi ex oculis, nefandissima, citius,
que nummis preditata recalcitras meis.
595   Quod dedi datum nollem, reliquum non dabo.
Chry. Si peccatum esset quod putatis, madide
adhuc essemus. Sed agite periculum,
introspicite: sicut ex balneo
exivimus, munde et nitide sumus;
600   nec videri, si placet, refugimus.
Theo. Abite, inverecunde, sceleste, fetide!
Abite, ni vultis experirier
nostri quam pugni sint hodie graves!
Chry. Res seria est. Quid agimus, Cassina?
605   Si nunc nos suspendimus, operam lusimus,
et ultra operam restim perdidimus,
atque his voluptatem creaverimus,
qui tamquam inimici nostro gauderent malo.
Vivamus potius et comedamus satis;
610   sic illis fiet egre plus quam velint.

: XIII :

Archimenides amator, solus

Arch. Parva res est voluptas in etate hominum,
at molestie quidem longissime.
Voluptati semper est meror comes;
humana ut sunt, nihil est perpetuum datum.

on earth are we going to find men like them? O gods, now we're
abandoned women, now we're widows! Alas! Now we'll have to
buy ourselves mourning dress — though you two should at least
pay for that!   590

Chrysis. And yet I'm sure my lover here won't leave me.

Theobolus. You'd better believe it, because I've already left you and
abandoned you to your precious stables. Get out of my sight,
you unspeakable whore, and be quick about it! How dare you
turn up your nose at me after I've lavished my money on you! I
wish I hadn't, but at least I'm not giving you what's left.   595

Chrysis. If we had committed the offense you think we have, we'd
still be sweaty. But look, check it out for yourselves; look under
our dresses: we're as clean and pretty as when we left the bath.
We won't refuse to be inspected, if that's what you want.   600

Theobolus. Get out, you shameless, thieving, stinking whores! Get
out, unless you want to find out today how heavy our fists are!

Chrysis. [*To Cassina*] This is getting serious. What are we going to
do, Cassina? If we hang ourselves now, the effort will be wasted.   605
And quite apart from the effort, we'll lose the cost of the rope
and bring pleasure to these two, who'll enjoy themselves at our
expense as though they were our enemies. Better to go on living
and keep filling our bellies. That will bother these two more
than they'd like to believe.   610

: XIII :

Archimenides, lover, alone

Archimenides. Pleasure is a paltry thing in the life of a man, but
miseries endure. Sorrow is always a companion to pleasure.
Nothing everlasting is given us, as is the way with human

615   Hoc ego plane iam nunc experior,
         hanc qui noctem mihi iocundissimam
         futuram rebar. En, que nunc est turbatio!
         Esuriales illi iam ducunt ferias.
         Cum caduceo, quasi Mercurius,
620   componere hos inimicos volui;
         iste mihi auscultarent, illi non audiunt.
         Sed quid ego amicorum causa crucier,
         si sponte sua dolent, cum possint fungier
         isdem, quibus ego fruor, voluptatibus?
625   Herebo iam his voratricibus modo,
         hisque me letum dabo atque subblandiar.
         Stultum est curis se vexare superfluis;
         viden ut vinum ingurgitant ebriole?
         Nihil est in his mestitie: sapiunt.
630   Cum his sapere volo, non cum illis desipere.
         En fortunatus ego, qui nubere
         uni putabam; iam nubam tribus!

: XIV :

Canthara lena, Charinus et Sedulius amatores

Can. Quis illic est qui nunc posticum movet?
Char. Amicus tuus.
Can.   Quis amicus?
Char.   Ego.
Can. Quis tu 'ego' es?
Char.   Charinus.

affairs. I now know this from experience. I thought tonight was 615
going to be a night of supreme pleasure. But look what a mess
things are in now! Those two are now celebrating the Festival
of Famine. I wanted to settle their disagreements with a wave
of my caduceus, just like Mercury. The women might have lis- 620
tened to me, but the men won't hear a thing I say. But why
should I torment myself about my friends' problems, especially
since they brought it on themselves, as they might have enjoyed
the same pleasures that I enjoy? I'll stick with these voracious 625
she-beasts for now, take my pleasure with them and fawn on
them. It's foolish to bother oneself with useless cares. Do you
see how those lady lushes are gulping it down? *They* certainly
aren't suffering! They're smart. I want to be smart like them,
not stupid like those friends of mine. I'm lucky, aren't I? I 630
thought I was going to bed with one girl, but now I'll be bed-
ding three of them!

: XIV :

Canthara, procuress; Charinus and Sedulius, lovers

[*The doorway of the brothel*]

Canthara. Who's that trying to get in the back door?
Charinus. Your friend.
Canthara. What friend?
Charinus. It's me.
Canthara. Who is "me"?
Charinus. Charinus.

331

635 *Can.*   Quis Charinus, amabo?
Char. Charinus qui Cassinam perit tuam.
Can. Qui sies nescio.
Char.   Scit Cassina qui siem.
Can. Quid tibi vis?
Char.   Intromitti postulo.
Can. Quam ob rem?
Char.   Quia videre illam cupio.
Can. Quid amplius?
640 *Char.*   Et condormire illi flagito.
Can. Quis tecum est?
Char.   Sedulius, amator Chrysidis.
Can. Quid poscit hic?
Char.   Idem quod ego peto.
Can. Quid dabitis?
Sedu.   Quecumque volueris.
Can. Auri dragmam postulo.
Sedu.   Dabitur maxime.
Can. Quando istuc erit?
645 *Sedu.*   Cras primo diluculo.
Can. Nisi nunc dabitis, operam perditis.
Sedu. Dabimus, ecastor; ne trepida, mulier!
Can. At in presentiarum volo dari.
Sedu. An nescis quales hic sumus viri?
650 *Can.* Bonos puto, sed non volo fallier.
Sedu. Nec scimus fallere, nec volumus.
Que bonis fit viris gratia, gravida est bonis.
Inescabis nos, si admiseris modo,
et optume fenerabis beneficium.
655 *Can.* Qui cavet decipi, vix cavens cavet;
sepe cautor captus est, dum cavisse putat.

Canthara. And who is Charinus, please? 635

Charinus. A man dying of love for your Cassina.

Canthara. I don't know you.

Charinus. Cassina knows me.

Canthara. What do you want?

Charinus. I want to come in.

Canthara. What for?

Charinus. Because I want to see Cassina.

Canthara. And what else?

Charinus. I'm asking to sleep with her. 640

Canthara. Who's that with you?

Charinus. Sedulius, Chrysis' lover.

Canthara. And what does this fellow want?

Charinus. The same thing I do.

Canthara. How much will you pay?

Sedulius. Whatever you want.

Canthara. I want a drachma of gold.

Sedulius. I'll have it for you.

Canthara. And when will that be?

Sedulius. First thing tomorrow. 645

Canthara. If you don't pay me right now, you're wasting your time.

Sedulius. We'll pay you, by Castor. Don't worry, woman!

Canthara. But I want it right now.

Sedulius. Don't you know the quality of the men you're dealing with?

Canthara. I think you are gentlemen, but I won't be cheated. 650

Sedulius. We don't even know how to cheat, nor do we wish to. Favors done to gentlemen are well rewarded. If you'll just let us in, the bait will be in our mouths, and you'll be well repaid, with interest.

Canthara. He who is wary of being cheated is wary of his own un- 655 wariness. Often the cautious man is taken in when he thinks he's being wary.

Char. At huius cras duplum dabimus tibi.

Can. Nunquam ego tam fui astuta aut callida,
quin bonum dari vellem in presentia.

660 *Char.* At si nihil est auri aput nos modo?

Can. Ite hinc et nummosi revertimini.
Interdictus amor est pauperibus.

Char. Quid, si arraboni dedero pallium ?

Can. Nihil facies.

Char.   Quid, si aureum cingulum?

Can. Admittam.

665 *Char.*   Accipe, sed servato probe.

Can. Ite huc; animam silendo premite,
ne illi verba vestra arbitrari queant
amatores, in scannis qui iacent, alii.
Pulcram, ecastor, fallaciam struimus;

670 at fallere non est fallere, nisi astus siet,
sed malum maximum, si venit palam.
Manete hic; ego vinum et cene particulam
ad vos afferam. Post Archimenidem
in hanc rem mihi conciliavero;

675 namque is etiam hic cum sua dormiet.

Sedu. Perge, lenarum omnium quas novi melior!

∶ XV ∶

Dyophanes amator, Congrio servus

Dyo. Quanto magis rem hanc animo repeto,
tanto egritudo resurgit auctior.
Siccine sublitum esse os decuit?

Charinus. Look, tomorrow we'll give you twice what you're asking.

Canthara. I've never been so cunning and clever that I've not preferred the bird in hand.

Charinus. But what if we don't have any money on us now?   660

Canthara. Then leave here and come back with the cash. Love affairs are not for poor men.

Charinus. Well, what if I give you my cloak as earnest money?

Canthara. No deal.

Charinus. Well, what if I give you this golden belt?

Canthara. In that case I'll let you in.

Charinus. Take it; but make sure you hold on to it.   665

Canthara. Go inside. But be quiet and hold your breath; I don't want the other lovers who are waiting, lying down on the benches, to overhear your talking. [*Aside*] By Castor, we're putting together a beautiful piece of deception! Yet a trick isn't really a trick unless some strategem is involved, but it's a disaster   670 if it's exposed. [*To the men*] Stay here. I'll bring you some wine and a bit of dinner. Afterwards, I'll ask Archimenides's advice about the plan, for he's here, too, to sleep with his sweetheart.   675

Sedulius. Let's do it. You're the best madam I've ever known!

: XV :

Dyophanes, lover; Congrio, servant

[*In the vestibule of the brothel*]

Dyophanes. The more I think this over the more my anxiety returns, and greater than ever. Should we really let ourselves be duped this way? Because when everybody finds out, we'll be

680 Quod cum scibitur, pulcre irridebimur.
Ad forum cum venerimus, omnes referent:
'Hi sunt, quibus heri verba sunt data'.
Sed quid tu nobis iam suades, Congrio?
Hiccine dormimus an imus domum?

685 Con. Manere necessum hic est, namque custodibus
observantur publicis omnes vie.

Dyo. At dormire hic non possum.
Con.   Ergo vigila.
Dyo. Ah, scelestas meretrices!
Con.   Scelestissimas
verius voces.
Dyo.   Cras illam multcabo male.
Con. Quid facies?
690 Dyo.   Crinibus in terram dabo.
Con. Recte.
Dyo.   Post hec, insultabo calcibus.
Con. Pulcre.
Dyo.   Linguam mox eripiam sibi.
Con. Viriliter.
Dyo.   Stat mens oculos eruere.
Con. Fortiter.
Dyo.   Ossa confringam quelibet.
Con. Sic meruit.
695 Dyo.   Quid, si enasare lubet?
Con. Probo.
Dyo.   Nec aures indulgebo sibi.
Con. Indigna est auribus.
Dyo.   At nunc irruo,
vel eras potius?
Con.   Cras melius censeo.
Dyo. Scin tu quid mihi alias obtigerit?
Con. Nisi dicas, nescio.

laughing-stocks. When we go to the forum, everyone will say, 680
"Here come those two who got hoodwinked yesterday." What
do you think we should do, Congrio? Should we sleep right
here or go home?

Congrio. You'll have to stay here; all the streets are being patrolled 685
by the police.

Dyophanes. But I can't sleep here.

Congrio. Then stay awake.

Dyophanes. Those swindling, wicked whores!

Congrio. They're as wicked as they come.

Dyophanes. Tomorrow I'm going to punish her good.

Congrio. What are you going to do?

Dyophanes. I'll pull on her hair and knock her to the ground. 690

Congrio. Good.

Dyophanes. Then I'll kick her.

Congrio. Perfect.

Dyophanes. After that I'll rip out her tongue.

Congrio. What a man!

Dyophanes. I have a mind to rip out her eyes.

Congrio. What strength!

Dyophanes. I'll break a few bones.

Congrio. She deserves it.

Dyophanes. What if I decided to cut off her nose? 695

Congrio. I say, do it.

Dyophanes. And I'm not going to spare her ears either.

Congrio. She doesn't deserve to have ears.

Dyophanes. Should I do it now or wait until tomorrow?

Congrio. Tomorrow's better, I think.

Dyophanes. Do you know what's happened to me on other occasions?

Congrio. Not unless you tell me.

337

700	*Dyo.*	Bachidem colui

Maguntie. Hec me frustra occepit habere;
ego dissimulare; illa me reposcere;
revertor. Dum cena coquitur, miles adest;
orat me Bachis cedere militi.

705   Ego irasci, illa rogitare magis
amplectitur, osculatur, tractitat.
Ego inter basiandum arripio dentibus
nasum et fugio.

Con.   Vah, militare facinus!

Dyo. At quid illud? Dixin tibi quo pacto Senis
dilaniarim mecam?

710 *Con.*   Plus milies.

Dyo. Accipe rursus atque audito ordinem.

Con. Iam me somnus opprimit, narra Theobolo;
is tecum vigilat. Si sim rex ego,
ex amantibus tantum deligam vigiles.

715   His ego in asseribus iacebo et dormiam;
vos vigilate, fidi custodes urbium.

Dyo. Haud iniquum optas. Res otium petit
quam incipisso. Nisi Theobolus mihi
aures dat, tibi vel dormienti referam.

: XVI :

Artrax coquus

720 *Art.* Iupiter, amas me, measque auges opes;
voluptates opiperas offers mihi;
cure sum tibi, tot das mihi ferias,
potationes, saturitates, gaudia!

Dyophanes. In Mainz, I used to go to a girl named Bachis. She   700
started to play fast and loose with me; I pretended not to notice; she reclaimed me, and I went back to her. Then while dinner was being cooked, a soldier showed up. Bachis begged me
to give way to the soldier. I was furious; she went on insisting.   705
She embraced me, kissed me, caressed me. While she was kissing me I bit off her nose and took off.

Congrio. Now that was a heroic act!

Dyophanes. Have I ever told you about the time in Siena I tore a
hooker limb from limb?

Congrio. A thousand times if not more.   710

Dyophanes. Let me tell you the whole story again in detail.

Congrio. [*Yawns*] I'm getting sleepy already. Tell your story to
Theobolus. He'll stay up with you. If I were king, I'd choose
only lovers for my night-watchmen. I'll lie down and sleep on   715
these benches. You two stay awake, my trusty night-watchmen!

Dyophanes. Well, that's fair. The story I started needs time to tell.
If Theobolus doesn't listen to me, I'll tell it to you, even if
you're asleep.

： XVI ：

Artrax, a cook

[*In the kitchen*]

Artrax. Jupiter, you love me and increase my riches. You bring me   720
sumptuous pleasures. I surely am under your care, so many are
the feasts, the drinking parties, the hearty meals and the joys
you bring me! But it looks like there's some question whether

Sed cena, ut video, adhuc restat dubia.
725 Edepol, ne ego me prius explevi probe!
At reliqui in ventre celle uni locum,
ubi reliquiarum ponam reliquias.
Proh, Iupiter, quam diversa sunt hominum officia!
Pars in amplexu meretricum iacet,
730 pars eiulando fortunam incusat suam.
Ego, quod optimum est, ventri consulo meo.

⁝ XVII ⁝

Canthara lena, Cassina et Chrysis meretrices

Can. Illi iam abierunt nunc hospites novi
expleti; sed assunt adhuc veteres.
Elevabo vocem: volo ut audiant.
735 Cassina, Chrysis! Quid agitis, paupercule?
Chry. Nil, ecastor, hac noctu dormivi misera!
Cas. Haud dubito, nam subagitata es probe.
Can. Quid obstat tibi?
Chry.   Qui me vexat amor.
Can. Cuius istic est amor?
Chry.   Theoboli.
Can. Quid tu, Cassina?
740 Cas.   Eodem modo pereo.
Can. Quid te cruciat?
Cas.   Dyophanis amor.
Can. Insulse, stulte, fatue bestie!
Illi vos temnunt, vos contra diligitis!
Ubi nunc verba que dicta sunt heri?
745 Emori prius velim quam illa tolerem.

this dinner is going to come off. By Pollux, it's a good thing I
stuffed myself first! But I still have room for leftovers — the left-   725
overs of the leftovers! By god, Jupiter, how varied are the occu-
pations of mankind! Some lie in the arms of courtesans; others
lament and blame their ill fortune. But as for me, I think of my   730
belly, the best occupation of all!

: XVII :

Canthara, procuress; Cassina and Chrysis, prostitutes

[*The bedroom, the following morning*]

Canthara. Those new guests will be gone by now, their desires sat-
  isfied; but the old ones are still here. I'll raise my voice; I want
  them to hear me. Cassina! Chrysis! What are you doing, my
  poor little dears?   735
Chrysis. I feel terrible, by Castor; I haven't slept a wink!
Cassina. [*Aside*] No doubt! You've been ridden like a horse.
Canthara. So why can't you sleep?
Chrysis. I'm being pummeled by love.
Canthara. Love for whom?
Chrysis. For Theobolus.
Canthara. And what about you, Cassina?
Cassina. I'm dying of the same malady.   740
Canthara. What's eating you?
Cassina. My love for Dyophanes.
Canthara. You stupid, foolish, idiotic creatures! Those two despise
  you, and you love them back? Have you already forgotten what
  they said to you yesterday? I'd sooner die than put up with
  words like that.   745

Chry. Quod ira dicitur, meminisse non decet.

Can. At illi ex animo dixerunt malo.

Cas. Non illi, sed amor locutus fuit.

Can. Ego, ut natu maior, sic sum sapientior;

750 auscultate mihi, si bene consulo.

Mittite hos aridos concubinos querulos;

ego alios dabo, formosos iuvenes,

potentes, divites, qui vos vestibus,

si vultis, aureis actutum vestient,

755 qui vobis et mihi bene facient.

Chry. Ah, mea Canthara, quid ais? Quid est

quod in mentem modo cecidit tuam?

Si possunt retro redire flumina

atque convexo sidera celo cadere,

760 potero et ego mei Theoboli

immemor esse.

Can.   Quid tu ais, Cassina?

Cas. Prius inter arandum pisces invenient

atque in arboribus summis ruricole,

quam meo decidat Dyophanes pectore.

765 *Can.* Nunquam rem facietis ambo, si viris

tam vultis esse fideles: hoc decet

si matronas, meretrices dedecet.

Chry. Quin sinis nos, ut volumus, vivere?

Can. Quia vos mendicas esse doleo;

770 assunt dites, qui vos amant, milites.

Cas. Incassum faris; stat fidem servare datam.

Can. Vino, non amore, bonum est uti vetere.

Cas. Enecas. Quin taces, dum fixas vides?

Can. Taceo; sed vos hoc agetis, si sapitis.

Chrysis. What's said in a moment of anger should be forgotten.

Canthara. But they spoke with such hatred!

Cassina. It wasn't them, it was Love that spoke!

Canthara. I'm older and wiser than you, so listen to some sound 750
advice. Get rid of these dried up, whining gigolos of yours; I'll
give you some other pretty young men, powerful and wealthy
men, who will, if you let them, dress you at once in golden gar-
ments and who will do well both by you and by me. 755

Chrysis. Ah, dear Canthara! What are you saying? What's come
into your head? Only when rivers flow backwards and the
stars fall from the vaulted heavens will I be able to forget my
Theobolus! 760

Canthara. And what do *you* say, Cassina?

Cassina. Peasants will find fish in their fields or on treetops before
Dyophanes will be expunged from my heart!

Canthara. You two are never going to turn a profit if you want to 765
be so faithful to men. This is how matrons should behave, not
courtesans.

Chrysis. Why won't you let us live as we wish?

Canthara. Because I'd be sorry to see you become beggars. There
are rich soldiers here who adore you. 770

Cassina. It's pointless for you to say more. We're going to keep our
word.

Canthara. It's good to love old wine, but not old lovers.

Cassina. You're killing me. Why don't you just be quiet, as you can
see we've made up our minds?

Canthara. I'll be quiet. But if you're smart, you'll do as I tell you.

: XVIII :

Dyophanes, Theobolus, Canthara, Archimenides

775   *Dyo.*   Audistin que ille inter se dicerent?

      Theo. Usque a principio omnia, et gaudeo.

      Dyo.   Quid ergo dicis?

      Theo.   Nos malos et illas bonas.

      Dyo.   Quid faciemus?

      Theo.   Revertemur in gratiam,

      orabimus veniam, supplicabimus.

780   *Dyo.*   An nescis quam dure iurarim, miser?

      Theo. Iurasti lingua, mens iniurata manserat.

      Dyo.   Ah, nefas est iusiurandum spernere!

      Theo. Nulla tenet amantes religio.

      Quia lingua iurasti, eadem ut deiures volo.

785   Ridet istec ex alto periuria Iovis.

      Dyo.   Siccine suades?

      Theo.   Et suadeo et imperito.

      Dyo.   Imperio qui malus est, minus est malus.

      Sed nostrum Archimenidem compellare placet.

      Heus, Archimenides!

      Ar.   Quis me vocat?

      Dyo.   Propera huc properanter.

790   *Ar.*   Hic etiam

      estis? Iussissem vos dudum accersirier,

      si scissem. Vah, quam vellem vos nosse omnia!

      Ut iurgate iste sunt invicem mulieres!

      Nunquam vos illis tam dilectos censueram.

795   *Dyo.*   Audivimus omnia. Sed quid nunc consulis?

      Ar.   Id quod res monet. Ne succensete Canthare

      si, quod lenam decet, admonuit probe;

: XVIII :

Dyophanes, Theobolus, Archimenides, Canthara

Dyophanes. Did you hear what they were saying to each other?   775
Theobolus. Every word from the beginning, and I'm delighted.
Dyophanes. What do you say, then?
Theobolus. That it's we who have been wicked and they good.
Dyophanes. What shall we do?
Theobolus. We'll try to get back in their good graces; we'll beg
   their forgiveness and fall on our knees before them.
Dyophanes. I feel terrible — or don't you remember my bitter   780
   oaths?
Theobolus. You swore only with your tongue, not with your heart.
Dyophanes. Ah, but it's wrong to go back on your word!
Theobolus. There's no religion that binds lovers. You swore with
   your tongue? Well then, unswear with your tongue! Jove on
   high laughs at perjuries such as these.   785
Dyophanes. Is that what you suggest I do?
Theobolus. I not only suggest it, I command it!
Dyophanes. He who does something wicked when following orders
   is less wicked. But let's canvass the views of our Archimenides.
   Hello, Archimenides!
Archimenides. Who's calling me?
Theobolus. Quick, come over here!
Archimenides. You're still here? I would have had you summoned if   790
   I had known. Oh, how I wish you knew all! How these women
   have been wrangling with each another! I never would have
   guessed they loved you so much.
Dyophanes. We heard it all. But what do you advise us to do now?   795
Archimenides. What the situation demands. Don't be angry with
   Canthara if she's given them good advice according to her
   lights; a madam isn't a madam if she's not wicked. It's she, in-

345

nam lena non lena est, si non est mala.
Eapse vos primam rediget in gratiam.
800 *Dyo.* Recte admones; suum facit officium.
Ar. Accede huc, Canthara; hos sui erroris penitet.
Can. Optimi vini veteris tres cados
in penam duint.[2]
Ar. Tu iam illas reconcilia.
Can. At puellis si dederint cingulum.
Ar. Dabitur.
805 *Can.* Et onustum auro bono.
Ar. Fiet. Vosque iam valete et plaudite,
spectatores optimi. Quid sibi fabula
hec nunc velit, scitis. Nam virtutibus
insudandum est; sint procul meretrices,
810 lenones, parasiti, convivia.
Virtus omnibus rebus prestat; nihil
illi deest, quem penes est virtus, viro.

FINIS EST

deed, who will return you to the good graces of your girl-friends.

Dyophanes. You're right. She was just doing her job.   800

Archimenides. Come here, Canthara. These two are sorry for their mistake.

Canthara. As their penalty they will have to give me three jugs of the best vintage wine.

Archimenides. Then you'll reconcile them with the girls.

Canthara. But they have to give the girls a belt.

Archimenides. Consider it given.

Canthara. Loaded with fine gold, mind you.   805

Archimenides. It shall be done. [*To the audience*] And, now, you, best of spectators, farewell and give us your applause. Know that the moral of the play is this: that you should work hard to be virtuous, stay away from courtesans, pimps, parasites and   810 wild parties. Virtue excels all things, and the virtuous man lacks for nothing.

THE END

EPIROTA

[*Epistola comitativa prima*]

1   Thomas Medius Hermolao Barbaro sal. d.

2   Numam Pompilium Romanorum regem commercium habuisse
cum Dea Egeria priscorum tempora crediderunt; que antiquitatis
commentitia exempla, si aetas nostra imitari soleret, multo modes-
tius te musarum alumnum potuisset fingere, cuius inclyta eruditio
et candidi animi ingenuae artes istam numinum educationem
usque quaque sapere et redolere videntur. Tot enim scientiarum
compos argumentum dederas, non sine alicuius numinis felici aura
te potuisse brevi universa illa consequi, in quibus singulis perdis-
cendis plerique studiosi defatigentur.

3   Sed quorsum hec de virtute tua strictim libata praeconia?
Nempe huc spectant, ut meam arguant inscitiam qui, cum te ta-
lem tantumque noverim litterarum censorem, haud tamen maies-
tate ingenii tui deterreri potuerim quin hanc novo modo conditam
fabellam tibi protinus legendam mitterem, ubi comoediarum insignibus tam licenter in scribendis iocis abuti visus sim et illa tam
insolita prosae orationi ausus sim affectare. Quas quidem ob res,
cum huiusmodi iocosae emulationis meae licentia reprehenderetur,
et eo quidem gravius quod tuum non reformidaverit acumen, ami-

THE EPIROTE

[*First Letter of Presentation*]

Tommaso Mezzo to Ermolao Barbaro,[1] greetings. 1

In ancient times men believed that Numa Pompilius, the king 2
of the Romans, used to hold converse with the goddess Egeria;[2]
and if we in our times were inclined to imitate these fanciful moral
illustrations of antiquity, one could do much worse than to imagine you as the alumnus of the Muses. For your celebrated erudition and the noble skills of your unblemished mind seem to carry
the full taste and fragrance of that numinous education. So many
are the disciplines of whose mastery you have given proof that it
could not have been without the happy inspiration of some divin-
ity that in so short a time you have acquired a knowledge of all the
disciplines, the individual study of which would have exhausted
the wits of most men.

To what end am I pouring out this encomium of your virtue in 3
summary fashion? Why, clearly it has the purpose of proving my
own ignorance. For though I knew the extent and quality of your
literary authority, I was nevertheless undeterred by your intellectual greatness and was unable to prevent myself from immediately
sending you this play to read. It is constructed in a new way, in
that I seem in writing jokes to have abused the characteristics of
comedies and to have dared, unusually, to employ prose. On this
account, although the license I have taken in the sort of humorous
emulation I have employed may be criticized, and the more seri-
ously as it did not shrink from your critical acumen, the principle
of friendship will defend my cause with the greatest confidence.
That principle will affirm it to be the privilege of friends that,

citiae ratio causam meam confidentissime defendit, amicorum esse affirmans, quaecunque ipsi audent cum intimis communicare, nec futurum cuiquam turpe aut vitio dandum inter paucos familiares quovis iocorum genere lusitare, nec negatum si libuerit cum necessariis ad imitationem usque poeticarum argutiarum comica amoenitate colludere.

4   Hac ergo defensiuncula (ut mihi visa fuit) probabili adductus, haud veritus sum quicquid otiosus luserim tibi mittere legendum. Quod si forte probaveris, paucis etiam amicis impertiam, sin secus, non deerit locus apud me ubi saeculum latitet. Sed de his hactenus. Ego te e patavino secessu nostris (ut arbitror) hominibus perutili vehementer expecto, atque in tuo adventu latinum Dioscoridem tuum veneratus amplectar. Vale.

[*Epistula comitativa altera*]

1   Thomas Medius Danieli Medio sal. d.

2   Solent multi doctissimi viri, mi Daniel, Hermolai Barbari eruditionem ut egregiam et singularem admirari, et eum natum ad illustranda litterarum studia existimare. Quam quidem opinionem ita probo, ut etiam affirmare non dubitem eius ingenii indolem illorum existimationem aliquatenus superaturam. Quibus sane ex rebus facile coniicere potes qualis etiam in rei publicae muneribus existimandus sit, qui et innato acumine perspicax et tot monumentorum exemplorumque omnis aevi copia instructus, nihil paene circumspectissimo ingenio suo non prospicere videtur. Huic sane excultae humanitati eius atque doctrinae incredibilis comitas atque festivitas adiuncta est; facetiarum, et id genus argutorum dictorum, estimator mirificus censeri solet.

whatever things they dare communicate with their intimates, it will neither be set down as shameful or vicious if they amuse themselves among a few friends with any sort of joke, nor will it be forbidden if they are inclined to sport and take pleasure in the comic manner with their companions in imitation of poets' verbal dexterity.

Induced by this plausible (as it seemed to me) little line of de- 4 fense, I have had the courage to send you to read the playthings of my leisure. If you approve of them, I may share them also with a few friends; if not, I shall find a place where they may lie concealed for posterity. So much for that. I am eagerly waiting for you as you leave that Paduan retreat of yours, so very useful (as I believe) to the Latin world; and on your arrival I shall embrace you, paying homage to your Latin Dioscorides.[3] Farewell.

[Second Letter of Presentation]

Tommaso Mezzo to Daniele Mezzo,[4] greetings.   1

Many men of great learning, my dear Daniel, are accustomed to 2 marvel at the erudition of Ermolao Barbaro as something outstanding and unique, and they consider him born for the task of elucidating the study of letters. And indeed, I agree with their estimate, so much so that I do not hesitate to assert that his intellectual gifts are going to exceed somewhat their estimate of him. Certainly from such testimony you can easily suppose the sort of value placed upon his gifts in the state as well, for his innate critical sense gives him such perspicacity, and his wealth of historical knowledge and moral exempla from every period give him such resources, that almost nothing seems to be beyond the foresight of his wide-ranging genius. Joined to this exquisite humanity and learning is an unbelievable graciousness and and genial wit, and he is generally considered a marvelous judge of the genre of witty sayings.

3   Cuius ingenii facilitate fretus (ut ad rem aliquando veniam)
hanc fabellam, audacius fortasse quam ratio exilitatis eius postula-
bat, ipsi legendam misi, nec poenituit tamen amicissimi iudicio
eius exilitatem subiicere. Quam, ne forte cuiusmodi esset require-
res, eius ad te misi exemplum, eo quidem libentius quod acre iudicium tuum in pensitandis ioculis et amoenissimi ingenii comita-
tem pernoveram, et quantus in omni sermone tum lepos tum
festivitas in acumine tuo vigeat. Leges igitur has facetiunculas nostras, eo quo semper solitus fueras animo scripta nostra lectitare.
Vale.

Argumentum

Anus Pamphila deperit Clitiphonem, quem pretioso cultu ornata
quasi sponsum ad delicias exspectat. Ille, mutuo Antiphilae amore
captus, variis frustrationibus vetulam eludit. Patruus interim Antiphilae, dum ipsam olim patria profectam quaeritat, Syracusas ex
Epiro venit, variis affectus molestiis. Suspectus interea Antiphilae
Clitipho nomine meretricii amoris accusatur. Inventa tandem
Antiphila a patruo et dote et marito donatur. Pamphila vero anus,
ut Clitiphonis copiam haberet, despecto a se Epirotae nupsit.

Relying on his good nature and wit (to come to the point) I 3 sent him this play to read, somewhat more boldly than its slender merits would seem to demand, and I was not sorry that I submitted these few leaves to his kindest of judgments. On the chance that you might wonder about the sort of thing it is, I have sent you a copy of it, the more willingly as I well know your penetrating judgment in evaluating humor and the graciousness of your own charming nature, and I know also how much your wit and your gaiety flourish in every form of speech and criticism. So read these little witticisms of mine in the same spirit that you always, as a rule, bring to my writings. Farewell.

Argument

Pamphila, an old woman, is dying of love for Clitipho. Adorned in expensive finery she awaits him as if he were her husband coming to make love to her. He is in the grip of a requited love for Antiphila and eludes the old hag by means of various delaying tactics. Meanwhile, the uncle of Antiphila, who some time ago left her homeland, comes from Epirus to Syracuse, where he experiences various troubles.[5] In the meantime Clitipho is suspected by Antiphila and is accused and charged with loving a courtesan. At last, having been found by her uncle, Antiphila is given a dowry and a husband. However, Pamphila, the old woman, in order to get access to Clitipho, is married to the uncle from Epirus whom she despises.

CHARACTERS[6]

Pamphila, *an old woman*	Syrus, *a slave*
Lesbia, *a handmaid*	Harpage, *a procuress*
Andria, *a midwife*	Erotium, *a courtesan*
Hegio, *an old man*	Clitipho, *Antiphila's fiancé*

: I :

Anus Pamphila, Lesbia ancilla

1 *Pa.* Sternite lectum in triclinio eburatum peristromate conchy-
liato, ubi meus genius mecum cubet. Ornetur thalamus basilice,
renideat atrium aulaeorum ornatu, ut ingredienti regi meo
bono cum omine statim omnia arrideant comitatemque erae
atque hilaritatem et elegantiam prae se ferant. Totae denique
splendeant aedes apparatu regio. Pulvinar, inquam, praecipuo
ornetur studio, ubi Iuppiter meus cubitet. Hae potissimum
stragulae sternantur, quae Cupidinis habent imaginem, cuius in
tutela ego atque ille sumus, ut auspicatiora omnia sint in aedi-
bus. Euge, quanta ego afficiar laetitia! Quantum in hoc angusto
pectore versabitur gaudium, cum meum genium ingredi meas
aedes aspiciam, nitidum, cultum, Alexandro illi Troiano simi-
lem! Pol, ego Helenen reginam neutiquam accusandam censeo,
si formosissimi hospitis specie capta amori temperare nequive-
rit. Sed deos quaeso, ut bene atque feliciter hoc mihi atque illi
vertat. Tu, Lesbia, ceteris ancillis hoc negotium ornandi aedes

Antipho, *his client*	A Musician
Damascenus, *the Epirote*	A Steward
A Citizen of Syracuse	Scapha, *a old nurse*
A Quack	Charinus, *a client*
An Innkeeper	Clitipho, *a Samian*

Scene: *Syracuse*

: I :

Pamphila, an old woman; Lesbia, her slave

[*Pamphila, coming out of her house, addresses her servants*]

Pamphila. Make sure that the ivory-covered bed in the dining- 1
room is spread over with that purple fabric, where my angel will
be lying down with me. Let the bedchamber be decorated in
kingly fashion, let the house sparkle with rich tapestries so that
everything may immediately smile with good omen when my
king arrives and bespeak a mistress' warmth, elegance and good
cheer. Finally, let the whole house be resplendent with royal re-
finement. Let the couch be decorated with special care where
my Jupiter may rest his limbs. Most important of all, get these
bed linens ready which are embossed with the likeness of Cupid, under whose protection both he and I are, so that everything in the house may be even more auspicious. Oh, good!
How happy I shall be! How much joy will stir in this poor
heart of mine when I see my angel enter my house, glowing
with youth, well-groomed, just like Trojan Alexander![7] By
Pollux, I think that Queen Helen would by no means be
blamed if she were unable to control her passion, captivated by
the appearance of so extremely handsome a guest! But please,
gods, let things turn out well and happily for me and for him!
Lesbia, leave the business of decorating the house to the other

relinque et mihi speculum affer et cistulam cum pigmentis, ut vicissim me ornem.

2　*Le.* Maxime.

Pa. At vos, quae solitae iam estis torpere desidia, nisi mihi hodie agiles expeditasque ad haec quae instant negotia vos praebueritis, et praeteriti languoris et huius dabitis negligentiae poenas.

Le. Hem, pertuli ut iussisti.

Pa. Frugi es. Obline os mihi, ut consuevisti, cerussa, tinge genas purpurisso, interpola faciem, ut memet non agnoscam in speculo.

Le. Faciam si nusquam te flectes aut versabis.

Pa. Statua non aeque riget ut ego astans rigebo.

Le. Ad istunc modum paulisper mane.

Pa. Maneo.

Le. Vah, tu vero serio riges. Resupina te aliquantum ut etiam sub mento te tingam.

3　*Pa.* Sub mento, pessima? Tam cito oblevisti malas ut etiam ad collum descendas? Ut suspicor, pigmentis parcis. Tempus est nunc scilicet parcendi offuciis, cum studeo aequare Nympha, ut Narcisso meo placeam?

Le. Quid, malum, parco? Paries non ita illitus est tectorio ut tu cerussa.

Pa. Indiligenter, inquam, os meum polis, transversas video in facie lineas, alias albicantes, nigricantes alias.

Le. Non mea culpa fit, era, illud neque tua.

Pa. Cuius ergo?

4　*Le.* Naturae. Quibusdam enim matronis cutis est laxior nec satis levis ad poliendum. Meum est enim tingere os, non fingere.

Pa. Hei mihi, oblita sum rugarum. Curre actutum ad obstetricem Andriam. Iube ut veniat ad me afferatque medicamina illa com-

slaves; you bring me a mirror and my cosmetic-case; it's my
turn to beautify myself.

Lesbia. Of course. 2

Pamphila. But the rest of you lazy, idle creatures, you'll pay for
your all your languorous neglect if you don't look sharp and be
quick about helping me with the business at hand.

Lesbia. [*Clears her throat*] Ahem, I've brought what you asked for.

Pamphila. You're a good girl. Now, put my lipstick on in your usual
way, put some rouge on my cheeks, touch up my face; I don't
want to recognize myself in the mirror.

Lesbia. I'll do it if you'll just stop bending around and turning
your head.

Pamphila. I'll stand stiffer than a statue.

Lesbia. Just stay that way for one minute.

Pamphila. I will.

Lesbia. Goodness, but you really are stiff. Lean back a bit, so I can
apply some make-up under your chin too.

Pamphila. Under my chin, you good-for-nothing? Have you fin- 3
ished coating my cheeks so quickly that you're already starting
on my neck? My guess is that you're not using nearly enough
make-up. I ask you, is this the time to spare the paint when I'm
eager to rival the nymphs so as to please my Narcissus?

Lesbia. [*Aside*] The devil I'm sparing the paint! Your house has
less plaster on it than your face has rouge!

Pamphila. You're being careless finishing my face: I can see lines
across it, some whitish, some darkish.

Lesbia. This isn't my fault, mistress, nor is it yours.

Pamphila. Well, whose then?

Lesbia. Nature's: some women have skin that's so flabby that it's 4
just not smooth enough to apply make-up to. My job is to color
your face, not reshape it.

Pamphila. Woe is me, I forgot about those wrinkles. Run as fast as
you can to the midwife Andria. Ask her to come to me and

planatoria, quibus os mihi complanet levigetque. Quid cessas? Festina!

Le. Evolo. Dii boni, quid era mea coeptat? Adulescens decrepita studet fieri, fingendam se obstetrici Andriae vult tradere. Gestio videre quisnam huic incredibili rei sit exitus.

: II :

Obstetrix Andria, Lesbia ancilla

5 *An.* Mitte rogitare quid in ea re nostra queat praestare sollertia. Mira atque incredibilia nonnumquam ingenia hominum excogitare solent et ideo novas in dies artes nasci vides, quae priscorum aetate nullae fuerant. Nihil est profecto quod temptando vestigandoque summis ingeniis aliquando non innotescat. Quod ad me artemque meam attinet, ego percalleo meaeque sollertiae esse profiteor canos tingere, nigros capillos rutilare, cutem rugosam erugare et cetera difficilia huiusmodi, quae ad ornatum et necessitatem mulierum spectant, curare.

Le. Peropportuna edepol vel fictrix vel ornatrix erae meae advenis. Mira sunt profecto, quae tua sollertia praestare possit. Sed dic, quaeso, quibus medicaminibus erugabis faciem erae meae?

An. Sunt illi firmi dentes?

Le. Nec firmi quidem nec infirmi praeter duos, qui iamiam casuri videntur et quoties screat toties agitur de re dentaria.

bring those emollient potions of hers to smooth out and de-wrinkle my face. What are you waiting for? Hurry up! [*Enters the house*]

Lesbia. I'm on my way. Good gods above, why does my mistress even try? The old bag is trying to be a young girl again; she wants to put herself in the hands of the midwife Andria for a makeover. I can't wait to see how this whole incredible thing gets played out.

: II :

Andria, a midwife; Lesbia, a slave

[*Andria enters on her way to Pamphila's house*]

Andria. Stop asking what our skills can accomplish in this matter. 5 Human genius regularly comes up with amazing and incredible things, and every day you see new arts being born which didn't exist in ancient times. Through trial and research there is noth-ing that can remain unknown to the greatest minds. As far as I and my skill are concerned, I have great experience and boast of my skill in coloring grey hair, lightening black hair, removing wrinkled skin and other difficult tasks of this kind which cater to the beauty needs of women.

Lesbia. By Pollux, your arrival to do my mistress's makeover is very timely. It's really amazing what your skill can do. But tell me, please, what potions will you use to de-wrinkle my mistress' face?

Andria. Does she have strong teeth?

Lesbia. Well, they're not exactly strong or weak, except for two of them which seem just about ready to fall out, and whenever she clears her throat things happen to her teeth.

An. Scrupulosissima sane cura siquidem, ut narras, non sine periculo screare possit. Edentulis difficilior curatio est. Sed quot annos nata est?

Le. Illa quidem non prodit annos suos, sed aequalem ego existimo sibyllae. Nulla sane est in urbe annosior illa.

6 *An.* Iugerum herbarum non erit satis huic rei, sed tamen nolo ut haec diffidat medelis nostris. Habemus, inquam, Lesbia, complanatoria medicamina plura, lomentum, ichthyocollam; perutiles sunt et radices lilii in vino coctae. Praecipue autem faciem purgat atque erugat cygni adeps. Fiunt etiam ex quibusdam aliis rebus diaplasmata,[1] quae cutem in hoc genere emendant, praecipue si lamina plumbea apponatur.

Le. Cave quaeso a lamina, nam actum erit de reliquiis dentium si apponetur.

An. Non sum admonenda.

Le. Sane Medeae Colchidis opera recognosco, cum tuas artes animadverto, quae suis medicaminibus Aesonem socerum ex sene iuvenem reddidisse fertur.

An. Procul dubio non sunt haec vulgaria. Sed abi, nuntia erae tuae me advenisse.

Le. Maxime.

7 *An.* Muliercularum credulitas est annona nostra et praedia rustica. Inde nobis victum, inde cultum et omnia necessaria comparamus. Cum enim mulierem cupidam et studiosam alicuius rei invenimus, quae plerumque et credula est, tunc illam morigeram nobis facimus, circumvenimus promissis, versamus ut molam trusatilem. Et licet id non praestamus, quod promittimus, simile tamen aliquid efficere videmur, et quod numquam

Andria. To hear you tell it, she has to be really careful clearing her throat so as not to endanger her teeth. Treatment of the toothless is more difficult. But how old is she?

Lesbia. To be sure, she never tells her age to anyone, but I'd guess she's as old as a sibyl. She's surely the oldest woman in the city.

Andria. A whole acre of medicinal herbs won't be enough for this 6 case. But I don't want her to doubt the efficacy of our treatments. I tell you Lesbia, we have lots of anti-wrinkle creams, blue powders and fish-glue; they are very useful, as are the roots of the lily cooked in wine. However, swan grease does the best job of cleaning and smoothing the face.[8] Also, we have scented powders made from certain other materials which clear up the skin, especially if a mudpack of lead is applied.

Lesbia. Please stay away from the mudpack: if you apply one of those, it will be all up with the rest of her teeth.

Andria. You don't have to remind me.

Lesbia. You know, your arts recall the magic of Medea of Colchis; it was through her herbal treatments that her father-in-law Aeson was returned to youth from old age.[9]

Andria. You're right; these treatments are not common knowledge. But go, tell your mistress I have arrived.

Lesbia. I will. [*Goes inside the house*]

Andria. It's the gullibility of these silly women that provides our 7 meal-tickets and our country houses. Their gullibility gets us our food, our dress, and everything that we need. In fact, when we find a needy woman who is eager for something, the kind who's also usually gullible, we wrap her around our little finger, cheat her with promises, and spin her around like the stone of a windmill. And although we don't accomplish what we promise, we nevertheless look like we're doing something similar, and we give the appearance of being on the point of delivering a product when we have no intention of ever finishing it. In the meantime, we find some excuse, say, that it's a cloudy day or that

361

facturae sumus, iamiam confectum tradere videmur. Causamur interim aut nubilum diem aut alicuius supervenientis malum oculum aut id requirimus ad medelam, quod nusquam gentium reperitur. Nos interea fruimur praediolo nostro et quotidianos fructus capimus. Mala profecto res, sed late patet hoc fallendi vitium, nusquam enim a rebus humanis dolus abest.

Sed ancillae me vocant, ingrediar atque ipsam dominam aggrediar. Concludam eam in conclavi atque eius faciem probe offuciis ornabo, ut dignoscere nequeas larva sit an matrona.

: III :

Anus Pamphila

8 *Pa.* Iam dudum asto cute probe curata atque ex sententia Clitiphonem exspectans. Non temere est quod ille rebus iam paratis ad id, quod ipse constituerat, tempus non venit. Mutavisse arbitror sententiam et me frustra habuisse. Maxime itaque vellem quam primum me hac exspectationis cura, quae pectus meum lacerat, solvi. Plus enim angitur animus, cum rebus incertis inter spem et metum fluctuat, quam si de re mala protinus certior fiat. Dolet enim ille quidem semel cognitis incommodis, sed dedolet rursus. At in re incerta distrahitur usque et scinditur et in anxietate perpetua versatur. Quam ob rem libet eius animum quam primum per litteras experiri, ut cognoscere aliquando possim dolendumne mihi sit ob eius perfidiam an laetandum ipsius fide.

some evil eye prevents us or that we need some ingredient in the treatment that exists nowhere in the world. At the same time, we enjoy the proceeds from our little country estates and pluck our fruits daily. Well, yes, it's wicked to deceive, but everybody does it; trickery is never absent from human affairs.

But the serving-girls are calling me. I'll go in and start on the mistress. I'll set her up in a separate room and paint her face so thoroughly that you won't be able to tell whether she's a matron or somebody wearing a fright-mask.

⋮ III ⋮

Pamphila, an old woman

[Pamphila stepping out from her house, very upset]

Pamphila. I've been standing here for a long time now, with my 8 skin perfectly made up and exactly to my liking, waiting for my Clitipho. There must be a good reason why he hasn't come at the time he himself fixed, after all these preparations of mine have been made. I think he's changed his mind and stood me up. I want most of all to be free of this anxious waiting that tears at my heart. The anguish of not knowing, of being tossed between waves of hope and doubt, is worse than learning the bad news right away. For once the heart learns of its misfortune, it grieves once, then puts an end to its grief. But in the midst of uncertainty it is pulled apart and dashed and is whirled about in endless worry. So I feel like testing his sentiments as soon as possible by letter, so I can find out definitely whether I'm going to suffer from his treachery or rejoice at his fidelity.

: IV :

Anus Pamphila, Lesbia, Hegio

9   *Pa.* Currito, amabo, Lesbia, atque hunc Hegionem senem vicinum nostrum evocato, qui ad Clitiphonem ocellum meum de hac re conscribat epistulam.

Le. Evolo.

Pa. Nimirum multis modis me sollicitant hae amatoriae litterae, quas ad Clitiphonem missura sum. Non enim vulgari ratione huiusmodi epistula scribi debet nec titubare uspiam potest sine flagitio, non enim oportet amatorem dicere non adverti. Sed eccum Hegionem, qui me in hac difficultate plurimum adiuvabit.

10   *He.* Salve, Pamphila.

Pa. Dii te ament, Hegio. Et mihi et tibi exhibeo negotium inepta his amatoriis litteris.

He. Si te istud non gravat, mihi quidem haud molestum est.

Pa. Cape stilum et tabellas, quaeso.

He. Factum. Iube modo quid scribam.

Pa. Corculumne meum fingam adversus eius perfidiam conqueri an animulum?

He. Neutrum censeo.

Pa. Quid? Mentem?

He. Multo minus.

Pa. Quid? Linguam contra pectoris eius iniquam voluntatem?

He. Quin tota cum illo toto non dimidiata agis, si quid tibi expostulandum est?

Pa. Morem tibi geram.

He. Loquere.

11   *Pa.* Scribito: 'Pamphilula Clitiphoni ocello suo ex animo salutem dicit.'

: IV :

Pamphila, an old woman; Lesbia; Hegio

Pamphila. I'd be obliged if you'd hurry, Lesbia, and summon that 9
old man, our neighbor Hegio, to write my letter about this to
Clitipho, the apple of my eye.

Lesbia. I'm on my way.

Pamphila. This love letter that I'm about to send to Clitipho worries me for many reasons. I mean, a letter of this kind shouldn't
be written in the common way, but clumsiness would be disgraceful: one mustn't overlook the fact that it's a lover who is
speaking. But here's Hegio, who'll help me a lot with this diffi-
culty.

Hegio. [*Enters*] Hello, Pamphila. 10

Pamphila. The gods bless you, Hegio. I'm so inept at writing these
love-letters that I'm exposing my private affairs to you.

Hegio. If it's no burden to you, it doesn't bother me either.

Pamphila. Please take a pen and your writing-tablet.

Hegio. Done; just tell me what to write.

Pamphila. To complain about his treachery, should I make out that
he's my "dear heart" or "the soul of my soul"?

Hegio. Neither, I think.

Pamphila. What then? "My mind"?¹⁰

Hegio. No, no!

Pamphila. What about "my tongue"? — against the wicked willful-
ness of his heart?

Hegio. If you're going to complain about something, why not do it
with your whole body, and address his whole body?

Pamphila. Fine.

Hegio. Go ahead, speak.

Pamphila. Write this down: "Little Pamphila greets her apple- 11
dumpling Clitipho from her very soul."

He. Quin Pamphilam te vocas, non Pamphilulam? Imminuere enim videris rationem amoris diminutione verbi.

Pa. Quo pacto?

He. Siquidem Pamphilae nomen 'totam in amore' et 'amicam amoris' innuit, Pamphilulam cum dicis, amoris quodammodo amiculam, non amicam asseris.

Pa. Hei mihi, si id flagitium imprudens fecissem! Perspicax usquequaque debet esse amator. Dele ergo, si quid scriptum est.

He. Delevi quod scriptum erat.

Pa. Ita dele ut nusquam appareat litura.

He. Factum.

12 *Pa.* Incipe rursus: 'Pamphila Clitiphoni ocello suo ex animo salutem dicit'.

He. 'Pamphila Clitiphoni ocello suo', addone 'ex animo'?

Pa. Hui, rogas? Atque 'ex corde' addendum erat.

He. Perge, absoluta est inscriptio.

Pa. Ascribe ergo . . .

He. Loquere quid.

Pa. 'Tuum admiror ingenium usque adeo efferatum esse . . .'.

He. 'Efferatum'? Grave est hoc verbum in amantem.

Pa. Gravius hic locus desiderat.

He. Perge.

Pa. '. . . Ut te neutiquam commoveat tanta exspectatio clientulae tuae'.

He. Nimium te iam summittis, quae modo superba eras.

13 *Pa.* Et summittendus et attollendus est, Hegio, animus amantis. At tu alioquin prudens, sed haec non calles amatoria.

Hegio. Why not just call yourself Pamphila instead of "little Pamphila"? Using the diminutive makes it seem as though you're lessening love's reckoning.

Pamphila. How am I doing that?

Hegio. Because the name "Pamphila" suggests "all for love" and "friend of love," so when you say "little Pamphila," you're saying that you are not a "friend" but a "small friend" of love.

Pamphila. Woe is me if I've thoughtlessly committed this shameful act! A lover has to be penetrating in so many ways! Erase it, then, if you've written that.

Hegio. I've already done so.

Pamphila. Erase it so that the erasure won't show.

Hegio. Done.

Pamphila. Begin again: "Pamphila sends greetings from her very   12 soul to her apple-dumpling Clitipho."

Hegio. "Pamphila to her apple-dumpling Clitipho"; do I add "from her very soul"?

Pamphila. Can you ask? And you should add "from her very heart" too.

Hegio. Go on. The address is finished.

Pamphila. Then write . . .

Hegio. Tell me what.

Pamphila. "I wonder that your attitude is so beastly."

Hegio. "Beastly"? That's a harsh word for a lover to use.

Pamphila. The context requires an even harsher word.

Hegio. Go on.

Pamphila. "That not even the great longing of your little client can move you."

Hegio. Now you're being too submissive, when before you were being proud.

Pamphila. The soul of a lover must be ready to assume both a su-   13 perior and inferior position, Hegio. Though in other respects you're a wise man, you're not too clever about love affairs.

He. Age, expedi reliqua.

Pa. Ascribito: 'Vides, ut amatoriis insignibus ornata incedo te dudum exspectans'.

He. Scriptum.

Pa. 'Nebulam excitat ardor amoris mei'.

He. Hui, Aetnaeos ignes narras! Quin ardores et fumos istos amatorios omittis? Et roga ut veniat nec pergat frustrari exspectationem tuam.

14 *Pa.* Perii misera! Frigidam ergo amatricem vis ut me profitear? Noli quaeso adversari.

He. Non adversor, mea quidem causa vel torrida esto. Perge, hoc scriptum est.

Pa. 'Nisi respexeris hodieque ad nos venias, nolo quicquam gravius ominari, non recte facies'.

He. Loquere.

Pa. 'Quare, anime mi, veni ocius: quem et aedes et domina et parietes ipsi aedium desiderant'.

He. Scriptum.

Pa. Ascribito: 'Vale, mi ocelle'.

He. Scriptum. Numquid aliud me vis?

Pa. Obsigna tabellas.

He. Factum. Vale, Pamphila.

Pa. Et tu, Hegio.

He. Haec Acheruntica vetula Acheruntem fortasse citius quam sponsum salutabit.

15 *Pa.* Perfer has tabellas, Lesbia, ocius ad Clitiphonem et soli sola legendas dato, observaque vultum eius, si noscere potes, qui sit illi animus ad hanc rem.

Le. Faciam.

Hegio. Go on, let's get on with the rest. [*Goes on writing*]

Pamphila. Write this: "You see how I pace about, embellished with the emblems of love, whilst awaiting you ever so long.

Hegio. Got it.

Pamphila. "The fire of my love begins to smoke."

Hegio. O my! Now you're describing the fires of Etna! Why not leave out those fires and amatory vapors? Just ask him to come and not to disappoint your hopes.

Pamphila. I'm wretched, I'm dying of love! And you want me to 14 avow that I'm a cold lover? Don't cross me, please.

Hegio. I'm not; go ahead and be scorching hot for all I care. Continue then; I've written that down.

Pamphila. "If you don't show some regard for me and come to me today, I don't want to predict something too unpleasant, but you won't be doing the right thing."

Hegio. Go on.

Pamphila. "Wherefore, my soul, come as quick as you can; both the house and your lady and even the walls of the house long for you."

Hegio. Got it.

Pamphila. Add the ending, "Farewell, apple of my eye."

Hegio. Done. Is there anything else you wish of me?

Pamphila. Seal the letter.

Hegio. Done. Farewell, Pamphila. [*Exiting to the side*]

Pamphila. And you, Hegio.

Hegio. [*Aside*] This little old woman with one foot in the grave will meet her maker long before she meets a husband.

Pamphila. Lesbia, take this letter very quickly to Clitipho and 15 make sure you give it to him to read when you are both alone. Watch his expression, if you can read it, to see what his response is to its contents.

Lesbia. Leave it to me.

Pa. Atque audi. Accusavit me quippiam Hegio, quod eum accersieram ad scribendam amatoriam epistulam?

Le. Nihil dixit.

Pa. Nihil plane?

Le. Sane nihil.

Pa. Abi, perge bono cum omine. Severius plerumque notant peccata amicorum hi, qui taciti rebus ineptis sunt arbitri, quam hi, qui liberius perperam facta effutiunt. Alteri enim stomachantes crimen tantummodo factum esse taciti conspiciunt; cuius culpa factum sit, quae plerumque latet, a nemine perquirunt; et sic amicos indicta causa gravius damnant. Alteri vero dum exprobrant vitia mordaci ioculo, plerumque etiam rationes purgantium admittunt, quibus habitis, quatenus succensendum aut ignoscendum sit amicis, optime tenent.

: V :

Syrus servus

16 *Sy.* Mirum in modum mens hominum in quiete nocturnis imaginibus adumbratur. Visus sum hac nocte videre eximio candore cygnum aedes nostras ingressum magna cum festivitate per domum volitare, nidum deinde sibi propere construere. Experrectus narravi hoc insomnium vetulae Scaphae, quae magno affecta gaudio 'procul' inquit 'dubio haec imago somnii bonam fortu-

Pamphila. Listen to me now: did Hegio find fault with me at all because I summoned him to write a love letter?

Lesbia. He said nothing.

Pamphila. Nothing at all?

Lesbia. Nothing whatsoever.

Pamphila. Go then and good luck. [*Lesbia departs*] Men who are silent onlookers of foolish behavior are generally more severe in condemning the sins of friends than are those who babble about improper actions with great freedom. The former look on in silence, taking it ill merely that a crime has been committed, and ask no one whose fault the crime was, a thing generally hidden. The latter, while reproaching vices with mordant jocularity, generally consider what the culprits say in justification of themselves, and taking this into account make good decisions about the degree to which one should take offense or forgive one's friends. [*Goes into her house*]

∶ V ∶

Syrus, a slave

[*Syrus coming from the house of Antiphila*]

Syrus. When men are asleep, their minds are enshadowed marvelously by nocturnal images. This last night I seemed to see a swan as white as snow enter our house with delight and fly to and fro through the house, then hastily build a nest for itself. When I awoke, I told this dream to the old nurse Scapha, who was seized with great joy and said, "Without a doubt, this sleep-image portends good fortune for us, Syrus, and I guess the gods will finally be looking out for us." But I think that this good fortune of ours is a long way off. For if Fortune was ever

16

nam nobis portendit, Syre, et nos tandem, ut conicio, dii respicient'. At ego longe abesse illam a nobis existimo. Nam si ventura aliquando esset, totiens iam invocata venisset. Sed quid nunc iam spei est, cum omnia tam nequiter adhuc provenire nobis videam? Primum omnium aere alieno olim obstrictus erus meus, Antiphilae pater, abiit ex Epiro in Siciliam scilicet commigraturus, incerto iam animo, quam urbem Siciliae incoleret. Conscendit ergo noctu clanculum navim cum tota familia. Medio in itinere morte interceptus est ex morbo qui eum in navi invaserat. Quod iam tum in Epiro nuntiatum esse certo scio a mercatore Epirota, qui forte, cum ille efflabat animam, e navi Tarentum solus advectus est piscatoria cymba.

17   Post id malum nos prosequimur cursum quem navis tenuerat. Advecti tandem sumus Syracusas. Hic patruus Clitiphonis, qui forte primus nos egredientes e navi fato appulsos sine spe, sine ope vidit, misertus malorum nostrorum hospitio nos recepit. Ibi Clitipho visam eram meam tali forma talique aetate misere amare coepit statimque pollicitus est eam se ducturum uxorem et hanc aediculam illi habitandam conduxit et suis nos alit impensis. Illam tamen non audet ducere indotatam. Triennium iam factum est postquam Dyrrachio discessimus, cum interea nemo nos respexit nec nuntium quidem ex Epiro attulit. Tota igitur salus nostra ab huius adulescentis fide pendet. Quae si novo aliquo amore immutari coeperit, quod iam maxime timendum est, quis iam dubitat nos funditus periisse? Sors ergo nostra proclivior est ad metum quam ad bonam spem.

18   Sed quidnam est quod haec lena Harpage acriter acclamitat? Papae! Filiam castigat suam hac fortasse de causa quod non maximum hodie fecerit quaestum. Libet subauscultare quid bella mater admoneat filiolam.

going to come to us, she would have come before now, as we've called upon her so many times. But what hope is there now, when everything seems to be going so badly for us? In the first place, my master, Antiphila's father, was tied down with debt even before he left Epirus to emigrate to Sicily, being uncertain at that time which city in Sicily he would make his home. With his whole family he took ship secretly at night. In the midst of his journey he was overtaken by death from a disease which attacked him on the ship. I know for a fact that the news of this then reached Epirus thanks to a merchant of that land who, while my master was breathing his last, chanced to be carried from the ship to Taranto in a fishing boat.

After this tragedy we followed the route the ship had been 17 taking, and were finally carried to Syracuse. Here Clitipho's uncle, who happened to be the first to see us leaving the ship, pummeled by fate, without hope, without resources, took pity on our misfortunes and received us as guests. In his house Clitipho, seeing that my mistress was so young and beautiful, fell desperately in love with her and at once promised to marry her, hiring this little house for her to live in and paying our expenses. Yet he didn't dare wed her without a dowry. It's been three years now since we left Dyrrachium and no one takes any notice of us nor has any news come from Epirus. So all our well-being depends upon the loyalty of this young man. If some new love should make him fickle, something we now fear, who could doubt but that we'll be entirely lost? So our lot leans more towards fear than hope.

But what is the procuress Harpage shouting about so an- 18 grily? Good grief, she's scolding her daughter! Perhaps the reason is that today she hasn't earned her full quota. I'd like to eavesdrop and learn why this lovely mother should chide her little daughter.

373

: VI :

Harpage lena, Syrus, Erotium meretrix

19 *Ha.* Quotiens edixi tibi ne sterilem quemquam inanemve, immo nec Iovem ipsum nihil afferentem, supplicem admitteres!

    Sy. Vale Iuppiter cum caelo tuo cumque horrendis tonitruis, si te supplicantem sine munere excludit lena!

    Ha. Quotiens emonui te, ut prospiceres in iuventa tibi, ne in senecta mendicares anus? Quod quidem malum si mihi iam vetulae eveniet, non immerito sorti meae accidisse fatebor, quoniam olim stulta dicto matris meae, ut tu nunc iam tuae, audiens non eram. Quae sapiens anus meam quotidie mihi in rapiendo negligentiam atque socordiam exprobrabat. Profanum atque sacerrimum genus meretrices apud omnes homines existimari affirmabat. Addebat etiam hoc peritissima mulier, neminem egentem aerumnosamque meretricem respecturum. 'Hostis est', inquit 'impudica mulier pudicae feminae, ridicula viris, nec quicquam est inope meretrice miserius'. Haec, pol, tibi saepius memoraveram; haec tibi, donec mihi obtemperes, milies repetentur. Proinde cavendum tibi censeo, ne, dum viris parcis, rem tuam perdas.

20 *Sy.* Vehementer incutit terrorem discipulae. Si hoc pacto vivitur, ut haec dictitat, ego quoque haud refragor dictis lenae.

    Er. Pol, iniuria me hodie accusas, mater, nec abstinentem me um-

: VI :

Harpage, procuress; Syrus; Erotium, courtesan

[*Harpage coming from her house with Erotium*]

Harpage. How many times have I told you? Don't take any cus-   19
tomers with empty pockets — not even Jove himself, if he
doesn't bring something!

Syrus. [*Aside*] Goodbye, Jupiter, along with your heavens and terrifying thunder, if a procuress turns you out for soliciting favors
without bringing a gift!

Harpage. How many times have I warned you to look out for
yourself when you're young, so that you don't end up begging
when you're an old woman? If that misfortune befalls me now
that I'm an old woman, I'll have to admit that I deserve it, since
I was so foolish as not to heed the words of my mother, as you
aren't heeding mine now. That wise old woman used to reproach me every day for my negligence and laziness in fleecing
clients. She used to maintain that all men considered courtesans a profane and execrable kind of person, and that knowl-
edgeable woman used to add that no one was going to be concerned with a needy and distressed courtesan. She said, "A
shameless woman is an enemy to a chaste woman, and mocked
by men; there's nothing more pathetic than a destitute whore."
By Pollux, I've reminded you of this often enough, and I'll keep
saying it a thousand times until you obey me. So I think you
should watch out that you don't lose your own means of support while you're giving discounts to men.

Syrus. [*Aside*] She's really terrifying that pupil of hers. If one lived   20
in accordance with her precepts, I too wouldn't gainsay this
madam's advice.

Erotium. By Pollux, your accusation is unjust today, mother, I've

quam ab exigendo quaestu nec verecundam uspiam in petendo novi, nec data umquam fuit rapiendi occasio, ut me in ea re temperarem.

Ha. Hei mihi, quid ego misera ex te nunc audio? Occasionem quaeritas in quaestu? Meretrix ipsa occasio est! Quid enim aliud est munus eius nisi, ut occasionem, ubi non est, faciat? An oscitanti tibi et desidi suppetet divinitus? Quin hanc ipsam vel detrahendi vel rapiendi opportunitatem, quam tu otiosa atque supina exspectas, nec hi plerumque, qui probi perhibentur, respuere solent; ob eamque rem haud fere quemquam intestatum mori audies in urbe, cuius centum non videas expetere hereditatem, alios cognationis iure, alios agnationis, alios alio iure agere. Censen iis omnibus simplicem deberi hereditatem? Uni tantummodo debetur, ceteri student rapinae.

21 *Sy.* Scelestiorem ego lenam nec vidi umquam nec audivi quidem nec quae magis verisimilia fingat. E ludo sophistarum profecta videtur. Vae illi, qui ad has commeabit, nisi pecuniae suae diligens custos erit! Oportebit enim ad eam servandam oculos habere in occipitio.

Er. Ubi, quaeso, mater, tua mandata neglexi?

Ha. Immo, nata, ubi, quaeso, integre servasti? Atque, ut omittam cetera, quid mihi nunc respondebis, quae non es ausa petere Clitiphonem promissum argentum pro palla?

Sy. Perii, hae insidiae Clitiphoni nostro locantur!

Er. Non, pol, mihi audacia, sed tempus deerat audendi. Qui enim intempestive audet, tempestive iacet.

never failed to extract my asking-price, and I've never, ever, been shy about looking for customers, and whenever I've had a chance to fleece them, I've never held back.

Harpage. Woe is me, what is this I'm hearing from you now, wretch that I am? You're *looking for* an opportunity to make money? A whore is *herself* an opportunity for profit. What else does a whore do but make opportunities where none exist? Do you think opportunity is going to present itself by divine intervention while you're sitting about yawning? Look, the opportunities for stealing and fleecing that you're lying about waiting to happen aren't usually sniffed at even by men who are held to be above reproach; that's why you never hear of practically anyone dying intestate in this city without seeing a hundred people going after his inheritance, some by right of marriage, others by right of lineage, and others by some other right. Do you think a simple inheritance is due all these people? The property is owed to just one person; the rest are just engaged in robbery.

Syrus. [*Aside*] I've never seen nor heard a more wicked madam, nor one who invents more plausible untruths. She's seems like a finished product of the schools of the sophists. Woe to the man who frequents these ladies and isn't careful with his cash! He'll need to have eyes in the back of his head to hold on to it!

Erotium. Please tell me, mother, when have I ever ignored your orders?

Harpage. No, you please tell *me*, daughter, when you've followed them to the letter. Not to mention anything else, what are you going to tell me now, when you haven't even dared get the money from Clitipho that he promised for your mantle?

Syrus. [*Aside*] I'll be damned, these traps are being laid against our Clitipho!

Erotium. By Pollux, it wasn't boldness on my part that was lacking, but the right time to be bold. The man who dares at the wrong time, goes begging when the time is right.

Ha. Argutule respondere didiceras.

Er. Vere magis quam argute.

Ha. Quid igitur obstitit ne promissum exigeres?

22 *Er.* Quasi non multa sint quae impudentem efflagitationem deterreant! An, praesente Agrigentinorum legato, quocum venit ad me hodie Clitipho, et de re publica verba faciente, commodum erat mihi efflagitare pallam?

Ha. Percommodum est, inquam, semper meretrici petere, dare numquam. Sed da, quibus de rebus sermo erat?

Er. De pugna ab Agrigentinis adversus Leontinos edita deque excursionibus Agrigentinorum et praeda ex vicis Leontinis facta.

Ha. Hui, tunc optima et perquam optima occasio erat petendi argenti pro palla, nisi tu tam insolens urbanarum artium et rudis esses!

23 *Er.* Imperita sum, fateor. Sed dic, quaeso, mater, quo pacto me a tam diverso sermone insinuare possem ad petitionem argenti?

Ha. Nunc iam incipio bene sperare de te, nata, quae virtutem parentum tuorum aemulari studes. Sed expediam quod quaeris.

Er. Cupio.

Ha. Numnam ubi populationes vicorum memorantur, captivorum et captivarum mentio facile fieri potest?

Er. Facile sane, sed quid tum?

Ha. Quid? Optares protinus alicuius magni ducis esse captiva potius quam parci amatoris amica hisque argutiis Clitiphonis par-

Harpage. You've learned to answer artfully!

Erotium. It's the truth, not artfulness.

Harpage. So what then did stand in the way of your demanding what he promised you?

Erotium. As if there weren't numerous obstacles discouraging me   22
from making shameless demands! Do you think it was a suitable time to ask him for a cloak, when the ambassador of
Agrigento was there — he came with Clitipho to me today —
when the two of them were talking about matters of state?

Harpage. I say it's always a highly suitable time for a whore to
make requests, and never a suitable time for her to bestow favors. But, tell me, what were they talking about?

Erotium. About the fighting between the Agrigentini and the
Leontini[11] and about the raids of the Agrigentini and the plunder they took from the villages of the Leontini.

Harpage. Aha! Then it was the best occasion, indeed the very best
possible occasion, for demanding the money for your mantle,
unless you're completely unfamiliar with and ignorant of the urbane arts.

Erotium. I am inexperienced, I admit. But, please, tell me, mother,   23
how could I possibly have led round to my demand for money
from a discussion of such a different tenor?

Harpage. Well, at last I begin to have some hope for you, daughter, since now you're eager to rival the virtue of your parents.
Let me explain what you're asking about.

Erotium. I'd like that.

Harpage. Certainly when the devastation of villages is alluded to,
can't a reference to the male and female captives easily be made?

Erotium. Of course, very easily. But what then?

Harpage. What then? You should immediately wish you were the
captive of some great general rather than the girlfriend of a
stingy lover; by these arts you may wittily reprove Clitipho's

citatem lepide exprobrares atque, ipso legato approbante ioculos, promissam pallam repeteres.

24　*Er.* Unde, quaeso, mater, haec tam abstrusa didicisti? An ab avia mea sollertissima muliere?

　　Ha. Magnam partem ab ea, verum addidit etiam mihi plura mea sollertia.

　　Sy. Haec retia Clitiphoni tenduntur! Dii vostram fidem, diram et detestabilem anum! Obstupefecit me suis vaframentis.

　　Ha. Praeceptis salutaribus te onerabo, nata, rationemque, si animum intenderis, tradam, ut, undecumque sermo incipiat, ad rem tuam facile vergat. Sic enim ad omnium sermonum genera lepidissima digressione penetrare poteris.

　　Er. Applaudo mihi, cui, quod a casu fortunaque expetendum erat, suppeditatur a matre, quae vicem hic Fortunae gerit.

25　*Sy.* Et ego Clitiphonis doleo vicem, qui in insidias, quas evitare nullo poterit pacto, inconsultius incidit.

　　Er. Sed maius institutio tua otium requirit, mater. Quam nec facilem ad docendum nec ad percipiendum perplanam esse intelligo. Nunc pro tempore velim expedias, mater, id, quod nunc te rogabo.

　　Ha. Hem absolvo quicquid quaesieris.

　　Sy. Vah confidentiam ingentem!

　　Er. Quid si de natura deorum sermo esset, quo pacto digressio inde commoda fieret ad efflagitationem argenti?

26　*Ha.* Non incongrua digressio, nata, ab eo sermone deduci potest. Nam ilico quaerendum esset tibi: 'Cur Ariadnae corona relata est in caelum? Cur Callisto? Cur multae aliae translatae sunt a

stinginess, and while the ambassador is applauding your little joke, ask again for the cloak you've been promised.

Erotium. Please, mother, where did you learn such secrets as these? Was it from my grandmother, that cleverest of women? 24

Harpage. A great part came from her, but my own cleverness added even more.

Syrus. [*Aside*] Ah, these are the nets cast for Clitipho! May the gods keep you safe from this terrifying and hateful old woman! She's amazed me with her clever strategms.

Harpage. I'll load you down with wholesome precepts, daughter, and if you pay attention, I'll tell you a way to turn any conversation round to your own advantage. In this way you'll be able to cut through any kind of discussion with a witty digression.

Erotium. I must congratulate myself that arts which must be sought from chance or good fortune have been supplied to me by my mother, who here plays the part of Fortune.

Syrus. [*Aside*] And I must grieve for the part Clitipho is playing, who has fallen unwittingly into traps from which there's no escape. 25

Erotium. But your training requires more leisure mother. I know it's not an easy thing to teach it and learning it is no straightforward matter, either. For the time being, I'd like you to clear up another question, mother.

Harpage. Ah, I'll solve whatever your problem is.

Syrus. [*Aside*] Good God, what enormous self-assurance!

Erotium. What if they're discussing the nature of the gods[12] — how is it possible to divert them from *that* subject to my demands for money in an appropriate way?

Harpage. There's a perfectly suitable way to digress from that subject, daughter. You must ask them straight off: "Why was Ariadne's hair carried to the sky?[13] Why was Callisto?[14] Why were so many other women carried to their heavenly seats by the gods? Clearly it was all thanks to love!" And when it 26

diis ad superas sedes? Amoris nempe gratia omnes!' Et cum satis constet Iovem donavisse mulierculas caelo ob amorem, ridiculum esse affirmabis illum homunculum dubitare bene merenti amicae dare pallam, qua amiciatur. Ac ne de singulis agam, nihil est, nata, tam diversum tamque abhorrens a sermone proposito, quod non ei apte et commode inseram.

Er. Hanc matrem decet auro expendi.

Sy. Actum est de Clitiphone.

27 *Ha.* Disce, nata, esse meretrix et, quando perhiberis facere quaestum, quaestum noli negligere. Multum autem iuvabit studia tua promptitudo linguae. Crede, inquam, mihi, nec nostri ordinis mulier nec orator publicus nec hi, qui politici volunt perhiberi, alicuius rei sunt, nisi haec calleant sciantque transgredi a sermone ad sermonem, ubicumque opus fuerit, commode et concinne, nullo interiecto hiatu, et casu, non studio, quicquid velint, proloqui videantur atque incidisse in eam rem quam affectant, non insiluisse ex abrupto credantur.

Er. Euge, mater, tuis admonitionibus triumphabo de parcis amatoribus. Geminas gerat vestes, qui posthac ad me venturus erit, nisi forte maluerit abire nudus.

Ha. Euge, nata, matrizas; salva res est.

28 *Sy.* Aperte haec affectat spolia ex amatoribus. Dubium non est quin propediem Clitipho e domo lenae exsiliat nudus confugiatque in domum nostram ridiculus.

Er. Sed tamen, si mendacibus aliquando credendum est, misit ad me postea Clitipho quendam, qui mihi nuntiaret se hodie mis-

emerges that Jove gave his little girlfriends places in heaven because of love, you will then be able to state how absurd it is that
that little fellow is hesitating about giving a deserving girlfriend
a cloak to wrap herself in. Not to go into every specific case,
daughter, there's nothing so at variance, so repugnant to the
subject at hand that I couldn't find an appropriate way to bring
it up.

Erotium. You're worth your weight in gold, mother.

Syrus. [*Aside*] It's all up for Clitipho.

Harpage. Daughter, learn to be a courtesan and when you apply   27
yourself to making a profit, make sure you do make a profit!
Readiness of tongue will aid your studies a great deal. Believe
me when I say it: neither a woman of our order nor a public orator nor even men who want to be reputed politicians are worth
anything unless they are clever enough to change the subject in
an appropriate and logical way whenever they need to, without
losing a breath. They should seem to be speaking about whatever they want to by chance, not artfully, and they should be
thought to have happened casually upon the subject they're
aiming at, rather than jumping towards it from across a chasm.

Erotium. This is great, mother! Thanks to your advice I'll triumph
over all those cheapskate lovers! The next one better bring two
sets of clothes when he comes to see me, unless he wants to
leave my house naked!

Harpage. This is great, daughter — you're acting like your mother;
all's well.

Syrus. [*Aside*] It's plain this girl is aiming to despoil her lovers. No   28
doubt before long Clitipho will come leaping out of this brothel
stripped bare and and the buffoon will come seeking refuge in
our house.

Erotium. Still, if lies are ever to be believed, Clitipho sent someone to me later who told me he was going to send the mantle to
me today so that I could examine it before he buys it, but that I

surum pallam mihi, quam scilicet inspiciam, antequam emat, verum inspectam, rursus remittam. Ego primum nihil illi credo, sed tamen si miserit, officium si nostrum faciam, non remittam.

Ha. Non es admonenda.

Sy. Cur cesso haec nuntiare erae meae, antequam aliquam surripiat vestem clanculum ab era mea, quam meretrici donet? Mihi autem dubium non est quin ille sit Clitipho, de quo illae aiebant, nam nudius tertius eum hinc egredientem solum vidi.

: VII :

Clitipho, Antipho cliens

29 *Cl.* Quantum ego corde capiam dolorem, quam misere crucier infelix, nec dicere nec enarrare quidem facile possum. Ut dii deaeque omnes illas veneficas perdant meretrices, quae mihi hoc negotium exhibuerunt! Nolo quicquam gravius in Clitiphonem sodalem meum dicere, qui horum malorum causa fuit. Aequius est me illa maledicta in me ipsum convertere, qui passus sum obsequendo sodali fieri miser.

A. Nescio quid iam de sodale conqueritur et se miserum praedicat.

30 *Cl.* Is, dum studet verba dare Erotio, ut intromittatur, simulat se illi pallam empturum. Incogitata ergo fallacia, venit ad me. Rogat ut Antiphilae meae pallam sibi ad paucas accomodem horas, quam amicae suae inspiciendam mittat, quam rursus mihi remittat: illo enim fuco sperare noctem mulieris. Impetravit, abstulit pallam, misit meretricibus. Illae, retorquentes fallaciam in auctorem, negant oportere vestem illam educi e manibus, quae

should send it back to him once I'd had a look at it. In the first place, I believe nothing he says, but even if he should send it, I'll do my duty and won't return it.

Harpage. You don't need *my* advice! [*Back to her house*]

Syrus. I'd better tell this to my mistress before he makes off with some of my mistress' clothing to give to his whore. I've no doubt that it's Clitipho they were speaking of, for I saw him coming out of this house alone three days ago.

: VII :

Clitipho; Antipho, his client

[*In the town square; Clitipho does not notice Antipho*]

Clitipho. I can hardly express or tell how much pain I'm in, how 29 wretchedly unhappy I am. May the gods and goddesses damn all these poisonous prostitutes who put me in this predicament! I don't want to say anything too harsh against my friend Clitipho,[15] who was the cause of these troubles. It would be more just to direct these curses against myself, since I was the one who allowed myself to become a wretch by obliging a friend.

Antipho. [*To himself*] I don't know why he's now complaining about his friend and claiming he's so miserable.

Clitipho. Being eager to hoodwink Erotium so that he can get in 30 to see her, he pretends that he's going to buy a mantle for her. Having thought up a trick, he comes to me. He asks me to lend him my Antiphila's cloak for a few hours, which he'll send to his girl for her to examine, then he'll return it to me; he hopes to spend the night with her using this trick. He made his pleas, took off with the mantle, and sent it to the courtesans. They turned the trick against him and said that the mantle shouldn't

iamiam emenda sibi esset. Sic ergo et Clitiphonem suis artibus ceperunt et me adiutorem fallaciae funditus perdiderunt.

A. Solent plerumque insidiantes opprimi suis dolis.

31 Cl. Ad id malum aliud insuper accessit: Syrus, Antiphilae servus, forte praeteriens, de via audierat lenam Harpagen cum filia altercantem. Constitit et multa in amatores nefaria consilia excepit. Inaudierat etiam pallam quandam esse hodie a Clitiphone Erotio mittendam. Quod ubi accepit Syrus, relicto coepto itinere, domum recurrit ut his de rebus monitas faceret mulieres. Antequam domum perveniret, a me vestis Antiphilae ablata erat. Ille rem omnem narrat ordine mulieribus. Crediderunt illae quod consentaneum erat eas credere: me esse illum Clitiphonem, qui pallam dederam meretrici. Coepit ilico vetula nutrix Antiphilae deorum atque hominum fidem clamare, meam accusare perfidiam, actum de alumna et tota familia vociferari. Antiphilam ipsam negant siccis esse oculis, quoniam se desertam a me clarissimo argumento opinetur. O me scelestum, o me perditum, qui commisi ut hostilem in modum viderer eam voluisse perdere, cuius tota salus a fide mea dependebat.

A. Miseret me profecto laboris huius, sed non audeo iam prodire, ne mihi aliis negotiis occupato aliquid iniungatur.

32 Cl. Sed quid nunc agam, incertum est. Adeamne ad eam, ut me de hac suspicione purgem? Operam perdam. Ita omnia consentanea sunt ad peccatum, ut, si profecto ipsa Veritas evolvere me innocentem ex hac criminis suspicione vellet, nequiret. Tum au-

be taken from their hands, as it's already being fitted for her. That's how they used their arts to take in Clitipho and to destroy me utterly as an accomplice in the trick.

Antipho. [*Aside*] It's common for tricksters to be ruined by their own tricks.

Clitipho. Another act of wickedness was added to that one besides. Syrus, the slave of Antiphila, chanced to be passing by and heard from the street the procuress Harpagê arguing with her daughter. He stopped and got an earful of their numerous wicked schemes against their lovers. He also overheard that Clitipho was going to send a mantle today to Erotium. When Syrus heard this, he abandoned his rounds and went back home to inform the women of what he'd heard. Before he arrived home, I had abstracted Antiphila's garment. Syrus told the women the whole story. They believed what it was plausible to believe: that I was the Clitipho who had given the mantle to the whore. At once Antiphila's old nurse began calling on the good faith of gods and men, blaming me for my betrayal, wailing that it was all up with her nursling and the whole family. They say that Antiphila was crying, since she believed she had the clearest possible proof that I'd deserted her. How wicked and depraved I was to perpetrate this crime, so that it seemed I wanted to ruin like an enemy the woman whose welfare depended entirely on my good faith. 31

Antipho. [*Aside*] Without question, this mess makes me unhappy, too, but I dare not come forward now; I'm occupied with other business and don't need him to saddle me with any more.

Clitipho. But I can't make up my mind what to do now. Shall I go to her to and make a clean breast of it? That's a waste of time; all the circumstances fit together so perfectly that even if Truth herself wanted to free me, innocent as I am, of suspicion of this crime, she wouldn't be able to do it. Then, too, I'm afraid that, if no one gets the mantle back quickly, the courtesans will pur- 32

tem vereor ne interim meretrices, si nemo est qui cito repetat, vestem intervertant. Atque adeo nescio an nunc quoque, cum mature requiram, quicquam proficiam. Quae si mihi pergent negare meum, introrumpam ipse in domum meretriciam et illis invitis et male habitis vestem eripiam. Deinde trecentas mihi dicas scribant. Certum est petere scelestam domum eo, quo iam institui, animo.

33   *A.* Non patiàr hunc hominem solum afflictari, operam illi dabo. Heus, Clitipho! Mane!

  Cl. Hem, quis me revocat properantem?

  A. Tuus Antipho socium laborum tuorum se adiungit. Mane!

  Cl. An novisti, quaeso, ea quae mihi obiecta sunt?

  A. Omnia modo ex te audivi. Sed nolo ut iratus adeas meretrices nec quicquam cum illis agas, antequam conveniamus Clitiphonem, qui eis dederat vestem. Eius est enim repetere, qui dedit. Tu nihil dederas, nihil a te repetendum est.

  Cl. Sic censes?

34   *A.* Sic censeo. Properemus ergo invenire Clitiphonem, cuius opera maximam nobis ad hanc rem expediendam facultatem dabit.

  Cl. Eamus, ut libet.

: VIII :

Epirota, Civis Syracusanus, Pharmacopola

35   *Ep.* Salve urbs optata, meorum profugium, ubi fratris filiam esse praedicant! Quam sane urbem salvus videre aut contingere

loin the garment. And I don't know whether even now, when I need to act quickly, I'll accomplish anything. If they go on refusing my request, I may break into that brothel myself and seize the garment whether they like it or not. Well, let them sue me three hundred times. I'm definitely going to make an attempt on their bawdy house with that intention in mind. [*Hurrying off*]

Antipho. [*Aside*] I really shouldn't let this man suffer by himself;   33
I'll help him out. [*Addresses Clitopho*] Hello, there, Clitipho, wait a moment!

Clitipho. Who's calling me back when I'm in such a hurry?

Antipho. Your Antipho is joining you to help you with your troubles, so wait up!

Clitipho. Please—do you know what I'm up against?

Antipho. I've just now overheard everything you've said. I don't want you to go near those whores when you're so angry or have anything to do with them until we've met with Clitipho, who gave them the garment. For it's the job of the man who gave it to get it back. You didn't give them anything, so you've no right to get anything back from them.

Clitipho. You think so?

Antipho. Yes, I do. Let's hurry then and find Clitipho; his services   34
will be our best bet to bring the matter off.

Clitipho. Then let's get going, please.

: VIII :

The Epirote; a Citizen of Syracuse; a Quack

[*Another spot in the town square where there is a crowd of people*]

Epirote. Greetings, city of my prayers, refuge of my family, where   35
they say my niece is to be found. I never really expected to see

numquam speravi, ita mare venti caelum in nos navigantes sae-
vierant. Quam ob rem, antequam incipiam fratris filiam per urbem quaeritare, recipiam me in aliquid diversoriolum, ubi corpus curem. Sed quis est, quaeso, ille, qui ex editiori loco verba
facit ad plebem? Exquiram iam ex proximo, tametsi nihil ad me
verba eius. Dic, sodes, tribunus est hic an aliquis subtribunus,
qui contionatur in foro?

36   *Ci.* Quid, malum, tribunus? Pharmacopola est, merus syco-
phanta.

    Ep. Pharmacopolae, obsecro, verba tam frequenti hominum coetu
audiuntur ac si responsa essent Sibyllae?

    Ci. Sic solitum est hic fieri.

    Ep. Malus videlicet mos. Sed quid ille nunc garrit? Non sua pote-
rit vendere pharmaca, nisi contionem advocet?

    Ci. Ille quidem non garrit, sed praesente hac homunculorum
turba suas radices illinit, quas mox vendat.

    Ep. Ego illum nihil unctitare video. Ambas tamen eius manus vi-
deo: dextram intentat loquens, laeva praegrandem radicem os-
tentat populo.

    Ci. Illam ipsam, quam vides nunc ostentare radicem, illinit iam,
cum loquitur.

37   *Ep.* Quo pacto loquens illinit? Nisi forte verbis illam tingat.

    Ci. Istuc ipsum, rem tenes. Verbis et quidem mendacibus illud
praestat. Nemo enim auderet emere quicquam, nisi illitum ab
eo prius esset hoc pacto. Cum enim satis illitum ab ipso et per-
litum ex sententia vident, certatim ruunt omnes ad merces et
ipsum fatigant emendo.

this city alive or to reach it considering how sea, wind and skies buffeted us during our voyage. So before I begin scouring the city for my niece, let me turn into some little inn where I can refresh myself. But I wonder who that man is up there who's addressing the populace? I'll ask the man next to me, though he hasn't said a word to me. [*He addresses the man next to him*] Tell me, if you wouldn't mind, is this some tribune or lesser official who's giving a speech in the square?

Citizen. What? A tribune? Like hell. He's a quack, nothing more 36 than a swindler.

Epirote. I beg your pardon, but is this dense crowd listening to the words of a quack as though they were responses from a sibyl?

Citizen. This is what usually happens here.

Epirote. Now that's plainly an evil custom. But what's he chattering about now? Can't he sell his snake-oil without calling an assembly?

Citizen. Oh, he doesn't just chatter; he smears on those herbal roots of his in the presence of this crowd of little folk, then sells the stuff afterwards.

Epirote. I don't see him putting on any ointment. But I do see both his hands: he's pointing with his right hand while speaking, and with his left hand he's showing this enormous root to the people.

Citizen. That root you see him holding up? That's the one he smears on now while he's talking.

Epirote. How can he apply his ointment while talking? Unless he's 37 soaking it in words.

Citizen. That's it—you've got it. He produces his effect with words, and lying words too. Nobody would risk buying anything unless the quack had smeared it on first in this way. When they see that he's put it on himself, really smeared it on in a satisfactory way, then they all race to fight over his merchandise. They wear the man out with their buying.

Ep. Cuiusmodi radices sunt istae, quas hic venales habet?

Ci. Radices sunt porcis praereptae et ob eam rem nullum invenies Syracusis suem obesiorem, nisi forte quis saginatur domi. Cibus enim aliis ad hunc usum praeripitur.

Ep. Dii boni, cur hoc pacto saepius elusi non sapiunt tandem?

38 *Ci.* Dicam tibi. Alii sunt qui nunc eluduntur, alii qui dudum elusi fuerant, alii porro qui eludendi sunt. Peregrini sunt omnes, confluunt in urbem et refluunt undarum more. Adde etiam credulitatem plebeculae, quae occasionem maximam fallaciis praestat.

Ep. Narra, obsecro, exactius, quo pacto hic ludibrio habet turbam.

Ci. Quid est opus ut ego narrem, cum tu ipsemet audire possis, si accedamus propius, quo pacto laudat suas herbas? Iactat antidota et anguem circumdat collo.

Ep. Accedamus ergo propius, ut aliquod ridiculum audiamus. Non enim negatum mihi arbitror, ut animum tot iam laboribus confectum hoc laxamenti genere leniam.

39 *Ph.* Ut occepi dicere vobis, iuvenes, in horto Hesperidum hanc herbam ortam fuisse aiunt. Innumeras illi virtutes esse constat, de quibus omnibus ipse periculum feci, et vos, si diis placet, hodie parva impensa periculum facietis. Eius maxima virtus est ad indicia furtorum. Nam citius manu continebit ignem is, qui furti noxa tenetur, quam radicem istam: cadit protinus e manibus, si eam ullo pacto tetigerit. Proinde in Mauritania, ubi haec nata fertur, nulli perhibentur esse fures, nisi forte qui post furtum statim fugam meditantur.

Epirote. Exactly what sort of roots does he sell here?

Citizen. The roots are snatched away from pigs, which is why you won't find really fat swine here in Syracuse, unless maybe there's one that's being fattened at home. In fact, food is taken away from others for this purpose.

Epirote. Good gods! If they've been tricked in this way so often, why don't they get wise to him in the end?

Citizen. I'll tell you why: the ones being fooled right now are 38 different from the ones who have been fooled before and from the ones that are going to be fooled in the future. They're all foreigners who flow in and out of the city like the tides of the sea. Then add the gullibility of the common herd, a trait which furnishes the maximum opportunity for chicanery.

Epirote. Please tell me more precisely how he goes about fooling the crowd.

Citizen. You don't need me to tell you — if we go up closer you can hear for yourself how he flogs those herbal remedies of his. He boasts about his antidotes and hangs a snake round his collar.

Epirote. Let's get closer, then, so we can hear something funny. I don't think I should deny myself this sort of relaxation to calm down my exhausted mind after all my troubles. [*They listen to the quack addressing the crowd*]

Quack. As I was starting to tell you, young men, they say this 39 herb was originally grown in the Garden of the Hesperides. It clearly has innumerable virtues, all of which I have put to the test, and you today, may it please the gods, will also test its power . . . for a small price. Its greatest virtue is a built-in theft-alarm. You see, somebody involved in thieving will sooner hold fire in his hand than this herb: it falls immediately from his hands if he touches it in any way. That's why in Mauretania, where this plant is said to have originated, there are reported to be no thieves except perhaps the ones who are planning imme-diate flight after their robberies.

Ep. Pusilla plantula! Fugavit iste omnes fures e Mauritania et docet ceteros esse negligentes in cavendis furibus, cum ipse sit in
custodiendis radicibus circumspectissimus.

40 *Ph.* Alia praeterea huic memoranda virtus: si quis eam vestibus
insutam gestabit, numquam malo leto peribit.

Ep. Deorum hic potestatem exigua radice compescit, ut, si Iovi libuerit garrulum hunc sycophantam perdere, prohibeatur radice,
cum in ea re vix Iuno ipsa adversari posset.

Ph. Vos appello, nautae, quorum maxime interest tutos esse, qui
salsos fluctus maris peragratis: factum est iam periculum eos,
qui hanc radicem gestant, numquam in aquis perire. Eam vel
gratis, si emere dubitatis, sumere licet.

Ep. Credo equidem illos, qui cum hac radice in mari perierunt,
non posse huius refellere mendacia, quia nusquam sunt, nec illos pariter, qui e naufragio evaserunt. Tum illud vide scelerum
caput ut homines ad impensam invitat simulando munificen-
tiam.

41 *Ph.* Si quis fortasse tantam naturae benignitatem non credibilem
ducit, meminerit eius, quod praeclarissimi auctores tradunt,
pisciculum quendam remoram nomine tantae virtutis ac roboris
esse, ut, si navem velo et fluctibus actam ore tetigerit, eam sistat
immobilemque a cursu praestet.

Ep. Immiscuit scelestus cum fallaciis suis summorum virorum
auctoritatem, ut ex eo uno dicto eorum sua ipse comprobet
mendacia.

Ph. Nemo dubitet hanc herbam contra ictus scorpionum plurimum valere, alvum sistere, calculos pellere, pectoris et cordis vi-

Epirote. [*Aside*] Such a tiny little seedling! It's driven all the thieves out of Mauretania and teaches the rest to be careless about preventing theft, while the man himself is extremely cautious about keeping his medicinal roots safe.

Quack. Moreover, it has another virtue worth mentioning: if 40 somebody wears it sewn into his clothes, he'll never die a painful death.

Epirote. [*Aside*] This charlatan even tames the power of the gods with his little root, so that if Jove wanted to destroy this garrulous swindler, the root would prevent him, although in this matter Juno herself would have trouble opposing him.

Quack. I appeal to you, sailors, you whose greatest concern is to be safe, you who traverse the salty waves of the sea: it's already been proved that those who carry this root with them never perish on the deep. If you're hesitating to buy it, I'll let you have it for nothing.

Epirote. [*Aside*] I would imagine that the men who have died at sea clutching this root never come round to gainsay the man's lies, and likewise with those who've escaped shipwreck. And look how this criminal mind gets men to pay him by shamming generosity.

Quack. If someone perhaps thinks such bounty on Nature's part is 41 unbelievable, he should remember what celebrated authors report about a little fish called a "remora," which has such power and strength that if it touches a ship under full sail with its mouth, it stops it dead in its course.[16]

Epirote. [*Aside*] This scoundrel mixes in the authority of the greatest men with his humbug and proves his own lies using a single saying of theirs.

Quack. Let no one doubt this herb's power to protect against the sting of scorpions, to stop diarrhea, to expel kidney stones, to relieve pains of the chest and the heart, to be a unique remedy

tia emendare, ad canis rabidi morsum unicum remedium esse, fluxum capillorum cohibere et pluribus aliis morbis mederi.

Ep. Hic sua sententia exigit omnes medicos a Syracusis, quorum universum quaestum hac una praeripit radice, cum ea sola omnibus medeatur morbis. Vah, quid ego nunc video? Collum suum circumvolvit colubro confidentissime! Cum mala bestia profecto commercium habet.

Ci. Pax est illi cum anguibus.

Ep. Sed quid nunc potat?

Ci. Toxicum.

Ep. Dignus est profecto hac potione. Sed vereor ne sorbeat Falernum.

42 *Ph.* Haec sunt antidota illa, turba mea, quae nec Mithridates ipse umquam excogitavit. Vidistis ut ante oculos vestros virus meracissimum bibi. Quantum quidem in eo est, ego sum mortuus, qui nunc loquor, iam dudum efflavi spiritum.

Ep. Utinam id verum esset!

Ph. Sed tamen auxilio huius antidoti salvus fiam et ab ostio Acheruntis revocabor ad vitam.

Ep. Stulte faciet mors, si perdiderit occasionem istam! Ego tamen illum non merum venenum, sed merum mulsum ebibisse arbitror. Quod illi male vertat! Sed abeundum est iam mihi, satis enim superque satur sum nugis eius.

Ci. Quo abis, hospes? Non manes, donec tribunus contionem dimittat?

Ep. Piget iam eius videre praestigias.

Ci. Ergo praestigiatorem hunc existimas?

Ep. Immo praestigiatorum magistrum.

Ci. Si audiendus tibi erit iterum, socium me tibi polliceor.

for the bite of a rabid dog, to prevent hair from falling out, and to heal many more diseases.

Epirote. [*Aside*] In his own opinion he's driving all the doctors out of Syracuse. Their whole source of income is going to be snatched from under their noses by this one medicinal root, since it alone cures every disease. O my, what do I see now? He's wrapped a snake around his neck with the utmost self-assurance. He'll surely make some sales with that evil creature.

Citizen. He's on friendly terms with the world of snakes.

Epirote. But what's he drinking now?

Citizen. Poison.

Epirote. That's just the drink for him. But I'm afraid it's Falernian wine that he's sucking down.[17]

Quack. These are antidotes, my friends, that not even Mithridates[18] himself ever dreamed of. You have seen me drink, before your very eyes, pure, undiluted snake venom. There's enough poison in there that the person who's talking to you now is dead; I've long since given up the ghost.   42

Epirote. [*Aside*] Would that were true!

Quack. Nevertheless, thanks to this antidote I'm safe; I've been called from the gates of Hell back to life.

Epirote. [*Aside*] Death is going to do something stupid if she loses this opportunity! But my view is that the man has drunk pure plonk, not pure venom. I hope it makes him sick! But I must be going now; I've had enough and more than enough of his nonsense.

Citizen. Where are you off to, stranger? Why not stay here, until the tribune dissolves the assembly?

Epirote. I'm tired of watching his chicanery.

Citizen. So you think he's a mountebank?

Epirote. To be precise, he's the arch-mountebank.

Citizen. If you'll only listen a little longer, I promise to keep you company.

Ep. Quid auctor es mihi, ut hunc iterum audiam?

Ci. Ego quidem nec hortor nec dehortor, sed, si tibi libuerit, ego tua causa non detrectabo munus.

Ep. Benigne facis. Vale, socie lepide.

Ci. Et tu, hospes.

Ep. Ego ad cauponam[2] recta pergam, ubi corpus quieti dem, nisi forte et ibi sycophantas offendam, qui perturbent otium.

: IX :

Caupo

43 *Ca.* Illum ego laborem vix laborem appellare soleo, ubi sola corporis opera usurpatur, animus difficultatis est expers, aut contra, ubi quiescente corpore animus in honesto simplicique negotio versatur. Verum enim vero hic labos plurimus, hic mera miseria, ubi utroque modo insudandum est, ut, cum habeas exercitum in multiplici negotio corpus, animum etiam ad meditationem malitiae fatiges. Velut caupones faciunt, qui et laboribus corporis impliciti sunt et dies noctesque animum sollicitum habent cogitantes sedulo, quo pacto caute insidiari possint hospitibus ita ut nec odium ex malefactis nec infamiam contrahant. Hic nempe mos est nobis, ut eos, qui diversuri sunt in cauponam, antequam veniant alliciamus; postquam venerint circumveniamus; si circumventi querantur, rursus et placemus. Itaque non plures colores excogitati sunt in scholis rhetorum, quam sunt a nobis ad hanc rem inventi, ut docte animos eorum tractare possimus.

Epirote. Why are you encouraging me to hear the man again?

Citizen. Really, I'm not encouraging or discouraging it, but if you want to, I'm at your service.

Epirote. You're very kind. Farewell, my charming friend.

Citizen. You too, stranger.

Epirote. I'll make my way straight to an inn where I can get some sleep, unless perhaps I bump into more of these hucksters there, too, who'll spoil my rest.

: IX :

Innkeeper

[*An innkeeper in front of his lodgings*]

Innkeeper. As a rule, I hardly call something work when the body 43 alone is engaged without any challenge to the mind, or on the contrary when the body rests but the mind is engaged in simple, honest business. But it's the worst labor of all, it's sheer misery, when you have to sweat both your mind and your body, so that your body's doing multiple tasks and your mind too gets worn out thinking up wicked schemes. That's what innkeepers do. They are involved in physical labor and they worry themselves day and night with tireless plans to lay traps for their guests that are without risk to themselves and that will not win them ill-fame or hatred for their wickedness. That's certainly our practice here: we ensnare the people who are coming to stay at an inn before they come; we cheat them after they've come; and if they complain about being cheated, we placate them again. Hence we've invented as many rhetorical devices for doing this as the schools of rhetoric ever dreamed up so as to negotiate skillfully with our customers.

44   Sed pro dii immortales, quantam ad me turbam venire video! Vix erit omnibus locus apud me. Hui, ducunt etiam citharoedum secum! Amoenitatis et Voluptatis sunt filii. Scio, crumena plena gravis solet esse iis. Amittam itaque illos inanes et
sine ponderis labore domum. Sed nihil malim, quam ut citharoedus hic oppignoraret cithatam. Subsequitur etiam eos nescio
quis peregrinus, lata zona cinctus et caerulea tunica: victima hic
nostra erit. Ego aliquantisper omittam hunc animi rigorem, ut
hospitalior advenientibus videar. Sed cesso illis quam lautissimam cenam parare, ut eos emungam argento.

: X :

Citharoedus, caupo

45 *Cit.* Nec durior quisquam caupo nec intractabilis magis in his ha-
bitat regionibus quam hic, apud quem diversuri sumus. Ferenda
est itaque eius morositas aequo animo. Nihil tamen malim,
quam ut aliqua insigni fallacia insidiari possem isti publico insi-
diatori, ut par meritis eius gratia referri posset. Sed congredia-
mur cauponem et cauponam. Faustum diversorium saluto.

Ca. Citharoedum et citharam, lepidissimum oblectamentum, ce-
terosque comites salvere iubeo.

Cit. Numquid liberalior aliquanto in nos eris, si lepidissimo ci-
tharae sono tuas deliniam aures?

But, by the immortal gods, what a crowd I see heading my   44
way! I hardly have room for them all. Ooh, good, they're even
bringing a performer with them who sings and plays the lyre!
They're sons of Charm and Pleasure. I know the sort: they
tend to find their purses too heavy. So I'll send them away from
my house with empty purses, lightened of their burdens.
There's nothing I'd like better than to get this musician to pawn
his lyre! There's some foreigner or other following them, belted
with a broad girdle and a sea-blue tunic; he'll be our victim. But
let me leave off these hard thoughts for a little; I need to seem
more welcoming to the new arrivals. However, I'll hold back on
getting a sumptuous dinner ready for them, so I can swindle
them of their silver.

: X :

Musician, Innkeeper

[*The travelers arrive at the inn*]

Musician. There's no innkeeper in these parts who is tougher or   45
    more intractable than this man with whom we are going to stay.
    So we have to put up calmly with his ill-temper. Still, I'd like
    nothing better than to cook up some brilliant plot against this
    well-known schemer so that he could be paid back in his own
    coin. But let us approach the innkeeper and his inn. [*He ad-
    dresses the innkeeper*] Greetings, O inn of good omen!
Innkeeper. I bid you welcome, musician, and your lyre, a most
    charming source of delight, and all your other friends.
Musician. Might it be that you'll be somewhat more generous to-
    wards us if I soothe your ears with the charming sound of my
    lyre?

46 *Ca.* Numquid magnificentiores in cauponem eritis, si suavissimo aliquo pulmenti odore nares vestras demulcebo?

Cit. Quid ad me fumus?

Ca. Quid ad me strepitus?

Cit. Par pari respondet. Missa istaec faciamus! Obsequendum est primum ventri, deinde confabulationis usurpemus.

Ca. Immo solutiones prius! Post id confabulari licet quantum vultis. Ego dapsilem vobis cenam dabo, sed admonendi non estis quanti vobis ea constabit.

Cit. Est unde solvatur tibi.

Ca. Ego hinc eo, ut eam et cito et laute vobis parem.

Cit. At festina!

∴ XI ∴

Citharoedus, dispensator, caupo, Epirota

47 *Cit.* Lautissimam cenam dedit nobis caupo, verum meminisse, quanti nos cenaturos dixerit, piget. Id ergo caveo nobis.

Di. Quid caves?

Cit. Ut vel parvi vel nihil nobis cena constet.

Di. Cura, amabo, nam nec pecuniae tantum reliquum est nobis, quantum hic exigit pro cena.

Cit. Aliquam in eum insignem technam machinabor, ut multem illum cena avaritiae exemplum.

48 *Ca.* I mecum, hospes, qui nostris pactionibus interfuisti, ut, si perplexari vellent uspiam isti more suo, tuo convincantur testimonio.

Innkeeper. Might it be that you'll spend in a more lordly way if I   46
   caress your nostrils with some extremely tasty appetizer?

Musician. What do I care about smells?

Innkeeper. What do I care about racket?

Musician. Like answers like. Let's forget about all that. First let's
   pay homage to the belly, then we'll have a jaw.

Innkeeper. No, pay up first. After that we can talk as much as you
   want. I'll give you a hearty supper, but you won't be told ahead
   of time how much it's going to cost you.

Musician. We have the cash to pay you.

Innkeeper. I'm going off to get your meal ready quickly and lav-
   ishly.

Musician. But hurry!

: XI :

Musician, Steward, Innkeeper, the Epirote

[*After the meal*]

Musician. This innkeeper provided us with a wonderfully lavish   47
   meal. But just remember, however much he charges us to dine,
   we don't like it. I'll manage it for us.

Steward. What are you going to manage?

Musician. That this meal costs us very little or nothing at all.

Steward. Please be careful. We don't have enough money left to
   pay what this man charges for dinner.

Musician. I'm going to come up with some brilliant device to fleece
   the man for the cost of the dinner and make an example of his
   greed.

Innkeeper. [*Entering with the Epirote*] Go with me, stranger; you   48
   were present at our bargaining, so if this lot try to muddle
   things up, as they usually do, they'll be refuted by your testimony.

Ep. Facile prodam, quod scio.

Ca. Numquid meministi me praedixisse cenam eximiam illis daturum?

Ep. Memini.

Ca. Et quid exigebam ab illis ob eam rem tenes?

Ep. Et id quidem.

Ca. Facilius obtinebo, si tu eos argues. Pravum enim genus sunt hominum: affabiles ieiuni, contumaces saturi, protervi, petulantes, oblocutores, praesertim in hospites. Atque ea de causa nolui ut cum illis discumberes.

Ep. Recte, pol, fecisti.

49 *Ca.* Sed aggrediamur hos mordacibus iocis, ut affabiles videamur. Salvere iubeo turbam edacem!

Cit. Salveto et tu vicissim, duritiae pater!

Ca. Te seorsum, citharoede, saluto, voracitatis exemplum!

Cit. Te appello, avaritiae specimen, decimator lagoenarum, quippe quas numquam plenas apponis, dilutor meri, surreptor hordei, suppostor pridianarum reliquiarum, a quo nec fides nec iusiurandum servatur!

Ca. Omnia haec vera sunt. Memorandae sunt vicissim, citharoede, virtutes tuae. Quid blateras, vulturinae sortis homo? Cuius venter per occasionem distenditur, quadraginta dies inedia laxatur, ad omnia coepta audacissime, qui expletus saepe, satur numquam fuisti.

50 *Cit.* Non est cauponis exprobrare edacitatem, nisi forte cogitaveris nos de tuo accipere.

Ca. Malo potius leto me exstinctum velim, quam micam panis de meo quisquam voret. Sed ioci causa illud.

Epirote. I'm ready to say what I know.

Innkeeper. You do remember, don't you, that I said I'd give them an excellent supper?

Epirote. I do remember.

Innkeeper. And you remember what I demanded from them for the meal?

Epirote. That, too.

Innkeeper. I'll get it from them if you're the one to accuse them. They're a perverse lot: friendly when they're hungry, willful when they've been fed; shameless, petulant, and abusive, especially towards strangers. That's why I didn't want you eating at the same table with them.

Epirote. By Pollux, that was the right thing to do.

Innkeeper. But let's join them with some biting jests, just so we look friendly. [*He addresses the diners*] Greetings to this voracious crew!

Musician. And greetings to you, too, father of austerity!

Innkeeper. I give *you* a special greeting, musician, O model of gluttony!

Musician. And I call upon *you*, O pattern of greed, decimator of decanters — for you certainly never set out a full flask — waterer of wine, burglar of beer, sneaky leaver of left-overs, you who never kept a pledge nor an oath!

Innkeeper. All of these things are true. And your virtues, musician, should in turn be recorded. What are you babbling about? You're like a vulture; your stomach gets stuffed when it can, then goes empty for forty days; every enterprise finds you as bold as brass; you're often filled up but never satisfied.

Musician. An innkeeper shouldn't condemn voracity, unless perhaps you had in mind that we should accept the meal at your expense.

Innkeeper. I'd rather be struck dead than let anyone eat a breadcrumb at my expense. Just joking of course.

Cit. At ego existimabam te hanc cenam largiturum nobis, si quis nostrum tuam torvitatem lepidissimo cantu oblectaret.

Ca. Hui, cantionum osorem postulas tu oblectare numeris?

Cit. Quid scis, an futurum sit, antequam audias? Iuppiter ipse delinitur cantu meo.

Ca. Noli, quaeso, mihi molestus esse. Tu, dispensator, age, numera, si vis, argentum!

51 *Cit.* Non feres obolum, nisi audies cantilenas nostras. Quarum si nullam probaveris, ilico tibi numerabitur argentum.

Ca. Redigis me, homo, ad insaniam, qui putas extorquere mihi cenam canendo, cum nec Musas ipsas canentes laudarem!

Cit. Hanc, inquam, tibi, caupo, feram condicionem: si annueris cantionem nostram tibi placere, cena nobis gratuita erit, sin negabis, protinus et quod debemus et quantum postulabis accipies.

Ep. Quid, quandoquidem ita instat, da illi hanc veniam, tu tamen usque pernegato. Et si metuis captiones, ad tertiam partem damni me ascribo socium.

Ca. Quando me ita omnes compellitis, accipiam condicionem. Sed matura!

Cit. Hem incipio.

52 *Ca.* Crispat etiam, si diis placet, vocem, ut me capiat! Vae capiti tuo!

Cit. Ecquid placuit tibi, caupo, cantilena nostra?

Ca. Ecquid modum facies dementiae?

Cit. Canam alteram.

Ca. Homo, operam, inquam, perdis, nam mihi nec Orpheus nec Amphion nec Arion canentes sine pecunia placerent. Illud vide, stolidus ut iactat caput cantando!

Musician. But I had the idea you'd make us a gift of this meal if one of us should amuse a grim character like you with a really witty song.

Innkeeper. Really! You're asking to amuse with your melodies somebody who hates songs?

Musician. How do you know what's going to happen before you hear it? Jupiter himself is charmed by my song.

Innkeeper. Please, I don't want to, I find music annoying. You, steward, please be so kind as to pay up!

Musician. You won't get a penny unless you listen to our songs. If   51 you don't like any of them, we'll pay you your money immediately.

Innkeeper. You'll drive me insane, man. You think you can extort a dinner from me by singing? I wouldn't speak well of singers if they were the Muses themselves!

Musician. I say, innkeeper, let me make a bet with you: if you should admit that our tune pleases you, the meal will be ours for free; if, however, you say that it doesn't please you, you'll immediately get twice what we owe you and twice your asking price.

Epirote. Well, since he insists, indulge him—but make sure you keep saying no. If you're afraid of losing the bet, I'll sign on for a third of the losses as your associate.

Innkeeper. Since you're all forcing me to do this, I'll take the bet. So get on with it.

Musician. Ahem. I begin. [*Sings*]

Innkeeper. Good god, he's even using vibrato to captivate me. The   52 hell with you!

Musician. I trust our song pleases you, innkeeper?

Innkeeper. I trust you'll put an end to this madness?

Musician. I'll sing another. [*Sings another song*]

Innkeeper. Look man, you're wasting your time. Neither Orpheus nor Amphion nor Arion[19] would please me with their singing if

Cit. Placuit haec tibi, caupo?

Ca. Immo, mehercle, displicuit!

Cit. Experiar tertiam.

Ca. Mea quidem causa vel centesimam, ego usque pernegabo.

53 *Cit.* At tu desine iam molestus esse cauponi, citharoede, gar-
riendo. Pactos iam, tibi dico, solve nummos! Num etiam haec
displicuit tibi?

Ca. Hahahae, immo perplacuit!

Cit. Gratia est habenda diis, cum ex multis tandem inventa est
una, quae tibi morosissimo placeret. Vale, caupo!

Ca. Hei miserum, quo abitis? Non ea ratione mihi placuisse affir-
mabam.

Cit. Testes sunt mihi tibi perplacuisse cantionem istam.

Ca. Curram recta ad praetorem.

Cit. Tuo arbitratu vel ad consules.

54 *Ca.* Num meministi tu, hospes, non ita pactum esse inter nos?
Quid ais? Taces, faex hominum!

Ep. Dramburi te clofto goglie.

Ca. Hei, mihi! Epirota me prodidit! Ille conscius fallaciae, tertiam
in partem damni se scripsit, ut me duabus partibus multaret.

Ep. Immo, caupo, si nescis, tota cena multatus es, nam ego ea lege
subscripsi, si pernegares, tu autem stulte et pueriliter annuisti.

Ca. Perii, miser! Etiam hic tergiversatur. Illi abierunt. Quid spei
est reliquum? Si apud praetorem hanc fallaciam conquerar, de-

there was no money in it. Look how the blockhead tosses his head while he sings!

Musician. Do you like this one, innkeeper?

Innkeeper. No, by Hercules, I hate it!

Musician. I'll try a third song.

Innkeeper. As far as I'm concerned, you can sing a hundred of them and I'll still say no.

Musician. [*To himself*] Stop annoying the innkeeper now, musician, 53 with your chatter. I tell you, pay him now the money we've agreed. [*To the innkeeper*] Now surely *that* tune is one you like?

Innkeeper. Ha, ha, he, now that's one I really like!

Musician. The gods be thanked, we've finally found the one and only tune that pleases you, you son of a bitch. Goodbye, innkeeper!

Innkeeper. Hey wretch, where are you going? I never said the song pleased me that way.

Musician. I have witnesses who'll testify that you found this tune extremely pleasant.

Innkeeper. I'm going right to the praetor.

Musician. It's up to you — why not the consuls while you're at it?[20]

Innkeeper. [*To the Epirote*] Surely you recall, guest, that this wasn't 54 our agreement. What do you say? [*To the diners, who are laughing uproariously*] Shut up, you scum!

Epirote. Dramburi te clofto goglie.[21]

Innkeeper. Woe is me! The Epirote has betrayed me! He knew it was a trick, he took the bet to pay a third of the damages so as to cheat me of the other two thirds!

Epirote. Actually, innkeeper, in case you haven't noticed, you've been bilked for the whole cost of the meal, since I only made my bet with the proviso that you'd go on saying no; but you acted like a stupid child and said yes.

Innkeeper. I'm done for, finished! Even this man is turning his back on me. They've gone; what hope do I have left? If I com-

ludar ab omnibus qui audient; eius contra laudabunt ingenium
qui eam commentus est; me deridebunt dignumque deputabunt
hac contumelia. Quid igitur faciam, nisi vel ut me suspendam,
vel procursum irae meae in hunc Epirotam perfidum proferam,
qui me in hos laqueos praestigiatorum coniecit?

: XII :

Epirota

55 *Ep.* Nihil ad hunc diem evenit mihi, quod non ab hariolo digre-
dienti domo praedictum esset. Multa sane tristia mihi portendi
affirmabat, antequam fratris filiam invenirem, sed tamen inven-
turum dictitabat. Quae omnia aequo animo patiar, dum eam
inveniam.

56 Atque ut omittam alios labores itineris, quos adhuc pertuli,
quot me contumeliis impurus caupo affecit, quod me supposi-
tum a citharoedo suspicabatur, ut concinnarem fallaciam, qua
delusus lepide fuerat! Testor mala mea: nec lepidiorem nec magis ridiculam sycophantiam factam umquam audisse memini.
Quid plura? Ego ipse miser, tot obrutus aerumnis, quoties in
mentem venit, rideo. Atque si dabitur ut salvus remeem in patriam, multos participes huius ioci faciam, praesertim cum non
ex audito quicquam, sed omnia meo periculo et meo magno
malo gesta narrare possim. Nam praeterquam quod omnium
generum maledicta mihi innocenti ingesserat caupo, sarcinulas
etiam meas in discessu meo subtraxit nec reddidit, donec partem damni meo, ut ille dictitabat, nomine suscepti pecunia mea
resarcirem.

57 Sed hoc plane vel ridiculum est vel ostenti simile, quod vates

plain about this trick to the police, I'll be the laughing-stock of everyone who hears about it; in fact they'll applaud the cleverness of the man who thought the trick up; they'll mock me and put me down as somebody who deserved this insult. The only thing left to do is hang myself or channel my anger against this treacherous Epirote, who threw me into the snares of tricksters.

: XII :

The Epirote

Epirote. Nothing has happened to me up to this very day which 55 was not predicted by the soothsayer as I was leaving home. He claimed that many truly bitter things were presaged for me before I would find my niece, but he repeated that I was nevertheless going to find her. And I'd suffer them all with tranquility if I could only find her.

Not to mention the other trials of the journey I've already 56 been through, how many insults that filthy innkeeper has subjected me to! He suspected the musician put me up to concocting the trick that so amusingly made a fool of him. I do solemnly declare to my own prejudice that I don't remember ever having heard of a funnier or more ridiculous piece of trickery. In short, though I'm myself a wretch buried in troubles, I laugh whenever I remember that. And if I'm lucky enough to return safe to my homeland, I can share the joke with many people, especially as I can tell everything that happened to my own peril and great detriment, not at second-hand. For in addition to the fact that the innkeeper heaped abuse of every kind on me despite my innocence, he also stole my wallet on my departure and refused to return it until I should reimburse him for that part of his loss which he's suffered, or so he kept saying, in my name.

But what my seer claimed was in the end presaged to me by 57

meus ad ultimum mihi fatis portendi asserebat: anum me decrepitam ducturum, unde maxima mihi fortuna immineret. Qui si addidisset malam, magis annuerem vaticinio. Deos, quaeso, ut meam sospitem inveniam filiam. Cetera, quae contingent, si tolerabilia sunt, aequo animo attollerabo.

: XIII :

Epirota, Scapha nutrix

58 *Ep.* Dum otium in caupona quaero, negotium inveni. Nullus in hac urbe locus sycophantarum praestigiis vacat, nec deversorium nec forum nec quisquam alius, ut arbitror, locus. Omnia sunt laqueis, omnia insidiis plena. Quam ob rem, quod faciendum est mihi in hac urbe, perpropere perficiendum censeo, ne mora opportunitatem praebeat sycophantis aggrediendi me. Sed ubi nunc primum eam, cuius causa huc veni, quaeram? Ubi investigem? Quos percontor, quos non percontor in alieno oppido nescio. Unum hoc certo scio: Syracusis illam esse. Ingrediar hoc templum Cereris deaeque supplicabo, ut indicium mihi faciat de filia, ubi exorabilem mihi spero deam futuram, quae olim pari iactata fuit infortunio in quaerenda Persephone. Sed conveniam ancillam hanc prius, quam otiosam in vestibulo templi astare video. Ex iis enim, quae abiectae sortis sunt, licet multa sciscitari, quae a gravioribus prohibet pudor.

59 *Sc.* Defessa sum circumspectando. Putaveram enim hic affuturum Clitiphonem cum sodalibus suis, ut assolebat. Sed illum ope-

the fates is really ridiculous or like a portent: he said I would marry a decrepit old woman, and from that marriage the greatest good fortune would be within my grasp. If he had said "bad fortune," I might have agreed with his prophecy. Please, gods, let me find my brother's daughter safe and sound. Everything else that happens, if bearable, I'll bear with tranquility.

: XIII :

The Epirote; Scapha, a nurse

[*The Epirote enters the temple of Ceres; Scapha stands in front*]

Epirote. While I was looking for peace in the inn, I found anything 58 but peace. In this city there's no place free from the tricks of mountebanks, neither the inn nor the forum nor any other place, or so it seems to me. Everything is rife with snares and plots. For this reason I've decided that what I have to do in this city I should conclude as quickly as I can; delay will only provide the chance for these swindlers to set upon me. But where now shall I seek her first, on whose account I've come here? Where should I look? Since I'm in a strange city I don't know whom to ask and whom not to ask. The one thing I do know is that Antiphila is in Syracuse. Let me just enter this temple of Ceres and supplicate the goddess to give me a sign regarding my niece. I hope the goddess will be moved by my entreaty, as she once suffered a like misfortune when looking for Persephone.[22] But first I'll approach this maidservant whom I see standing in the vestibule of the temple, doing nothing. You can find out a lot from persons of low condition which shame prevents weightier personages from telling you.

Scapha. [*To herself*] I'm tired of being on the lookout. I had 59 thought that Clitipho would be here with his friends, as usual.

ram magis dare novo amori arbitror, nunc praesertim cum gratior est meretrici ob donatam pallam.

Ep. Sed proloquar quasi ignorem cuius dei templum sit. Mulier,
estne hoc fanum Cereris?

Sc. Erilis patriae habitum recognosco. Est.

Ep. Proh dii immortales, nosciton ego hanc?

Sc. Iuno regina, eri fratrem Damascenum conspicor?

60 *Ep.* Scapha es fratris ancilla? Quid obstupuisti? Tibi dico, resi-
pisce! Improviso conspectu meo attonita consiluit.

Sc. Oh oh oh!

Ep. Responde, mitte fletum! Ego veni ut vos servarem.

Sc. Tam diu passus es nos desertas?

Ep. Ego non sum passus; sed sors ita tulit. Sed hoc unum mihi
responde: valet Antiphila?

Sc. Valet.

Ep. Diis habeo gratiam! Ubinam ea est? Qua est usa fortuna hactenus?

Sc. Adulescenti nobili conciliata est.

Ep. Hem!

Sc. Quam ducturus est uxorem sine dote, tametsi non audeat adhuc adversantibus cognatis illud efficere.

Ep. Dos dabitur illi amplissima.

Sc. O fortunatam adventu tuo eram meam!

Ep. Duc me ad eam!

Sc. Sequere, salus nostra!

But I think he's devoting his efforts to his new love, especially now that he is more in favor with his whore because of the mantle he gave her.

Epirote. I'll accost her by pretending not to know which god the temple belongs to. Woman, is this the shrine of Ceres?

Scapha. [*To herself*] I recognize the style of dress of my mistress' homeland! [*To the Epirote*] It is.

Epirote. By the immortal gods, don't I know this woman?

Scapha. Queen Juno, is it Damascenus, the brother of my master, that I'm seeing?

Epirote. Aren't you Scapha, the maidservant of my brother? Why 60 are you fainting? Wake up, I tell you! [*To himself*] Astonished by seeing me unexpectedly, she's speechless.

Scapha. Oh, oh, oh!

Epirote. Talk to me, stop crying! I've come to put myself at your service.

Scapha. Why did you let us be abandoned for such a long time?

Epirote. I didn't, but that is what destiny allowed. But tell me this one thing: is Antiphila all right?

Scapha. She's fine.

Epirote. I give thanks to the gods! Where on earth is she? How has fortune treated her?

Scapha. She is betrothed to a noble young man.

Epirote. Well, well!

Scapha. He'd marry her without a dowry, but he doesn't dare do so over his relatives' objections.

Epirote. He'll get a very rich dowry indeed.

Scapha. O how fortunate my mistress is that you've arrived!

Epirote. Take me to her!

Scapha. Follow me; you are our savior!

: XIV :

Antipho Clitiphonis sponsi cliens, Pamphila anus, Lesbia

61 *A.* Salve, nympha Nereis et habitu et facie!

Pa. Propior fortasse habitu quam facie, nam si qua mihi fortuna erat, eam dentium hebetavit dolor. En adhuc fomentorum vestigia in ore!

A. Laboras ergo ex dentibus?

Pa. Et male quidem.

A. Ex inopia credebam potius.

Pa. Quid dixti?

A. Male, inquam, factum, sed verbis Clitiphonis tibi salutem nuntio.

Pa. Utinam esset id, quod spero! Ain? Clitipho te misit?

62 *A.* Ipse, atque obsecrat, si se ames, ne huic condicioni, quam daturus est tibi, adverseris.

Pa. Ego unam exspecto ab eo condicionem, quam si laturus es, non est opus rogatu.

A. Paucis tibi expediam quicquid est.

Pa. Id, pol, percupio.

A. Olim ille quandam virginem compresserat, cuius nunc patruus ex Epiro venit.

Pa. Epirotane?

A. Sic. Rescivit rem omnem, coegit Clitiphonem eam ducere.

Pa. Male factum, perii!

: XIV :

Antipho, a client of Clitipho the fiancé; Pamphila, an old woman; Lesbia

[*A street in front of the houses of Pamphila, Antipho, and Harpage*]

Antipho. Greetings, your dress and appearance resemble those of a 61
sea-nymph!

Pamphila. My dress perhaps more so than my appearance; for whenever I have had any ill fortune, the pain of it weakens the appearance of my teeth. Look, I still have the remains of the poultice on my mouth.

Antipho. Your teeth are still bothering you?

Pamphila. And really badly.

Antipho. [*Aside*] I think it's really the lack of teeth that's bothering you.

Pamphila. What did you say?

Antipho. [*Loudly*] I said, that must really bother you. But I bring you greetings from Clitipho.

Pamphila. [*To herself*] O, may my dreams comes true! [*To Antipho*] You said Clitipho sent you?

Antipho. The very man himself, and he asks, if you love him, that 62
you don't reject the proposal he is going to make to you.

Pamphila. I'm waiting for just one proposal from him; if that's the one you're making, there's no need to ask.

Antipho. I'll explain it to you briefly.

Pamphila. By Pollux, I'd like that very much!

Antipho. At some time in the past Clitipho had sex with a certain virgin, whose uncle has now arrived from Epirus.

Pamphila. A man from Epirus?

Antipho. Yes. He knows the whole story, and is forcing Clitipho to marry his niece.

Pamphila. That's terrible! It's all over for me!

A. Dotem ei amplissimam dedit, nam ditissimus est.

Pa. Hoc etiam permolestum.

63   *A.* Clitipho tui percupidus, quoniam duas habere uxores non licet, rogat te ut ipsi affini suo nubas atque commigres hodie domum, ut te prope habeat et videat.

Pa. Hui quid dixti, obsecro? Ut nubam Epirotae?

A. Nempe nobili, robusto, opulentissimo, ubi in eodem, si volueris, cubili esse poteris cum Clitiphone.

Pa. Minime gentium! Epirotae, quem pro famulo, ita me dii
ament, vix vellem uti?

A. Tu, Pamphila, de hac re etiam atque etiam cogita. Nam si du-
cet aliam — expetitur enim a pluribus divitiarum causa — frustra
postea desiderabis amissam occasionem atque perpetuum inter
vos dissidium erit.

64   *Pa.* Ah, noli ominari dissidium! Dii meliora!

A. Ego quidem non ominor, sed commemoro quod futurum est.
Quid respondes? Quid taces?

Pa. Hui, feram ego latam Epirotarum zonam et semiplotia illa et
tunicas tritas caeruleas? Non possum, Antipho!

A. Vide quid facis.

Pa. Sed tamen, ne dissidium inter nos fiat, necesse est semiinvi-
tam annuere.

A. Nunc sapere videris.

65   *Pa.* Abi, Antipho. Nuntia Clitiphoni me modo missuram ad eum
ancillam, quae illum de hac re certiorem faciat.

A. Vale ergo, Pamphila nostra, si nostra pateris esse.

Pa. Excutis lacrimas, cum alienationem a vobis commemoras.

Antipho. He's giving Clitipho a very rich dowry, as the uncle is a very wealthy man.

Pamphila. This is really upsetting!

Antipho. Clitipho wants you a lot, but since he can't marry two 63 wives, he's asking you to marry the uncle and move to his house today, so that he'll have you nearby and be able to see you.

Pamphila. Oh dear, please — what is that you said? That I should marry this man from Epirus?

Antipho. He's really a fine, healthy, very rich man, and you'll be able to be in the same bed with Clitipho when you want.

Pamphila. Not a chance! So may the gods love me, I wouldn't want this Epirote for a slave, let alone a husband.

Antipho. Pamphila, you should think about this matter carefully, for if he marries the other woman — and many people are asking him to for the sake of the money — you'll be sorry later you lost the chance and there will be a permanent rift between you and Clitipho.

Pamphila. Ah, don't foretell any rifts! Heaven forbid! 64

Antipho. I'm not foretelling anything, I'm telling you what's going to happen. What do you say? Why don't you answer?

Pamphila. Ugh, could I put up with that broad girdle the Epirotes wear, those clogs and those worn blue tunics? I just can't, Antipho!

Antipho. Consider what you're doing.

Pamphila. Well, I don't want there to be any rift between us, so I'll have to give my consent, half-hearted though it is.

Antipho. Now you're being smart.

Pamphila. Go, Antipho, and tell Clitipho that I will soon be send- 65 ing the Epirote a maid-servant who will give him the news.

Antipho. Then, farewell, our dear Pamphila, if you will allow yourself to be called ours.

Pamphila. You make me cry when you remind me about being separated from you.

A. Unum hoc scio, te numquam nos deserturam.

Pa. Abi, lenocinium habet lingua tua, lenocinaris ultro, cum loqueris.

A. Vale ergo, futura nostra!

Pa. Placet omen, vale et tu. Abiit ille. Perii, misera! Invita volo.
Heus Lesbia, accede! Paululum secreto volo tecum colloqui.

Le. Praesto adsum.

Pa. Eamus in conclave, ut commodius his de rebus loquamur.

Le. I, sequor.

: XV :

Lesbia, Charinus cliens Clitiphonis Samii

66 *Le.* His nimirum solet Fortuna commoditatibus plerosque affi-
cere, quas si auderent ipsi optare, levissimi ineptissimique habe-
rentur. Quam ob rem desino iam mirari, si quae mulieres suae
sortis immemores alta incredibiliaque animo suo vel optant vel
sperant. Posse enim cuiquam evenire quod cupit, annuente fortunae libidine, quae rebus humanis moderatur, vident.

Ch. Quid est, quod Lesbia, relicta lana et colo, disserit de fortuna? Auscultabo quid velit sibi haec oratio.

Le. Vel haec quis non prodigiosa existimet, quae Clitiphoni hodie
evenere?

Antipho. I know one thing: you will never desert us.

Pamphila. Go, you have a tongue like a pimp's; when you speak, you're pimping in your own interests.

Antipho. Fare you well, then, our future! [*Exits*]

Pamphila. I like that omen; farewell to you also. He's left. I'm miserable, I'm finished! I will without being willing. Hey, Lesbia, come here! I want to talk with you a bit in private.

Lesbia. I'll be right there.

Pamphila. Let's go into this chamber so we can discuss the situation better.

Lesbia. Go ahead, I'm right behind you.

∶ XV ∶

Lesbia; Charinus, a client of Clitipho of Samos

[*In front of the house of Clitipho, Charinus in the background*]

Lesbia. There's no doubt that Fortune generally grants many men 66 advantages like these. If they themselves dared pray for such advantages, they would be reckoned frivolous and ineffectual in the extreme. That's why I've stopped being surprised that there are women who so are forgetful of their own lot in life that in their hearts they hope and pray for exalted and unbelievable things. For they see that anybody can get what they want so long as it suits Fortune's fancy—she who controls human affairs.

Charinus. [*To himself*] Why is it that Lesbia, abandoning her wool and distaff, is giving a lecture on Fortune? I'll just listen in on the subject of her oration.

Lesbia. Indeed, who wouldn't think that the things that have happened to Clitipho today are a prodigy of nature?

Ch. Nempe de Clitiphone narrat Archimedontis filio nostri Clitiphonis sodale, qui amat peregrinam illam, cuius palla missa fuit
Erotio.

Le. Anus haec era mea illum iam pridem deperibat. Vel ut amicum vel ut virum illum expetebat.

Ch. Obsequentissima amatio!

Le. Munera pretiosissima missitabat Clitiphoni; praeter munera
nihil gratum erat.

Ch. Recte dictum! Nihil amat, qui ingratum amat.

67 *Le.* Docte tamen et callide animum vetulae tractare, rem procras-
tinare, benigne loqui, ad rem vetulae cupidissime, frustra tamen
inhiare. Illam vero alteram, quam ex animo amabat, ducere palam indotatam non audebat. Inter has rerum difficultates ecce
insperato advenit huius puellae patruus ex Epiro, vir opulentis-
simus. Invenit illam Clitiphoni collocatam, firmat nuptias, dotem ingentem dat. Quid multa? Clitiphonem modo pauperem
maximarum divitiarum compotem facit.

Ch. Gaudeo, mehercle, bene evenire Clitiphoni!

68 *Le.* Compulsus deinde a Clitiphone, hic affinis eram meam vetulam uxorem petiit.

Ch. Scio quo res evadet: accersita in domum Clitiphonis vetula
blanditiis compilabitur.

Le. Illa primo respuebat connubium, Epirotarum fastidiens genus. Deinde, ut Clitiphonis copiam haberet, annuit nuptiis et

Charinus. Surely she's talking about Clitipho, the son of Archimedon — the companion of my Clitipho — the one who's in love with that foreign woman, whose mantle was sent to Erotium.

Lesbia. This old lady, my mistress, has been desperately in love with Clitipho for a long time, and was after him to become either her lover or her husband.

Charinus. Now that's an obliging approach to love-making!

Lesbia. She kept sending him the most expensive gifts, but nothing beyond the gifts was welcome to him.

Charinus. Well said; the person who loves an ingrate loves nothing.

Lesbia. Nevertheless, he manipulated the heart of the old woman 67 cleverly and shrewdly, while postponing their affair with fine words, all the while thirsting to get hold of the old girl's property, but in vain. Meanwhile, the other woman, whom he truly loved, he didn't dare marry without a dowry. In the midst of all these problems, behold, from out of the blue Antiphila's uncle from Epirus shows up, who's a man of great wealth. He discovers that Antiphila is betrothed to Clitipho, confirms their nuptials, and presents him with a huge dowry. To make a long story short, he makes Clitipho, who shortly before was a pauper, the beneficiary of an enormous fortune.

Charinus. By Hercules, I'm delighted that things have worked out so well for Clitipho!

Lesbia. Then, at Clitipho's urging, this uncle of his sought my old 68 mistress' hand in marriage.

Charinus. I know how the story will end: the old girl will be summoned to Clitipho's house where she'll be robbed blind with flattering words.

Lesbia. At first, she rejected the marriage, turning up her nose at the idea of marrying an Epirote. Then, to get amorous access to Clitipho, she gave her approval to the wedding and went from being unwilling to being extremely eager for marriage. Hence

423

ex invita facta est cupidissima nuptiarum. Misit ergo me ad eum ut renuntiarem nullam per se fieri moram nuptiis. Sed cui iam dubium erit quin era mea suis divitiis beatum faciat Clitiphonem, qui, duplici auctus fortuna; regem Attalum, ut opinor, divitiis provocare poterit?

Ch. Cur ego cesso Clitiphonem hoc impertiri gaudio, quem solide gavisurum tanta sodalis fortuna certo scio?

Le. Pulsandum iam est ostium Clitiphonis. Heus, heus! Aperite ostium! Ego sum, Lesbia!

: XVI :

Clitipho sponsus, Clitipho Samius, Charinus cliens Clitiphonis Samii

69 *Clsp.* Multa gratulando verba fecisti, Clitipho, ubi animum erga me tuum ab ineunte aetate perspectissimum frustra explicare conatus es. Visus es enim, quod est luce clarius, ostentare. Satis quidem novimus nos inter nos, proinde et istam meam, quantulacumque est, fortunam communem tibi mecum, si libuerit, esse volo.

Clsa. Amice, mehercule, et perbenigne loqueris, Clitipho. Verum ego satis dives sum, cum te video ditem, et fortunatus, cum te fortunatum aspicio. Tibi etenim cum bene est, mihi ipsi perbene esse existimo.

Clsp. Missa ergo nunc istaec faciamus et, quod magis instat, hilarem hunc agamus diem. Sed Charinum tuum venire ad nos video admodum hilari vultu.

she sent me to him to bring back the message that the nuptials should not be delayed on her account. But will anyone now doubt that my mistress has made Clitipho blissfully happy with her riches? The man has doubly increased his good fortune; in my view he could challenge King Attalus in riches.[23]

Charinus. Why am I being so slow to share this joy with Clitipho? As his crony, I'm certain he's going to be overjoyed at this great good fortune.

Lesbia. I must knock now on Clitipho's door. Hello, hello, open the door! It's me, Lesbia!

: XVI :

Clitipho the fiancé; Clitipho of Samos; Charinus, his client

[*The street in front of all three houses*]

Clitipho F. You've said a lot in the course of congratulating me, Clitipho; you've tried in vain to make clear to me how your love for me has been tried and true from earliest youth. Indeed, you seem to be making a parade of your loyalty, that's clearer than daylight. Well, we know each other quite well, so I'd like you to share this good fortune of mine, modest though it is, if that's what you want.

Clitipho S. By Hercules, you speak like a true friend and with great kindness, Clitipho. But it's riches enough for me to see you rich, and I'm fortunate when I see you blessed by Fortune. Indeed, when things go well for you, I consider that they are going very well for me too.

Clitipho F. Well, let's drop all this now. The most pressing matter is to enjoy this day. But I see your Charinus coming towards us, looking very cheerful.

69

Clsa. Laetus, est, ita me dii ament, valde ob ea, quae tibi feliciter evenerunt.

Clsp. Novi iam pridem animum hominis.

70 *Ch.* Salve, Clitipho! Tuis me commodis gaudere te credo credere.

Clsp. Credo. Sed tuum est nunc, Charine, nisi quid te detinet, ut mihi operae aliquantum hodie des.

Ch. Quid est opus?

Clsp. Ut cures accersendos tibicines et qui hymenaeum canant, conducendos cocos, emenda obsonia largiter, ornandas aedes. Magno enim cum apparatu has nuptias celebrari volo et, quod admonendus non es, ne quid parce aut sordide fiat!

Ch. Potin es, ut quiescas et sponsam tuam cures et mihi totam hanc curam nuptialem committas?

Clsp. Non addam verbum.

71 *Clsa.* Septem hominum impigrorum munus fungitur Charinus solus in huiusmodi negotiis gerundis.

Clsp. Novi hominem.

Ch. Apparatum scilicet vis magnificum?

Clsp. Magnificentissimum! Hem tibi ergo marsupium: cui non parcas, dum omnia opipare instruantur.

Ch. Dictum satis. Accingar negotium.

Clsp. Bene ambulato.

Ch. Bene valeto.

Clsp. Vidistin adhuc, Clitipho, hunc affinem meum peregrinum?

Clsa. Nondum vidi.

72 *Clsp.* Si alloqueris hominem, haud censebis illum in barbarie natum. Peringenuos habet mores et, quod magis novum est, urbanitatem maximam in sermone.

Clitipho S. He's really happy, so may the gods love me, because things have turned out so happily for you.

Clitipho F. I've long known the man's character.

Charinus. Greetings, Clitipho! I trust you believe I rejoice in your good fortune. 70

Clitipho F. I do. But it's your job now, Charinus, unless you have some other commitment, to give me a bit of help today.

Charinus. What do you need?

Clitipho F. I need you to take care of summoning the pipers and those who sing the marriage-song, to see to the hiring of cooks, the buying of food for a feast, and the decoration of the house. I want these nuptials to be celebrated with great pomp, and—I hardly need tell you—nothing must be done cheaply or in a vulgar fashion.

Charinus. Why don't you just relax and attend to your bride, and put the whole responsibility for this wedding in my hands?

Clitipho F. That's just what I wanted to say.

Clitipho S. Charinus all by himself performs the work of seven energetic men in matters such as these. 71

Clitipho F. I know the man's abilities.

Charinus. Let me ask you, do you want a magnificent display?

Clitipho F. As magnificent as possible. Here, take my purse. Don't be stingy with it, so long as everything's prepared sumptuously.

Charinus. Say no more. I'll get started on the business.

Clitipho F. Have a good stroll.

Charinus. Farewell to you both. [*Departs*]

Clitipho F. Have you seen this foreign relative of mine yet, Clitipho?

Clitipho S. No, not yet.

Clitipho F. If you talk to the man, you'll hardly believe he was born in a barbarous country. He has the manners of a nobleman and, what is even stranger, his conversation is highly urbane. 72

427

Clsa. Vulgo sunt ingenia et virtutes. Sed de verbis tuis habebit Pamphila quocum maxime se oblectet. Nam te auctorem harum nuptiarum audivi.

Clsp. Hahahae, ipse fui!

Clsa. Bellum conciliatorem! Nisi maxima esset in hoc viro facilitas, non ita facile id ab eo impetrares.

73 *Clsp.* Facilis, Clitipho, et obsequens est et perbenignus et quem, ita me dii ament, magni facio. Is non diu amisit liberos et uxorem in Epiro, et totum iam animum in Antiphilam fratris filiam convertit et me maxime colit. Quem ego contra percolo.

Clsa. Usus es eius facilitate et obsequio non in levissima re neque inani. Una iam fiet, ut arbitror, domus Pamphilae cum tua.

Clsp. Una plane, et omnia communia.

Clsa. Proventum feliciter est.

Clsp. Cur non imus visum hominem intro et sponsam meam?

Clsa. Eamus, sed haereo, Clitipho.

Clsp. Quid haeres?

Clsa. Pudet me uxoris tuae, quod eius pallam Erotio misi, quae nondum remissa est.

74 *Clsp.* Vah, meminisse praeterita illa, quae cognita iam sunt omnia et sedata? Bona fortuna, Clitipho, aequiorem animum hominibus praestat. In tenuissima re si accedit malum, minus tolerabile videtur. Nunc, cum nobis propitii sint dii, alius animus est nobis. Pallulam illam habeat sibi Erotium. Te autem nec amice nec benigne facere dicam, nisi hac mea fortuna communiter mecum uti velis.

Clitipho S. Intelligence and virtue are found everywhere. But your words suggest that Pamphila will have a man whose company she'll enjoy. Indeed, I've heard that you proposed the idea of their nuptials.

Clitipho F. Ha, ha, he, I did indeed!

Clitipho S. Well, you make a fine marriage agent! Unless this man has the greatest good nature, it won't be so easy to persuade him to marry her.

Clitipho F. He is good-natured, Clitipho, and obliging and very 73 gracious and one upon whom, may the gods bless me, I set great store. Not long ago he lost his wife and children in Epirus, and now his whole concern is for Antiphila, his brother's daughter, and he holds me in the highest esteem. And I have great regard for him in turn.

Clitipho S. You are imposing on his good nature and sense of obligation in no trivial or empty matter. As I understand it, your household and Pamphila's are going to be combined.

Clitipho F. Really combined, with everything in common.

Clitipho S. It has turned out happily.

Clitipho F. Why don't we go inside to see the man and my bride?

Clitipho S. By all means. But one thing makes me hesitate.

Clitipho F. What's that?

Clitipho S. I'm ashamed to see your wife because I sent her mantle to Erotium, which she hasn't yet returned.

Clitipho F. Oh, she won't remember all that in the past; it's now all 74 found out and laid to rest. Good fortune, Clitipho, brings calmer emotions. When times are bad, misfortunes seem less tolerable when they happen to you. Now, since the gods are looking kindly on us, we take a different attitude. Let Erotium keep that little mantle for herself. I'll say you are being unkind and unfriendly if you don't want to share this good fortune of mine with me

429

Clsa. Gratiam habeo, Clitipho. Si usus erit, faciam. Sed ingrediamur tandem, percupio enim videre hunc affinem tuum.

Clsp. Eamus. Et non multo post videbis etiam Pamphila novam nuptam.

Clsa. Et illam quidem haud perinvitus.

Clsp. Intus exspectabimus Charinum et quod est reliquum nuptiis, intus transigetur.

FINIS

Clitipho S. Thank you, Clitipho. If I need to, I'll do that. But let's go in at long last; I really want to meet this relative of yours.

Clitipho F. Let's go. And not much later you'll even see his new bride, Pamphila.

Clitipho S. I'm not totally unwilling to see her, either.

Clitipho F. We'll wait for Charinus inside. And what is left to do for the nuptials, shall be performed within. [*Both exit to the house of Antiphila*]

THE END

Note on the Text

The Latin text of the *Paulus* is based on the edition of Alessandro Perosa (1983), reproduced by the kind permission of Leo S. Olschki Editore. Readers interested in the manuscript evidence for the text and its textual tradition are advised to consult this excellent edition with its full critical apparatus. Some slight departures from Perosa's text are given in the Notes to the Text. I have also consulted the useful translation of Michael Katchmer (1998), whose renderings I have sometimes adapted. My notes too are in part indebted to Katchmer's work.

The Latin text of the *Play of Philodoxus* is based on the edition of Lucia Cesarini Martinelli (1977), reproduced by kind permission of the Istituto Nazionale di Studi sul Rinascimento in Florence. The text survives in two redactions, an earlier redaction datable to 1424 (when Alberti was twenty years old) and a definitive redaction composed between 1434 and 1437 (see Cesarini Martinelli, p. 113). The earlier redaction was that printed by Aldus Manutius the Younger in 1588, while the later redaction was published in the Salamanca edition of 1500 and in Bonucci's *Opere volgari* of 1843. The textual variants between the two redactions are many and substantive (see Grayson 1954, pp. 291–93, cited in the Bibliography), and, according to Cesarini Martinelli (p. 115), "cast light on the process of maturation in Alberti's style in the period of his youth." Cesarini Martinelli's edition presents both versions of Alberti's play side-by-side, but for this I Tatti edition we give only the second, more polished version of Alberti's play. Readers interested in the textual evolution of the play and the manuscript evidence for the text are advised to consult the excellent edition of Cesarini Martinelli. Some minor changes to Cesarini Martinelli's text are noted in the apparatus.

The first redaction of the play included as prefatory matter only the prologue of Lepidus and the argument, while the second redaction dropped the Lepidus prologue, retained the argument, and added the dedication to Leonello d'Este and the Commentary. For this edition I

have included the Lepidus prologue from the first redaction for the convenience of the reader.

The Latin text of the *Philogenia and Epiphebus* follows that of Francesca Rosselli (1965, 1997). The latter is not a critical edition, being essentially a transcript of a single (rather corrupt) manuscript with readings cited from a second codex of no evident authority. More than forty manuscripts of this text survive, and it would be highly desirable to have a proper critical edition of it. For this I Tatti edition James Hankins, the series editor, prepared a provisional text based on the two witnesses cited by Rosselli, Florence, Biblioteca Medicea Laurenziana Ashburnham 188 (*A*) and Paris, Bibliothèque Nationale lat. 8364 (*P*). The readings reported from these MSS are cited from Rosselli's apparatus and are not based on fresh collations. As Rosselli's text is often defective, many readings have had to be inferred from the excellent Italian translation of Perosa (1965), which was based in turn on an unpublished critical text ("testo critico provvisorio") prepared by his student, Giovanna Maria Mura (see ibid., p. 137). Mura's text unfortunately could not be consulted.

The Latin text of Aeneas Silvius Piccolomini's *Chrysis* is based on the edition of Enzo Cecchini (1968), reproduced here by permission of Sansoni Editore, Florence. The edition of André Boutemy (1939) has also been consulted as well as the Italian translation of Perosa (1965).

The Latin text of Tommaso Mezzo's *The Epirote* is based on the edition of Graziella Gentilini (1983), reproduced by permission of Longo Editore, Ravenna. The textual evidence for the *Epirota* consists of a *codex unicus* (Reggio Emilia, Biblioteca Municipale, MS Vari E 160, s. XV ex. or s. XVI in.), which I have examined *in situ*, as well as an incunable and three editions from the Cinquecento. I have also consulted the edition of Ludwig Braun (1974), which contains as well a German translation of the text.

Included in both the codex and the *editio princeps* is Mezzo's letter of presentation to Ermolao Barbaro, placed before the text of the play, and a

letter to Daniele Medio, placed after it. I have prefaced the Latin text with these two letters. The text of the letters is taken from the Braun edition, though the punctuation and capitalization has been modernized.

In all five plays, the scenic indications and stage directions, added in the English translation within square brackets and in italics, are those of the present editor. Lists of *dramatis personae* have been supplied at the beginning of each play, and paragraph numbering has been introduced in the prose plays. Slight adjustments to the punctuation of all five plays have also been made.

Notes to the Text

❦❧❦

1. *sc.* pignoris

2. *The manuscripts have* ante *after* preterquam *which is bracketed by Perosa.*

3. *This scene division is not in Perosa's text but is implied by the dialogue.*

4. postea *ed.*

5. *The codices indicate a speech by Papis but leave a blank space for the dialogue.*

THE PLAY OF PHILODOXUS

1. *In the notes (p. 226) to her edition, Cesarini Martinelli suggests the reading* Doxia *instead of the* Doxam *of the MSS that she prints in the text proper. But impersonal* inquit *seems the more likely reading in the absence of a* se *as the subject of* velle.

2. *Reading* de bibundo *for* debibundo *("tasting") in accordance with Cesarini Martinelli's suggestion (p. 226).*

3. *sc.* iis, *a Plautine form.*

4. *Cesarini Martinelli makes this interrogative:* Cessas? *This whole aside makes no sense in context and should perhaps be obelized.*

5. *Cesarini Martinelli gives* voluptas, *possibly an unattested syncopated form of* voluptates; *conventional accidence would seem to require* voluptates.

PHILOGENIA AND EPIPHEBUS

1. iudicium *ed.:* indicium *inferred from Perosa's* indizio

2. exulabit *ed.:* exsultabit *inferred from Perosa's* spiccato il volo

3. intelligio *ed.*

4. pro *ed.*

5. ad *ed.:* (venuto) da (me) *Perosa*

6. huic *ed.*

7. *possibly one should read* concentu

8. miseratus tibi *P:* miserear et *A:* (che cessino codesti tuoi) affanni *Perosa*

9. dicis *ed.:* (come dalle case di) Dite *Perosa*

10. descendens te et *ed.:* (Basterà che) tu discenda *Perosa*

11. splendidor *ed.*

12. deberi *ed.:* deleri *inferred from Perosa's* cancellarsi

13. abiecit infelicitas *P:* habeat infelicitatis *A*

14. mediam *ed.:* in diem *inferred from Perosa's* per la vita.

15. *possibly one should read* intra limen: *Perosa has* (Varco) la soglia di casa

16. namque *ed.:* E non (sono stata io sola) *Perosa*

17. adiurata *ed.:* ammirare *Perosa*

18. nostro *ed.:* Nostra figlia *(as subj.) Perosa*

19. ventri *P:* venter *A:* pensa alla pancia *Perosa*

20. si *P:* et *A:* se *Perosa*

21. Non *ed.:* noi stessi *Perosa*

22. damno nobis *P:* damno *A*

23. ut stipes *P:* ut propter stipes *A*

24. opertam *P:* operatam *A*

25. foras *P:* in feras *A*

26. sim *P:* sum *A*

27. solicitudine *ed.:* solitudine *inferred from Perosa's* se rimango sola

28. *Rosselli's text is missing this final line of the scene; it is inferred here from Perosa's* EUFONIO: Vado.

29. hoc perripiat *ed.:* me praeripiat *inferred from Perosa's* se costei mi portasse via prima del tempo.

30. operabor *ed.:* dovrò attendere *Perosa*

31. pricides *ed.*

32. *Perosa translates* sono perduta! *as though reading* disperdo

33. nunc *ed.*: *Perosa* non

34. donabis *ed.*

35. que *A*: cum *P, ed.*

36. inquet *A*: inquiet *P*

37. preterea *ed.*: (rievocare) il nostro passato *Perosa*

38. Et vero veriorem *ed.*: Dice una verità sacrosancta *Perosa*

39. qui *ed.*: le cose (che hanno conosciute) *Perosa*

40. At quid *A*: Atqui *P, ed.*

41. laudare *ed.*

42. apte *A*: apertum *P*: aperte *inferred from Perosa's* apertamente

43. humanum est *P*: humana sunt *A*

44. ais *P*: vis *A*: (Tu che ne) dici *Perosa*

45. eos *ed.*

46. quod senescam *P*: persenescam *A, ed.*

47. dicis *P*: dicit *A, ed.*: Dici *Perosa*

48. pur *sic ed.*

49. commodi *ed.*

50. laveris *ed.*: Alleggerendo *Perosa*

51. Principi *ed.*: Innanzitutto *Perosa*

52. aut *ed.*: affinché *Perosa*

53. hic *ed.*: d'ora innanzi *Perosa*

54. quando *ed.*

55. ne *ed.*

56. promisum *ed.*

57. more *ed*: morte *Perosa*

58. exacta *ed.*

59. probe *P*: principali *A*

60. atque *ed*: affinché *Perosa*

61. verbum *ed.*: Ma *Perosa*

62. alium *ed.*

63. iure *P*: in te *A*: e poi *Perosa*

64. adnuttat *A*: adnuctatur *P*: (affinché io) sia ricevuto *Perosa*

65. quidam *ed.*

66. in *ed.*: eunuco *Perosa*

CHRYSIS

1. *Possibly one should read* melobiba

2. *Cecchini's edition assigns this speech to Archimenides; it is given to Canthara, more plausibly, in Perosa's Italian translation.*

THE EPIROTE

1. *Sc.* diapasmata

2. cauponem *ed.*

Notes to the Translation

PAULUS

1. I.e., he uses the comic, not the tragic form.

2. The canonical day was divided into twelve hours, from sunrise to sunset. The hours were arranged in groups of three, from Tierce (the first three hours after sunrise) to Sext (six hours), Nones (nine hours), and Vespers (the last three hours before sunset). Thus, "in tertiam," here is rendered as 9:00 A.M. At line 67 the phrase "noctem ad quartam," is translated as 4:00 A.M., i.e., the fourth hour after midnight.

3. Presumably his law degree.

4. Perhaps an allusion to the famous thirteenth-century canon lawyer, Dinus de Mugello (d. 1303), who taught at the University of Bologna.

5. A doctrine most famously associated with Aristotle.

6. Compare the device in Terence's *Heautontimorumenos*, where Clinia pretends to run off to join the army, only to return secretly after a few months (a parallel noted by Katchmer).

7. One of the four main gates of the old town of Bologna; see Staüble, *La commedia*, p. 10.

8. Alluding to Aristotle's famous theory in *Politics* VII that geography affects character, so that intemperate regions of the world, especially Asia, produce more slavish characters. Line 221 suggests the Stichus is a Turk, or more likely (given the usual sources of slaves in Renaissance Italy) a Tartar. The name Stichus was a common slave name in antiquity and was the title of a play by Plautus.

9. An allusion to the ancient maxim *corruptio optimi pessima*, "the corruption of the best is the worst form of corruption."

10. Sentio is presumably Paulus' father.

11. Medieval and Renaissance lectures were always on set texts which were read and commented on in class; the texts were divided up into *puncta* or starting points for each day's reading.

12. This subplot is never developed, a fact which some scholars take as evidence the play was left unfinished.

13. The difference in behavior between a slave (like Stichus) and a hired servant (like Herotes) was often remarked upon in Renaissance Italy.

14. The humor of the lines is more evident in Latin, as the words for "to be ruined," "to die" and "to pine away from love" *(perire)* are the same as the word for "to have an orgasm."

15. Legal language *(visus et habitus)* for a prisoner who has appeared before a judge and is being held for trial.

16. See Boccaccio, *Decameron* 6.10.

17. The text seems to be incomplete here; a reply by Papis is also indicated in the MSS but is not specified; this is further evidence that the play was never completed (see note 12 above).

18. A near-quotation of Cicero's *De amicitia* 56: "The value a man sets on himself is the value his friends should set upon him" *(quanti quisque se ipse facit, tanti fiat ab amicis)* — but significantly altered.

THE PLAY OF PHILODOXUS

1. Leonello d'Este (1407–1450), marquis of Ferrara from 1441 until his death.

2. Meliaduse d'Este (1406–1452), brother of Leonello and a close friend of Alberti's since at least 1435, when they were together in Florence. Alberti dedicated his *Mathematical Exercises (Ludi rerum mathematicarum)* to Meliaduse.

3. In Greek.

4. Throughout the Commentary, Alberti refers to the character Doxia as Doxa, the transliteration of the Greek noun for "glory," while through most of the play he refers to her using the typonymic Doxia. This is one of several changes to the names of characters that Alberti appears to have

made in the last stages of revising his text. Cesarini Martinelli notes that the name Phrontisis from the first redaction was changed in the second redaction, first to Phronisis, then to Phroneus; but that Alberti failed to correct Phronisis to Phroneus in every case. Cesarini Martinelli further remarks (p. 139): "In the final pages of the codex [Estensis 52, a manuscript of the second redaction with autograph corrections], from folio 22r onwards, the names Doxia and Phimia are sporadically emended to Doxa and Phemia. Phroneus, Doxa and Phemia are forms that appear in the Commentary, where moreover one reads Alethia instead of Alithia and Aphthonus in place of Ditonus. The elimination of itacisms and the search for a word with a Greek etymology for the one character, Ditonus, that retained a name with a Latin root shows that Alberti had progressively improved his scanty knowledge of the Greek language." In this edition of the play proper, as distinct from the prefatory matter, we adopt Alberti's predominant spellings: Doxia, Phroneus, Phimia, Alithia, and Ditonus.

5. In the play itself they are *virgines*, maidens, rather than matrons.

6. An allusion to the old saw *Veritas Temporis filia*, "Truth, the daughter of Time," for which see Aulus Gellius 12.11.7 and Apuleius, *Metamorphoses* 8.7, among other texts.

7. Lorenzo Alberti died in 1421. After studying classical literature from about 1416–1418 at the famous humanist school in Padua of Gasparino Barzizza (1360–1430), Leon Battista Alberti continued his education at Bologna, where he learned a little Greek from Francesco Filelfo (1398–1481), the best Italian Hellenist of the mid-fifteenth century. Alberti received his doctorate in canon law in 1428 from the University of Bologna.

8. The great Alberti scholar Cecil Grayson (1954, p. 291) identified this friend with the ribald Latin poet Antonio Beccadelli, called "il Panormita," on the basis of an ambiguous allusion in a letter from Panormita to Paolo Toscanelli, but this identification is rejected on good grounds by Cesarini Martinelli, p. 111, n. 3.

9. This prologue, masquerading as the work of the (otherwise unknown) comic poet Lepidus, is given immediately below, after the Commentary, as it appeared in the 1424 redaction of the play (see Note on the Text).

Alberti used the name Lepidus again for the cynical interlocutor of his *Intercenales*, short dialogues modelled on Lucian, which were probably also begun during his student days in Bologna.

10. On the meaning of *caesius* as equivalent here to "nearly blind," see Cesarini Martinelli's notes, pp. 228–229 (the first redaction calls Ditonus *quasi caecus*).

11. Proverbial expressions, meaning to trade in worthless goods.

12. Lit. "men of the people," a medievalism. In late medieval Italian cities, the middle classes, known as the *populares* in Latin, were organized militarily to help fellow citizens resist attacks from the powerful.

13. That Ditonus' house has a tower is an example of a "medieval" detail in an otherwise classicizing scenography; see also the next note.

14. A barber who doubles as a surgeon is another "medieval" touch.

15. A pun: "speaking with the stomach," ventriloquating, referring probably to the rumbling of an empty stomach.

16. I.e., the eternal life of the gods, immortality.

17. Lit. "(an old man) thrown off a bridge," an inkhorn term derived from Paul the Deacon's epitome of Festus; see Cesarini Martinelli, p. 232.

18. An attendant of a Roman magistrate; here Chronos plays the part of a Roman judicial magistrate, who is also in charge of the corn supply.

19. Possibly a joke with the *double entendre* meaning "I'll dive into this tavern for a beer."

20. Transliterated Greek for "beautiful speaker"; Calilogus seems to be Chronos' scribe and clerk in the former's capacity as magistrate; presumably they are checking the records of the grain-supply as referred to in the previous scene.

21. I.e., she is free to marry Fortunius, as the sequel shows.

22. I.e., Swift-of-foot.

23. Translating "Quid tum?," Alberti's personal motto, a phrase often found in his works as a kind of hallmark.

24. *Plaudite hoc meo bono* might also mean "applaud this good work of mine" and thus constitute an appeal of Alberti the playwright to his audience.

PHILOGENIA AND EPIPHEBUS

1. The plot of Pisani's play is strongly reminiscent of Plautus' *Casina*. The device of a concubine who is passed off as a virgin is also found in Boccaccio, *Decameron* 2.7. Yet the language of *Philogenia and Epiphebus* makes free use of Terence, and the play as a whole is best seen as a Terentian pastiche.

2. See Esther 1.20–30.

3. Nicomius is rejecting the Stoic doctrine that the wise man is always the same. The name "Nicomius" recalls "Nicomachus," Aristotle's son and the dedicatee of the *Nicomachean Ethics*; Aristotle's ethical doctrine teaches that, in order to achieve the virtuous mean, one's behavior will have to vary in accordance with time and circumstances. Yet below Epiphebus identifies Nicomius' maxims as Stoic.

4. Terence, *Phormio* 1.4.26.

5. An apparent reference to Petrarch's most popular prose work, the *De remediis utriusque fortunae* (*On the Remedies for Good and Bad Fortune*).

6. The text seems to be more than usually corrupt here: we translate Perosa's *le capita come a quelli cui viene servita una cena, dove non sai da che piatto incominciare.*

7. Fors Fortuna is the ancient Roman goddess of good luck, bringer of fertility, particularly associated with the life of women.

8. Source not identified. The sentiment is typical of poetry in the courtly tradition of *dolce stil novo*.

9. See especially 2.3.9 and 3.7.34, but this is a general theme of the work.

10. See Virgil, *Georgics* 1.2. Grape vines were often trained around trees in premodern times, rather than on trellises as in modern vineyards.

11. A small town twenty miles from Pavia, which, as Perosa pointed out, shows that the action of the play is set in Pavia.

12. The text is more than usually corrupt at this point; Perosa's Italian has been translated: *Accontentarlo poi, é anche un obbligo di pietà.*

13. The Etruscan god of marriage, whose name became the name of the marriage procession in ancient Rome, when the bride was led from her parents' house to her new home; the name of Talassius or Talassio is invoked in nuptial songs. See Livy 1.9.

14. The following speeches suggest that the character of Alphius may be Emphonius in disguise; another, perhaps more plausible possibility is that Alphius is the second friend of Epiphebus who hid Philogenia after she had left Emphonius' house (see above, §§63 and 71).

CHRYSIS

1. In the single manuscript of this text the names of four persons are written in abbreviated form next to the didascalia in scenes 2, 5 and 6. These are apparently historical personages, of which three have been plausibly identified in the literature (see Cecchini, p. x, note). "Eich" (Sedulius) seems to be Johann von Eich, a diplomat and imperial representative to the Council of Basel, later Bishop of Eichstatt and an important monastic reformer; "Iacobus" is likely to be Jakob Widerle or Wiederle, a chancery official; and "W. T." (Archimenides) is probably Wilhelm Tacz, an official of the imperial chancery who had offended Enea Silvio; he is referred to in Pius II's *Commentaries* (1.11.3) as "a Bavarian who hated all Italians;" see Pius II, *Commentaries*, vol. 1: *Books I-II*, ed. and tr. Margaret Meserve and Marcello Simonetta (Cambridge, MA, 2003), p. 46. It has been suggested that these were figures that Enea Silvio wished to satirize in his play, or less plausibly, that they performed the relevant parts in a court production of the play. That the scene is Basel is inferred from lines 160–167.

2. 25 to 38 kg of gold in the ancient Greek coinage, so a very large sum.

3. An allusion to the ancient philosophical maxim, *Nosce teipsum*, Know thyself.

4. Marcus Porcius Cato (95–46 BC) was a man of unbending character and absolute integrity, "the conscience of Rome," as Livy called him, "equally above praise and vituperation." Cicero wrote a panegyric on him,

and Dante devoted much of his first canto in the *Purgatorio* (lines 31–108) to Cato. The wit of the line is more evident in Latin, as the word for pimp, *leno*, is a near-rhyme with Cato.

5. This and the following line are to be taken in a *sensus obscoenus*.

6. I.e., men who took second wives after their baptism: see Gratian, *Decretum*, dist. 26, cap. 2: *Qui ante baptismum habuerit unam, et post baptismum alteram, ordinandus non est.*

7. The Eumenides ("the kindly ones") were ancient Greek divinities responsible for avenging crimes, especially crimes against the bonds of family. The play of Aeschylus entitled *The Eumenides* could not have been known to Enea Silvio.

8. The Armagnacchi were mercenary troops loyal to the d'Armagnac faction in France; in 1444 the king of France, Charles VII, at the request of the house of Hapsburg-Austria, sent them into Switzerland where they devastated the lands around Basel; in the battle of Saint Jacob-en-Birs (24 August 1444) they killed more than 1500 Swiss soldiers.

9. The Council of Basel broke with Pope Eugene IV in 1438 and nominated an anti-pope, Amadeus VI of Savoy, known as Felix V; the schism lasted until 1448. The "gentlemen of the toga" (*togati*) probably are to be identified with the members of the Council of Basel, which was meeting during the time Enea Silvio was composing this play.

10. An impeccable Stoic sentiment, broadly Senecan in flavor.

11. In antiquity it was considered a sign of intemperance to drink wine without mixing the denser wines of that time with water or other non-alcoholic liquids.

12. A large, two-handled drinking cup.

13. Another name for Bacchus.

14. The legal language here suggests that Archimenides is being imagined as a lawyer or barrister, a suggestion reinforced by the meaning of his name in Greek, i.e. "champion"; see note 1.

15. Perhaps with a *double entendre*, as *rimare*, to probe into crevices, and *irrimo*, to practice fellatio, are closely related morphologically.

16. Celaeno was one of the Harpies; the name means "black cloud."

17. Boccaccio has a similar remark, that the lips are not less soft for having been kissed.

18. I.e., with cold cash.

19. As the patron deity of courtesans.

THE EPIROTE

1. Ermolao Barbaro (1454–93) was an illustrious Venetian humanist and scholar, most famous for his emendations to Pliny the Elder's *Natural History*, known as the *Castigationes Plinianae*. Mezzo's play contains some near-quotations of the *Natural History*, a fact which testifies to the close relations between the two humanists. Barbaro's interest in Roman drama is shown by his attempt to complete the lost scenes in Plautus' *Amphitruo*.

2. Numa Pompilius was the legendary successor of Romulus as founder of Rome; his peaceful reign was regarded by later writers as a Golden Age. Legend said that he received counsel from the goddess Egeria, from whose sacred spring the Vestals drew their water.

3. Dioscurides of Anazarbus, Greek physician of the first century AD, author of a treatise on medical drugs, known in Latin translation as the *De materia medica*. Barbaro's "Latin Dioscurides" almost certainly refers to Barbaro's commentary on Dioscurides, the *In Dioscuridem corollarii*, first published in 1516, but composed about 1481–82, shortly before the publication of *The Epirote*.

4. Nothing is known of Daniele Mezzo, though he was probably an older contemporary and relative of Tommaso; see Braun's 1973 edition of the text, pp. 9, 13.

5. Epirus was a region in northwestern Greece north of Macedonia, roughly equivalent to modern Albania, considered semi-Greek or barbarous by the ancient Greeks, and therefore also in Roman literature. There was a major migration of Albanians to Southern Italy in the later fifteenth century after the conquest of Albania by the Turks; they were not a popular immigrant group.

6. Besides the play's other Plautine features, Mezzo's two characters, Clitipho of Syracuse and Clitipho of Samos, although unrelated to each other, inevitably recall the twins in the *Menaechmi*. The misunderstanding caused by the confusion of identities is the source of the complication in both works. Mezzo's play, again like Plautus', contains a *meretrix* named Erotium.

7. I.e. Paris, the abductor of Helen in the Homeric legends.

8. A near-quotation from Pliny the Elder, *Natural History* 30.30: *praecipue tamen faciem purgat atque erugat cygni adeps.*

9. In the conventional version of the Medea myth, Aeson, the father of Jason, was brought back to life by bathing in a cauldron of water filled with magic herbs that Medea had prepared.

10. With a suggestion of *double entendre*, as the diminutive of *mens*, mind, is *mentula*, i.e. a phallus.

11. Two cities which, like Syracuse, were founded by the ancient Greeks in Sicily.

12. *De natura deorum* is the title of one of Cicero's graver philosophical dialogues.

13. The constellation, Corona Borealis, was said to have been formed from Ariadne's hair.

14. Callisto was a nymph in the service of Artemis (Hera) and who so angered the goddess that Artemis changed her into a she-bear. She wandered about in this form until her son Arcas came upon her while he was hunting and would have killed her with his spear had Zeus not changed Callisto into the constellation Ursa Major and Arcas into Arctophylax.

15. His namesake Clitipho of Samos.

16. Pliny the Elder, *Natural History* 9.40.

17. A wine from Campania celebrated by the ancient Roman poets, particularly Horace.

18. Mithradates VI Eupator, king of Pontus (c. 131 - 63 BC), was a much-feared opponent of the Romans; he was supposed to have made himself immune to poison by fortifying his food with antidotes.

19. Famous singers in Greek mythology. Orpheus was a pre-Homeric bard who was so marvelous a player of the lyre that wild beasts were spellbound by his music; Amphion played the harp with such skill that stones were drawn into their places during the building of the walls of Thebes; and Arion, according to Greek myth, was a poet from Lesbos who, when thrown overboard on a sea journey to Corinth, used his song to charm a dolphin into carrying him to shore.

20. The praetor in a Roman town is generally responsible for police matters, while a consul would be a kind of mayor or chief magistrate.

21. According to Braun's edition of this text (see pp. 27–28, 123), the words are Albanian for "Please shut your mouth!" Braun points out the parallel with Plautus' *Poenulus*, where the character Hanno speaks his native Punic in several places.

22. Ceres, identified with the Greek god Demeter, had a daughter Persephone by her brother Zeus, who was abducted by Pluto.

23. The Attalids were a dynasty in the third century BC who acquired Pergamum in Asia Minor and gained an important strategic alliance with Rome. The dynasty came to an end in 133 BC when Attalus III bequeathed his lands and power to Rome. The wealth of the Attalids was legendary and Pergamum the most celebrated city in Asia Minor.

Bibliography

❧❧❧

COMPLETE EDITIONS

PAULUS

K. Müllner. "Vergerios Paulos, eine Studentenkomödie." *Wiener Studien* 23 (1900–1901): 232–57.

In Amalia Clelia Pierantoni. *Pier Paolo Vergerio Seniore*. Chieti: Stabilimento Arti Grafiche, 1920.

In Vito Pandolfi and Erminia Artese, eds. *Teatro goliardico dell'Umanesimo*. Milan: Lerici, 1965, pp. 47–119. Reprint of Müllner's edition with a facing Italian translation.

Sergio Cella and Francesco Semi, eds. "P. P. Vergerio il Vecchio: il *Paulus*." *Atti e Memorie della Società Istriana di Archaeologia e Storia Patria*, 14, n. s. (1966): 45–103. Latin text with an Italian translation.

Alessandro Perosa. "Per una nuova edizione del *Paulus* del Vergerio." In *L'Umanesimo in Istria*, Vittore Branca and Sante Graciotti, eds., pp. 273–356; text on pp. 321–56. Florence: Leo S. Olschki, 1983.

THE PLAY OF PHILODOXUS

Comedia Philodoxeos Leonis Baptiste. Salamanca: Juan Giesser, 1500. Second redaction.

Lepidi comici veteris Philodoxios fabula ex antiquitate eruta ab Aldo Manutio. Lucca, 1588. First redaction.

Anicio Bonucci, ed. *Opere volgari di L. B. Alberti per la più parte inedite e tratte dagli autografi*, 1: XIII–XVII and CXX–CLXVI. Florence: Tipografia Galileiana, 1843. Second redaction.

Lucia Cesarini Martinelli, ed. "Leon Battista Alberti, *Philodoxeos fabula*: edizione critica." *Rinascimento*, n.s, 17 (1977): 111–234. Both redactions.

PHILOGENIA AND EPIPHEBUS

Ugolinus Parmensis Philogenia. Toulouse, ca. 1476.

In Vito Pandolfi and Erminia Artese, eds. *Teatro goliardico dell'Umanesimo*. Milan: Lerici, 1965. Text by Francesca Roselli with a facing Italian translation by Erminia Artese, pp. 171–285.

Philogenia et Epiphebus. Rome: Torre d'Orfeo, 1997. A reprint of the Roselli text with Artese's translation.

Chrysis

André Boutemy, ed. *Aeneas Silvius Piccolomini. Chrysis: comédie latine inédite*. Collection Latomus, 1. Brussels: n. pr., 1939.

Ireneo Sanesi, ed. *Enea Silvio Piccolomini. Chrysis*. Nuova collezione di testi umanistici inediti o rari, 4. Florence: Olschki, 1941.

In Vito Pandolfi and Erminia Artese, eds. *Teatro goliardico dell'Umanesimo*. Milan: Lerici, 1965. The Sanesi text with a facing Italian translation by Erminia Artese.

Enzo Cecchini, ed. *Enea Silvio Piccolomini. Chrysis*. Florence: Sansoni, 1968.

The Epirote

Thome Medii Patricii Veneti Fabella: Epirota. Venice: Bernardinus de Celeris de Luere, 1483.

Comedia Thome Medii Veneti que Epirota inscribitur. Oppenheim: [Jakob Köbel], 1516.

Comedia Thome Medii Veneti que Epirota inscribitur. Leipzig: Jacobus Thanner, 1517.

Thomae Medii Patricii Veneti fabella Epirota. Adiecta est in calce libelli Ioannis Pici Mirandulae ad ipsum Thomam Medium de hac fabella epistola. Mainz: Ivo Schoeffer, 1547.

Ludwig Braun, ed. *Thomae Medii Fabella Epirota*. München: Wilhelm Fink Verlag, 1974. Humanistische Bibliothek, Reihe II, Texte, Band 8. Critical edition with a facing German translation.

Graziella Gentilini, ed. *Teatro umanistico veneto: la commedia*. Testi e studi umanistici, 1. Ravenna: Longo Editore, 1983. Critical edition, pp. 21–45, with an Italian translation, pp. 47–69.

TRANSLATIONS

Paulus

Into Italian:

In Pandolfi and Artesi, *Teatro goliardico*, as above.

In Semi and Cella, "P. P. Vergerio il Vecchio," as above.

In Alessandro Perosa, ed. *Teatro umanistico*, pp. 55–85. Milan: Nuova Accademia Editrice, 1965. Based on an unpublished critical text by Giovanna Maria Mura.

Giuseppe Secoli. "Il 'Paulus' di Pierpaolo Vergerio il Vecchio." In *Studi Vergeriani*, pp. 23–33. Trieste: Centro Pedagogico della Regione Friuli Venezia Giulia, 1971. Originally translated in 1959 from Müllner's Latin text.

Into English:

Michael Katchmer, *Pier Paolo Vergerio and the Paulus, a Latin Comedy*, pp. 105–137. New York: Peter Lang, 1998.

The Play of Philodoxus

Into English:

Joseph R. Jones and Lucia Guzzi. "Leon Battista Alberti's *Philodoxus* (c. 1424): An English Translation," *Celestinesca* 17.1 (1993): 87–134.

Philogenia and Epiphebus

Into Italian:

In Alessandro Perosa, *Teatro Umanistico*, as above, pp. 138–181.

In Pandolfi and Artesi, *Teatro goliardico*, as above, and the reprint of 1997, as above.

Chrysis

Into Italian:

In Alessandro Perosa, *Teatro Umanistico*, as above, pp. 181–209.

Ettore Barelli, tr. *Enea Silvio Piccolomini: Criside*. Milan: Rizzoli, 1965.

The Epirote

Into Italian:

In Gentilini, *Teatro umanistico veneto*, as above.

Into German:
In Braun, *Thomae Medii Fabula*, as above.

SECONDARY LITERATURE

Paola Andrioli Nemola, Giuseppe Antonio Camerino, Gino Rizzo, Paolo Viti, eds. *Teatro, scena, rappresentazione dal Quattrocento al Settecento: atti del convegno internazionale di studi, Lecce, 15–17 maggio 1997.* Galatina: Congedo, 2000. With an article on the *Chrysis* by Sondra dall'Oco, pp. 67–72.

Eugenio Battisti. "La visualizzazione della scena classica nella commedia umanistica." In *Rinascimento e Barocco*, pp. 96–111. Turin: Einaudi, 1960.

Lucia Cesarini Martinelli. "Metafore teatrali in L. B. Alberti." *Rinascimento*, ser. 2, 29 (1989): 3–51.

George E. Duckworth. *The Nature of Roman Comedy.* 2nd ed. Norman: Univ. of Oklahoma Press, 1994.

Anthony Grafton. *Leon Battista Alberti: Master Builder of the Italian Renaissance.* New York: Farrar Straus Giroux, 2000. Includes discussion of the *Tale of Philodoxus.*

John McManamon. *Pier Paolo Vergerio. The Humanist as Orator.* Tempe, Arizona: Medieval and Renaissance Texts and Studies, 1996.

Giorgio Padoan, "La commedia rinascimentale a Venezia: dalla sperimentazione umanistica alla commedia regolare." In *Storia della cultura veneta* III/3, pp. 377–465. Vicenza: Pozza, 1981.

Alessandro Perosa. *Teatro umanistico.* Milan: Nuova Accademia Editrice, 1965.

Jon Pearson Perry. "A Fifteenth-Century Dialogue on Literary Taste: Angelo Decembrio's Account of Playwright Ugolino Pisani at the Court of Leonello d'Este." *Renaissance Quarterly* 39 (1986): pp. 613–43.

Mary Hieber Sabatini. "The Problem of Setting in Early Humanist Comedy in Italy: A Study in Fifteenth-Century Goliardic Theatre." *Studi urbinati di storia, filosofia e letteratura* 48 (1974): 5–70.

Eckehard Simon. *The Theatre of Medieval Europe: New Research in Early Drama.* Cambridge: Cambridge University Press, 1991.

Antonio Staüble. "Un dotto esercizio letterario: la commedia *Chrysis* di Enea Silvio Piccolomini nel quadro del teatro umanistico del Quattrocento," *Giornale storico della letteratura italiana*, 142 (1965): 351–367.

———. *La commedia umanistica del Rinascimento.* Florence: Istituto Nazionale di Studi sul Rinascimento, 1968.

Paola Ventrone, ed. *Le Tems revient: Feste e spettacoli nella Firenze di Lorenzo il Magnifico.* [exhibit catalog] *Firenze, Palazzo Medici Riccardi, 8 aprile–30 giugno 1992.* [Cinisello Balsamo]: Silvana, 1992.

Paolo Viti. *Immagini e immaginazioni della realtà: ricerche sulla commedia umanistica.* Florence: Le lettere, 1999.

Index

ॐ§ईॐ

References are by play and paragraph number or line number ("n" refers to notes to the translation). Lowercase Roman numerals refer to pages in the Introduction. The comedies are abbreviated as follows: Pa *(Paulus)*, Px *(The Play of Philodoxus)*, Pg *(Philogenia and Epiphebus)*, C *(Chrysis)*, and E *(The Epirote)*. LB and LM refer to the letters of Tommaso Mezzo to Ermolao Barbaro and Daniele Mezzo, respectively, that precede *The Epirote*.

Accademia Pontaniana, xiv
Accademia Romana, xiv, xvi
Aeson, E6
Africa, Px53
Agrigento, E22
Alberti, Leon Battista, viii, xiii,
    xiv, xix–xx, xxi, xxii, xxv
Alberti, Lorenzo, Px6
Alexander, E1
Alighieri, Dante, C96n4
Alphius, xv, Pg91
Amphion, E52
Apollo, Px76
Apuleius, Px3n6
Archimedon, E66
Aretino, Pietro, ix
Ariadne, E26
Arion, E52
Ariosto, Ludovico, ix
Aristotle, xxii–xxiii, Pa111n5,
    214n8; Pg2n3
Armagnacchi, *French troops*,
    C161
Athena, C578

Attalus, E68
Aulus Gellius, Px3n6

Bacchus, Pg28; C218, C226
Barbaro, Ermolao, LB1, LM2–3,
    E1
Barzizza, Gasparino, ix, Px6n7
Basel, Cn1
Beccadelli, Antonio, "il
    Panormita," xiv, Px7n8
Boccaccio, Pa804; Pg1n1; C412n17
Bohemians, C208
Bologna, Pa443; Px6
Bracciolini, Poggio, x, xvi
Brunelleschi, Filippo, xix

Calfurnio, Giovanni, x
Calliopius, xv–xvi
Callisto, E26
Casteggio, Pg56
Cato, C96
Celaeno, C344
Ceres, Pg28; E58
Chian, *wine*, C209

Cicero, Pa863n18; Pg51; E25n12
Climarchus, Px56, Px75
Cogo, Niccolò del, xvii
Cupid, Pg20; C334; E1
Cusanus, Nicolaus, x

Decembrio, Angelo, xxvi
Dioscurides of Anazarbus,
    LB4
Donatus, x
Dyrrachium, E17

Egeria, LB1
Eich, Johann von, Cn1
Eleanora of Aragon, xiv
Epicureans, Pg23
Este, Alfonso I d', xiii
Este, Ercole II d', *duke*, xiii, xiv
Este, *family*, ix, xiii
Este, Leonello d', xiii, Px1
Este, Meliaduse d', Px2
Esther, book of, Pg1n2
Ethiopians, Pa215
Etna, E13
Eumenides, C158

Falernian, *wine*, E41
Ferrara, viii, xiii, xiv, xvi, xvii
Festus, Px103n17
Filelfo, Francesco, Px6n7
Florence, xi–xii, xxiii
Fors Fortuna, Pg40
Frenchmen, C176, C492
Furies. *See* Eumenides

Ganymede, C76
Germans, Pa223; C176

Gratian, C145n6
Guarino da Verona, ix

Helen, E1
Hercules, xiii
Hippocrates, Pg25
Hrotsvitha of Gandersheim, ix,
    xxiii
Hymenaeus, Pg84

Juno, Pg84; C566, C577; E59
Jupiter (Jove), xiii, Px80, 121;
    Pg84;C565, C578, C728, C785;
    E19

Leontini, E22
Lepidus, xxii, Px13
Leto, Giulio Pomponio, xiv–xvi,
    xx
Liber. *See* Bacchus
Lippo Topo, Pa804
Livius Andronicus, xv
Livy, xv

Machiavelli, Niccolò, ix
Mainz, C701
Mars, Px17
Mauretania, E39
Medea, E6
Medici palace, xvi
Meleager, xiii
Mercury, C620
Merula, Giorgio, xi
Mezzo, Daniele, LM1
Mezzo, Tommaso, viii, xviii, xxii,
    xxv, xxvi
Milan, ix

Mithridates, E42
Modena, xiii
Mugello, Dinus de, Pa58n4

Naples, xiv
Narcissus, E3
Negri, Francesco, xxix
Nestor, C584
Nicholas V, *pope*, xv
Numa Pompilius, E2

Ops, C580
Orpheus, E52

Padua, ix
Palazzo della Signoria, Florence,
    xvi
Panormita. *See* Beccadelli
Paris, C76
Paul II, *pope*, xiv
Paul the Deacon, Px103n17
Pavia, ix, xii, Pg56n11
Persephone, E58n22
Persians, Pg1
Petrarch, viii, Pg28n5
Piccolomini, Enea Silvio (Pius II),
    viii, xi, xxii, xxiv–xxv
Pisani, Ugolino, viii, xii–xiii, xv,
    xxi, xxii, xxv, xxvi
Pius II. *See* Piccolomini, Enea
    Silvio
Plautus, vii–xi, xiii, xiv, xvi, xvii,
    xxi–xxvi, Pa153n6; Pgn1
Pliny the Elder, LB1n1, E6n8,
    E41n16
Pluto, Px18
Poliziano, Angelo, x, xxiii

Ponte alla Carraia, Florence, xi
Pucci, Antonio, xi–xii

Ravenna Gate, at Bologna, Pa164
Regio, Rafaele, x
Riario, Pietro, *cardinal*, xiv
Riario, Raffaele, *cardinal*, xiv, xv,
    xvi, xx
Rome, viii, xix, xxv

Seneca, vii, xv
Sforza, Alfonso, xiii
Sforza, Anna Maria, xiii
Sicily, E16
Siena, C709
Sixtus IV, *pope*, xiv
Stoics, Pg2n3, 4; C182n10
Strasbourg, x
Sulpizio da Veroli, xvi, xix, xx
Swiss, C163
Syracuse, xxvi

Tacz, Wilhelm, Cn1
Taranto, E16
Terence, vi, viii–xi, xiii, xv, xvi,
    xviii–xix, xxi–xxiv, Pgn1, Pg5n4
Thalassius, Pg84
Tiber, Px79
Toscanelli, Paolo, Px7n8
Treviso, Pa850
Turks, Pa221; C208
Tuscan, Pa786, Pa852

Venice, xiii
Venus, Px17, 47; Pg6, Pg14, Pg20,
    Pg23, Pg28; C10, C83, C234,
    C566

Vergerio, Pier Paolo, viii, ix–x, xi,
     xix, xxi, xxii, xxiv
Vespucci, Giorgio Antonio, xvi
Villani, Giovanni, xi
Virgil, Pg52n10

Vitruvius, xvi–xxi

Widerle (Wiederle), Jakob, Cn1

Zabarella, Francesco, xxiv

Publication of this volume has been made possible by

The Myron and Sheila Gilmore Publication Fund at I Tatti
The Robert Lehman Endowment Fund
The Jean-François Malle Scholarly Programs and Publications Fund
The Andrew W. Mellon Scholarly Publications Fund
The Craig and Barbara Smyth Fund
for Scholarly Programs and Publications
The Lila Wallace–Reader's Digest Endowment Fund
The Malcolm Wiener Fund for Scholarly Programs and Publications